THE LAST CALIPH

T.L. WILLIAMS

First Coast Publishers

Also by T.L. Williams

Cooper's Revenge

Unit 400: The Assassins

Zero Day: China's Cyber Wars

www.tl-williams.com

Acknowledgements

Writing is a solitary pursuit, but it is through the interactions that I have with subject matter experts, colleagues, friends and family, publishing professionals, and readers, that my books come to life. I owe a debt of gratitude to so many who have encouraged my love of writing. To the Florida Writers Association and Florida Authors and Publishers Association, who, through annual conferences, writing workshops, and national literary award competitions have strengthened my craft. To my editor at Type Right Editing, Alex Melone. To my colleagues at the Central Intelligence Agency, the Federal Bureau of Investigation, Homeland Security, local law enforcement, and the U.S. military, who fight the good fight against terrorism every day. Their vigilance, unwavering dedication, and unparalleled professionalism keep our nation secure. To my critique group – Kenneth Overman and Judith White, who provided invaluable help as first readers. To the Central Intelligence Agency Map Library for their generous consent to use the Middle East map herein. To my design team at Expert Subjects, especially Heather UpChurch who designed the book interior and Jason Alexander who designed the striking cover. But above all I thank you, dear reader, for your unwavering support.

T. L. Williams
Ponte Vedra Beach, Florida

To my wife and soul mate,

Carol

With love

Printed in the United States of America

Publisher's Note
This is a work of fiction. The people, events, circumstances,
and institutions depicted are fictitious and the product of the
author's imagination. Any resemblance of any character to any
actual person, whether living or dead, is purely coincidental.

The publisher is not responsible for websites (or their content)
that are not owned by the publisher.

Publisher›s Cataloging-in-Publication Data provided by Five
Rainbows Cataloging Services

Names: Williams, T. L., author.
Title: The Last Caliph / T. L. Williams.
Description: Ponte Vedra Beach, FL : First Coast Publishers, 2019.
    | Series: Logan Alexander.
Identifiers: LCCN 2019900004 | ISBN 978-0-9884400-1-2 (paper-
    back) | ISBN 978-0-9884400-2-9 (ebook)
Subjects: LCSH: Terrorism--Fiction. | Terrorism--Prevention--
    Fiction. | United States. Central Intelligence Agency--Fiction.
    | IS (Organization)--Fiction. | Suspense fiction. | Spy stories.
    | BISAC: FICTION / Thrillers / Terrorism. | FICTION /
    Thrillers / Espionage. | FICTION / Thrillers / Suspense. |
    GSAFD: Spy stories. | Suspense fiction.
Classification: LCC PS3623.I5643 L37 2019 (print) | LCC PS3623.
    I5643 (ebook) | DDC 813/.6--dc23.

Epigraph

*"The Islamic caliphate cannot be restored by force.
Occupying a country and killing half of its population...
this is not an Islamic state, this is terrorism."*

Grand Imam of Al-Azhar

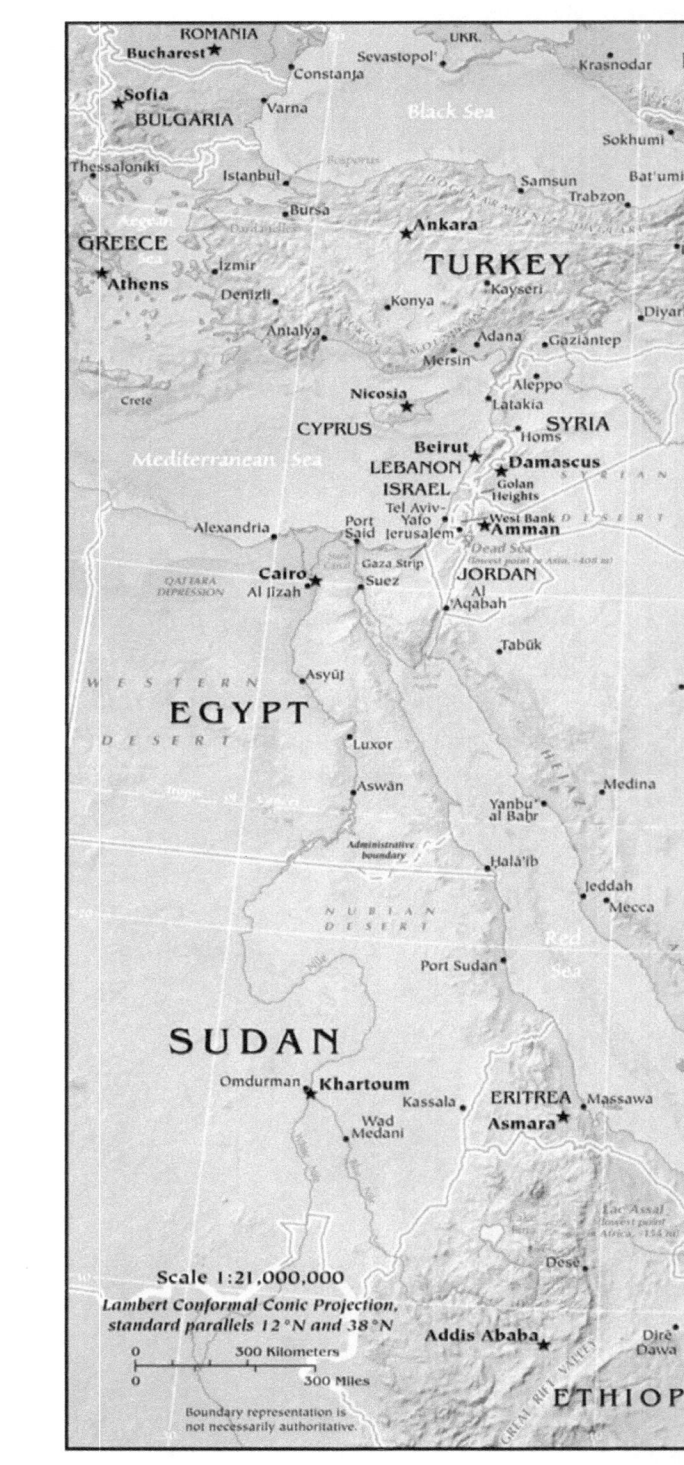

Scale 1:21,000,000
Lambert Conformal Conic Projection,
standard parallels 12°N and 38°N

0   300 Kilometers
0   300 Miles

Boundary representation is
not necessarily authoritative.

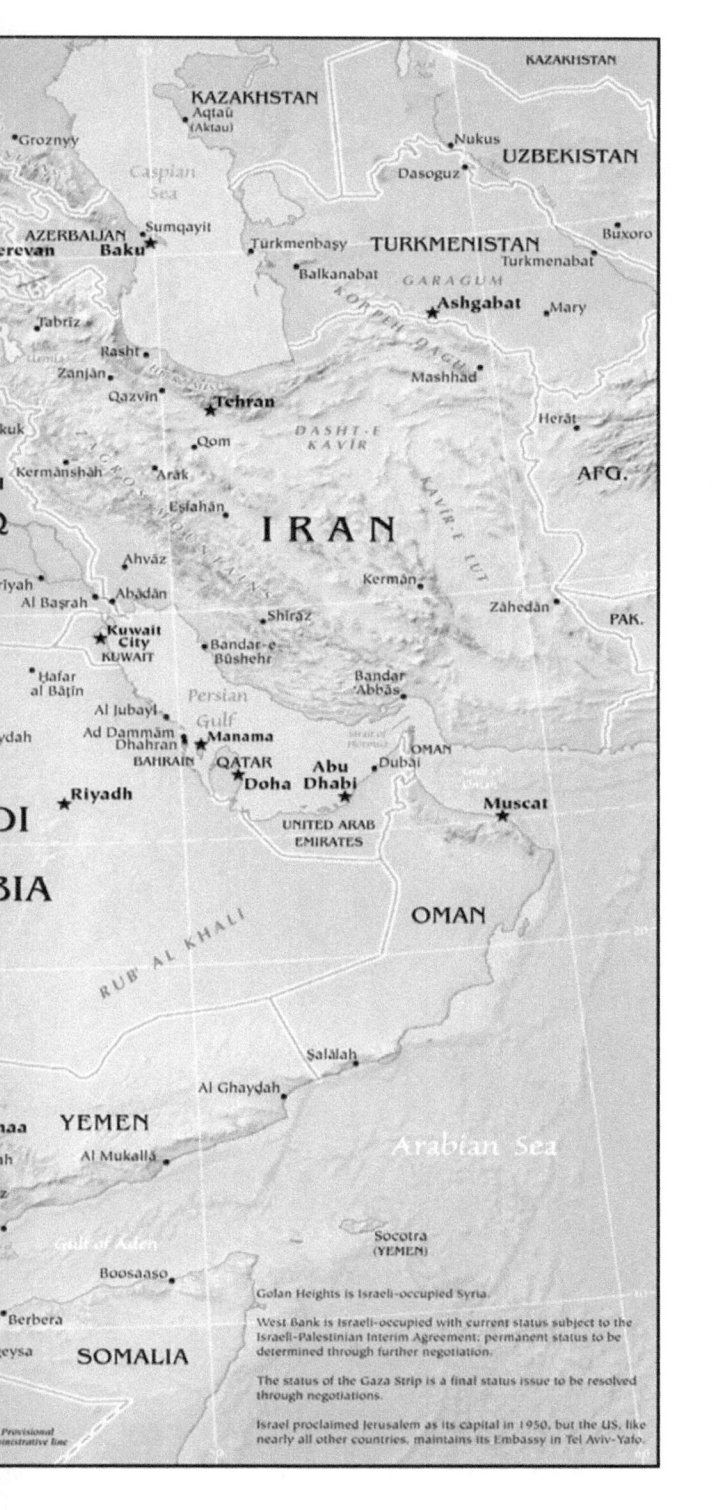

KAZAKHSTAN

Groznyy

Caspian
Sea

Aqtaū
(Aktau)

Nukus

Dasoguz

KAZAKHSTAN

UZBEKISTAN

AZERBAIJAN
Yerevan   Baku

Sumqayit

Turkmenbaşy

TURKMENISTAN

Turkmenabat

Büxoro

Balkanabat

GARAGUM

Ashgabat

Mary

Tabriz

Rasht

Zanjān

Qazvin

Tehran

Qom

Mashhad

DASHT-E
KAVĪR

Herāt

AFG.

rkuk

Kermānshāh

Arāk

Esfahān

IRAN

KAVĪR-E LŪT

Ahvāz

Kermān

irīyah

Al Başrah

Abādān

Shīrāz

Zāhedān

PAK.

Kuwait
City
KUWAIT

Bandar-e
Būshehr

Bandar
'Abbās

Ḥafar
al Bāţin

Al Jubayl

Persian
Gulf

aydah

Ad Dammām
Dhahran

Manama

BAHRAIN

QATAR

Doha

Abu
Dhabi

Dubai

OMAN

Muscat

Riyadh

DI

3IA

UNITED ARAB
EMIRATES

OMAN

RUB AL KHALI

Salālah

Al Ghaydah

naa

YEMEN

ah

Al Mukallā

Arabian Sea

zz

Gulf of Aden

Boosaaso

Berbera

geysa   SOMALIA

Socotra
(YEMEN)

Provisional
administrative line

Golan Heights is Israeli-occupied Syria.

West Bank is Israeli-occupied with current status subject to the
Israeli-Palestinian Interim Agreement; permanent status to be
determined through further negotiation.

The status of the Gaza Strip is a final status issue to be resolved
through negotiations.

Israel proclaimed Jerusalem as its capital in 1950, but the US, like
nearly all other countries, maintains its Embassy in Tel Aviv-Yafo.

Chapter 1

"You're actually serious about this, aren't you?" Aaron Cousins, CIA's deputy director for operations (DDO), fixed his flinty gray eyes on Logan Alexander with a penetrating stare that, in the case of a lesser man, would surely elicit powerful feelings of self-doubt. He toyed with the letter of resignation before him, his manner revealing the depth of his exasperation with the young operations officer.

"Why now? You've just pulled off one of the most elaborate operations against a hard target in the history of this Agency. Hell, what you and your team achieved was nothing short of amazing. Not to mention the amount of effort and cost that went into establishing Alexander Maritime in Hong Kong."

Logan allowed the DDO's praise to permeate the reflexive shield he'd erected. The significance of his team's accomplishment was not lost on him. He knew thwarting China's Zero Day attack against the U.S. was a significant coup for the intelligence community. It was the catalyst, when all else was said and done, for bringing the government, private sector, and military together in support of legislation establishing the most comprehensive cybersecurity bill in the nation's history.

Despite their achievements, though, over the last year, he found himself questioning his commitment to long-term government service. And notwithstanding his devotion to the Agency, and his early success, there were times when the bureaucracy and Washington politics made it difficult to stay focused on the mission.

A recent family tragedy was all it took to push him over the edge, the driver behind today's meeting with Cousins.

He sighed inwardly as he contemplated the events leading to today's face-off. His wife, Zahir, had suffered a miscarriage in her third trimester, the result of a confrontation with a Chinese ministry of public security (MPS) intruder who had broken into their Hong Kong apartment, knocking her down when she surprised him by returning home earlier than usual from her teaching job.

Logan had rushed her to the emergency room, shaken up and spotting. After the doctor examined her, he prescribed a period of bed rest. Her situation appeared to normalize after a few days, and the medical staff was able to detect a fetal heartbeat at the follow-up visit.

But something had gone terribly wrong at the beginning of the third trimester. Logan drove her to the hospital early one evening following a family Christmas trip to Thailand. She was experiencing heavy bleeding, and as they wheeled her into the emergency room at Adventist Hospital. Logan's throat constricted, and he fidgeted in the waiting room with his head in his hands, praying to God. An hour later, the doctor emerged from the ER.

"The baby was stillborn," she said.

"But—up to now, everything seemed to be all right." Logan could feel his emotions rising.

"We moved her to a private room so we could induce labor. The medical term for what we found is placental abruption. It happens when the placenta separates from the uterine wall. This is what was causing the heavy bleeding. We don't always know what causes the placenta to separate. Often, it's trauma or injury to the mother's abdomen.

"I see from your wife's medical record she was admitted to the ER during her first trimester with an injury resulting in vaginal bleeding. The attending recommended bed rest. Follow-up pre-natal visits indicate she and the baby were doing well."

The doctor made a helpless gesture with her hands. "I'm sorry."

The rest of the evening evaporated in a blur. Logan and Zahir held the lifeless body of their daughter until it was time to say goodbye. The ride home from the hospital was painful. Zahir was disconsolate, sobbing until back at their apartment. She fell into a fitful slumber once she lay down in bed.

Now, Logan held up his hands in front of the DDO as if to ward off a blow. "It's Zahir. The shrinks won't clear her for overseas duty. She's depressed, and I think deep down, she blames the Agency because she believes this would never have happened if we'd been living in the States."

"Where is she now?"

"We're staying in Arlington with her parents."

"Look, why don't you take some time off? Don't do anything rash. When she gets better—"

"I've already closed out everything I was working on, and we packed up our apartment before we left Hong Kong. We're heading back to Boston at the end of the week. Maybe—" Despite Washington's caustic political climate and Zahir's health concerns, he had to admit he loved the work.

"What are you thinking?" Cousins asked.

"Take some time off to spend with her. Hopefully, her condition will improve, and she can go back to teaching in the fall."

"She was at Boston University, right?"

"Yes. In their Arabic language program, Academy for Arabic Teachers. Depending on how she's doing, I plan to ease back into work at Alexander Maritime. I've put some feelers out with a couple of my old navy pals, and there's some contract design work we have a shot at getting."

He shrugged his shoulders. His degree in marine architecture from the U.S. Naval Academy had served him in good stead ever since a battlefield injury in Afghanistan ended his navy SEAL career over six years prior.

"I'll tell you what I'd like to do." Cousins was creasing Logan's memo between his fingers. "I'm going to authorize an extended leave of absence. It'll be for one year without pay. If at the end of that time, you want to come back to work, you know you'll be welcome. If you're still on the fence, we'll accept your resignation. No harm, no foul."

"Thanks, boss." He felt a lump rise in his throat. He doubted he'd be back, but it didn't hurt to placate Cousins and at least give the appearance of leaving the door open to his possible return. He stood and shook the DDO's hand before nodding to the secretary, Marge Givens, on his way out the door.

He wasn't prepared for the deflated sensation that overwhelmed him as he took the elevator down to the first floor and walked through the main foyer. He paused before the granite CIA emblem in the entryway, inscribed with the words "Central Intelligence Agency, United States of America." It depicted the head of an eagle, a shield, and a 16-point compass star, representing strength, defense, and intelligence from around the globe.

He let his eyes wander to the white Alabama marble memorial wall etched with 129 stars, commemorating Agency officers who lost their lives in the line of duty. U.S. and CIA flags flanked the wall, and in the middle, beneath the stars, was the book of honor, which depicted the star and year of death for each memorialized officer. In many cases, the names were included, but for some, they would forever be cloaked in secrecy, lest their disclosure endanger ongoing operations they might have been involved in. He saluted the memorial, turned, and hurried out of the building.

As he walked, he felt a burden lifted from his shoulders. It was a fact, the initial impetus for his decision to leave the Agency was Zahir's health. The Office of Medical Services (OMS) made it clear her condition was frail; she would have to undergo counseling and a battery of psychological tests before they would even consider signing off on another foreign field assignment.

On one level, he understood her hostile feelings towards the CIA. After all, the MPS officer who broke into their apartment wouldn't have been there if he wasn't suspicious about Logan's real occupation. What worried him more, though, was the possibility that Zahir's aggravation might, over time, be directed less at the Agency and more towards him. He couldn't bear the thought of their relationship unraveling because he put duty before family.

He'd heard of marriages failing over the death of a child. No amount of counseling could get those couples back together if they weren't devoted to making it work. Their relationships were damaged beyond repair, endless recriminations spiraling into resentment, resulting in a peevish coexistence leading to separation or worse yet, divorce.

On one level, he felt he was already betraying her, letting her take the fall with the Agency brass about his decision to leave. But he knew himself well enough to realize what had really been gnawing at him for the last year was the recognition that he was at his best when he alone called the shots. He was used to having more autonomy than the CIA customarily gave its officers. In the field, operations officers saw themselves as the pointy end of the spear, and they had considerable leeway in making operational decisions on the spot as circumstances demand. Back in Washington though, you were just a cog in the wheel.

His deal with the Agency was as good as it got for government work, but with Washington politics and the inner workings of the Agency's ever-changing bureaucracy, personal autonomy was fast becoming a scarce commodity. Add to that, congressional oversight and the Director of National Intelligence's propensity to meddle in just about every facet of the Agency's work, he could understand his recent surge of disgruntled feelings. He was more "go it alone" than "team player."

He followed the sidewalk around the south parking lot to his rental car. His in-laws lived in nearby Arlington, Virginia, a fifteen-minute drive from headquarters. He was feeling melancholy as he navigated through their leafy neighborhood. He made the turn onto 32nd and pulled around to the back of the Parandeh's residence.

His in-laws' 7,000-square-foot home was just around the corner from the Washington Golf and Country Club. When he first met Zahir, he had no idea her family was so wealthy. His mother-in-law was a favorite niece of the deceased

Shah of Iran, Mohammad Reza Pahlavi. During the sixties and seventies, before he was ousted from power by Islamic revolutionary, Ayatollah Khomeini, her family salted away millions in Swiss bank accounts from Iranian oil exports.

Zahir's parents followed on the exiled monarch's heels in 1979, establishing themselves in northern Virginia with other Pahlavi family expatriates, many just a stone's throw from Langley. While most of them settled in for the long haul, the former Shah was later banished to Egypt after Islamic militants stormed the U.S. Embassy in Teheran, taking 52 American diplomats hostage.

When he and Zahir first met, she had just been evicted from her family's home, after they discovered she was pregnant, the result of an amorous relationship with Logan's younger brother, Cooper. She and Cooper fell in love while working together in Iraq. When Cooper was killed in an IED attack while on patrol in Ramadi, Zahir was sent back to face her family in the U.S. in disgrace. She found temporary refuge in Boston with Logan's younger sister, Millie. Over the next year, she and Logan, who had moved to Boston to set up his maritime consulting business, fell in love and married.

As he rounded the back of the house, he spotted his father-in-law, Nima, working in the potting shed in the backyard. Things had been decidedly cool between him and his in-laws when they first met. Thirty-five years in the U.S. had done little to soften the bitterness of being exiled from their homeland, despite the fact their circumstances in the U.S. would elicit feelings of envy from most Americans. Then, to add to their disappointment, their daughter married outside of her faith—to a Catholic. It was almost more than they could tolerate.

Not too long after their marriage and the birth of their son, Cooper, named for his biological father, his in-laws' attitude towards them softened. Ali, Zahir's older brother, was the sole holdout. He remained somewhat aloof. Working in New York City as a marketing executive for the National Basketball Association (NBA), he didn't have much contact with them. Ali was a conservative Muslim; he worshiped at the Masjid al-Farah mosque in Tribeca and once confided to Zahir he felt at odds with the Imam's message of tolerance and reconciliation, which he felt was out of touch with today's reality. Logan was wary of Ali and kept his eye on him.

The Parandehs did not discuss religion around the family dinner table. They were moderate Shias, who raised Ali and Zahir according to the Quran. Zahir was non-practicing, and Logan suspected Ali was either self-radicalized or headed in that direction. *It's a good thing my brother-in-law has no idea what my actual occupation was for the past several years*, he thought.

He spotted Cooper helping his grandfather in the potting shed. "Hey, guys, what's going on?"

"Daddy!" Cooper dropped what he was doing and ran over to greet him. Logan scooped him up and walked over to the potting bench where his father-in-law was at work. The structure resembled nothing like most people's idea of a garden shed. It had the feel of a small cottage from Washington's Mt. Vernon estate. Plank siding, a copper roof, and columns across the front gave it a decidedly genteel appearance.

Nima worked as a civil engineer in Iran until his late twenties, when his father died of a sudden heart attack, and he stepped up to take over the family business, Parandeh Civil Engineering Corporation, one of the largest construction companies in Teheran. Ten years later, he and his young family left for the U.S., where he wasted little time establishing a flourishing consulting business. He retired five years ago and spent most of his free time planning and planting flower beds around their Arlington estate.

He wiped his hands on his work pants and shook Logan's hand. "I've lost my helper," he joked as he tickled Cooper's ribs.

Cooper kicked and shrieked with laughter. "Stop, Babar."

Logan put his wriggling son down and looked at the

mound of potting soil, seedling flats and peat pots stacked on the bench. He picked up a small plant and sniffed it. "What's this?"

"Celosia. That one's called Chinatown. Bright red when it flowers. I'm going to put them in the bed over by the back of the patio. We get full sun there, and we can admire them when we're sitting outside."

Cooper lost interest in the conversation and was already on his hands and knees, crawling after a wriggling worm. "How's Zahir doing today?" Logan asked. She was still sleeping when he left the house at 7:30 for his meeting with Cousins.

Nima rubbed his brow and stared off into the distance. "She and Rosana took a walk. They're meeting Rosana's sister in Georgetown for lunch. They left just a few minutes ago." He started to say something and stopped.

"What?" Logan searched his father-in-law's face.

"We're worried about her. I hope time heals these wounds." He paused a moment before continuing. "You know, we lost a child as well." Nima's lip quivered, and Logan could tell he was fighting to maintain his composure.

He was startled by his father-in-law's admission. Zahir never mentioned a third sibling. He struggled to find the right words. "I'm sorry. Zahir never said—"

"She didn't know. It was the year after Rosana and I were married. Our first child. The same thing happened, a miscarriage in the third trimester. We held him." His voice cracked, and he looked away. He picked up a pot and began to scoop in potting soil.

"It took Rosana over a year to recover from her depression. Afterward, we never talked about the baby. It was too painful. For both of us." He extracted one of the Celosia from a flat and transferred it to the pot, covering the roots and tamping down the mixture.

"I asked Rosana this morning if she'd be willing to talk with Zahir about her experience. Maybe knowing her mother went through the same thing would help her overcome her grief."

Logan gave his father-in-law a hug. He felt him tense up in response to this uncharacteristic display of intimacy. The Parandehs weren't given to overt manifestations of emotion. "I hope so. She needs something," he said.

"It'll be hard for her to talk about it because, even after all these years, those feelings are still raw, but she'll do it. The worst thing for a mother is to lose her child. Watching one suffer is almost as hard." There was a faraway look in Nima's eyes as he turned back to his potting.

Logan was struck by the melancholy expression on his father-in-law's face and the plaintive tone of his voice. It was apparent decades after his loss, the pain was as fresh and poignant as the day it happened. Was this his and Zahir's fate? Would bitterness and disparagement define their lives going forward or would love win out? His stomach twisted as he caught a glimpse into a rancorous future.

Cooper was tugging at his jacket. "What's wrong, Daddy?"

Logan crouched down so he was at eye level with his son. He drew him in and kissed him on the cheek. "Everything's just fine, buddy. Everything's just fine."

Chapter 2

Logan felt a twinge of nostalgia as he strode into his office complex at Fan Pier, located on the waterfront in South Boston. It had been three days since his meeting with Aaron Cousins. Boston was where he first hung out his shingle, after leaving the navy six years ago. From the looks of it, not much had changed at One Marina Park Drive. There was a new concierge behind the reception desk. Miguel, the old one, had moved on apparently, replaced by a young woman who was a dead ringer for the R&B vocalist, Alicia Keys. Her name was Tammi, according to the stitching on her blouse.

"Good morning, may I help you?"

"Morning. I'm Logan Alexander, of Alexander Maritime. You must be new. Last time I was here Miguel was still running the concierge desk."

"That's been a few months. Miguel got an offer from the Ritz-Carlton he couldn't turn down."

"Here? In Boston?"

"Yes, head concierge at the Ritz on Boston Common."

"I'll have to look him up. I wanted to let you know I have a temp coming in later this morning from Manpower. My permanent secretary won't be back in town until later this summer. So, we'll see how the temp works out. I don't know who they're sending but just so you know to expect her."

"Thanks, and welcome back, Mr. Alexander. Please let me know if I can do anything for you."

"Thank you."

As he rode the elevator up to his office suite, he thought about his secretary, Alicia Gomez. She had followed him to Hong Kong, but when he broke the news he and Zahir would be returning to the States early, she asked for her old job back in Boston if he still needed her. Alicia expected to remain in Hong Kong until her commitment was up in June but did not plan to extend beyond then. She enjoyed her job in Asia but didn't like being so far away from her family in California.

When he entered the office, he paused a moment to take in the view of Dorchester Heights and Boston Harbor. Water taxis skimmed along the harbor surface. They didn't run as often as cabs and were more expensive at ten bucks per passenger, but being able to take a boat, any boat, to work was a big plus as far as he was concerned. He loved being on the water.

He had come up to Boston by himself on Sunday. "I think Cooper and I will stay in Virginia another week," Zahir said.

"Why don't you come with me?" For a moment the thought of leaving them made him feel guilty, but the fact was he could use the time to get his office squared away and open up their apartment, which had necessarily been in mothballs since their transfer to Hong Kong.

As if reading his mind, Zahir continued. "You need time to settle in, and we'll just be a distraction." Although he was in and out of Boston while assigned to Hong Kong, his main reason for keeping the office open was the Agency continued to pay the lease to support his cover legend—that he was a Boston-based marine architect looking to get into the China trade.

Neither he nor Zahir wanted to rent out their apartment while they were away. It would have made sense to do so financially but dealing with tenants could be a hassle and then there was the issue of having to put most of their things into storage.

He sat down and powered up his computer to check his messages. When his email opened, he was surprised to see a name he recognized at once, although he had not been in touch with the man for years—Nayef Al Subaie.

Logan had met Nayef just after his brother Cooper was killed in the Ramadi attack in Iraq. A Kuwaiti businessman, he was one of his sister's clients. Her law firm represented the Al Subaie's business interests in the U.S. He hadn't thought of Nayef since his last trip to Boston. It had coincided with the anniversary of Cooper's death. He and Millie had been having a glass of wine in her apartment, reminiscing about old times.

"I saw Nayef last week," she said. "We went out to dinner after we finished our business, and he started talking about Hamid. He was kicking himself for not talking him out of going to that Iranian terrorist camp with his cousin."

Hamid was Nayef's son, killed by Iranian assassins after they discovered he was working for Kuwaiti intelligence and had played a role in an attack on one of their military facilities.

"Mohammed?" Logan asked. "Remember, the Iranians turned Hamid's cousin into a *jihadi* after one of their operatives spotted him on the Hajj in Mecca.

"Nayef shouldn't blame himself. Hamid was working undercover for Kuwaiti intelligence. Nayef knew it and was well aware of the dangers he would be facing going to Iran. The intel people planted him in the camp because it was a great opportunity to find out what the Iranians were up to. No one could have predicted how it played out—that Mohammed would blow himself up. Or that we would go in there, destroy their training camp, and kill an Al Qaeda bomb maker."

"Didn't you also kill the camp commander?" she asked.

"Yeah. Colonel Barzan Ghabel. If it weren't for Hamid shooting him, Ghabel would have killed Zahir and me. I think that's what really pissed the Qods Force off. That's why they sent their assassins from Unit Four Hundred after us."

Logan roused himself from his reverie and read Nayef's email. Every time he got together with Nayef, things got interesting. The Iranians murdered Hamid a year after the attack on the terrorist training camp, and Nayef persuaded him to join forces with Kuwaiti intelligence to hunt down the killers.

The ensuing manhunt took him and a team of special forces operatives to Europe, South America, and back to the U.S., where they ultimately killed the assassin in this very office.

His daydream was interrupted by the ringing of his phone. "Hello?"

"Hello, Mr. Alexander? This is Tami downstairs. I have a Mrs. Grady from Manpower coming up. You mentioned you had a temp coming in today?"

"Great. Send her up."

He scanned the rest of Nayef's email.

Dear Logan,

Much has happened in the world since we last talked. I recently spoke with Millie, who told me you would soon be returning to Boston. I'm in New York this week and will be flying up to Boston on business tomorrow. I would love to see you again. We have a lot to talk about. Please let me know if you're available.

Your friend,
Nayef

Logan gazed out the window. What was Nayef up to? What did he mean by, "We have a lot to talk about?" Nayef wasn't one for idle chatter. He'd just have to wait and see. He posted this reply:

Dear Nayef,

It's been a long time! I just got back Sunday. I'd love to get together with you. Zahir and Cooper are visiting her parents in Washington for another week, so we'll have to fend for ourselves. Do you remember where our apartment is on Porter Street?

Give me a call if you need directions (617) 629-8813.
Logan

As he hit the send button, the doorbell rang. Logan got up from his desk and admitted a middle-aged woman, carrying an oversized shopping bag. Beverly Grady was a native Bostonian. She was of sturdy build and a straightforward, no-nonsense manner. At slightly over five feet in height, including the hot-rollered bouffant hairdo, lacquered in place with more hairspray than should be legal, Mrs. Grady proved to be a charmer.

Logan showed her to the reception desk in the outer foyer. The Red Sox pennant she strung from a bookshelf behind her desk was a testament to her passionate fandom, and the delicate matching porcelain teapot and cup placed on a credenza made the room hers. Within ten minutes she was up and running. They chatted for a few minutes about her duties and the likelihood Logan would require her services for approximately two weeks.

He spent the rest of the day clearing out his inbox and reaching out to past clients to let them know he was back in town. Alexander Maritime's bread and butter was its consulting work for Navy's Special Warfare Command. You would think it would be lucrative work, but defense contracts were hard to come by these days given the never-ending acrimony between the White House and Congress over the president's spending priorities. Military spending spiked after 9/11and continued to climb for years before peaking in 2010. Since then it was down 20 percent and headed south. Besides, the government sequester was only making things worse. Who knew? Maybe the Republican administration would make good on its pledge to increase military spending.

As he started to shut it down for the day, his eyes fell on a cherry wood shadowbox displaying navy SEAL memorabilia on a drop leaf table across from him. In it were his SEAL insignia, challenge coins, and his KA-Bar tactical fighting knife.

Seeing it put him in a reflective mood. He knew from the moment he set foot on the grounds of the U.S. Naval Academy as a young plebe, he wanted to major in marine architecture. During his years at Navy, the school was ranked as the top public liberal arts college in the country. By the time he graduated, he not only had a solid marine architecture education, but he was also steeped in the history of the academy and its expectations for graduating midshipmen, who would constitute the next generation of navy and marine corps leaders.

He leaned back in his chair and smiled at the memory. It hadn't been easy. But it wasn't all work and no play. There were plenty of good times, too. Besides academics, the navy encouraged student participation in school athletics. As an all-state quarterback at Montpelier High School, he was heavily recruited to play Navy football. The competition was fierce, and he realized early on he didn't stand a chance of winning the starting quarterback position. He had good hands, size, and speed, though and made the transition to wide receiver, where he was a varsity starter for three years.

He picked up a picture on his desk and studied it. It was a snapshot of Millie and Cooper, who came down to Annapolis with their parents for his last Army-Navy game. They were standing in front of Bancroft Hall after the victory over army for the ceremonial ringing of the Bridge of Nations Bell. The bell is a replica of the original one brought back to the U.S. from Japan by Commodore Matthew Perry and is rung to celebrate Navy's exploits against Army.

Life was much more straightforward in those days. Cooper had still been in high school, and Millie had been applying to colleges. Dad's lumber business was thriving, and it had been pre-9/11, before America lost its innocence.

Logan got up from his desk and stretched. Looking at his watch, he was surprised to see it was already four-thirty, time to call it a day. He needed to pick up a few things at the store and then stop by the ABC for some wine. Although Nayef was Muslim, he had picked up a few Western habits when he studied in the States in the 1980s, including an appreciation for good wine.

His cell rang as he left the office. It was the garage on Condor Street where he was having his car serviced. It was ready. If he hurried, he could pick it up before they closed for the day.

He said goodbye to Mrs. Grady and waved to Tammi on his way out the door. Hailing a taxi, he gave the cabbie the address for Bill's Garage. Settling back into his seat, he stared out the window. A few blocks from Fan Pier he thought he recognized a face in the crowd, a woman walking towards the pier. He craned his neck as they sped through the intersection. He was usually pretty good with faces, but he was drawing a blank with this one. He shrugged and shifted back in his seat, watching the cars speed by.

The cab made good time. This driver knew his way around, managing to shave ten minutes off the trip by using side streets. He pulled up in front of the garage with 20 minutes to spare. Logan paid the fare and hurried inside.

Fifteen minutes later, he was on his way to an ABC store near his apartment. As he fiddled with the radio, searching for 102.5 FM (WKLB Country), he couldn't stop thinking about that face in the crowd. Then it hit him as he replayed a scene from the past in his head. He was in a darkened apartment building in Caracas, Venezuela. Lying on the floor in front of him was the twitching body of a Unit 400 assassin he had just shot with a taser moments earlier. He and his special ops team had been tracking her partner, Hamid's killer, for weeks, and he had just managed to elude them.

The laser lodged in her neck, and it was unclear if she would survive the injury. After they finished searching the apartment, they checked her vitals and made an anonymous phone call to the police, tipping them off to where they could find the injured woman.

Could it be that the figure he had spotted on the street was that woman? The resemblance was uncanny. She was the spitting image of Azar Ghabel, wife of the slain Qods Force colonel, Barzin Ghabel, and Unit 400 accomplice.

Chapter 3

Azar Ghabel walked south along Fan Pier's waterfront promenade, occasionally stopping to photograph the view. It was early spring, and Boston was enjoying an unseasonably warm respite from a harsh winter. Runners sped by, wearing t-shirts and shorts. Couples holding hands strolled along the red paver walkway.

Her non-stop Porter Airlines flight from Toronto Island Airport to Boston arrived on time and check in at her Jamaica Plain hotel under the assumed name, Alice Sherazi, was uneventful. Her three years living in Toronto, which she used as a base to deploy on various operational missions to South America, made today's trip seem relatively routine.

The journey she began several years ago was the result of a bizarre sequence of events she never could have imagined. She was a young army wife living in Bandar Deylam, Iran, a small port city near the Persian Gulf, where her husband, Barzin, commanded a military base that served as a secret facility for the Qods Force.

Bandar Deylam was a far cry from her hometown of Shiraz, once the capital of Iran and birthplace of the renowned Persian poets, Saadi and Hafez. She studied at Shiraz University, where her father was a respected professor.

Her life began to unravel in 2011, the year her father died of a heart attack followed only weeks later by the murder of her husband in a terrorist attack on his army base. The loss of the two most important men in her life left her feeling disconsolate. In her mourning, she began questioning life's capricious twists and turns.

Azar's mother, ever dependent upon her spouse of 35

years, struggled to come to grips with the solitary life of a widow in the months following his death. Soon Mama's health began to decline, and she, too, succumbed to the inevitable.

It was at this point when she was feeling most vulnerable, her husband's deputy, Major Tahmouress Samadi, reached out to her. He was not on duty the night the base was attacked, and thus managed to avoid the fate of his commander. In the weeks and months following Barzin's death, Samadi stayed in touch with her, even after he was transferred to Teheran.

The following year Samadi was promoted to colonel and appointed chief of Unit 400. Whether motivated by a sense of guilt or obligation to her husband, she never knew, but she was shocked and surprised when she learned he had recommended her to Qods Force commander, General Salehi, during a recruitment drive to sign up women for the elite force. The scheme was to assign the new recruits to support roles, or, in her case, assassins-in-training. Salehi's ultimate goal was to shake up the unit and give it non-traditional capabilities.

The Qods Force commander was said to be an idea man, and rumor had it the Ayatollahs paid attention when he spoke. She remembered a talk he gave shortly after completing her introductory training. He described two new initiatives just getting underway, in which the new recruits were to be assigned prominent roles. The first step was expected to give a boost to jihadists, by supporting a lethal spinoff to Al Qaeda in Iraq, *al-Dawla al-Islamiya fil Iraq wa al-Sham*, more commonly known by the sobriquet, the Islamic State, which had been gaining traction in the war-torn country since 2007.

"The Americans and their pawns will never suspect the Qods Force is working with the Sunnis," he said. "Of course ISIS is our enemy, and we must take every precaution to keep our cooperation with them under wraps. It would be a public relations nightmare for our leaders if this arrangement were ever disclosed. But we will use ISIS for our own purposes—to weaken Iraq, and in the process, defeat the Great Satan.

"Then when the time is ripe, before they destroy Iraq, we will turn on ISIS, and reclaim our rightful role as the most powerful Islamic republic in the world." He slammed his fist down on the desk and glared at them as if to challenge anyone's objection to his prophetic declaration.

At the time she was being indoctrinated, Azar was dubious about Salehi's vision. She met a couple of like-minded skeptics among the other trainees. Although it was dangerous for them to do so, they often shared their ideas in marathon discussions dragging late into the evening in their barracks.

"We all know the price Iran paid throughout the eighties in its decade-long war with Iraq," one raven-haired beauty said.

"It's true," Azar said. "By attacking Iran, Saddam Hussein thought he could put us in our place and establish Iraq as the leading Gulf state. This approach just happened to serve the interests of America, and the other Western countries who were no longer friends of Iran, given what happened to the Shah."

"But then Saddam did something very foolish," added Patrice, who was from Mashad. "He invaded Kuwait. All of a sudden, Iraq was on the wrong side of the Americans, and Saddam's allies became his enemies."

"Yes. Just the excuse the Americans needed to gain a foothold in the Gulf," Azar said. "Remember, between 1990 and 2004 America was either plotting against, bombing, or invading Iraq," she added.

A lengthy period of foreign occupation followed two devastating wars. Finally, in June 2004, the Iraqi Governing Council named Iyad Allawi prime minister.

Some in Iran thought the Americans would leave after that, but they were needed to prop up the new coalition government. It was during this period Salehi began to develop his idea of supporting ISIS. The timing just happened to coincide with Unit 400's recruitment of Azar. She remembered her initial conversation with Colonel Samadi.

"Look, Azar. Salehi's idea is to form assassination cells in strategic locations outside of Iran, from which his people could deploy on missions within their assigned region. We're going to send you to Venezuela for your first assignment. You'll be paired up with an Iranian-American by the name of Nouri Khorasani."

"Where will we live?"

"Caracas. You'll lease an apartment there, and we'll help you get established."

Azar was introduced to Nouri by Samadi during a hotel meeting in the Venezuelan capital. She remembered thinking he was young, but he had a proven track record. He worked with her to hone her skills and later they became lovers.

Three weeks into their assignment, Nouri was deployed to Mexico for a fast-breaking operation. The day he left, some men broke into their apartment and were waiting for her when she returned. All she remembered was being shot in the neck with a taser. She remained in a coma for several days and when she came to, she was told she was recuperating in a Caracas hospital.

"Where am I?" she asked.

"The Centro Médico de Caracas," the nurse replied.

Azar looked at her surroundings. She was apparently in a hospital room, and the woman speaking to her was no doubt a nurse, but she had no recollection of how she had gotten there.

"What happened?" she asked.

"You were attacked at your apartment. We received an anonymous tip you were injured. The doctors believe you were shot with a taser. Someone will be in to see you in a little while. Just rest for now." She patted Azar on the arm.

Azar still felt disoriented, but the memory of the attack was beginning to come back to her. She remembered returning to the apartment by herself because Nouri was on his way to Mexico. She recalled going inside and getting a tingly sensation warning her something was not right; that was when they attacked her. Whoever "they" were. It must have been at least two assailants because she was haunted by the memory of going after one of them with a knife, and then being shot in the neck with the taser. She sensed movement just before it happened, but she couldn't remember what the attacker looked like.

After her condition stabilized, Azar was medically evacuated to Iran where she underwent an extended period of therapy before she was able to return to work. During those months, Azar learned Nouri was in America to finish the job he had begun when he took out Hamid Al Subaie, scion of the wealthy Kuwaiti Al Subaies.

Something went terribly wrong, here in Boston, Azar thought. Nouri was killed, plunging to his death from the office building in front of her. She shielded her eyes as she gazed up at the gleaming structure, trying to imagine how terrified he must have been as he plummeted from the building to the pavement below. Did he take in the water taxis plying the harbor, or the yachts rocking in their slips in the nearby marina as he fell? Could he read the horrified expressions on the faces of the pedestrians strolling along the promenade? Did the thud his body made when it hit the sidewalk reach the recesses of his brain before the lights went out? She prayed he was dead before hitting the ground, sparing him the horror of that moment.

Azar didn't have any business being here in Boston today. She was on her way to New York City to vet an Iranian-American she was in touch with through a jihadist chat room she managed for ISIS. But she felt drawn to this spot.

She sighed as she dropped her hand and turned towards the sound of a passenger jet taking off from Logan Airport. She watched the JetBlue aircraft climb at a steep angle, straining to overcome gravity as it momentarily disappeared into the clouds and then re-emerged, the sun reflecting off its fuselage.

Azar steeled herself against the luxury of giving in to emotion after her father's and husband's deaths. She remembered the numbness of her anguish in each instance, incapable of rational thought as she wallowed in self-pity.

Since then, she was inured to the violent nature of her occupation, and the sudden, often gruesome, deaths her victims endured. This hardened her to the violence she often inflicted on others, deadening all human sensitivity. Thus, she was unprepared when the sudden onslaught of grief overwhelmed her as she took in the scene of Nouri's final moments. What had she become?

Tears flooded her eyes, and she stumbled as she turned away from the building. A young man walking by caught her arm as she tripped over an uneven spot on the sidewalk.

"Are you all right?" he asked. He released her arm, a look of concern on his face.

"Yes." She pulled back and kept moving. Her head began to clear as she walked away from the pier.

Perhaps it was foolish of her to come here, to pay homage to her partner, teacher, and lover. She couldn't afford to let her emotions rule her actions. She had work to do in New York and needed to be entirely in control. Considerable effort went into establishing her Alice Sherazi persona in Toronto, and she couldn't afford any missteps.

When her Unit 400 bosses initially proposed Canada as her base of operations, she resisted. But she came around after they told her, although Canada suspended diplomatic relations with Teheran in 2012 over international terrorism concerns, Immigration, Refugees, and Citizenship Canada continued to keep the gates open to qualified Iranians seeking Canadian citizenship. Over 95,000 Iranian expatriates were living in Canada when Azar moved into Toronto's Little Teheran neighborhood.

Maybe, in a different environment, she would be able to reclaim a part of herself that was all but gone. She would never again be the innocent coed of her university days, nor even the person she was when she first met her husband. But the cold-blooded assassin she had become was, in turn, slowly eating away at her humanity.

A young couple seated on a park bench locked in a passionate kiss was oblivious to her and everyone else. A few steps further, she stopped and gazed over the harbor, trying to reconcile her feelings with who she was.

Her bosses in Unit 400 took great pains to craft her new identity. They felt it was prudent, in light of Canada's designation of the Qods Force as number one on a list of international terrorist organizations. Iran stood out, even in the company of groups like Hamas, the Taliban, Hezbollah, and Islamic Jihad. For her to be successful, there could be no linkage between Azar Ghabel, Unit 400 operative, and Alice Sherazi, a newly arrived immigrant.

Azar felt mostly ambivalent when Samadi first outlined the details of his plan for her. With both of her parents and husband gone, she had no lasting ties to her birthplace. She was given a fabricated cover legend incorporating many of the details of her early life in Shiraz so she could speak with familiarity about her hometown.

Building on a childhood interest in photography, Azar completed the equivalent of a masters of fine arts in photography program while she was in Teheran, with the objective of immigrating under Canada's criteria for self-employed people. The Qods Force helped her build up an impressive portfolio as she submitted her work to the "right" places for publication. By the time she applied for her residence permit, she had a professional credential and two years' experience as a freelance photographer under her belt.

Azar glanced back at the couple on the bench. The young man caressed his girlfriend's face with both hands while gazing into her eyes. Azar continued to walk, quickening her pace to distance herself from the two lovers.

After she arrived in Canada, Azar rented an apartment with one bedroom plus a den near the Yonge/Steeles area in north Toronto. It was anonymous enough with over a hundred and fifty apartments in two towers. The complex had been built with privacy in mind. Each unit was on two floors, and the front door of each was staggered, so no two main entrances opened onto each other. The nearest public transportation was only two blocks away, and there were plenty of stores, restaurants, and coffee shops in the neighborhood.

Azar converted the den into a photo lab. Her freelance photographer job afforded the flexibility necessary for frequent trips abroad. Most of her travel was to South America; if this trip to the U.S. was successful, she expected that she would be spending more time here in the months ahead.

Azar checked her watch. She was booked on the 12:10 p.m. Acela Express from South Station. It was only 10:15, but she needed to check out of her hotel and retrieve her bag, so she decided to take a cab to Jamaica Plain. A taxi pulled up, and she gave the driver the name of her street. As she settled into her seat, she thought about the day ahead. It was three and a half hours to New York's Penn Station. When she got in, the first order of business would be to pay a visit to the NYC Mini Storage facility in the Bronx.

One of Samadi's support assets had rented a five-by-five-foot unit there in one of Azar's alias accounts. Inside the unit, she would find cash, alias documentation, an assortment of weapons, and a cell phone. Azar would store her Alice Sherazi documentation and personal cell phone there and pick up what she needed for her New York stay.

She told the driver to wait while she checked out of the hotel and retrieved her bag. Twenty minutes later, her taxi pulled up in front of South Station. She pawed through her purse for a twenty and told the driver to keep the change. Once inside, she purchased a bottle of water and a piece of fruit at a kiosk and made her way to the platform.

As she mentally plotted her day, she began to feel that slight tingle of adrenaline coursing through her bloodstream. It was game on.

Chapter 4

Zahir called Logan to let him know she and Cooper would spend a few more days with her parents. He thought she sounded less tense than when they last spoke. Maybe the talk with her mother helped after all. He had just hung up when the doorbell rang.

What struck him the most when he opened the door was how much Nayef had aged. When they first met over six years ago, the Kuwaiti billionaire was slim, sporting a thin, wispy mustache. There was an urbane, sleek demeanor about him. The man standing before him today was 20 pounds heavier, wore a bushy goatee, glasses, and had gray streaks running through his hair. Nayef was in his early fifties but could easily pass for someone ten years older.

They shook hands. "Nayef! Please come in."

"Logan, how are you?" The Kuwaiti businessman walked inside, and Logan showed him to two armchairs with a view of the city.

"Here, let me take your jacket. Would you like a glass of wine?" He hung the jacket over the back of a chair and then walked over to a sideboard with glasses and a bottle of wine.

"Please."

He poured a generous portion of a Malbec into Nayef's glass and then helped himself. The two men settled into their chairs. Nayef took an appreciative sip of his wine and visibly relaxed. "Ah. That's good, he said."

"How's Nisreen?" Nisreen was Nayef's wife, an accomplished novelist and women's rights activist in Kuwait. Logan first met her following the successful conclusion of the operation against Unit 400, years before.

"She sends her love. She was hoping to join me on this trip, but the publisher is pushing her to finish a new book due out this fall. How's Zahir? And your son?"

"They're fine, considering."

Nayef gave him a quizzical look.

"We lost a child in January," said Logan. "It was unexpected. A baby girl. She died stillborn. It's been hard."

Nayef set his glass down and leaned forward in his chair. "I'm sorry, Logan. I didn't know. Millie didn't say anything."

"No, she wouldn't. Zahir's been depressed. We thought it would be better for her to be closer to family, so we left Hong Kong. Just last week in fact."

"And how about you?" Said Nayef. "We men are supposed to be strong, but we have feelings, too." He seemed lost in thought for a moment, then continued.

"When Hamid died, it was one of the hardest things I've ever had to deal with. Way worse than losing a parent. I don't think you ever completely get over it. You develop coping mechanisms to deal with the pain. Some people handle it better than others. "What are you going to do?"

"We'll try to get on with our lives here. I'm not planning any travel for a couple of months. I'll work from home a couple of days a week to make sure she's doing okay. If she's up to it, she'll probably go back to teaching at BU in the fall. We're going to homeschool Cooper for the remainder of the year. We'll enroll him in a Montessori program down the street in September."

"How about your business? Did you close your office in Hong Kong?"

Nayef wasn't aware he was working for the CIA, and there was no reason to let him in on that secret. Besides, Alicia, Norm Stoddard, and Bruce Wellington were still running operations in Hong Kong. They would eventually phase out their office there, but probably not until next year sometime. Meanwhile, he would stick with the story he'd worked out with headquarters.

"China's a tight market to crack. Not everything's

transparent, so it's hard to know what to believe. We primarily do maritime consulting. So far, our bread and butter here at home has been working with U.S. Navy Special Operations Command on some of their requirements. He took another sip of wine, set his glass down, and continued.

"I wasn't naïve enough to think we'd be winning any Chinese military contracts going into this, but China's doing a fair amount of commercial shipbuilding, too. Everything from luxury yachts to fishing boats. They even have an icebreaker in the works because of their interest in Arctic exploration."

"So, you're focused on the commercial market?"

"We are. I just think it's too hard for an outsider like us to crack the military side in China."

"Not only that," said Nayef. "There are things as a foreigner you just don't understand. Kuwait does billions in two-way trade with China annually. We started trading with them in the fifties, and over time, we've gotten to know them pretty well. But corruption, cronyism, currency manipulation, all of these can hurt your bottom line. You need to be very careful."

"We'll probably give it another year. If things don't pick up, everything else being equal, we'll pull back from Asia and stay closer to home."

He offered Nayef more of the Malbec. After refilling his own glass, he set the decanter down on the sideboard and returned to his seat. Toying with his drink, he wondered what was on Nayef's mind. He knew for sure his friend hadn't reached out to him to talk about trade with China. He didn't have to wait long.

"Logan, I wanted to talk to you about a growing terrorism concern in Kuwait, although not only Kuwait. I'm talking about Islamic State specifically. As you know, my family has played a vital leadership role in Kuwait's modernization. We have a written constitution, freedom of speech, and fair elections. We're considered progressive in the Arab world.

"But in the last couple of years, I've been troubled by a

mentality among some of our leaders, fostering what your treasury department calls a "permissive jurisdiction" for terrorist fundraising. There are people in power who have shown an inclination to look the other way when these questionable practices come to light. And in some cases, there are those who actively promote them.

"We're concerned about the activities of ISIS, not only in Kuwait but regionally. They're becoming more powerful by the day with their fundraising and recruitment activities."

"I hate to say it Nayef, but that's old news. If I remember correctly, your nephew was radicalized that way. Somehow a recruiter got hold of his name and approached him when he made the Hajj to Mecca.

"It's true. Mohammad met the wrong people. Not ISIS. We know it was the Iranians and possibly Al Qaeda. But I think he was already disaffected. It didn't take much to turn him away from his family and towards *jihad*.

"There have been many studies on what it takes to radicalize someone. It's become fashionable in the West to blame Islamic extremism on Islamic orthodoxy. But I believe this is an over-simplification.

"You have to admit, Nayef, the Hajj could be fertile ground for *jihadi* recruiters. Last year alone something like three million Hajjis made the pilgrimage. Some of them are bound to get recruited."

"Maybe you're right. I remember when I made my own Hajj over thirty-five years ago." He had a far-off look in his eye.

"What was it like?"

Nayef paused as he thought back to the events of that week long ago.

"It's a big commitment for the average person, with the travel costs and time off from work. Every year the Hajj begins on the eighth day of *Dhul Al-Hijah*, which is the twelfth month in the Islamic calendar. It translates roughly as "possessor of the pilgrimage" in English. I made the Hajj with my father and uncle." He gazed off into the distance.

"I know the Hajj has been going on for almost fourteen

hundred years, but why is it so important to Muslims?"

"In the year six thirty-two, just before his death, the Prophet Mohammed made what has been called his 'Farewell Pilgrimage' to Mecca. For this reason alone, the practice has great significance for Muslims. But more than a commemoration of Mohammad's pilgrimage, we also believe the rituals we celebrate during the Hajj commemorate Hagar and Ishmael's survival in the desert. You may recall from your own studies of scripture, the prophet, Abraham, left them there to avoid the fury of his first wife, Sarah, who could have no children, and was jealous because Hagar, her maid, had borne Abraham a son.

"When Abraham returned to the desert after some time to check on them, he learned they had discovered a well, which later became known as *Zam*, making it possible for them to survive their ordeal. Not only were they surviving; they turned the well into a flourishing business, bartering water in exchange for food from travelers.

"Abraham built the Kaaba as a shrine to Allah and to give thanks for his intervention in the protection of Hagar and Ishmael."

"Today, would there be many opportunities for *jihadis* to find new recruits during the week?" Logan asked.

"It would be difficult for someone to pursue a radical agenda there. That kind of activity would go against the whole purpose of the Hajj. In one sense, there is a feeling of equality among the Hajjis. Everyone wears *Ihram*, a kind of white garment, and an effort is made to strip away differences. Characteristics like social status, nationality, and ethnicity are deemphasized."

"But, Mohammed's case begs the question."

"I'm not saying it doesn't happen, or that such contacts couldn't take place on the margins. I'm just saying I doubt large numbers of young men are being recruited while they are on the Hajj. Besides, they're too busy.

"The first day begins with the *Umra*, a kind of purification ritual. We started at a place called Miquat, which is near Mecca. There we bathed, put on the *Ihram*, and made our intentions for the pilgrimage known. Afterward, we recited prayers while walking around the Kaaba seven times. This ritual is called the *Tawaf*.

"When we finished circling the Kaaba, we drank some water from the sacred well, and then walked back and forth between the Safa and Marwa hills seven times."

"What's the point of all that?"

"It represents Hagar's search for water and prayers to God to save her and Ishmael from dying in the desert."

"But that was just the beginning of our week. Over the next several days, we traveled to Mina, the valley of Arafat, and Muzdalifa, where we made sacrifices, prayed to God and participated in a ritual to cast out Satan."

"What kind of sacrifices?"

"We stood in the desert sun for an entire day. We threw stones at pillars in Mina called *Jamraat*. These represent the devil. We sacrificed a lamb. And we had to shave our heads.

"We finished our pilgrimage on the twelfth day of the month. I remember making one final *Tawaf* in Mecca and standing there with my father and uncle asking for God's forgiveness. It was uplifting.

"But let's set that aside for now. Getting back to ISIS. What's been happening in Iraq has had us worried for several years, but now ISIS is operating in our own backyard."

"How so?"

"There is compelling evidence ISIS was behind the bombing of a Shiite mosque in Al Ahmadi last month. Our security people have arrested what they are calling an 'ISIS cell' in Kuwait City who they believe may be behind it."

"How many people?"

"I think it was five. I'm not sure. It was made up of both men and women."

"Are they cooperating with the police?"

"No. These people are devoted *jihadis*. They would rather die than betray their associates. But the authorities did retrieve cell phones and computers from them, and they are in the process of exploiting those now.

"Besides this, I was speaking with my Uncle Ali last

week. You remember meeting him in Kuwait?"

"Yes, of course." Ali Al Subaie was the moneyman behind the Bandar Deylam operation. A Kuwaiti financier, he set up offshore dummy accounts to cover funding and acquisitions for the covert operation Logan mounted against the Qods Force.

"Ali is concerned about irregular financial transactions he sees taking place with greater and greater frequency, especially fundraising for charities, in the mosques. It hasn't helped our government has refused to acknowledge the severity of this situation. In fact, they are a big part of the problem. Last year, the national assembly had the nerve to appoint a person with known ties to terrorism finance to a minister-level position in the government."

"I know. Treasury has been pressuring Kuwait to tighten up its financial regulations to make it harder for these people to use the financial system to move money around. They've sanctioned some people and blacklisted others." Logan jumped out of his seat and began to pace around the room.

"Logan, ISIS isn't getting the majority of its funding from these kinds of transactions. They're selling tankers full of oil they've stolen from Iraqi oil fields near Mosul and Syrian oil fields near Deir Ezzor. Some estimate they're selling on the order of a hundred thousand barrels a day. Others say it's less, maybe half as much.

"Ali told me his sources in the Iraqi Finance Ministry believe ISIS is getting twenty-five dollars per barrel. At a hundred thousand barrels per day, they're banking on the order of seventeen million dollars a week."

"Who's buying it? We have a lot of allies in the region. It has to be hard for ISIS to move this much product." Logan frowned as he considered the possibility U.S. allies would place a higher premium on cheap oil than their mutual security.

"Believe it or not, our security people believe much of it goes right back into Syria. I assume ISIS is using a portion of it to fuel their own war effort. But there's also strong evidence President Assad is purchasing much of it. ISIS doesn't have any refining capabilities. They are just selling the crude to Assad, and it gets moved to refineries the regime controls in the western part of Syria."

"What do you think of the Russian claims that Turkey is buying up the ISIS crude for refining in Turkey?"

"Ali is convinced the Russian allegations are suspect. He believes Turkey has minimal unauthorized refining capability. The majority of their oil production is through a company called Tüpras. It was state-owned until 2006 when it was privatized. I know it has been fined in recent years for price gouging and unfair trading conditions, but Ali feels, even if they wanted to, it would be too risky for them to accept ISIS crude into their refineries."

"I doubted the Russian theory from the outset," Logan said. Moscow made those accusations right after Turkey shot down one of their bombers near the Syrian border. The Russians will say anything to make the Turks look bad."

"Whether the Turkish angle is correct or not, we know ISIS is funding much of its activity through the sale of stolen oil. Someone is refining it, and someone is buying it. It will take international cooperation and a willingness to impose sanctions where needed to cut off this stream of oil. That is for governments to deal with.

"What I really want to talk about is something else." Nayef took a deep breath and fixed his eyes on Logan. "ISIS is recruiting *jihadis* in the U.S. They want to set up a fifth column made up of ISIS cells to attack America."

Chapter 5

The expression on Logan's face belied the queasy feeling twisting his insides as he digested Nayef's words. The world had seen the shocking videos of beheadings, listened to the ominous threats spewed from the mouths of ISIS psychopaths, and watched in helpless dismay as the extremists occupied enormous swaths of territory in Iraq and Syria. Recent efforts by the U.S. military and Iraqi forces to drive ISIS out of the occupied territories were putting a dent in the ISIS offensive. But ISIS was persistent, continuing to fight on many fronts against all odds. There were recent provocations in Libya and Afghanistan as well as increasing numbers of ISIS-inspired attacks in the U.S. and Europe. These disturbing assaults were forcing law enforcement and the intelligence community to double down their efforts to contain and eradicate the terrorist group.

But to suggest ISIS had the wherewithal to launch a campaign on the scale Nayef was intimating, inside the U.S., was absurd. Or, was it? If nothing else, Logan had learned not to underestimate the enemy when he was deployed to Afghanistan. And ISIS was cut from the same cloth as Al Qaeda.

Kuwait didn't come across as a reliable source of actionable intelligence on terrorism to most of the people he knew working the issue, indeed not a consequential player on the world stage, but the Al Subaies had been doing business all over the globe, especially in the Middle East, for decades. Their successes could be measured by the enormity of their holdings, which even in the company of the wealthiest Arab sheikhs, were substantial. The Al Subaies hadn't reached the pinnacle of the business world by fumbling their way to the top. They were in the know. And when Nayef spoke, it made sense to pay attention.

"Where's this coming from, Nayef? We've heard the threats. ISIS has mastered social media and has been effective with their propaganda campaigns. But to imply they could establish infrastructure here seems like a stretch."

"Do you have a good handle on ISIS, Logan? Do you feel as though you understand them?"

"Since I got out of the navy, I can't say I've had any unique insights, other than what I read and see in the news. I know ISIS grew out of Al Qaeda in Iraq and the U.S. has portrayed them as some kind of evil JV team, not as well organized as Al Qaeda. They are despicable, and they've inflicted damage, usually in graphic, inhumane ways. But I think we've assumed they wouldn't have staying power over the long run. Don't you think moderate Muslims will eventually rally against them?"

"The West can't grasp the fact ISIS actually appeals to a certain demographic. Most of us in the Middle East tend to see them as psychopaths, but they actually have core religious beliefs and adhere to established religious doctrine." Nayef's expression was ominous.

"They're doomsday believers. They have embraced an apocalyptic vision of the world, pitting their brand of Islam against everyone else, especially Jews and Christians. Their own self-survival is far less important to them than pursuing their radical, destructive agenda." Nayef toyed with his wine glass for a moment and continued.

"Their point of view isn't a modern one. You would have to search all the way back to the sixth century, the time of Mohammed, to put it into context and to understand how they're interpreting the Quran in today's world."

"When you say apocalyptic are you talking about the final days? The Day of Judgment?"

"Yes," Nayef said. "Just as Christians believe in the hereafter, so, too, do the followers of ISIS. They just have a different belief in how to get to paradise." Nayef stood and stretched. He walked over to the windows and looked out over East Boston as the city lights came to life. He paused in deep thought before returning to his theme. Turning back to Logan, he continued.

"We now know the so-called leader of all Muslims, the Caliph, is an Iraqi by the name of Abu Bakr Al Baghdadi. So little is actually known about him he is often referred to as 'the invisible sheikh.'

"Baghdadi's sermon at the Great Mosque in Mosul in 2014 announced the establishment of the Caliphate and his appointment as the Caliph. He laid out a broad agenda and called on all Muslims to follow him."

"Obviously that hasn't happened," Logan said. "Although it's surprising how many *jihadis* have responded to his call."

"I will say this. Most mainstream Muslims reject Baghdadi's call to action. The people stuck under ISIS control in Syria and Iraq number perhaps seven million. But how many of them are true adherents? Look how many people have left their homes and everything they own to get away from ISIS.

"It's also impossible to know how many foot soldiers ISIS has. The estimates are all over the map, ranging from a low of twenty thousand to a high of one hundred thousand. The real number is probably somewhere in between."

"But getting back to their belief system, what is it they really believe?" Logan involuntarily clenched his fists in anger.

"Let's start with their attitude towards other Muslims. ISIS is a Sunni-based group. They believe many Shiite practices are in violation of the Quran and so to them, all Shia believers are considered apostates. According to their interpretation of Sharia law, these people should be killed. That's somewhere around a hundred and seventy million Shia, give or take."

"So essentially," said Logan, "if ISIS considers Shiites to be apostates, that doesn't leave much hope for everybody else. It's ISIS against the world." He shook his head in disbelief.

"Pretty much. And apparently anything it takes to reach ISIS's goal can be justified through Sharia law; they are a throwback to the sixth century. Practices like crucifixion, rape, slavery, and beheadings were commonplace during Mohammed's time. These modern-day adherents actually believe they have a moral justification for committing such offenses."

Logan found it hard to keep the emotion out of his response. When he finally spoke, his voice was steely. "That's disgusting. What ISIS is doing to Christians and Jews amounts to ethnic cleansing. *The New York Times* reported last year was the worst in modern times for Christian persecutions. Over 7,000 people were killed in a single year. ISIS isn't just murdering Christians though; it's also driving them out of places where they've lived for thousands of years."

The two men were silent as they contemplated the dismal state of the world. Logan joined Nayef by the window and looked out at the city. Logan spoke first.

"I just don't understand how ISIS is flourishing. How can they expect to recruit Americans to carry out these attacks in the U.S?"

"Let me tell you about a briefing I attended just last week," Nayef said. Our security people told me last year, thirty-two people in the U.S. said they would like to help ISIS by conducting an attack in America."

"Where's that coming from?"

"The FBI filed charges against them. Your legal attaché in Riyadh briefed our Ministry of Interior last month. He brought some people from Washington to interview the suspects from the mosque bombing. Before they left, they offered a broader ISIS briefing to our security people.

"Five of those who said they would like to help ISIS were actually in direct contact with them, and four others thought they were talking to ISIS but in reality, it was the FBI. Four others succeeded in carrying out three separate attacks in Texas, Florida, and California."

Nayef continued. "According to the FBI, there were

many more, perhaps hundreds, with a different agenda. They didn't necessarily want to carry out attacks in the U.S. They were trying to get to Syria or Iraq and join ISIS as foreign fighters. *Jihadists.*"

"You hear about some of these cases, but I thought the number was lower than that," Logan said.

"The FBI told us they have over one thousand active investigations against U.S. citizens sympathetic to ISIS," Nayef said.

"A lot of these leads must be coming from social media," Logan said.

"Yes, Twitter in particular. The initial contact often takes place there, and at some point, ISIS moves the conversation to a secure messaging program like CryptoCat or ChatSecure. Other apps like Wickr and Surespot automatically destroy a message after it's encrypted. And since no record resides on the service provider's server, the authorities can't retrieve those conversations."

"I know law enforcement has developed a profile of what these people look like," Logan said. "The New York City Police Department's intelligence unit says from what they're seeing, the majority of ISIS supporters in the U.S. are American. They're young. Maybe twenty-six years old on average. And they're male."

"I saw a similar study conducted by researchers at Georgetown University," Nayef said. "They concluded the ISIS supporters in the U.S. are a diverse group. They span the socioeconomic spectrum. Some had only a high school education, and others had graduate degrees."

Abruptly changing the subject, Nayef asked, "Do you remember when we helped you and your team procure alias passports for the Bandar Deylam operation?"

"Yes. Why?" Logan was taken aback by the question. Kuwait's security service had obtained official-looking Canadian passports so the team could travel in alias from the U.S. to Kuwait, where they trained for their incursion into Iran.

"When our security people processed the team's

paperwork, as a matter of routine, they conducted background checks based on your original documentation. This information included contact information for next of kin, parents, and siblings."

"Yes. I vaguely remember filling out those forms. So?"

"This information was entered into the security service's databases. Typically, it would be archived after five years, but for some reason, it wasn't. When our researchers are conducting name traces, they run the names against everything in the database."

"You and Zahir were not yet married when you traveled to Kuwait. Is that right?"

"Right. It wasn't until the following year."

"She was entered into the system under her maiden name, Parandeh," Nayef said.

"Yes. I'm sure she was. But what's this about, Nayef?" Logan sounded exasperated as he waited for Nayef to make his point.

"Last week, Zahir's name came up during a routine name trace."

"We've done some international travel over the past few years, so I'm not surprised."

Nayef's expression was ominous. "The information was not about Zahir specifically, it was about her brother, Ali. Ali Parandeh."

Logan felt his stomach lurch as Nayef uttered those words. He waited for his friend to continue.

"Ali Parandeh was approached by an ISIS spotter last week. It looks as though he's in the early stages of being radicalized."

Chapter 6

Ali Parandeh bore a close resemblance to his father, Nima. He was in his late thirties. Despite his slight frame and short stature, he had a rugged quality about him. A shock of black hair was combed over to one side, and a full mustache framed his upper lip. He was sometimes mistaken for Italian, with his olive complexion offset by brooding eyes the shade of night.

Ali enjoyed a privileged childhood, growing up among the other wealthy Iranian expatriates in the Washington, D.C. area after his parents decided to flee the upheaval known as the Iranian Revolution in 1979. He was four years old when his mother and father abandoned Teheran in favor of the leafy Arlington suburb in northern Virginia where they now lived. As he grew older, the images of their old neighborhood in Teheran dimmed, now reduced to a pencil sketch where once they had been a full tapestry, rich in texture.

Besides their close physical resemblance, Ali shared one other quality with his father, a deep yearning for his lost homeland. Ali didn't understand the root cause of this feeling. It wasn't rational. Other than the disruption caused by being transplanted at the age of four, where he had to learn a new language and make new friends, his early years were care-free and unremarkable by most standards.

His parents were conservative Muslims. By this, he didn't mean they were zealots. They kept halal, attended prayer services at the Islamic center on Mass Avenue in the district, and insisted he and his sister, Zahir, learn the Persian language and participate in a Sunday program in Islamic and Quran studies at the Arlington Islamic Center.

He attended Washington-Lee High School, where his exploits on the soccer field earned him the nickname of Hejazi, after Nasser Hejazi, the world-famous Iranian goalkeeper who gained recognition in World Cup play years earlier, right around the same time Ali and his parents were fleeing the Iranian Revolution.

Following high school graduation, Ali attended the University of Virginia (UVA) in Charlottesville, where after his second year, he decided to take the entrance exam for admission to the university's undergraduate business program at the McIntire School of Commerce. Unlike his father, Ali wasn't drawn to a career in civil engineering. He was interested in business, though and purposely chose a marketing concentration with the goal of securing a position with an international firm following graduation.

He returned to Washington for a year after college but soon realized New York City was where he needed to be if he was going to amount to anything. After five years of bouncing around the marketing world, he landed his dream job. He was hired as the senior coordinator for international marketing for the NBA. He was based in New York City but did a fair amount of travel to Asia and Latin America, where the NBA was working closely with local marketing teams to develop programs consistent with the NBA's brand. Just this month alone, he had meetings in Brazil and Mumbai.

Thanks to his mother's inheritance and the family's investments in oil during petroleum's heyday in Iran, money was never a problem. He owned a two-bedroom apartment in Chelsea, just down the street from the Chelsea Market and kept a BMW 750L for weekend trips out of town.

At the moment, he was on his way to the market to pick up breakfast. The building housing Chelsea Market formerly belonged to the National Biscuit Company and dated back to the 1800s. Like many of his fellow New Yorkers, Ali did little cooking at home, preferring to avail himself of the plentiful choices of street food, take-out, and restaurants in the city. He strolled into the market and walked down to Abby's Bakery. They had everything in there, but his favorite was their Semolina-fennel-raisin bread.

"Let me have a loaf of that." He gestured, pointing to the rack of fresh loaves.

"That'll be $4.37," the cashier said as she slid the loaf into a sleeve and folded over the end. "How've you been?" She smiled. "I haven't seen you in a couple of weeks."

"Traveling," Ali said. "Just got back from Rio yesterday."

"Oh. Welcome back."

"Thanks." He pocketed his change and as he turned, held the warm loaf up to his nose and inhaled its yeasty fragrance. His mouth began to water, so he reached inside and tore off a small chunk, which as usual, never failed to satisfy. Weaving around the throng of early morning commuters, he made his way to the Smiling Barista, where he purchased an Espresso with milk.

Looking at his watch, he saw it was 7:35. Time enough to relax and enjoy his breakfast. He found an empty table and sat down, basking in the tide of humanity bustling through the marketplace.

As Ali ate, he entertained himself with a game, letting his imagination run free as he scanned the crowd, now and then zeroing in on a face, trying to foretell what was in store for that person in life. Of course, he had no way of knowing anything about these people. But there was always something foreboding about his reflections.

A young middle school student carrying a violin case became a budding virtuoso, whose prospects seemed limitless until he was struck down with leukemia at the age of 13, surrendering to it the following year. An ebullient 17-year-old girl destined for Smith College would succumb to opioid addiction in her freshman year and would spend the next eight years in and out of rehab, her skeletal frame and vacant eyes, a shell of her former self. Two Hispanic immigrants, flush with their first pay from a day job on a construction site in the Bronx, would be assaulted in a back alley, blocks from where he sat for resisting a mugger's demand for their money. One would be shot down, and the other grievously wounded.

He seldom wondered about these morbid concoctions. He never resisted them. In fact, he welcomed and even embellished on them. Sometimes he felt if he allowed his ruminations to give way to action he would be diagnosed as a bona fide psycho, but self-restraint always triumphed. He was but a voyeur to his own depraved imagination.

That is until today. The old factory clock suspended from the ceiling registered eight-ten. Just enough time to meet his Uber ride for the drive to West 39th Street, where there was an internet café. He needed to get there in time to log in to an eight-thirty chat session a new friend from the mosque had set up for him. He was intrigued by the private nature of the contact. Akbar warned him never to log into this chat from his home computer. He gave him the address of the internet café and told him to log into jitsi.org, using their off-the-record encryption feature.

"You will find what this person has to say, very much in line with your thinking," Akbar said.

Ali exited the market onto 9th Avenue as his ride pulled up. He didn't have to wait for long considering the time of day and the fact a light spring drizzle had begun while he was eating breakfast.

"West 39th. Between 8th and Avenue of the Americas."

"All right."

The driver pulled into traffic, and Ali settled back into his seat. The rain was beginning to pick up. Pedestrians were pulling out umbrellas and running for cover. As he was riding, Ali reminisced about the life-changing meeting, just a week ago, with his new friend from the mosque, Akbar.

Their encounter had happened the day before his trip to Rio. He had been attending weekly prayer services at the Masjid al-Farah mosque in Tribeca, and as usual, found himself disenchanted with the Imam's cliché message. His sermons promoted a doctrine of moderation, of harmony. *He must have been living under a rock for the last twenty years,* Ali thought, not to feel some anger over the way Muslims were treated in the U.S.

He remembered one sermon in particular. The cleric was speaking on the subject of patience. One quote the Imam took directly from Allah stuck with him. *"Oh, you who believe, seek assistance through patience and prayer; surely Allah is with the patient."*

He wasn't able to get the words out of his mind for the rest of the sermon, because to him, it was a call to capitulate, to remain passive. Muslims were being advised to keep their heads down and pray Allah would take care of everything. Meanwhile, thousands of their brothers were being slaughtered all over the world, victims of senseless bloodshed.

As Ali stood fuming outside the mosque after prayers that day, he was distracted thinking about an image from an ISIS video he watched the night before. In it, ISIS militants had beheaded four Kurdish *Peshmerga*, literally, those who face death. ISIS had captured these Kurdish fighters near the town of Sinjar in the Talafar district of northern Iraq.

He hadn't turned away from the screen as he watched the brutal ritual unfold. It took place in a desert setting, devoid of any evidence of human habitation. An ISIS militant waved a flag buffeted by the desert wind. At the top, the black and white banner, often associated with ISIS, but not unique to the group, proclaimed in Arabic, "There is no God but Allah." Beneath were the words, "Mohammad is the Messenger of Allah." It gave affirmation from on high to what the group was about to do.

The four *Peshmerga* captives wore matching orange jumpsuits. Their hands were secured behind their backs, as they knelt before their captors. Behind each man stood an ISIS executioner, clad in black robes and hoods leaving only their eyes exposed. Each grasped a serrated fixed-blade combat knife in his hand. As they listened to the ISIS commander read the charges against them, the prisoners stared straight ahead, betraying no emotion other than an occasional nervous licking of the lips. When the attack came, it was swift. Flashing knives, severed heads, and rivers of blood staining the desert sand.

"So, what did you think of the Imam's sermon?"

Ali roused himself from his reflections. Standing before him was a man about his age, perhaps a few years older. He considered ignoring the question. Everyone knew the NYPD and FBI trolled the mosques looking for radicals. They even had informants among some of the Muslims who worshiped there on the payroll. But something about the man's demeanor caused him to drop his guard.

"We have an image problem," he said.

"What do you mean?"

Ali inclined his head towards the mosque. "He's preaching a message of patience and prayer. That doesn't sound like a call to action to me."

"What do you propose?"

"I'm not sure. You know, we only make up about one percent of the population here."

"You mean in New York?"

"No. I'm talking about nationwide. One percent."

"So?"

"There are fewer Middle Easterners here than African Americans. It took a civil war for blacks to get their freedom, and there's still a double standard in how they're treated. We don't stand a chance."

Ali didn't give a shit about African Americans, but their plight helped him make his point.

"You know, not all the Imams are like this one. I think the ones here in the city are kind of covering their asses. They stick to the Quran, but they know 'Big Brother' is looking over their shoulder, so they don't preach anything provocative.

"You ought to listen to this one Imam who's in Kuwait. His name is Hassan Al Sadiq."

"How did you hear about him?" He pulled out a business card. "By the way I'm Ali."

"Akbar. Hey, you want to grab a cup of coffee? I think there's a café near here."

The two men had walked to a Starbucks on Hudson Street. After they ordered, they took their coffees and sat in armchairs, where they continued their conversation.

"So, you were saying?" Ali asked.

"What? Oh, how I heard about Al Sadiq. It's kind of funny, but it was a little bit like me running into you today. I came out of prayers once last year, and I was really pissed about something the Imam said. He was telling us the NYPD and Department of Homeland Security called a meeting of all the senior Imams in the city. He went and got this big lecture from the cops saying the religious leaders were part of the problem and needed to start using their voices to counter the more radical Imams who were preaching hatred.

"NYPD basically told them they were being co-opted, and if they didn't get with the program, the city was going to make life hard for them," Akbar said with a scowl. "Anyway, I was steaming, just like you, and I ran into this dude who told me about Al Sadiq. I've been in touch with him for about six months now, and he's the real deal.

"I'm not afraid to tell you though, I'm paranoid. I initially listened to Al Sadiq's webcast at home, but the first time I actually reached out to him with a question, I used an internet café. I've got a good job, and I don't need the NYPD knocking on my door and giving me shit. So, I'm just saying. If you're not happy with what you hear at Masjid al-Farah, maybe you need to give this a try." He held out a folded piece of paper.

Ali had slipped it into his pocket.

* * *

After work that night, Ali stopped at the New York Public Library and researched some of Al Sadiq's writings. One quote, taken from one of his online posts, seemed to sum up his philosophy.

"The West needs to accept the fact Islam is the fastest growing religion in the world. Decadent democracies will be destroyed in time, and Sharia law will prevail. The Caliph will see to it his Caliphate stretches to the ends of the earth and the infidels will become our slaves."

He read several more postings but deferred following up because of his trip to Rio. He had a jam-packed week there, during which time he worked out the specifics of a deal between the NBA and Brazil's national basketball league. It gave the NBA national-level control of all advertising, marketing, and merchandising in Brazil. His bosses thought he could do no wrong after the ink dried on that agreement.

Ali's thoughts turned to the present as his car swung onto West 39th and pulled up to the entrance of the internet café. He paid the driver and consulted his watch. Five minutes until he would actually be able to hear from the Imam himself. He hurried inside.

Chapter 7

A zar stowed her bag in the overhead luggage rack and settled into her seat in the quiet car on the 12:10 p.m. Acela Express. She wasn't planning to use any of her electronic devices so as to avoid leaving a digital trail from Boston to New York. To stay occupied, she had brought a New York City guidebook along to study.

The train picked up speed, and within seconds, they emerged from the station into bright sunlight. The rail yard seemed to go on forever before giving way to graffiti-covered abutments separating the tracks from the urban squalor crowding up against them.

As they hurtled south, the countryside opened up. Here and there one caught a fleeting glance over backyard fences into suburbia. Passing through Connecticut, she was surprised to catch brief glimpses of the ocean, but these quickly gave way to fields as they moved west and inland. Before she knew it, the three-and-a-half-hour trip was over as they eased into Penn Station. She exited the station onto West 31st where it took her 15 minutes to flag down a taxi.

"The Bronx," she said to the driver, as she settled into the back seat.

"Where in the Bronx, lady?" he asked. "It's a big place."

She pulled the address of the mini storage facility out of her pocket. "942 Johnson Avenue in Riverdale."

The driver grunted and pulled into traffic. He took several turns before merging onto New York 9-A south, exiting onto the Henry Hudson Parkway, which brought him into the Bronx. Twenty minutes later, he pulled up in front of the mini storage facility, a ramshackle two-story brick structure with roll-up doors.

"Do you want me to wait?" he asked, studying her through the rearview mirror.

"No, thanks. I might be awhile." Azar paid him and went into the building. She still had 30 minutes before they closed. It would be convenient to have him wait, but since she would be emerging from the storage facility with a different identity, she thought it best to cut any ties to the traveler just in from Penn Station. It might not make any difference but playing it safe would cost her no more than a minor inconvenience.

Azar mounted the stairs to the second floor, walked down a narrow corridor to unit 2-AA. The light switch was on the right. After closing the door firmly and locking it from the inside, she took stock of the room's contents. Metal shelving lined one wall. On each shelf sat a footlocker secured with a combination lock. She dialed the combination on the first locker from memory and lifted the lid to reveal a cache of weapons and ammunition. After a minute spent examining the contents, she removed a Glock 9mm, two magazines of spare ammo, and a tactical fighting knife.

From a second footlocker, she withdrew $5,000, leaving behind about $35,000 in small denominations—more than enough to cover her expenses for this trip. Whenever possible, she would try to use cash instead of credit cards to minimize her credit trail. You never knew who might be watching, and it was much easier to cover your tracks going in than trying to explain a complicated electronic footprint after the fact.

The third locker contained her alias documentation—passport, driver's license, credit cards, and pocket litter. She carefully withdrew all of the Alice Shirazi documentation from her purse, placed it in the footlocker and removed the documents for her new identity—Alice Meens.

Finally, she read a note tucked into an envelope inside the locker containing emergency contact instructions, should she run into a problem. The letter also gave the address for a short-term rental in Brooklyn where she would be staying. If things worked out according to plan, she could be spending several days a month in the city. Staying in a safe house would lessen her travel footprint and again, limit the number of credit card transactions she would have to make.

She closed the unit, making sure each footlocker was secure and exited the building with five minutes to spare before closing time. Consulting a subway map included in the note, Azar discovered Metro North Station was only a few blocks away on Johnson Avenue. Towing her roll-aboard, she set off in that direction. It felt good to be outside in the breezy, spring air. Crossing Edsall Avenue into Spuyten Duyvil she saw signs for the Hudson Line.

Azar purchased a fare card; she had a twenty-minute wait until the next train. The station was adjacent to the Hudson River, and since it was so pleasant, she decided to remain outside. Overhead was the Henry Hudson Bridge. She craned her neck to take in the uppermost steel arches, estimating it was over three hundred feet tall in the middle.

Checking her guidebook, she learned the bridge was supposed to be built in 1906, but people in the neighborhood resisted the idea, thinking it would adversely affect their property values. It took nearly three decades of lobbying, but finally, in 1935, construction began. Completed in just one and a half years, it became the longest masonry arch bridge in the world at the time, over two thousand feet long. Built with two decks, it was capable of carrying seven lanes of traffic. She snapped several photos and then stowed her camera.

As she closed the camera bag, she sensed something was not right. Looking up, she observed two young men—one Caucasian and one black—walking towards her. Suddenly, they stopped ten feet short of where she was standing. Looking around, Azar realized she was alone on the platform with these two troublemakers.

The black kid spoke first. He thrust his hairless chin out, thumbs hooked in the loops of his frayed black jeans. "Hey sister, what you doing out here?" he asked.

"Yeah, what you doing?" The white kid echoed his

companion's question.

"I'm not looking for any trouble," she said. "Why don't you just go about your business?"

"You hear what she say, James? She don't want no trouble."

"Well, you got trouble, sister." The white kid smirked. "My man don't never lie, do you, Paisley?"

"No sir, I sure don't."

Azar was mostly worried about attracting unwanted attention from law enforcement. Given her training, the two juvenile delinquents confronting her were in far greater danger than she.

"Paisley. Isn't that a girl's name?" she asked. "Why don't you boys just go home? Your mama's probably looking for you."

"You shut your mouth," Paisley seethed. He had a wild look in his eyes, and Azar wondered if he was high on something.

"Yeah, bitch. Shut up," James said.

When they rushed her, she was ready. Years of training as an assassin kicked in. As they closed in, Azar felt the familiar rush of adrenaline. She slid to one side to dodge Paisley, then spun as smoothly as a ballet dancer to deliver a flawlessly aimed kick to James' groin. He screamed and collapsed in a heap, howling in pain as he grasped his crotch. Paisley regained his footing and closed on her, sensing she was off balance. He was mistaken.

Azar tugged the blade from its sheath concealed in the small of her back. She could care less about this menace to public safety but decided not to kill him. When Paisley lunged again, she feinted to the left then leaped to the right, slashing the side of his face from ear to chin. It wasn't a lethal cut, but he began to bleed profusely. Her attacker stopped mid-stride, realizing he was wounded. He looked confused, then stricken, as his hand came away from his face covered in blood.

"You crazy bitch!" He whipped off his shirt and held it to his face.

Meanwhile, James was showing no sign of recovery as he moaned and rocked back and forth on the platform.

"Next time you might want to think twice before you mess with a woman," Azar said. She heard the train approach the station. Grabbing the handle on her bag, Azar walked towards the nearest car. She looked back over her shoulder and addressed the two men.

"I'm getting on this train. If you know what's good for you, you won't try to follow me. If you do, there's more where this came from." She pointed to where her knife was stashed.

Inwardly, she trembled as a result of the sudden violence and her seemingly preternatural ability to wreak havoc at will. The doors hissed open and out spilled a half-dozen passengers, who gawked at the human wreckage on the platform. As she boarded, she looked out the window to see what the two men were doing.

Paisley crouched in shock, a dull look on his face as he tried to stem the tide of blood seeping through his shirt. James pulled himself into a slumped position, his face contorted in pain as he attempted to get to his feet. He made brief eye contact with Azar, and then doubled over, retching.

Azar collapsed into a seat next to a young woman surveying the spectacle on the platform. "What happened to those guys?" she asked, eyeing Azar warily.

"I don't know. Must have been a gang fight or something."

"Bloods," the woman said. "They look like Bloods. Used to be they was just in LA, but now we got 'em here in New York. That one guy's bleeding pretty bad."

Azar shrugged her shoulders. "Long as they don't mess with me," she said.

"You can say that again," the woman replied. She slid closer to the window and went back to her magazine.

The ride into Brooklyn took over an hour, including a single line change where Azar transferred to the Seventh Avenue Express towards Flatbush, exiting the train at Hoyt Street by Fulton Mall. Looking at the station map, she found the intersection of Hoyt and Livingston, just a short hike from where she stood. Ten minutes later she walked up the three flights of stairs to apartment 3-B.

The one-bedroom, furnished apartment more than met her needs. She wouldn't spend much time there anyway, but she was not immune to some creature comforts. A red brick fireplace dominated one wall in the living room. It was sunny, and the oak floors in all the rooms glistened as though recently polished.

She found the bathroom, stripped off her clothes, and waited for the water to heat up before stepping into the steaming shower. She felt decadent as she luxuriated in the hot stream cascading over her body. She didn't expect to feel this tired since she rarely experienced fatigue while on the road. Perhaps it was the encounter with those two muggers; it had been years since she last used her skills in self-defense.

Her mind wandered back to her first kill. Nouri was teaching her the art of knife fighting shortly after they deployed as a two-person team to Caracas. They were sparring hours on end, and she was exhausted from the effort, but she refused to allow him to see how much of a toll it was taking on her body. Finally, one evening, when he felt she was ready, they targeted a scumbag drug dealer Nouri recognized on the outskirts of Caracas, Barrio Nuevo Tacuga, a slum on the west side of the city.

That evening, they were following the unsuspecting pusher from a distance as he made his rounds, dispensing drugs. When the time came, Azar approached him, feigning interest in buying some of his product, but he became suspicious and turned on her. In the resulting scuffle, she plunged her knife into his kidney.

Initially, she felt no remorse, nothing. Moments later though, the enormity of her actions penetrated her facade. She was confused by her initial lack of emotion over taking a human life. Granted, the thug was a low life with no redeeming qualities. But still, he was a living, breathing being.

It was the night she first offered herself to Nouri.

Somehow, in her mind, by sacrificing her body to him, she expunged her guilt and felt whole once more. But in reality, she knew she had crossed a line with what would be the first of many kills—one from which there was no turning back.

She toweled herself off and selected a pair of salmon-colored chinos and matching pullover top to wear. Refreshed, she walked into the kitchen and put on a pot of water to boil. Later, sipping tea in the living room, she began to plan for the next day. There was much to do.

Chapter 8

Logan stood on the pitching deck of *Fish Sniffer* a 38-foot Glenn Holland Downeast Cruiser. The 450 horsepower Caterpillar diesel inboard's throaty roar thrummed with reassuring constancy as they cut through the frothy white spray.

It was 6:00 a.m. on Saturday morning, and he, his dad, brother-in-law, Ryan, and two buddies from his former navy SEAL unit were heading out for a day of fishing on Captain Willy Blacklock's charter. Willy was a grizzled veteran of five deployments to Iraq and Afghanistan. He was a SEAL comrade who returned to his native Boston after leaving the navy and was pursuing a life-long passion for running his own fishing charter business.

Willy fished in and around Boston Harbor from the time he could sit on his granddad's lap with a light fishing pole in his hands. Logan remembered a story Willy told about the time his granddad let him take the family's 12-foot Boston Whaler for a solo ride in Hull when he was just seven years old. It was one of the sweetest moments of his youth. That's when he decided that he wanted to be a sport fisherman.

"What's running, Willy?" Logan shouted to be heard above the reverberations of the engine. He warmed his hands on the travel mug Willy handed him just after they boarded.

The captain kept his eyes on the channel. "Striped bass and blues are running pretty good," he said. I had a customer and his son out last weekend who pulled in a big mother of a striper. Weighed almost forty pounds."

"Forty!"

"Yep. Getting fat on all those pogies and herring cruising

through here. This guy was maybe, oh I don't know, three-and-a-half maybe four feet long."

"Blues are pretty good, too, although it's a little early. They don't really start coming through 'til June. You want to give your dad a thrill? I got some live pogies and herring in the bait well. Put a live one on one of them medium action spinning rods, and he won't know what hit him."

Logan grinned at the thought. His dad wasn't exactly a wimp when it came to physical exertion. Harry Alexander owned and operated Green Mountain Lumber for over 30 years, and he was in the yard more often than behind the desk. He could hold his own, even with the younger guys.

Logan looked to the starboard side where his dad was standing. He and Ryan were joking with Le Brian Delray and Ed "Blackjack" Wozolski, his two SEAL buddies and not coincidentally, veterans of the operation against the Iranian terrorist training camp.

Willy stayed the course, pointing *Fish Sniffer* in the direction of Castle Island. There were a few other early risers on the water, but for the most part, boat traffic was light. As they got closer to the island, Willy switched on the fish finder.

"Lot of times you can see the stripers on the surface hitting herring. I'm not seeing any action topside right now. Let's see if we can pick up a herring school down below."

"Wow, look at that," Logan exclaimed. A big ball materialized on the screen. It was swirling and moving beneath and all around them.

Willy squinted at the screen. "See that water column?" He pointed to a section of the display. "Looks like they're at about fifteen—twenty feet."

Willy scanned the sonar and pointed to several arching shapes coming in above and behind the ball. "Those are stripers starting to hit on the herring," he shouted over the drone of the engines. "Let's get some lines out and find out if they're biting."

Logan was a frequent guest on the *Fish Sniffer*, so he knew where Willy stored his gear. He headed over to the rod locker, calling out over his shoulder, "What rods are you thinking about using?"

"I've got them medium action spinning rods rigged with 14-pound test monofilament line."

"You thinking plugging or jigging?"

"Depends. We can do lures or bait fish. Find out what the boys want to do. Wait a minute." He thought for a minute. "I'd say live bait right in here. They're not hitting on the surface, so we'll probably have better luck fishing off the bottom."

Logan walked over to where the others were standing. "Looks like we're in a pretty sweet spot right in here. Willy's going to troll just inside the channel. He recommends using bait fish for now."

"Is that what you're using?" Le Brian asked. The former navy SEAL was from Longmeadow, a suburb of Springfield in western Massachusetts. He hadn't done much fishing growing up.

"I'm thinking baitfish," Logan said. "Willy says they hit pretty good on it. A customer he took out last weekend caught a forty-pound striper on pogies."

"That settles it," Harry exclaimed. "I'm going with pogies."

Logan pulled five rods out of the rod locker and handed them to Wozolski, who passed them around to everyone else. He reached into a tackle box and pulled out a bunch of pyramid sinkers and a half-dozen long leaders. He rummaged around but didn't see any floats.

"Hey Willy, where are your floats?"

"Oh, they're in the Cabela's bag in the galley. Guess I forgot to stow 'em when I came aboard this morning. Those five- and seven-inch Little Joe's should do the trick."

Ryan went to the galley in search of the floats, and everyone else walked over to the bait well and began baiting their hooks.

Logan had done some freshwater fishing with Cooper and his dad growing up, but they didn't do as much salt water fishing given their distance from the coast. There was no comparison though. Being out on the water like this was the best.

Ryan returned with the floats and handed them around.

Le Brian examined his float. "Is this to keep an eye on where your line is?" he asked.

"Partially," Logan explained. "But mainly it's to keep the bottom feeders like crabs and skate from stealing your bait.

"Here. Let me show you how to rig this thing." He attached the sinker to the monofilament, and then put a float on one of the long leaders and affixed it to the line near the hook using a clinch knot. Reaching into the bait well, he pulled out a wriggling pogie. Grasping the fish in his left hand, he threaded the treble hook through the fish's snout.

"There. You're all set." Le Brian moved back over to the starboard side of the boat and made a passable cast.

The sun had been up for over an hour. It burned the early morning mist away, revealing a cloudless blue sky. The sea was calm as Willy cut the throttle back to four knots per hour and began trolling in 20 feet of water.

The men spread out around the boat. Logan was standing next to Wozolski on the port side. Ed was from Princeton, New Jersey.

"Did you do much fishing when you were a kid, Ed?"

"Yeah. We were about an hour, hour and a half from Sandy Hook. My uncle lived up there, and he had a boat. We spent a lot of time around Raritan Bay, used mostly sandworm baits. I think the biggest striper I ever got was twenty-two pounds. That's about average for there. I was sixteen." There was a faraway look on Ed's face, and Logan shared the moment with him in silence before they cast out their lines.

"You're never going to believe who came over to see me the other day," Logan said.

"Who?"

"Nayef Subaie."

"That's a blast from the past. What's he up to?"

"He was here on business. You know Millie's law firm

handles all of the Subaie's U.S. legal work? Anyway, he wanted to talk so he came over to the apartment and we spent a couple of hours together."

Wozolski listened as Logan described in detail, Nayef's account of ISIS's fundraising and recruiting activities in Kuwait.

"The real ass-kicker is he thinks my brother-in-law's in the process of getting himself radicalized." He checked the tension on his line and reeled in a couple of feet.

The revelation produced a soft whistle from Wozolski. He knew Zahir from their work together on the Iran operation and was vaguely aware of her strained relationship with her brother after she got pregnant out of wedlock.

"This is the same guy who basically disowned Zahir after she got pregnant?"

"One and the same. Name's Ali. We thought he mellowed out a little bit after we got married. Moved to New York and got a dream job doing marketing for the NBA, but he's never warmed up to me. It's not like he's hostile or anything. Maybe he's just not the warm and fuzzy type. I know he and Zahir aren't as close as they were growing up. I don't even know if he's close to his parents."

"What makes Nayef think Ali's becoming radicalized?"

"The Kuwaitis were running some background checks having to do with ISIS, and his name came up. It seems he's been in touch with a supposed ISIS spotter trolling for fresh meat at Ali's mosque in New York. The Kuwaitis are pretty certain he's linked to ISIS."

"How's he know him?" Ed asked.

"I guess they go to the same prayer service. From what Nayef said, it sounds as though he just put some feelers out there. Ali told Zahir he was attending prayer services at this mosque in Tribeca. I looked it up, and the Imam there has a reputation for being moderate. Most likely, this guy spotted Ali there and tried to turn him on to an Imam working for ISIS in Kuwait. Name's Hassan Al Sadiq."

Ed's float disappeared from sight, and a sudden tug on the line almost ripped the rod from his hands. He set the drag, and let the fish run, fighting the temptation to begin reeling him in.

"Man, that sucker hit hard," Logan said.

"He's a big one," Ed shouted. The reel hissed as line streaked out. He checked the tension as his rod arched beyond its specs without snapping in two. It appeared to be doubled over from where Logan stood.

He pulled his own line in and gave Ed a wide berth so he could fight the fish. It sped ahead of the boat, stripping off 100 feet of line before turning and racing back towards them.

"He's pissed!" Ed shouted. "I can feel him trying to spit out the hook," he huffed, as the big fish thrashed around.

Logan's dad got a hit on the starboard side, and then Ryan and Le Brian got in on the action. Everybody started yelling at once.

Logan recast his line off the stern as Willy continued to stroll along at about four knots per hour. There was a big grin on his face as the men continued to battle the stripers for the next 20 minutes.

"Damn," Le Brian exclaimed, as his fish slipped the hook and the line went slack. "He got away."

"Don't just stand there, man," Ed shouted.

Le Brian jumped into action, reeling in the line. He pulled another pogie out of the bait well, baited the hook, and recast into the channel.

"Look at you!" Logan chuckled. "You look like you've been doing this all your life."

"I'm going to get me one of these suckers this time," Le Brian said.

Logan felt a hit on his rod. He waited for a second before setting the hook; stripers like to nibble around the edges before feeding. He didn't have to wait for long. The fish took the bait and ran with it. Thirty minutes later, Logan was still fighting a pitched battle. Despite the morning chill, he was dripping in sweat, surprised by the fish's tenacity. When he finally reeled it in, he was both excited and disappointed. The striper easily weighed 30 pounds, meaning it was most likely a cow since they tend to get heftier than the bulls.

"What do you think, Willy, keeper or not?" he shouted.

Willy had Ryan take the helm for a minute as he walked back to the stern to examine Logan's catch. Although it's practically impossible to tell the difference between males and females without resorting to dissection, the larger ones generally are female.

"That's a cow," he announced, shaking his head. "Look how big she is. She could have a million eggs in her. Or more. Back she goes."

Logan tossed his writhing catch back into the water, as Willy scurried back to relieve Ryan at the helm.

"You want a beer?" Logan asked Ed. There was an ice chest full of cold beers on the port deck. He retrieved half a dozen beers and handed them around before resuming his conversation with Wozolski.

"Nayef had more on his mind than just telling me about Ali. He seems to think ISIS is gearing up to recruit a fifth column of jihadists here in the U.S. Some of these recruiters are working out of Kuwait, but they operate virtually from just about anywhere. Maybe even in the U.S.

"I'm going to get in touch with Peter Breen over at the Boston Police Department. I got to know him pretty well when we were trying to track down Nouri Khorasani. I heard Breen moved out of homicide and is running this unit Homeland Security set up over there, the Boston Regional Intelligence Center (BRIC). I want to find out if what Nayef's saying rings true."

"And, if it is?" The look of resolve in Logan's eyes answered his question.

"Count me in, whatever you decide."

Logan smiled. "I thought you might say that. Le Brian said the same thing when I talked to him yesterday."

Chapter 9

Peter Breen was just finishing up Logan's tour of the BRIC. Logan must have visited five or six different fusion centers during his time as a navy SEAL, and this one had DHS's imprint all over it. In their most basic form, they're intel units set up by DHS and the FBI to facilitate sharing of information between key federal agencies, the military, and state and local governments. Boston was considered a major urban area fusion center, as opposed to one handling issues statewide.

Breen led Logan into his private office and offered him a cup of coffee. While he was busy getting the drinks, Logan studied the former detective. Years ago, Peter was assigned to investigate his friend Hamid's murder. As he got to know him, Logan discovered Peter wasn't your average gumshoe. You could tell he really cared about the victims and their families. You hear stories about the caring ones who burn out. They get ground down by the demands of the job, retiring with a stack of cold case files, embittered by a broken criminal justice system. But Breen seemed to have beaten the odds. Not only did he survive, but it also looked as though he was thriving.

The BRIC chief picked up where he left off as he passed a coffee cup to Logan. "We opened our doors in 2005, falling under the jurisdiction of the Bureau of Intelligence and Analysis here at Boston Police Department (BPD). You can think of us as a hub in the Metropolitan Boston homeland security region. Because we have liaison personnel assigned to the BRIC, it's much easier for us to reach into other organizations like the state police, emergency medical services, the fire department, DHS, and the FBI.

"We're organized into four separate groups: intelligence, field operations, technical services, and critical infrastructure and support services."

"Sounds like a big job, Peter."

"If all I had to do was concentrate on the work it wouldn't be so bad," he said. "But there's a lot of politics in this job." Logan detected a note of frustration.

"You mean some of the bad press you've gotten?" A couple of years earlier the BPD, especially the BRIC, was taken to task in the *Boston Globe* when it was revealed they monitored the activities of protestors and speakers who participated in Occupy Boston street demonstrations.

Breen's unit was criticized by the American Civil Liberties Union for employing tactics reminiscent of the McCarthy era, when political dissent was considered unpatriotic. The public hue and cry didn't seem to adversely impact Breen's rise in the BPD, but the fact that he brought it up, showed the criticism still rankled.

"Yeah. The bleeding-heart liberals in this town would rather we sat on our butts doing nothing, instead of kicking some terrorist ass. What we do makes it a hell of a lot easier to fight crime and stay ahead of the bad guys."

He abruptly changed the subject. "What's going on with you? Seems like you went off the grid for a few years. Heard you were working in Asia, right?"

"Yeah. We set up an office of Alexander Maritime in Hong Kong to see if we could crack the China market, but it's pretty tough. They hold all the cards. You can compete for commercial maritime projects, but you don't stand a chance of getting anywhere near the military side. We've still got some reps out there to finish up several jobs, but we'll probably be closing it down by next summer."

Logan wasn't about to tell Breen about his CIA affiliation; that would have to remain under wraps. But he decided to reveal his role in tracking down Hamid's killer because of a budding plan taking shape in his mind, following his meeting with Nayef.

"You remember a story in *The Wall Street Journal* a few

years ago entitled, "Iran's Secret War: Qods Force Reign of Terror?"

Breen stroked his chin. "I didn't pay much attention to it at the time, but after I moved into this job, I remember reading about it. Blew the lid off of the whole issue of Iranian support for terrorism, right? Something to do with a bomb school for terrorists?"

"That's it. Well, I was the one who put together the special ops team responsible for taking out that terrorist camp."

Breen leaned back in his chair and regarded Logan with more than just a little curiosity. At last, he spoke up.

"That explains something I've wondered about for several years. I remember when Kuwait briefed us on the background information they had on Nouri Khorasani. I knew Hamid's family was well connected, but I could never establish any linkage between Khorasani and your friend. Why would someone working for the Qods Force murder this Kuwaiti fellow? It never made any sense. But if it was paybacks for an attack on their secret training camp, it's beginning to make sense. Is that what happened?"

"Logan nodded. I tried to tell you everything I could at the time to help your investigation, but we were about to put boots on the ground in Iran, and we couldn't take a chance our plans would leak to the Iranians."

"Fair enough. I get it. The only thing I can't figure out is why you're telling me this now." There was a calculated look in his eye as he studied Logan.

"You met Hamid's father, Nayef, right after he was killed. You're right. The family is very well connected. They run a billion-dollar global enterprise, and they're plugged in all the way to the top echelons of Kuwait's government.

"You remember meeting the director of operations for their intel service, don't you? Thamir Alghanim? He's a close family friend of the Al Subaies. He was like an uncle to Hamid. Anyway, Thamir told me they were onto the Iranians and their terrorist training program early on. They still keep an eye on them."

Breen's secretary poked her head in to remind him

about a meeting at the FBI field office in 30 minutes.

"Have Stan bring a car around to the front entrance. I'll be there in fifteen minutes." He turned his attention back to Logan. "Sorry. You were saying…"

"We were talking about Kuwait and the Iranians. Nayef came to see me the other day about something else. It has to do with issues Kuwait's having with ISIS. Apparently, there was an attack against a Shiite mosque in Kuwait City about a month ago. The police arrested five people and have been interrogating them. They're pretty sure all of them were members of an ISIS sleeper cell."

Breen didn't seem surprised by this revelation. "I saw the initial intel reporting on the attack. Kuwait's been on everybody's radar because of the amount of terrorist financing they do. Who was it?" Breen searched his mind for a minute. "Oh yeah, Treasury recently published a white paper on Kuwait's terrorist financing. They call it one of the most permissive environments for terrorist financing in the world."

"Yeah, that's what Nayef told me," Logan said. "It's a big embarrassment for them, but the government can't seem to get a handle on it. Much of the action happens in the mosques through fundraising for 'charities,' but the biggest problem is the lax approach their government takes to regulating financial transactions."

"There's very little we can do about it from where we sit," Breen said. "Unless we start to see dirty money flowing into the U.S. It's pretty much up to the diplomats and the U.N. if they want to consider sanctions or something along those lines."

"No, I get it. And that wasn't really the main thing Nayef wanted to talk about."

"What was it, then?" Breen asked.

"Nayef thinks ISIS is on a recruiting spree. There are extremist clerics all over who are trying to stir things up. He said the Iranians may be involved, although it seems far-fetched to me, given they're mostly Shia, and ISIS is a Sunni organization. And besides, Iran has openly denounced ISIS and is working with Assad and others to defeat them. To tell you the truth though, I wouldn't put it past the Qods Force to team up with anybody if it serves their objective."

"What's the U.S. angle?" Breen inquired.

"He thinks ISIS is going after disaffected youth here in the U.S. The idea is for them to set up ISIS sleeper cells capable of running terrorist operations against the homeland."

"We know ISIS is already here," Breen asserted. "The bureau's tracking hundreds of ISIS threats—people who want to go to Syria to commit *jihad*, people who want to mount attacks here at home, or others who just want to spread ISIS propaganda. We have a handful right here in Boston we're monitoring."

Logan had already made up his mind to not raise Ali's name with Breen. He wanted to talk to Zahir first or maybe even get third-party confirmation Ali was up to no good, before taking any action.

"I figured you were on top of it. Nayef's a friend, and there are times I pick up stuff from him. Could be useful to you." He shrugged his shoulders. "The Kuwaitis have an official liaison relationship with the bureau, but you know how it is; even the best of friends don't always share everything."

Breen pulled a business card out of a desk drawer and scribbled a number on it. "That's my direct line. Call me anytime."

"Thanks, Peter." They exchanged cards, and the two of them walked to the main foyer.

"How's your family doing?" Sorry, we got so wrapped up I forgot to ask about them."

"We're good. We had a rough time towards the end of our stay in Hong Kong. Zahir had a miscarriage. She was in her third trimester, so it was pretty tough. She's still visiting with her parents down in D.C."

"I'm sorry. Please give Zahir my condolences. I hope she's feeling better soon."

The two men shook hands. As he turned to leave BPD's headquarters building, Logan spotted a bulletin board with several notices posted. One caught his attention right away. Entitled *Standing Up for Peace*, it described a recent rally held on the steps of the Islamic Society of Boston Cultural Center. There was a photo of the BPD commissioner along with several members of an organization called Veterans for Peace, offering support for the Muslim members of their community.

"That's a switch," Logan mused. He thought back to the recent presidential election; the xenophobia voiced by some of the candidates was reminiscent of Mussolini's fascist pronouncements in the 1920s. And yet here was Boston, standing in solidarity with its Muslim neighbors, despite suffering a major terrorist attack a few years back by a couple of radicalized Chechen immigrants on the very day of the Boston Marathon.

There was also a print out of crime stats for the previous 24 hours throughout the city. Couple of stabbings, five street robberies, five vehicle thefts, 14 vehicle break-ins, and five residential break-ins. *Note to self: Check the alarm system on the car.*

As he left One Schroeder Plaza, he noticed it had warmed up. He took off his jacket and switched his phone off silent. Almost immediately, it rang. It was Zahir.

"Hi, Sweetheart. How are you doing?"

There was a long pause before she responded. "Logan?"

"Yeah. What's up? How's Cooper?"

"He's fine. He's out in the yard helping Dad plant some flowers."

"You'll never believe who I just talked to. Remember Detective Breen from BPD? The one who was helping us find Hamid's killer? He said to say hi."

"Where'd you run into him?"

"I reached out to him."

"How come?"

"It had to do with a conversation Nayef and I had the other day about terrorist financing in Kuwait. He was in town on business, so I had him over to the apartment for drinks."

"Was Nisreen traveling with him?"

"No. He was by himself. He said Nisreen's working on a book with a tight deadline."

As he was walking, he spotted a sign for the Hurly Brewing Company. There was a beer garden set up outside, and a few people were drinking beers and relaxing in the afternoon sun. He found a table and ordered a Liberty Lager.

"How are you feeling?"

There was a long silence. When Zahir spoke, she sounded weary.

"I don't know. I…" Her voice trailed off, and in the quiet, he could sense her torment.

"Why don't you come home, sweetie? If you want, I'll fly down tomorrow so you won't have to travel with Cooper by yourself."

"No. I think I need a break."

"What do you mean?"

"I mean I need a break from us."

The gravity of her words lingered in the air for a moment before their full import registered. "From us?" Logan asked.

"Yes."

"But—"

"Just for a while. I need time to think." Her words rushed out. "I just can't stop thinking if we hadn't been in Hong Kong, none of this would have happened. That guy wouldn't have broken into our apartment. Everything would be all right."

"You don't know that. This could've happened anywhere."

"But it didn't. It happened there. In our home."

"So, you blame me?" He heard the sharp intake of her breath.

"I'm not sure. What I do know is I don't want to be put in that position again. I know you. How long will it be before you start to resent me for having to quit your job? You did quit your job, didn't you?"

"You know I did. I told you the DDO offered to give me

a year off without pay to think it over."

"I know that's what you said."

"This is ridiculous. You know I love you. I only want to do what's best for you. For our family."

"Tell me why Nayef came to see you."

"I told you. We got to talking about terrorist financing through fundraising in Kuwait's mosques."

"Is Iran involved?"

"I'm not sure. The IRGC may be, but it looks like ISIS."

"Why are you involved?"

"I—" His voice faltered. He couldn't lie to her.

"Something came up. It may be nothing, but I have to check it out."

"Tell me."

"It's your brother."

"Ali? What's this have to do with him?"

"His name was mentioned. Kuwait's investigating a radical Imam in Kuwait City. Ali's been in touch with this guy named Akbar at his mosque in Tribeca who they suspect is a spotter for ISIS. There may be a connection."

"Are you saying Ali's involved with ISIS?" The shock in her voice was palpable.

"I don't know for sure. I told Nayef I'd look into it." There was silence on the other end. When Zahir spoke, her voice was strained.

"It would kill my parents if it's true. Have you told anyone?"

"No, of course not. But I have to do something. I can't just ignore it."

"I know." Her tone was resigned. He could sense her torment as he waited for her to continue.

"Call me if anything comes up."

"Zahir?" Only silence. And then he realized she'd hung up. He slumped in his chair, and the signaled the waiter for another beer. And when he finished that one, he ordered another. But the alcohol did little to deaden his torment. First, he had lost a child and then his job. And now he seemed to be on the verge of losing the woman who gave his life meaning.

He paid the tab and struggled to his feet. As he set out in the direction of Porter Street, his resolve hardened. He was going to get to the bottom of Ali's contact with ISIS and blow the lid off of anything ISIS thought it could do in the U.S. And then he was going to get his family back.

Chapter 10

Ali strode into the cybercafé. There was a coffee bar staffed with one barista offering a selection of lattes, cappuccinos, and regular coffees. In the center of the room, were six round tables where several customers were using their personal electronic devices to access the complimentary WIFI to log onto the internet. Along two walls, there were a dozen computer workstations available to rent. Only three of them were occupied.

Ali asked for a twenty-dollar debit card from the barista and ordered a medium-sized French roast coffee. After he paid in cash, he sauntered over to one of the workstations, sat down, and swiped his card to begin the session.

Azar was one of three people occupying computer workstations in the café. She arrived early and staked out a spot offering a decent vantage point from which to observe the other customers. She noticed the man right away when he came through the door. Teheran didn't provide a good enough description of the target to positively ID him, but there was a good chance the most recent arrival was her man. He was definitely Middle Eastern, maybe even Iranian. He was in his late thirties, handsome, with olive skin and a bushy mustache. She would receive a definitive confirmation from her bosses via text message if he logged onto the webcast.

ISIS was much more sophisticated in the way it vetted volunteers than just a few years ago when she first started working with them. Although the organization tended to project a thuggish, barbarian image to the outside world, their leadership made good use of technology and proven recruitment tactics to help maximize the success of their online targeting campaigns. In other words, they were smarter than their actions indicated, and shouldn't be underestimated.

To expand their reach, ISIS adopted techniques espoused in an Al Qaeda manual entitled *A Course in the Art of Recruiting*. Azar read the 51-page handbook when she first came on board and deemed it to be little more than a crash course in the art of brainwashing. But, it *was* effective. The primer was designed to guide field *jihadis* through a tightly scripted step-by-step process of identifying, assessing, indoctrinating, and eventually recruiting new members into their organization.

This approach extended the reach of any brother with access to an internet connection to targets across the globe. Typically, the group's initial recruitment efforts were via social media, where a broad swathe of potential volunteers was exposed to the organization's philosophy, activities, and successes.

ISIS recruiters trolled the internet, and once they identified potential conscripts, they engaged them in discourse about Islam. These initial exchanges were innocuous enough, always downplaying Western media's reporting on the organization's activities. Over the course of weeks and sometimes months, the jihadist recruiters would follow their instruction manual, gradually reeling in their targets.

In the case of America, ISIS was challenged by its lack of proximity to potential recruits. Of course, the safest way to meet them in person was to encourage their travel to a safe zone ISIS controlled, where they could be vetted away from the prying eyes of the authorities. But, visiting these areas posed its own challenges, a red flag inviting the scrutiny of Homeland Security and the FBI. More often than not, ISIS was constrained to operating in the murky world of cyberspace, where it was difficult, if not impossible, to discern at the beginning, the actual beliefs and intentions of the would-be jihadists reaching out to them.

They found, for example, the devious tactics employed by Homeland Security and the FBI initially thwarted their recruitment efforts. Many times the authorities, or their surrogates, were lurking behind the scenes, waiting to pounce when ISIS made direct contact with aspiring recruits. It was a setup from the very beginning. Several brothers were sitting behind bars as a result of these sting operations.

Nowadays, it was standard procedure for ISIS to vet new enlistees online before meeting them face-to-face. This is where the Qods Force proved to be more than helpful. With their resources and years of conducting covert operations, professionals like Azar could minimize the risk of exposing the recruiters to U.S. authorities.

The Qods Force took extra precautions to protect its operatives' identities because their work for Unit 400 made them such valuable assets, although, given the incident in Caracas, it was doubtful Azar would ever be tapped to do wet work again.

In her current role, great care was taken to compartment each stage of the vetting process to shield her from others involved in the operation. For example, the spotter who initially contacted Ali outside of the mosque in Tribeca had no knowledge of her identity nor that she was inside the internet café with the target at this very moment.

Likewise, the three-man surveillance team waiting outside the building set to follow Ali when he emerged from his internet session, didn't know where she was, although if they were smart enough, it probably wouldn't be too hard for them to figure out. The plan called for her to text a description of him and signal when he was leaving so they could tail him, making it pretty obvious she was inside the café too.

She took a sip of her hot chai and looked at the time. Eight-thirty. Her phone vibrated. It was a confirmation text from the technical crew in Tehran monitoring the webcast; Ali was signed in. It must be the man with the mustache. She texted a description of Ali to the team leader outside so he could begin to set up surveillance coverage.

Azar tuned into the program so she could follow along and see if Ali telegraphed any visual clues indicating his reaction to the Imam's message.

Al Sadiq began by paying homage to an Imam in the U.K. who was recently charged by the British government for inciting listeners to support ISIS.

"Let it be a reminder—Muslims everywhere are being persecuted by their oppressors. In England, Imam Abadi is being persecuted simply for stating his opinion. He said, and I quote:

'Sharia over Democracy
Submission over Freedom
Khalifa over Secularism
Jihad over Oppression
Allah over the Queen'

"For this, a man of faith is being persecuted by the British authorities. We must unite behind him and support all of our brothers. The West has gone out of its way to spread lies about Islamic State. Let me set the record straight. But don't take it from me alone. You can find the truth about our way of life anywhere. Abadi has even written about it on social media. See for yourself." A link to the Imam's Twitter account appeared on the screen, and a voice-over intoned the following message:

"All of our brothers and their families are taken care of because of the sacrifices they are making in the name of the Caliph. Their living expenses are covered, including rent and utilities, and we give them a subsistence allowance for food. No one has to be concerned about their health; we provide free medications and physical exams."

Al-Sadiqe resumed speaking, listing several other benefits not mentioned in Abadi's recitation.

She tuned out and looked over in Ali's direction. He was sitting at the computer in rapt attention, absorbed in the Imam's words. He took out a pen and paper and was scribbling notes. His reaction was not uncommon—blind infatuation with the sermons of these charismatic Imams.

She considered herself to be a devout Muslim, although

ISIS's message didn't resonate with her. Given her upbringing as the only child of a respected university scholar, she grew up being encouraged by her parents to think for herself. Her husband was much more of a traditionalist, so she tempered her opinions, particularly in light of Iran's post-revolutionary atmosphere, after they were married. And while nowadays she maintained an outward veneer of conservatism for her Unit 400 bosses, Azar sometimes found herself harkening back to the days of her youth.

She read Al Qaeda's recruitment manual and was surprised they made such a fuss about identifying volunteers who didn't have a broad grounding in the Quran, or who for that matter, weren't even believers.

Guess they don't trust these novice recruiters to go up against Muslims with a strong theological base, she surmised. They wouldn't be able to argue the subtler points of the Quran, making them ineffectual when trying to persuade someone to leave the comforts of home for a life of *jihad*.

Even the word *jihad* was corrupted. The Quran didn't actually define *jihad* as a "holy war." ISIS and many before them bastardized the concept because *jihad* was really more about personal struggle and survival than it was about a crusade.

She recalled a discussion with her father when she was in her late teens. Papa was discussing the Iran-Iraq War, which took place when she was still a little girl.

She was an only child, and he made time every Saturday to discuss her studies. They were sitting on the brown and red Shiraz carpet in the living room of their university-provided apartment. She closed her eyes and could envision herself running her fingers along the edges of one of the three medallions filling the center of the rug, luxuriating in the tactile pleasures of the wool pile. They were waiting for Mama to bring in two cups of *chai*, the strong black tea Persians love to drink. She could almost smell the cardamom and rosewater Mama always added to the teapot.

"Military force is the least desirable way to resolve conflict," her father said. "Our leaders have recourse to many other approaches before they must resort to war."

"For instance?" she pressed him.

"Diplomacy, economic sanctions, political pressure. These are all preferable to warfare. Ultimately though, there are times when war is the only way.

"Even though Ayatollah Khomeini used the pretext of a holy war to battle Saddam Hussein, given his attacks on Shiites, in reality, the war was more about who would emerge as the dominant geopolitical force in the region in the years ahead. Iran or Iraq?

"Baghdad was pressuring Teheran, and so Khomeini had no problem convincing the other Iranian clerics to go along with his views. It's true some, including Grand Ayatollah Yazdi, later on tried to convince him to find a peaceful resolution. But Khomeini felt he had the support of most religious scholars because the country was at risk, and war was the only way to repel Saddam. The conditions were ripe for justifying the charade of a holy war."

"But over time, didn't he lose the support of the people? The economic hardships and loss of life must have been terrible," she said.

"Khomeini made martyrdom a virtue. He argued by withdrawing our troops precipitously, he would deny the chance for martyrdom to our fighters. To him, martyrdom was more precious than life itself."

She sensed rather than saw movement to her left. Looking up from her reverie, she was surprised to see the target gathering his things and preparing to leave. She was so engrossed in her reflection she had lost track of time.

Target preparing to depart, she texted the surveillance team leader with additional details. *Male, dark, black hair, mustache, medium height, gray pants, yellow shirt, blue jacket.*

Ali logged off of the internet and began walking out of the café. Azar remained in her seat. She didn't want to tie her movements to his departure. Her phone lit up briefly, and she relaxed as she saw the notification she was waiting for.

Target engaged.

Azar didn't realize how tense she was. There was a big push to recruit Americans, and, although she was ambivalent about being seconded to ISIS for this effort, she wanted to be successful. ISIS was already reaping the benefits of its recruitment program in Europe. It had already led to several successful attacks in Paris, Belgium, and Turkey; plans for attacks in the U.K., Greece, and Germany were also well underway.

Lax border controls made it easy to move around Europe. ISIS also managed to run some recruits into Europe via refugee channels, but this avenue was receiving greater scrutiny and couldn't be counted on. All in all, the program in Europe was yielding a good return on investment.

But now the emphasis was on taking the fight to the Americans. And not just to Americans anywhere. Sure, there was often collateral damage against Americans in these inspired and directed attacks taking place in Europe. But the Americans were fond of talking about protecting the homeland. What better way to strike terror into the hearts of these people than walloping them at home? And there was a delicious kind of irony in using Americans to kill other Americans. ISIS was eager for more successes like the mass shootings in San Bernardino and Orlando, where scores of victims died.

Azar glanced at her watch. Thirty minutes had passed since the target's departure. Several other people had come and gone since he took his leave, so she decided it was safe for her to depart; she planned to take a cab to the Meatpacking District. Azar didn't expect to hear back from the surveillance team until this evening at the earliest, and there was work to do.

Chapter 11

Ali departed the cybercafé for his office. There was a mid-morning conference with the NBA's strategic planning team to go over the results of his meetings with the local marketing crew in Rio; he needed to be on time.

The NBA was fighting an uphill battle to gain market share in Brazil. Realistically, there was no way basketball was ever going to displace soccer in popularity. *Futebol*, as the Brazilians called it, was just too ingrained in their blood. But to lose out to volleyball, which was Brazil's second most popular spectator sport, would be nothing short of embarrassing.

His significant breakthrough last week was the result of months of hard work. The deal guaranteed the NBA a big slice of the pie in Brazil's basketball operations and player development.

The South American colossus already had a small number of pros playing in the NBA. If anything could lure more Brazilians to the sport, it would be the opportunity to cheer on their hometown heroes. And for young Brazilians, it would plant the seed that they too could realize their fantasy of playing in the big leagues.

Ali was well prepared for the strategic planning session. And it was a good thing because right now his mind wasn't on basketball. He was in turmoil, going over word-for-word Imam Al Sadiq's message. On one level he was mesmerized by the charismatic cleric's webcast. It was powerful. Not like the drivel he'd come to expect from his own Imam in Tribeca. But on an intellectual level, he felt severe reservations about many of Al Sadiq's claims.

Looking up, he realized he had been wandering as he

confronted his reaction to Al Sadiq's dogma. He flagged down a taxi and gave the driver the NBA's Corporate Office address on Fifth Avenue.

As Ali settled into the back seat, he thought back to the many weekends when, as a child, he and Zahir attended Islamic and Quran studies at the Arlington Islamic Center near their home. Their parents insisted they receive a solid grounding in Farsi and religion. Although he complained at the time, he had to admit it provided a firm foundation in Islam they wouldn't otherwise have received.

This very grounding was causing him to question some of Al Sadiq's assertions. He knew from his teachers, for example, that it was essential to read the Prophet Mohammad's writings in their historical context; otherwise, it would be easy to misinterpret his real meaning. Ali gazed out the window of his taxi, so absorbed in his ruminations he failed to notice the surveillance vehicle with three men trailing behind his cab.

He went over what he had learned about Al Sadiq before his Rio trip. Much of it seemed to be taken from Al Qaeda's playbook. For example, the way the cleric talked about apostasy. The Quran teaches that one who leaves the faith is an apostate. But Al Sadiq insisted upon a much stricter interpretation of the word. His writings emphasized the designation should apply not only to those who leave the faith but also to anyone refusing to follow Sharia law.

In one recent account, Al Sadiq discussed the 2014 establishment of the Caliphate headed by Abu Bakr Al Baghdadi. Ali was intrigued by Al Baghdadi, an Iraqi who grew up in the Sunni-dominated town of Samarra, north of Baghdad. He was an impressive football star as a young man but later turned to religious studies, pursuing a PhD at the Islamic University in the capital.

And it was in this person, this Caliph, Ali discovered yet another significant inconsistency in ISIS dogma. Al Baghdadi surrounded himself with a group of Salafists during his university years, and it was these religious cohorts who influenced him the most. Salafists are Muslims who take a fundamentalist approach to Islam and seek to follow the example of the Prophet Mohammed and his earliest followers in everything they do.

Ali rubbed his neck. All this ruminating about ISIS was giving him a headache. He was thinking back to a world religions course he took at UVA his second year. His professor was explaining some of the schisms in Islam.

"Many equate Salafism with Wahhabism, but Salafists decry the comparison," he said. "Wahhabism has been the state religion of Saudi Arabia for two centuries, and it too purports to adhere strictly to the teachings in the Quran."

Ali accepted the fact Salafists came in many stripes and colors. Years before Al Baghdadi announced himself as Caliph, he became a jihadist Salafist, one who encourages *jihad* without bothering to determine if the Quran's traditional conditions for declaring holy war merit such a call to action.

The jihadist Salafists' beliefs stand in stark contrast to those held by traditional Salafists, who look to the pure teaching of the Prophet Mohammed as their guide. And while Al Baghdadi's world-view may be rooted in traditional, fundamental Salafism, his barbaric behavior in recent years was a shocking contrast to everything Ali remembered learning about Islam during his formative years.

Ali's life seemed to be one of wrestling with demons. It was his curse. He was unable to fathom the source of his discontent. He usually blamed his troubles on being uprooted at an early age and forced to adapt to a society that viewed Muslims with a certain amount of trepidation, particularly after 9/11. He was in his second year at UVA when the planes flew into the World Trade Center and the Pentagon. Attitudes towards Muslims, never particularly beneficent anyway, became lukewarm, if not hostile, in the days and weeks following the attack.

He frowned as the contradictory nature of his membership in two "one percent" clubs came to mind. He was in the top one percent of Americans by wealth, but at the same time, as a Muslim in America, he belonged to a minority making up only one percent of the population.

He realized they were turning onto Fifth Avenue and approaching Olympic Tower, home to the NBA's New York offices. He slipped the driver a 20 and told him to keep the change. As he walked towards the entrance, he spotted a messenger bag he liked in the adjacent Armani Exchange window display. With all of his recent travel, his old messenger bag looked worn. This one was made of pebbled black leather. A steal at $200. He made a note to pick one up on his way home.

Ali rode the elevator up to his floor, stepped out, and went straight to the conference room adjacent to Phil Stanton's office. Stanton was the senior vice president for Global Marketing Partnerships. This was his meeting. For some reason, the NBA Mission Statement, which calls for integrity, teamwork, respect, and innovation, flashed before his eyes as he stepped into the room. These were the four pillars of the association's code.

A few other people were milling around inside, waiting for the meeting to begin. Aaron Black, senior vice president for International Business, a couple of attorneys from the general counsel's office and Sally Provo, vice president for Latin America. He poured a cup of coffee from the buffet and sat down next to Sally.

"Nice job in Rio, Ali." She gave him a thumbs up. "I spoke with the commissioner last night. He was very impressed with the progress you made on your trip."

"It wasn't too hard to sell. The Brazilians know if they want to take it to the next level, they'll have to work with us. I told them we've been doing this for seventy years, and we've learned a few things about running a professional basketball organization along the way."

"I invited their head of operations and player development for a visit next month. We'll be heading into the playoffs, so we can take in a game or two, loosen him up, and then have a day or two of working meetings. We need to figure out how we're going to implement our plan."

"Make sure you're joined at the hip with legal from the

get-go. We don't want any hiccups down the road."

"No problem."

Stanton called the meeting to order and then asked Ali to report on his trip to Rio. His presentation was on his laptop. He connected the video cable to the VGA port on his computer and the other end to the VGA input slot on the projection panel.

The introductory slide was an image of the Brazilian flag and the number 200 million written below it. Ali began speaking. "The first thing I want to emphasize is there are over two hundred million people in Brazil. That represents a huge target pool of future NBA fans."

He clicked to the next slide. "Our primary partner in this arrangement is going to be The *Liga Nacional de Basquete*. They've only been in operation for eight years, so you know they're eager to build on our expertise and successful business model.

"One area where we already see an immediate impact is in our Jr. NBA program. I visited a shantytown, Rocinha, which has a population of 180,000, while I was down there. The Jr. NBA Center we're funding in Rocinha opened last month and students are already receiving better coaching and playing ball on refurbished courts. Also, we brought in twenty of our portable kits with removable flooring, scoreboards, and baskets, to move around to different locations. This will extend our reach beyond Rio to some of the other municipalities."

"Have we identified those yet, Ali?" Sally asked as she shifted her attention from the slide to Ali.

"I've asked the *Liga* to give me a list of recommendations," Ali said. "We should have those in a couple of days, and then we can huddle to see where we can expect to have the greatest impact. Remember we selected Rocinha for our first center because of its proximity to Rio and our ability to monitor their program. We should learn enough from our experience there to feel confident about branching out down the road."

Ali clicked on the next slide. It and several others

depicted the abject poverty of the slum. Unpaved, dirty alleys with decrepit tin-roofed shacks pushed up against each other. Chickens and near-naked children strutted through a stream spewing garbage.

"Moving on. Another theme we touched upon is the great marketing opportunity we have to build on Brazil's performance on the international stage in the last couple of years. While they only placed ninth in the last Olympics, their national basketball team won gold in the Pan American Games, beating Canada in the finals. We discussed several marketing strategies to take advantage of the deep interest Brazilians will have in a sport where they have a real chance to come home with the gold medal."

He talked for 20 minutes and spent an additional 15 minutes answering questions. There was a lot of energy in the room. The NBA was eager to see this program take off because going international was one of the most promising areas for basketball growth.

After the meeting, he was packing up his computer when Phil Stanton stopped by to shake his hand. "Nice work, Ali. The commissioner's very impressed with the progress you're making with the Brazilians. If this takes off, it'll become the model for the rest of our global marketing efforts." He slapped him on the back as he walked out.

"I see a fat bonus in your future," he called over his shoulder.

Ali couldn't restrain a grin despite the lingering angst over his early morning tryst with Islamic extremism. Maybe he should just forget about the jihadist BS, find a girlfriend, get married, and settle down.

He spent the rest of the afternoon catching up on emails, pulling together his travel accounting, and putting the finishing touches on a trip report he started writing while on his return flight from Rio.

On his way out after work, he stopped in the Armani Exchange and purchased the black messenger bag.

"Very stylish," the salesgirl, said. "Nice choice. Is it a gift?"

"No, it's for me. I might just wear it out of here if you don't mind tossing out this other one."

"Sure." She waited while he pulled out his laptop and a couple of other items from his old bag and stowed them in the new one. He adjusted the shoulder strap and appraised himself in a nearby mirror.

"Nice." He handed the woman the other bag and departed the store. He was going to head for home and crash. His trip must be catching up with him. As he hailed a cab and folded himself into the back seat, he failed to notice the three men following him fall into line behind his taxi.

Chapter 12

Logan boarded the 4:00 p.m. Delta shuttle from Boston to New York. As usual, it was overbooked, and the airline was offering appealing incentives for people to give up their seats. He wasn't tempted, though. He needed to see his brother-in-law. He had to find out for himself if Nayef's warning about Ali's flirtation with Islamic extremism was accurate.

An hour later he was deplaning at La Guardia's Terminal C. He had reached out to Ali the night before on the pretext of having business in the city to see if they could get together. Ali suggested catching a basketball game at the Garden. He had tickets to a Knicks/Bulls game and invited Logan to accompany him. Logan's pass would be waiting for him at the will call window in the Garden's box office on 7th Avenue. Ali was in meetings until late afternoon and wasn't sure he would make it for the opening tip-off but promised that he would catch up with him there.

The game was scheduled to begin at 7:30. Rather than wait to see if Ali wanted to grab a bite to eat later, Logan decided to catch an early dinner at Katz's Deli, which was about 20 minutes from Madison Square Garden. He hadn't gorged himself on one of their famous hot pastrami sandwiches in years. The world-famous eatery opened for business in 1888 and prided itself on its unique position in New York's culinary landscape.

The restaurant's fame extended beyond New York City, Logan recalled. A Jewish buddy of his in Boston ran an annual fundraiser for his synagogue, importing Katz's pastrami and making up sandwiches for sale in the neighborhood at $10 a pop. There were never any leftovers to worry about.

His mouth began to water as he thought about it.

"You can let me out here," he told the driver as they turned onto East Houston Street. There was a line snaking around the front of the red brick building, festooned with the name "Katz's Delicatessen" in garish red neon lights, but it was moving pretty fast. When he was seated after a fifteen-minute wait, he ordered a pastrami sandwich with potato salad on the side and a Brooklyn Lager. He didn't even have to look at the menu.

The thing about Katz's pastrami was, instead of curing their meat for 36 hours like most places, they would take as long as 30 days to make sure the meat was just right.

He grinned as he took note of a sign on one wall announcing, "Where Harry met Sally. Hope you have what she had. Enjoy," a reference to actress Meg Ryan's famous fake orgasm scene in the movie *When Harry Met Sally*.

Zahir would be all over me if she knew I was packing in this much meat, he thought, as the waiter delivered his meal. There must have been a pound of pastrami stacked up on this monster. Thinking about her made him lonely so he pushed the thought away rather than allowing it to linger, as he usually would have.

After eating, he walked up to Essex and caught the M line to 34th Street and 6th Avenue and then walked a block to the Garden. He retrieved his ticket at the box office and found his seat.

One of the perks of Ali's job was his access to tickets to all kinds of sporting events. And tonight's seats were great, mid-court below the first walkway. He and Ali's relationship could best be described as lukewarm from when they first met. It undoubtedly went back to the fact Zahir got pregnant when she and his brother, Cooper, were dating while they were stationed together in Iraq. Cooper was planning to propose when he was unexpectedly killed in an IED attack.

These days, Ali's attitude towards them was more mellow than malevolent. Logan hadn't been in touch with him since their return from Hong Kong. The week before, Ali was traveling and had only just returned. He called Zahir when he found out about the miscarriage, and when Logan talked to him, he empathized with their loss.

Tip-off was five minutes away when he spotted Ali working his way through the crowd to their section. He was carrying two drinks and waved as he climbed up to their seats.

He handed Logan one of the drinks. "Hey, how you been?"

"Not bad. Still trying to get settled."

"What time did you get in?"

"Four-thirty. I stopped by Katz's and grabbed a sandwich. Wasn't sure what you were thinking about for food."

"That's good. I ate a big lunch. Probably a good idea to skip dinner." He rubbed his stomach and grinned.

"How're Zahir and Cooper? They in Boston?"

"No, Zahir wanted to spend a little more time with your folks." He was pretty sure she hadn't said anything to her brother about their separation, and he wasn't about to bring it up now. Maybe he was delusional, but he was counting on her to rethink her decision.

"Thanks for the ticket. Great seats."

"Yeah, not bad. Pretty rotten year for the Knicks though."

The Knicks were struggling both at home and away this year. Injuries and over-dependence on one franchise player to carry the load was not a winning formula. They were ranked 13th out of 15 teams in the Eastern Conference. Coming into tonight's contest, they were on a 14-game losing streak, which prompted some fans to show up wearing paper bags over their heads as a token of their embarrassment. Tonight, the Knicks had already turned the ball over twice, and they weren't even five minutes into the game.

"How are things at the NBA?" Logan asked.

"Except for these bums, pretty good," he said. He talked about his Rio trip and his expectation the NBA would become a more significant presence in Brazilian basketball in the months and years ahead.

"I'm surprised the commissioner hasn't tapped you to

handle the Middle East account," Logan said. "You still speak Farsi, right?" It was a long shot, but he was hoping this gambit would prompt Ali to talk about the region and segue into a discussion about ISIS.

"We've got a senior vice president in London responsible for Europe, the Middle East, and Africa. The league wants to do more there. I think there's interest. We're working with our media partners to make programming available in a handful of Middle Eastern markets."

"I heard they're already talking about a pre-season game in Abu Dhabi next year," Logan said. "I imagine the security concerns must be a nightmare for something like that."

Ali looked as though he wanted to say something, but he held back. Logan decided to take the plunge. "I remember how crazy it was in Afghanistan when I was over there, but now with groups like ISIS coming in where there are power vacuums in Syria and Iraq, who knows if they'll ever get back to any kind of normal life." He hoped Ali would take the bait.

Ali took a deep breath and then blurted out what was on his mind.

"It's all screwed up over there. The Sunni-Shia divide, angry young people, corrupt dictators, and one war after another. It's the perfect place for an organization like ISIS to do what they do. They can harness the anger and like you said, take advantage of the power vacuum to get away with pretty much anything."

"I just don't get where they're coming from," Logan said. "Before I went to Afghanistan, the navy put my unit through some area fam modules. One was on Islam. I'm certainly no expert, but what ISIS is doing seems out of touch with what the Quran says. What do you think? Zahir told me your parents sent you to religion classes when you were kids."

The Knick's small forward intercepted an errant Bulls' pass and was sprinting down court. The fans went wild. The man sitting behind Logan leaped to his feet and began waving his arms, forgetting his cup wasn't empty. Cold beer sprayed across the row where they were seated. Several people jumped to their feet and berated the embarrassed culprit.

"Bum."

"Sit down."

"Take his beer away."

"He doesn't have any beer left."

This last comment elicited a laugh from the crowd, and the sheepish offender offered an apology. Security was moving towards their section, but once they noticed the fans had settled down, they backed off.

"Where were we?" Ali asked.

"ISIS," Logan said.

"Right." He took a moment before responding. "They're smart. They know just enough theology to be dangerous. The problem is there aren't many activist Muslims who are moderate. You have all these milk toast Imams in the U.S. who've been co-opted by the establishment and are afraid of making waves. And then you have the opposite extreme like this Imam I heard about."

"Who's that?"

Ali hesitated before speaking. "His name's Al Sadiq. He's an Iraqi cleric based in Kuwait. He does these podcasts, and it's all about *jihad* and supporting ISIS."

"How'd you find out about him?" Logan took a casual sip of his drink and glanced around to see if anyone was listening. The Knicks had just scored inside the paint on a fast break and for the first time were leading. The crowd was on its feet as it looked like the hometown team might be headed to the locker room with the slimmest of leads at the half.

"This guy I met after prayers a few weeks ago. Akbar. We talked, and he thought I would be interested in hearing Al Sadiq's message. Funny thing though, he really emphasized I shouldn't listen to the podcast from home. He mentioned a cybercafé, so I went there."

"Hey, you want another drink?"

"Sure."

"Ok. My turn."

Logan walked out to the concession area, angling through the throng of excited fans. His conversation with Ali was going better than he expected, and he wanted a minute to frame his thoughts before pushing him any further. Logan ordered a beer for himself and a soft drink for Ali. While he waited, he went over Ali's revelation.

It appeared to him ISIS was in the early stages of recruiting his brother-in-law. He couldn't be sure, but it seemed like a typical recruitment operation. A spotter reached out to him in a neutral place and directed him to a cybercafé, where his actions couldn't be monitored by the authorities, but just might be watched by an observer inside the café.

From what Ali said, it didn't sound as though he was inclined towards ISIS's ideology. Like most Muslims in the U.S., he probably experienced a lot after 9/11. Zahir talked about it some—the dirty looks she got from her classmates in college, the innuendos, sometimes from people she'd known all her life that she wasn't trustworthy, that she came from the same gene pool as the Al Qaeda fanatics who murdered thousands of innocent people, the shame that her religion was hijacked for such an immoral purpose.

By the time Logan got back to his seat, the game was underway. He handed Ali his drink.

"Thanks."

They watched the game in silence for a few minutes and then Logan spoke up. "Look, Ali. I'm a little worried about what you told me."

"What do you mean?" Ali turned to him with a puzzled look.

"I've heard of this Imam. Al Sadiq."

"What?"

"Yes," he said. "I don't know if you remember my friend Hamid Al Subaie?"

"The one who was murdered?"

"Yes."

Ali looked confused. "What's that have to do with Al Sadiq?"

"I got to know Hamid's family pretty well, and I've stayed in touch with his dad, Nayef. Millie's law firm handles the Al Subaie's legal work in the U.S., and whenever he comes over on business, we get together." Logan went on to describe his conversation with Nayef and the fact Ali's name was mentioned as someone who might be in touch with the Imam.

"Are you keeping tabs on me?" Ali's face darkened, and he looked angry.

"No, it's not like that. When Nayef raised your name, it was in the context of a broad investigation into Al Sadiq's role radicalizing foreigners who are attracted to the idea of *jihad*. There are over a thousand people in the U.S. who are under investigation because they support ISIS or want to go to Syria and fight."

Ali's face relaxed. "I don't think it's anything like that. I mean, I'm not happy with what's going on right now, but I'm not crazy. I came away from the podcast thinking Al Sadiq is a persuasive guy who might appeal to someone who doesn't know much about the Quran. But, growing up with it…" He swallowed hard and shook his head. "They've basically hijacked Islam to justify what they're doing."

"We agree on that. But I'm willing to bet even though you can see through the BS, they're still interested in you. ISIS takes a long-term approach to these things. I wouldn't be surprised if they had someone in the café with you monitoring your reaction to the podcast. They may even have some people following you."

"Why would they do that?"

"They've been burned, particularly in the U.S. Not so much in Europe, although with the recent attacks there, ISIS sympathizers have been coming under a lot more scrutiny.

"ISIS wants to make sure you're not working against them. That you're not the FBI posing as a prospective recruit."

"So, what do you think I should do?" He was nervously tugging at his mustache.

Logan tensed. Ali's response to what he was about to

propose could make all the difference in thwarting ISIS's plan to carry out terrorist attacks on American soil.

He gripped Ali's shoulder. "I think you should play along with them for a while."

"But, I thought you said—"

"Just for a little while. What I really want is for you to introduce me to Akbar. I want him to think I'm ripe for *jihad*."

Ali's mouth gaped open in surprise. He swallowed hard and looked away for a moment.

"I don't understand." He turned a questioning face towards Logan.

"Let's just say, once a navy SEAL always a navy SEAL."

"Are you working for the government?"

"No. I've done a couple of projects with Nayef before, and I have a good friend in the BPD. I need to work out some details first, so don't say anything to Akbar yet. Will you do this?"

Ali exhaled and nodded his head. "Yes. Yes, I will."

Chapter 13

Logan, Le Brian Delray, and Ed Wozolski were just finishing a 10K run along the Boston waterfront. It was one of those perfect spring days in New England. The sky was a brilliant blue, unmatched by any hue on the color wheel. It was 65 degrees cool, and not a wisp of a cloud floated across the endless reaches of blue bordering on indigo.

Logan invited Le Brian and Ed to Boston for the weekend to gauge their reaction to his request for help targeting ISIS sympathizers in the U.S. Years ago, Logan recruited the two navy SEALS to participate in a clandestine operation targeting an Iranian terrorist training facility, so they had a history working together.

Logan had a lot of respect for the two men, but they weren't his first choice for this job. If he had his druthers, he would have reached out to Norm Stoddard and Bruce Wellington, two special ops buddies who had also participated in the Iran operation and who later on helped him track down the Iranian assassin, Nouri Khorasani, after he murdered Hamid. Stoddard and Wellington were also in Hong Kong with him, but both were committed to ongoing operations there, at least through the end of the summer.

"You guys want to check out this brewpub I found a couple weeks ago? The Hurly Brewing Company. They've got a beer garden out back."

"Let's do it."

Fifteen minutes later, they were being seated outside on a tree-shaded terrace. They decided to eat an early lunch and ordered burgers and a pitcher of spring lager. The beer came out right away. Ed let out a satisfied burp after taking a long swig of the brew.

"So, when's Zahir coming up?" he asked.

Logan dabbed at a wet spot on the table to buy time. He was uncomfortable talking about their recent separation. "I'm not sure. She and Cooper are still at her parent's place." He knew it sounded lame. *What the hell? These guys are like brothers.* He took a deep breath and exhaled.

"The truth is she's really messed up over the miscarriage. The hell of it is she blames me because we were in Hong Kong. In her mind, it never would have happened if we weren't there. She wants to separate for a little while."

"Whoa, man. Sorry to hear that." Le Brian reached over and patted him on the back. "Is she coming back or what?"

"I hope so. She's not herself right now."

"What do you hear from Stoddard and Wellington?" Ed asked.

Logan appreciated Ed's tactful change of subject. In truth, it stung every time he thought about Zahir and the possibility he might lose her.

"They're both good. Wellington's tying the knot in July."

"No!"

"Yep. Another one bites the dust. Name's Adèle. She's from Sweden."

Le Brian whistled. "Man, I thought Wellington was going to be the last Lone Ranger. I never pegged him to be the marrying kind."

"It took someone special. Adèle runs marathons, rides motorcycles, and looks like Uma Thurman," he said. She was probably ten years younger than the American actress, but the resemblance was uncanny.

There was a lull in the conversation, and he leaned in.

"Have you guys thought any more about ISIS since we talked last time?"

"ISIS? Shit, those are some crazy mothers," Le Brian said.

"I kind of like the marine corps quote making the rounds on the internet," Ed said.

"Which one?"

"You know the one about it being up to God to decide

whether or not to forgive ISIS but that it was up to the marines to make sure they make it to the meeting?" Logan and Le Brian laughed.

"Oh yeah. Sounds like a quote I saw on some message boards before we nailed Bin Laden," Logan said.

"Did you end up talking with your detective buddy? Breen?" Le Brian asked.

"Yeah, and it was a real eye-opener," Logan said. "We all know ISIS or at least some ISIS supporters are already here. But what shocked me was how many people the FBI has under active investigations who support ISIS."

"You mean real *jihadis*?" Ed asked.

"It runs the gamut. People who want to go fight in Syria. Others just want to give them money. Some want to help them get their message out. There are over one thousand active ISIS investigations going on at this very minute, all across the country."

Le Brian whistled softly. "That many?"

Logan nodded his head. The men ordered another pitcher of the lager. After the waiter refilled their glasses, he continued.

"I went up to see my brother-in-law in New York the other day."

"This the one you said might be self-radicalizing?" Ed asked.

"That's the one. And if you can believe what Ali says, he listened to a webcast by this Imam Nayef told me about. Hassan Al Sadiq. He's the one the Kuwaitis have their eyes on. Al Sadiq's an Iraqi living in Kuwait who may have been involved in a terrorist attack there. A couple sitting at the next table both swiveled their heads to look at the three men. Logan leaned forward and lowered his voice.

"Ali says he was turned off when he heard Al Sadiq's spiel. Look. He's a frustrated guy, but he's not stupid. He understands ISIS and all these terrorists have basically hijacked Islam and twisted its meaning to serve their own warped vision.

"Ali and Zahir had religious education growing up in

Virginia. Their parents were pretty conservative. So, they know their Quran. And Ali didn't have any trouble poking holes in this guy's dogma."

"So, why's he even listening to him?" Ed asked, toying with his glass.

"I think something happened to him after 9/11. A lot of Muslims in the U.S. became scapegoats for what a handful of people did. I think it twisted his thinking. Made him bitter. Maybe even resentful.

"I can't say I really understand him," Logan said. "But this talk we had the other day was the first time I felt like we ever really connected."

"So, what are you thinking?" Le Brian nudged him.

"I think what we're seeing is a classic ISIS recruitment approach. We know how they do this. ISIS probably has spotters trolling the places where Muslims hang out. From what Ali told me, this guy named Akbar came up to him after prayers a few weeks ago and got him to talk about their Imam, who's a mainstream cleric, not a radical. Akbar put some feelers out and must have liked what Ali had to say. Steered him to a jihadist website and then let this Al Sadiq guy do his thing. I wouldn't be surprised if they had someone in the internet café monitoring Ali's reaction to Al Sadiq or maybe even shadowing him to verify that he's not working for the FBI."

"You mean like a sting operation?" Le Brian asked.

"Yeah. You've probably read about some of the cases the Bureau's prosecuted."

"So, what's the play? What are you thinking?" Ed motioned to the waiter for another pitcher of beer.

"The first thing was to convince Ali to help me out. From what he said, he's already decided not to follow up with Al Sadiq. For now, he's agreed to stay in touch, but not make any commitments. The key thing he's agreed to is to introduce me to Akbar."

Le Brian's eyes glinted with interest. "What's going on in there?" He tapped his temple with his forefinger.

"I think if I can meet Akbar, I can figure out if he really

is a spotter for ISIS and dangle myself to him."

"In your true name?" Le Brian asked.

"No. Too risky. We know the Iranians figured out my identity after Bandar Deylam. The Qods Force penetrated the Kuwaiti intelligence service, and their agent tracked me down and ID'd me based on the first trip I made to Kuwait. He had a lookout working at the airport, and it was easy for him to locate the car service and the hotel they took me to. I was traveling in my true name, so it was a simple process of elimination."

"How are you going to pull this off? It sounds as though ISIS has some resources. They at least have people here who want to help them out. Do you think they could check on your story?" Ed gave Logan a doubtful look.

"I don't think we have a handle on their capabilities here. We've seen the kinds of operations they're capable of executing in Europe—a lot of planning, operational cells, money, and weapons. And we're starting to see more of that in the U.S. but not to the same extent.

"We have to assume they can do some rudimentary background checks, maybe even put people out on the street to check out these volunteers before they get in too deep." He paused for a moment while the waiter refilled their glasses and set the pitcher on the table.

"Can I get you anything else?" he asked.

"No. I think we're good," Delray said.

After the waiter was out of earshot, Logan continued. "Nayef is willing to bankroll this, at least initially, and Breen said he was open to working with me off the books to see how far I can take it."

The one thing Logan didn't mention was his plan to reach out to the Agency. CIA didn't typically dangle its people in front of targets, but they might just be intrigued by the possibility of getting an inside look at ISIS. And hell, if Zahir were to go through with this separation, it would get him back in the saddle and take his mind off his private hell.

Ed interrupted his reverie. "What's the end game? I mean, let's assume you can get yourself recruited, and that's a big if." Ed hesitated. "What are you going to do after that?"

"Try to find out if there are any imminent threats," Logan said. "Beyond that, see if we can figure out if ISIS has any infrastructure here. Are they just depending on lone wolves to carry out attacks, or are they really trying to set up cells as some kind of fifth column they can activate when they choose to?"

Logan clasped his fingers together and ran his thumbnail over the rough edges of his front teeth. "Who knows? If we're lucky enough, we might even get a chance to take the fight to ISIS where it'll hurt them the most."

"You mean Syria?" Le Brian asked.

"Syria, Iraq, Afghanistan. Wherever we get a chance to go after their leadership."

"That would be a ballsy move," Ed said. "But, look how long it took us to get Bin Laden and the resources we dedicated to it. You're not going to have that level of support."

"Not initially," he said, as an image of Langley flashed before his eyes. "But I don't want to rule out anything. More important though is I need to know if I can count on both of you."

Le Brian and Ed looked at each other, and both nodded. Ed spoke first. "I'd do anything for you, brother. Just tell me what you need."

"Same here," Le Brian said. "Where do you want to start?"

"I've got a little homework to do before I reach out to Akbar. I need to take a page from one of these law enforcement undercover operations—set up a backstopped secret identity, probably not in Boston, but someplace like Fall River or New Bedford. That way I won't have to worry about bumping into anyone when I'm operating undercover.

"When I'm ready, I'll get Ali to set up a meeting with Akbar in New York. I'll give you plenty of lead-time, but when I meet him, I'd like you to be there. See if anything squirrely is going on in the background. Find out if Akbar brings anybody to the meeting. That sort of thing. Best-case scenario, he agrees to put me in touch with Al Sadiq and then I can shift the focus from New York to Boston and see where it goes.

"I have no idea how fast this will move once I establish contact with Al Sadiq. I don't want to play it like I'm overly eager."

"I agree," Ed said. "I think playing hard-to-get will be less alerting."

"All right. We'll leave it at that. I'll get things set up with Nayef, and when I'm ready to meet Akbar, I'll give you a heads up." The men paid their bill and started back towards his apartment.

"You guys still interest in catching a baseball game?"

"Who's playing?" Le Brian asked.

"Red Sox and Indians. We've got a couple of hours before game time. Time for a shower. It's only fifteen minutes from the apartment to the park, so we don't have to rush."

The three friends headed back to Porter Street. The lazy Saturday afternoon belied the turmoil brewing beneath the surface. The turmoil that would change their lives forever.

Chapter 14

A zar walked along the crowded streets, trying to capture in her lens the colorful parade, replete with steel drum bands, marching school children, and young people on stilts as they sashayed through the picturesque town of Alajule, Costa Rica, just north of the capitol, San José.

She flew in from New York two days earlier, following her visit to the cybercafé, for this photo assignment. Her work in the city was finished for the time being. The surveillance team was still compiling information based on their shadowing of the target, and she expected to hear back from them any day. Once she had their report in hand, she would be able to recommend next steps, if any.

Azar used an e-doc drop box to exchange information with the team leader. To protect her identity, he was unable to contact her independent of this mechanism. These one-way exchanges could be cumbersome, but in the event of an emergency, she was able to communicate with them on a near real-time basis to resolve any pressing issues.

Standing in Juan Santamaria Plaza, she zoomed in on the eponymous historical national monument, a bronze likeness of the young hero, who lost his life in the Battle of Rivas in 1856. The monument was a shrine for Costa Ricans, who revered the young martyr. A second statue was erected in front of the national congress building in San José, and even the international airport bore his name.

Azar left the square and strolled through the central market. She needed to find a battery for her watch. She passed butcher shops, flower stalls, and several fish markets before finding a kiosk selling watches and offering watch repair. The proprietor, a curmudgeon who barely acknowledged her, glanced at the timepiece and pawed through a plastic box containing batteries before finding the right size.

"Fifteen hundred colons," he said.

Azar signaled she didn't understand, and with an exasperated sigh, he wrote the figure down on a slip of paper. She dug through her bag, found the correct amount and handed it to him.

She needed to check her drop box to see if there was an update from the team leader. There was an internet café near the central park, and she began to walk that way. Alajuela was often referred to as the "City of Mangos" because of the abundance of mango trees in the city center. She detected a distinctly musky odor as she entered the park. It was strong but not unpleasant.

As she walked through the spacious greens, she could see off to one side, a large church. *That must be Alajuela Cathedral,* she thought. A quick reference to her guidebook confirmed her hunch. It had been built over a period of 80 years, beginning in 1782 and was finally completed in 1863.

Exiting the park to the north, Azar found the internet café. She purchased an access card and logged into her e-doc account. The drop box signaled there was a new document for her to view.

When she opened the attachment, she saw there was a four-page report as well as several photos. This team was very professional. Sometimes Unit 400 picked up retired private investigators who would work for anyone as long as they were paid. They worked on the clock and didn't ask any questions. Suspicious spouses were the typical clients in this line of work.

She read their report with growing interest. The subject, Ali Parandeh, was a young executive with the NBA in New York City. He was from the Washington, D.C. area, although it looked as though his family emigrated from Iran in the late 1970s. *Must be monarchists.* She frowned. So many Iranians loyal to the Shah fled Iran after the revolution. Many of them settled in the D.C. area.

Ali graduated from public high school in Arlington, and

then attended the University of Virginia, where he majored in business. After a brief stint in Washington, he moved to New York and accepted a position with the NBA doing marketing in South America.

Her interest piqued when she read he spent some time in Brazil, as recently as a week ago. It made her feel nostalgic as she thought back to her time in Caracas with Nouri, where she learned her craft. But then her thoughts turned dark as she recalled Venezuela was also where her life began to unravel. She was attacked there and later medevacked to Teheran for treatment and a lengthy period of rehab.

The pictures included outside shots of the NBA headquarters offices, Ali's apartment building in Chelsea, and candid shots of the young Iranian on the street. One picture of Ali and a tall handsome stranger coming out of Madison Square Garden caught her attention. The lighting was not very good, but the profile shot of the unidentified man seemed familiar to her. He was handsome, over six feet tall, judging by how much he towered over Ali and bore a distinctly military bearing.

She dismissed the thought. *People are always seeing someone they think they know*, she mused. She logged out of her e-doc account, collected her belongings, and left the internet café. It was afternoon and the light breakfast she ate at the hotel left her stomach growling. She found a small restaurant off the park offering typical *Tico* fare. She asked for an order of *gallo pinto* (black beans and rice), which was the staple of most Costa Rican diets, and a piece of *corvina*, the sea bass common in the waters off the coast of the Caribbean nation.

As she ate her meal, Azar was thinking about Ali. He seemed to have everything going for him. What was leading him down the path of radicalization? If indeed that was what was going on here. Some of the older American Muslims she knew of were activists, motivated out of compassion for fellow Muslims, or who themselves had been falsely accused of something.

But the younger ones, and Ali may or may not fall

into this age group, were different. They might initially be moved to do something because of a perceived injustice, but because they often didn't have a very good grounding in the Quran or in Islamic practices, they come across *jihadist* websites designed to fan the flames of their anger. And that's when they become ripe for recruitment.

She signaled her waiter and asked for a cup of tea.

"Be careful, Ma'am; it's very hot," he warned when he brought it to her moments later.

Azar blew on the liquid and took a tentative sip, burning her lips. She set the cup aside to cool and turned her thoughts back to her target—Ali Parandeh.

The spotter at the mosque in Tribeca, Akbar saw something to make him think Ali fit into this mold. His initial report described a conversation in which Ali decried the moderate approach of the Imam at their mosque, and the passive role America's Muslim clerics tend to take in defense of Muslims under attack.

It would be interesting to know if he had family or friends who were in some way persecuted for their beliefs. If most of his family remained behind in Iran, it was possible they didn't fare well following the revolution, particularly if they were closely associated with the pro-Shah monarchists.

But Muslims persecuting other Muslims generated a different kind of angst than Muslims dying from American drone attacks. Sunnis and Shias had been at each other's throats ever since Muhammed's death in the year 632, when fighting erupted over who would be his successor. The Sunnis wanted Abu Bakr, Muhammad's father-in-law, while the Shias were inclined towards Ali ibn Abi Talib, Muhammad's son-in-law.

Azar thought back to the history lesson every Muslim child could recite. Over the next several decades four Caliphs emerged—Abu Bakr, Omar, Othman, and Ali, but the persistent question of whether the Caliph should be appointed by the Muslim State or follow Muhammad's hereditary lineage remained unresolved centuries later.

She used a piece of flour tortilla to sop up the remaining sauce from her *gallo pinto*. Her taste for South American cuisine was acquired when she lived in Caracas. She took one last sip of her tea and signaled the waiter to bring the bill.

As she walked outside, it occurred to her there was another factor causing adolescent Muslims to radicalize. It was why ISIS was enjoying so much success in Europe. Young Muslims were failing to assimilate into the foreign societies purporting to give them refuge—places like Belgium, France, Germany, Sweden, and the U.K., where most of them were relegated to menial jobs, with few opportunities for advancement.

Their prospects for a normal life with a career, marriage, and family were futile, fueling anger and resentment, which ISIS so brilliantly exploited. But the situation in America was unique. The U.S. accepted fewer refugees from the wars in the Middle East than their European allies. And the changing political climate in the U.S. made it unlikely they would be accepting many more in the years to come. Compounding this reality was America's geographic location. It was much less accessible to refugees than Europe.

So, what is behind the upsurge in radicalization among American Muslims? Azar wondered. Much of it had to do with the backlash from the attacks on 9/11 more than anything else. She suspected most Muslims living in America were politically moderate, but by virtue of their Islamic identity, were viewed with suspicion by many Americans, associated forever with the Al Qaeda martyrs who destroyed the Twin Towers. Was Ali one of these? An Islamic moderate cast as a villain by American society?

She guessed he would have been in his late teens or early twenties on 9/11. If he were already in college, living away from home, where would he have turned for support? It was a good chance Ali was a victim of this kind of discrimination. People like him were good candidates for radicalization. They were often isolated in their adopted land, turning to family and insular Muslim communities for support.

Ali was obviously successful at work. The PI's found an NBA press release naming him as the marketing rep responsible for developing the NBA's partnerships in Latin America. They referenced news accounts of the NBA's growing presence in Brazil and Colombia. But there was a paucity of detail about his life outside of work. There didn't seem to be a girlfriend in the picture, nor any friends for that matter, aside from the picture of the handsome stranger accompanying him at Madison Square Garden. *Maybe he is gay,* she thought. But even if he was, his friends or lovers would be somewhere in the picture. It was still early. More details would inevitably emerge the longer they investigated him.

If ISIS was successful in recruiting Ali, it was unlikely they would be interested in using him as a foreign fighter in Syria or Iraq. He would be much more valuable right where he was in New York City. She let her imagination run free. He didn't have any travel restrictions, and with his status as a respected member of one of America's best-known sports franchises, it was unlikely he was on law enforcement's radar.

The next step would be for her to personally take Ali's measure. She would give it another week or so to see if the PIs developed additional insights into his background or relationships that could influence ISIS's decision whether or not to move forward with his recruitment.

When they could, ISIS liked to meet these foreign recruits in person, the better to test their mettle. She knew of one case where a British recruit was actually introduced to "the invisible sheikh," Abu Bakr Al Baghdadi, in Iraq. The Caliph so inspired the young foreigner he agreed to return home to spearhead a chemical attack in London.

The plan called for the new recruit to identify a rail shipment of chlorine transiting London or any other major urban area in the U.K., and to sabotage the shipment so as to cause a major spill.

With tons of chlorine dumping into the streets, the impact would resemble a mustard gas attack on the population.

It was anticipated many people would die after coming into physical contact with the chemical, but many more would die from exposure to its vapors.

The plan was foiled when Britain's domestic security service, MI 5, was tipped off by an informant who was suspicious of the newly recruited *jihadist*. MI 5 placed him under surveillance and put a tap on his phone, gathering sufficient evidence to obtain a warrant for his arrest.

She checked her watch. She had a 3:30 p.m. flight back to Toronto. It would be good to be home again for a few days. Maybe she would have enough time to catch up on her backlog of photographs to print before she returned to New York.

Chapter 15

Peter Breen appeared dubious when Logan told him about his meeting with Ali. "You sure he's not playing you?" Breen asked. "You said yourself you two haven't been close ever since you and his sister got hitched." He raised a skeptical eyebrow as he bit into his grinder.

Logan and Breen were having lunch at the BRIC chief's favorite hole-in-the-wall sandwich shop in Southie. Logan ordered a *spuckie*, preferring the smaller Italian roll to the twelve-inch baguette draping over both ends of Breen's plate.

Logan figured if he was going to go after ISIS, he couldn't take the chance of anyone spotting him coming in and out of BRIC headquarters. From now on, he and Breen would keep their rendezvous to a minimum and meet only in out-of-the-way places.

"Yeah, I'm pretty sure," Logan replied. "The thing with Ali is he's a really righteous guy. He's also the product of a fairly conservative religious upbringing. He honestly believed when Zahir got pregnant, she was a disgrace to the family name. He's mellowed out a bit since then though. He even has the occasional beer."

Breen is proving to be helpful in more ways than one, Logan thought. He was a useful sounding board for ideas, and he had already pulled his connections with the DMV to fast track issuance of an alias driver's license in the name of Tim Hudson, which was the name Logan was using for his approach to Akbar. Breen also called in a favor with a buddy working at the Registry of Vital Records and Statistics to issue a birth certificate corresponding to his actual year of birth, in the Tim Hudson alias.

With these two documents in hand, Logan was busy pulling together additional backstopping to bolster his cover story. And, true to his word, Nayef's Uncle Ali used his banking connections to set up an offshore account in the Cayman Islands Logan could tap into through a third party, for operational expenses. He found the Al Subaies to be unfailingly generous. The $50K initial deposit was a measure of how eager they were to tackle the ISIS problem.

Logan's cell phone rang. Looking at the number, he recognized it was his former secretary, Alicia Gomez. He excused himself from the table to take her call.

"Hey, where are you?" he asked.

"D.C., I got in a couple of days ago. Headquarters decided to close down the Hong Kong office a few months earlier than planned. We weren't that busy, and they knew I was interested in moving on, so they let me cut my tour short."

"What are your plans?"

"If the offer's still open, I'd like to come back to work for you." She hesitated. "That is if you still need me."

"Boy, do I need you," he said. Her timing was perfect. He could trust Alicia to cover for him at Alexander Maritime while he was busy getting the ISIS operation off the ground.

"Look, we need to talk. Come on up and get settled in and I'll explain what we have going on. How about Stoddard and Wellington?"

"They're still up in the air. I'll tell you about it later."

"All right. I'll see you, next week?"

"That's perfect. See you soon."

He walked back to the table and sat down. "Where was I? Oh, I remember. I'm planning to rent a place in New Bedford. It's close, but far enough away I won't have to worry about running into anyone I know when I'm operating in Tim Hudson mode."

"Did you find anything yet?"

"I think so. I put in an application for a one bedroom on Dartmouth Street. They're supposed to get back to me this afternoon. I'm a little worried because Tim Hudson doesn't have much credit history, but money talks."

"How much is it?"

"It's only eight fifty a month. Furnished."

"Not bad. Let me know if I can do anything for you. If you run into any problems, we can do credit backstopping."

"Ok. Thanks."

"Oh. One other thing. How are you planning to portray yourself in this Tim Hudson persona?"

"I've been giving it a lot of thought. I want it to appeal to ISIS but keep it low maintenance. Something simple. I think I can use my military background to present myself as a private security consultant doing personal security training. Firearms training, tactical driving, security awareness. Basically, tailored programs for businesses or high net-worth individuals."

"Take a look at this." Logan pulled a tablet out of his backpack and opened it up to a website he was building for this business concept. It wasn't live yet, but there was enough content there to give Breen an idea.

"Pretty slick, Logan. I didn't know you were so talented."

"You haven't seen anything yet," Logan said with a laugh.

Breen clicked through the tabs. "This ought to appeal to them. Particularly if they're trying to recruit you to go do *jihad* someplace like Syria or Iraq. Like a mercenary."

"Or maybe right here," Logan said. "We know they're interested in hitting the U.S. They'll want people with military training to put together effective operational scenarios. Attacks that will kill a lot of people."

"If you look at some of the 'lone wolf' incidents ISIS is taking credit for in the States, they've inflicted some damage, even killed a lot of people, but there hasn't been anything truly catastrophic," Breen said. "Think about it. The biggest mass murder since 9/11 was in Las Vegas in 2017."

"You're talking about Stephen Paddock at the Mandalay Bay?" Logan asked.

"Yep. Killed fifty-nine people and injured over five hundred others. They called it the worst mass shooting in U.S. history. And it was the work of a single gunman," Breen grimaced.

"Do you think Paddock was inspired by ISIS, Peter?"

"Who knows? ISIS claimed credit for it at the time. But no one could prove Paddock had any connection to them. It's been how long? Over a year? Still a mystery.

"We may never figure out what caused him to go on a rampage like that. What we do know is ISIS is working overtime to hurt us at home. We don't think they have what it takes to inflict a lot of damage now. But it may be just a matter of time before they do." Breen looked grim.

"What kind of people do you see ISIS reaching out to?" Logan asked.

"It's a strange phenomenon. Defies labels. Remember last time we talked I told you we were tracking a dozen ISIS sympathizers right here in Boston? They're all different. Professionals, high school dropouts, young, old, Muslim, non-Muslim." He shrugged his shoulders. "Hard to quantify."

The two men finished their lunch. After paying the bill, they stood outside the restaurant talking.

"Let's stay in touch," Breen said. "A phone call once a week. Anytime, if there's an emergency, or you have imminent threat information."

Logan handed Breen a slip of paper with a "clean" cell phone number written down, making sure he understood it was the number he was using for his Tim Hudson alias.

Logan returned to his office and gave his temp a week's notice. He spent the rest of the afternoon clearing out his inbox and answering phone calls. There was a message from Zahir, asking him to give her a call.

She picked up on the first ring. "Logan?"

"Hi, Sweetheart. How are you? How's Cooper?"

Her voice sounded detached. "We're fine. We're ready to come home this weekend."

His pulse raced. "That's great! I—"

"No. You don't understand. Nothing's changed."

"You're right. I don't get it."

"I want you to move out."

"What?"

"I'm sorry, I just can't—"

"Can't what?"

"Can't handle it."

He groaned inside. Zahir was hurting, and there didn't seem to be a thing he could do to ease her pain. She seemed bent on this separation.

"What are you going to do?"

"BU wants me to teach the summer semester. I think I need to get back to work. To take my mind off everything. Off—"

"The baby?"

"Yes," she said.

"All right. I'll have my stuff out by Friday. But what about Cooper? I want to see him."

Zahir was noncommittal. He said goodbye, feeling a sense of finality when she hung up.

It was a good thing he was going to be busy for the foreseeable future. With too much time on his hands, he wasn't sure he could deal with it.

He turned his thoughts to a more immediate problem. How could he piggyback on Ali's connection with Akbar naturally without revealing their real-life relationship?

It occurred to him Ali's NBA affiliation might offer a plausible scenario. He played with the idea in his head. They were close to the same age and might have known each other in high school. After graduation, they went their separate ways but reconnected when he was doing some private security jobs for two players on the Boston Celtics. Ali heard about him and reached out a couple of years ago; since then, they tried to get together at least a couple of times a year.

At one of their infrequent meetups, he (allegedly) confided to Ali, his disaffection with the military after he was summarily released from active duty status following his wartime injury.

Just might work, he thought. As he was mulling it over, his Tim Hudson phone rang, and Vicki, his realtor, advised him his application for the apartment on Dartmouth Street had been approved.

"Great," he said. "I'll stop by tomorrow to sign the lease. Will I be able to move in this weekend?"

"I don't see why not. The apartment's vacant. As soon as we get the security deposit and first month's rent, it's yours."

"All right. Will you be in the office tomorrow morning? Say, ten?" He could hear the sound of her flipping through her planner.

"I've got a showing at nine, but I should be back in the office by ten. If I'm not, one of the other realtors can handle it. We'll take cash or a money order. It comes to seventeen hundred. I'll make sure she knows where the keys are."

"Okay. See you then."

It wouldn't take him long to move in. He wouldn't be taking anything for the most part except for clothes, some books, and bathroom stuff. He was going to have to be very careful about how he managed his dual identity, mainly after he established contact with Akbar.

He decided to use a rental van to move his stuff from Porter Street to New Bedford. He would drive a long surveillance detection run between Boston and New Bedford to make sure no one could link the two. He planned to keep his own car at Porter Street and lease wheels for Tim Hudson.

Logan was satisfied with the way things were coming together. All of this early planning could make the difference between success and failure downstream. Once he made contact with Akbar, it would be game on. If ISIS bit, there was a good chance they would throw everything at their disposal to vet him. Maybe even bring in an outsider to size him up. It was obvious they were already active in Boston. Breen said so himself. But did it extend much beyond the dozen or so cases the BPD had on the books?

"Mr. Alexander?" It was Beverly Grady, his temp.

"Do you need me for anything else today?"

Logan thought for a moment. "No, I think we have it

under control. Do you need to leave early?"

"I have to pick up a few things. We're having a party for our granddaughter. She just found out this week she was accepted to the naval academy."

"Congratulations." Logan got up from his desk, beaming with pleasure. "So, she's going to be a midshipman? You should be proud. I spent some of the best years of my life at Annapolis."

After she was gone, Logan stood by the window looking out over Boston Harbor. He wasn't generally given to melancholy, preferring to face down adversity and set the world right through his own efforts. But there was only so much one person could do when it came to relationships. He would just have to be patient. He returned to his desk.

One task he needed to tackle sooner than later was an application for Tim Hudson's passport. Although he didn't expect to be traveling anytime soon, Logan wanted to be ready if the opportunity presented itself. He discovered the U.S. passport agency took six to eight weeks to issue a new document, and they would only expedite it if there was proof of pending travel. Checking online, he found the name of an expediting company. They used a registered courier to speed up the process. For $200 beyond the $170 new-passport fee, they would deliver his papers within a week.

Using his Tim Hudson internet account, he pulled together the information for the application and found a drugstore not far from his office offering passport photos. While he was out, he received a call back from the registered courier. They provided him with FedEx shipping instructions and told him they had reserved a slot with the U.S. passport agency. Barring any complications, he would have his new passport in the mail by early next week.

Now there was just one more thing. Logan needed to give Aaron Cousins a call. He was glad he left the door open with the Agency because it was starting to look like he might need their help.

Chapter 16

Logan wasn't sure how the Agency would react to news he was partnering with local law enforcement and a Kuwaiti businessman against ISIS. The CIA liked to maintain primacy in foreign field operations, and this one was already beginning to get complicated. At a minimum, the CIA would feel compelled to bring in the FBI for any portions of the operation taking place on U.S. soil, given the memorandum of agreement governing CIA and FBI's respective mandates.

He knew the DDO would be intrigued by the possibility of penetrating ISIS, whether in the U.S. or abroad. It was one thing to recruit an ISIS terrorist and turn him against the organization, but quite another to have a CIA officer working on the inside of the despised group. Logan was circumspect in his call to the DDO's chief of staff, merely saying he had an urgent matter to discuss with his boss.

He took a JetBlue flight from Boston to Reagan National, picked up a rental car, and drove the 12 miles to headquarters. There was a delay getting into the building because he was on leave without pay, and the office of security couldn't locate his records. After two phone calls, they figured it out and issued him a no-escort badge.

His meeting with the DDO was brief and to the point. Logan brought Cousins up to speed on everything that had transpired since their last meeting, including Nayef's revelations about his brother-in-law and Logan's subsequent meeting with Ali.

"So, let me get this straight," Cousins said. "Your brother-in-law has been in touch with ISIS or at least a radical Imam sympathetic to ISIS who may be angling to bring him on board."

"It's preliminary. Ali was approached by this guy who's probably a spotter for ISIS at his mosque in Tribeca. A guy by the name of Akbar. He pegged Ali as someone frustrated with the way Muslims are treated in this country. And he is. It probably goes back to 9/11 when he was a student at UVA. He experienced the changed attitudes, the sideways glances, the feeling of being an outsider after the attacks.

"But I think once he established contact with this Imam, Hassan Al Sadiq, he saw through the BS. He was turned off by the pitch. He told me he wasn't planning to pursue it."

"But you convinced him to introduce you to Akbar." It was a statement rather than a question.

"Yes, sir."

Cousins turned to his chief of staff, who was busy taking notes of their conversation. "Dave, call Jason and see if he is available to meet with Logan once we're done here."

Logan suspected Jason was Jason Summers, the renowned chief of CIA's Mission Center for Counterterrorism, known by most as CTC. Jason made a name for himself after 9/11 by relentlessly prosecuting the war on terror in a very personal way.

And it was personal. Jason's first wife, Pam, was killed in the attack on Tower I of the World Trade Center. She worked as an analyst out of the Baltimore office for one of the leading global financial firms and by chance was in New York for meetings the day the planes hit the towers. She never made it home.

As Logan was wrapping up his meeting with the DDO, Cousins raised a question Logan dreaded answering.

"I need to know if we move on this, you're not going to be distracted, that you can give it your full attention. How are things at home?"

Logan paused a long moment before answering. "Zahir wants a separation. She's moving back to Boston this week and asked me to move out. She blames me for what happened in Hong Kong. I hope it's just a question of time before she comes around, but there aren't any guarantees."

Cousins stood and stuck out his hand. "I'm sorry, Logan. And I hope you're right. As far as ISIS goes, it's an intriguing situation. I'd like to hear from Jason before making a final decision. At first blush, I'm inclined to be proactive. We would probably have to brief the BRIC chief, Breen, on your intel affiliation, but I am disinclined to bring the Kuwaitis in, especially since you're dealing with a private citizen, not the government.

"Oh, and Logan, we might as well get you back on the books. Once I hear back from Jason, we'll update your clearances and have HR activate your file."

"Thanks, boss." Money hadn't been an issue since he and Zahir got married. She was independently wealthy. But with their relationship on the rocks, he could definitely use the income.

Logan left the DDO's office and walked down to the counterterrorism center. Summers' secretary led him into a small conference room, advising him the CTC chief was on a scheduled conference call. She thought it would be ten minutes at most.

He took a look around the room. There were maps of the Middle East and photos of key regional leaders on one wall. On the opposite side, there were photos of what looked to be CIA officers in the field. Scrutinizing them, he saw they were CIA officers killed in the line of duty by acts of terrorism. There was Johnny "Mike" Spann, a former marine corps officer killed in Afghanistan in 2001, and Jeremy Wise, a former navy SEAL, who died in the Camp Chapman bombing in 2009. There were others. Too many others.

"That's what motivates me every day I come to work."

Logan turned around. He had never met Jason Summers, but his reputation in the Agency was legendary. He was a bear of a man, swarthy, curly gray hair receding from an expansive forehead. His soft skin stood in sharp contrast to the brooding blue eyes that would have speared lesser men. He grasped Logan's hand in a vice-like grip and led him over to the conference table.

"Aaron tells me you might have a line into Al Sadiq?"

"It's very preliminary. I think we've identified a spotter he's using to go after targets in a New York mosque." He went on to explain Akbar's approach to Ali and Ali's agreement to broker an introduction to the ISIS spotter.

"I think I've come up with a scenario that'll appeal to ISIS given their efforts to recruit foreign fighters." He went on to describe his war service as a navy SEAL and his forced retirement due to his medical disability.

"I figure I can play the disaffected vet. A lot of guys get out and are bitter. I actually had it pretty easy. The VA did a great job getting me through rehab, and the transition to civilian life wasn't all that hard. Was I disappointed about the way things turned out? Yeah, I was disappointed. But hey, I was back on my feet."

"This is going to be interesting," Jason said. "ISIS is becoming more aggressive in their recruitment efforts. They have extensive resources to fund these campaigns because they're plundering Syrian and Iraqi oil and unloading it on the secondary market. We see them using social media effectively, which extends their reach way beyond their typical target base. And they're becoming more selective, which makes me think they're doing more vetting of these people than they were able to as little as a year ago. They're actually pretty sophisticated.

"There was a volunteer who reached out to us last year. Guy whose brother was killed because he raped some girl, and her father, who was an ISIS commander, went after him. Anyway, this guy said ISIS is using Al Qaeda's playbook for identifying and targeting new recruits.

"But more than that, we've seen some cases where they're using contract hires to help them vet some of these candidates before they bring them on board. One of these contractors reached out to the bureau a couple of months ago when he became suspicious over a job he was offered. He was a retired security officer with his own security company. Anyway, something about this client just didn't add up, so he reported it to the bureau.

"They reached out to us, and we got a FISA court

approval to go after the client's computer and phone. He was a little sloppy, and it didn't take too much homework to figure out what he was up to."

"What was it?" Logan asked.

"The usual. Any information out there in the public domain, occupation, residence, relationships. It was pretty basic stuff, actually. They weren't interested in taking a deep dive into anyone's background."

Logan explained the steps he was taking to bolster his cover identity. "You think it will stand up?" he asked.

Jason tapped a pen against the table top and scrunched up his eyebrows in concentration. "My gut tells me, yes, but the reality is we're still figuring this one out. It's not like we're flush with ISIS assets reporting on their M.O. If you establish contact with ISIS, you'll be breaking new ground.

"How soon do you think you'll be ready to go?"

"A week, maybe two? I'm moving into a new apartment in New Bedford this week. I need to think through how I can backstop my business as a security consultant in case they do try to run that down."

"We can help you with that. I can get you set up with an LLC in Massachusetts and backdate the year it was incorporated to fit your cover legend. We also have some friends over at the VA and can generate a phony military record to cover your years in the navy. We'll fast track both of those, so they'll be in place in a few days." Jason was making a to-do list on a yellow legal pad.

"Let's see. You mentioned the Kuwaitis were throwing some money at this. We can launder that money to make it look like you have legitimate clients. Anything else?"

"Commo. I need something solid. I don't expect to get the Cadillac of commo systems like I had before."

"I'll have the office of technical services see what's in the inventory. We don't like to mix apples and oranges, so we wouldn't necessarily issue you the same thing you were using in Hong Kong."

"One other thing. There were a couple of other guys working with me out of a commercial office we set up over there. I know they're shutting it down, but I'm not sure if the DDO has identified anything specific for them. I also had a secretary, who reached out to me yesterday, and she wants to come to work for me.

"I'm thinking these guys could be a support element for me, working out of my Alexander Maritime office in Boston. The two operations officers have special ops backgrounds and experience working in high-threat environments."

"Let me talk to Aaron. See if he has tapped them for anything else. Did you have something specific in mind?"

"We could start off by having them surveil my meeting with Akbar to see if anybody else shows up. I haven't thought much beyond that so far."

"I'll run it by Aaron and call you in a couple of days with an update on these action items." The two men exchanged contact information and said goodbye.

As he was driving off the headquarters campus, Logan found himself following the route to the Parandeh's home in Arlington. He parked his rental car a half-block from the house and sat there, uncertain of what had compelled him to come to the neighborhood, especially since his conversation with Zahir left little doubt about how she felt about him.

As he sat there thinking about their situation, he saw Zahir and Cooper on the front lawn. Cooper was kicking a soccer ball around, and Zahir was making a halfhearted effort to block his shots on an imaginary goal. For a moment, he felt the urge to join them, but he restrained himself. He would respect her wishes, even though it was breaking his heart.

Chapter 17

Ali was strolling south along High Line Park, away from Chelsea, en route to the Meatpacking District, where he was meeting Logan for coffee. The elevated pedestrian promenade, formerly known as The West Side Freight Line began on Gansevoort Street in Greenwich Village and meanders above the city streets northward in the direction of Chelsea.

Built in the 1930s, the original viaduct served the community as the principal rail line transporting all manner of goods to and from the docks in Manhattan. Within three decades, trucking surpassed rail as a means of moving freight, and the elevated passageway fell into disuse and decay. It was reclaimed in 1999, as a "rails to trails" restoration project, and New Yorkers now savored its lush gardens and meandering pathways.

Ali exited the park and took the elevator near the Tiffany and Company Overlook down to the street level. He and Logan were supposed to meet at a coffee shop on West 16th Street called Barista at 8:30. Five minutes later, he slid into a seat at a table in front of the shop. There were a half-dozen other empty tables with striped umbrellas providing shade.

"Hey, Logan. How you doing?" He signaled to a waitress to bring him a menu. "You going to eat anything?"

"Sure. I could have some breakfast. You been here before?"

"Yeah. The chef makes an egg 'toastie' with avocado and Gruyere cheese that's pretty good. Also, all the baked goods are homemade."

The two men ordered and after the waitress brought their coffees, settled back to savor their steaming mugs.

"How was your flight?"

"The usual. TSA's totally hosed up security in Boston. You used to be able to count on getting through in no more than thirty minutes, even at peak times, but now you're looking at one to two hours."

"I talked to my dad yesterday. He mentioned Zahir and Cooper are moving back to Boston."

"Yeah. Zahir's coming up alone first. Cooper's spending another week with your parents." Logan paused. He wondered what Nima had told Ali about his and Zahir's separation. He didn't have to wait long to find out.

"Dad said you and Zahir are splitting up."

"Unfortunately, that's where we are. Your sister said we needed a break. I don't think she's forgiven me for dragging her off to Hong Kong. She's convinced everything would have been all right if only we'd stayed in the U.S."

"What do you think?"

"Who knows? She could just as easily have been mugged walking down Mass Ave."

"Did they ever catch the guy, or figure out what he was after?"

"No. The police over there are too busy dealing with triads and gang violence."

"I hope you can work it out."

"Thanks. So do I."

"Changing the subject, where do we stand on an introduction to Akbar?" Logan asked. "Are we still good to go?" He held his breath. "Come on Ali," he whispered to himself.

"Yeah. The more I think about it, the most natural encounter would be after Friday prayers. Of course, there's no guarantee Akbar will be there. He doesn't seem to travel much though. I see him there pretty much every week.

"Do you want to try to meet him today, since you're already here?" Ali asked.

"Sure. I'm as ready as I'll ever be." Logan said. He proceeded to brief Ali on the cover story he planned to use with the ISIS spotter. When he was done, Logan stressed how crucial it was to keep Akbar in the dark about their actual relationship.

"I don't want him to find out we're related," he said. "These are some evil people, and I want to take every precaution to protect the family."

"Whatever you say," Ali said. "Let me go over your story one more time just to make sure I've got it right. Your name's Tim Hudson, and you're a high school friend of mine. We went our own ways after graduation but ran into each other after you provided some security services to a couple of NBA players in Boston." Ali seemed to grow more confident as he recited the cover legend.

"We got to talking, and you mentioned you were struggling with how you were forced out of the navy because of your injury in Afghanistan. You started to question U.S. involvement in the Middle East and wanted to learn more about Islam, so you reached out to me."

"Not bad," Logan said. "Do you think he'll bite?"

"Based on what you told me, you're just what they're looking for. You're mad at the system. You're looking for something, and you don't have a deep grounding in Islam. ISIS will probably figure they can manipulate you."

"I hope so," Logan said. "I think it's essential Akbar initiate the discussion about getting hooked up with Al Sadiq. I want him to feel as though I'm putting out feelers, but I don't want to give the impression of being overly eager.

"You sure you're comfortable doing this tonight?" Logan asked. It was Friday, and he was primed.

"Sure. It'll be interesting to see how Akbar reacts and if he gives you the same spiel he gave me." Ali checked his watch. "I need to get some work done. Looks like the commissioner liked my recommendations for increasing our visibility in Brazil. We're going to meet him formally next week and lay out a timeline for going forward."

"That's great, Ali. Sounds like you're making some headway."

The two men paid their bills and stood up. "What time do you want to get together?" Logan asked.

"Prayers are at five-fifteen. Let's meet in front of the masjid at five p.m."

"Masjid?"

"Oh, sorry. We don't use the word 'mosque.' It's 'masjid,' which means 'place of worship' or 'to bow down.'"

"It's on West Broadway, right?"

"Yes. Two forty-five West Broadway."

"This'll be a first for me. Anything special I need to do to get ready?"

"No. You're dressed fine. When we go in, we'll take off our shoes. Before we enter the prayer hall, I'll wash up. You don't have to bother because you won't be saying the prayers. We'll sit on the floor in the prayer hall. Just make sure you don't point your feet towards the Qibla."

"What's that?"

"You'll see. It shows the direction the faithful are supposed to pray. All over the world, Muslims are praying in the direction of the Kaaba, in Mecca."

"You can just sit there during prayers. The Imam will lead us. He'll recite verses from the Quran, but everyone else will follow along silently."

"Alright. I think I have it."

"Okay. See you at five."

Since he had several hours to kill, Logan decided to do something he'd meant to do, but somehow hadn't found the time—visit the 9/11 Memorial. The national September 11 Memorial and Museum was located at the World Trade Center site, where the Twin Towers had once stood. It was about a forty-five-minute walk to the memorial, and he decided to take the hike since he had time to kill.

For Americans, modern terrorism's most devastating occurrence was the 9/11 attack on the World Trade Center, where 2,977 victims perished. Logan's mood turned somber as he paid his entrance fee and began strolling the grounds. Where the north and south towers once shot up to the heavens, two one-acre pools now glistened in the late morning sun. Water cascading from two towering waterfalls drowned out the noise of the city.

As he got closer, he could see the names of the deceased inscribed on bronze plates affixed to the pool walls. So many names. Standing before one grouping, he whispered the names aloud, forging a brief, albeit intimate connection with those people. *What is it about names, written in blood, that invokes such depth of feeling?* he wondered?

Hundreds of swamp white oak trees shaded the plaza, but he was searching for one tree in particular known as the "Survivor Tree." It was a Callery pear tree that almost didn't survive the attack. Planted near Church Street in the early seventies, shortly after the World Trade Center first opened for business, the Survivor Tree barely endured on that fateful day. Badly charred, it was more dead than alive when it was discovered in the rubble. The tree was rescued and replanted in a Brooklyn nursery, where it was brought back to life, and then replanted in a place of honor on the plaza.

Logan located the tree; it was the only one with metal fencing around it to prevent people from touching its shallow furrows. As he gazed up, he imagined the heat and rubble flying every which way, after the planes crashed into the towers. When rescuers spotted the tree as they began cleaning up the mess, there was only one healthy limb, and few gave it any chance of surviving. But here it was, 30 feet tall, a tribute to nature's resilience over chaos. It was a survivor.

Logan felt heavy hearted as he walked through the plaza and entered the 9/11 museum. He was drawn to an exhibit entitled "Witness at Ground Zero." A French photographer by the name of Stephane Sednaoui lived in an apartment on Great Jones Street, not far from where he now stood. Over the course of several days, as he participated in the rescue effort, Sednaoui captured over 500 images of Ground Zero. The pictures, depicting the heroic efforts of first responders, volunteers, and others, were akin to Dante's depiction of hell in *The Divine Comedy*.

Ruptured steel beams leaned at improbable angles. Rubble and human remains comingled in an endless display of man's cruelty. Shocked rescuers stood, arms akimbo, surveying the daunting task before them.

Logan felt a brief stab of remorse that he was no longer out there, protecting the homeland from his favorite position, the front line. He recalled the times when he was a navy SEAL and was always the first to volunteer to be on point whenever the team deployed on patrol. Going after ISIS was the closest he could get to recapturing that feeling now.

Walking through the memorial exhibition was perhaps the most difficult. Photographs of the victims, biographic profiles, and audio recordings from family, friends, and colleagues told a poignant story of what the nation lost that day. One teenaged son eulogized his father with such depth of feeling, it moved Logan to tears. "Whew," he said as he emerged from the exhibit into the sunlight. Looking at his watch, he saw it was already 4:30. He decided to walk, calculating it would only take him about 15 minutes to reach his destination.

He spotted Ali outside the main entrance to the masjid. As he walked towards him, Logan was thinking about his upcoming encounter with Akbar. It was the beginning of Ramadan, and this time of year typically evoked an outpouring of piety from Muslims as they sought to renew their devotion to Allah.

ISIS, hoping to build on this religious fervor, recently urged all Muslims to initiate attacks against non-believers in Europe and the United States. It was a time for jihad, and the Caliph's spokesperson encouraged ISIS supporters to take the fight to the Crusaders. Almost as if on cue, violence erupted at different locations in Europe and the U.S.

"Hey Logan," Ali said as he drew near. Let's find a place. Akbar typically sits in the same spot each week, so we can try to be near there and then see if we can bump into him after prayers.

"Sounds like a plan."

The two men entered the masjid. Logan waited while Ali performed the purifying ritual. There were several built-in benches with adjacent faucets and drains. He washed his hands, face, and feet, dried them off, and then steered Logan towards the prayer hall.

Ali greeted several people near where they sat down.

Logan recognized the Arabic greeting. As-Salaam alay kum (Peace be with you), to which the respondent replied, Wa alaykum as-salaam (and with you be peace).

A moment later, Ali whispered the translation of the call to prayer:

"God is most great. God is most great. God is most great. God is most great. I bear witness that there is no god but God. I bear witness that there is no god but God. I bear witness that Muhammad is a messenger of God. I bear witness that Muhammad is a messenger of God. Hasten to prayer. Hasten to prayer. Hasten to success. Hasten to success. God is most great. God is most great. There is no god but [the One] God."

After the call to prayer, those assembled recited the first chapter of the Quran, the *Al-Fatihah*.

"In the name of God, Most Compassionate, Most Merciful. Praise be to God, Lord of the Worlds. The Most Compassionate, the Most Merciful. Ruler of the Day of Judgment. Only You do we worship. Only You do we ask for help. Show us the straight path. The path of those whom You have favored, not that of those who earn Your anger, nor those who go astray."

At this point, the Imam rose and walked to the pulpit. He was younger than Logan expected—late thirties, and he was slim, with a neatly trimmed beard. Ali bent towards him and whispered, "Over the course of Ramadan, which goes on for 29 to 30 days, Muslims will recite the entire Quran."

Today the Imam focused his sermon on the issue of charity and encouraged the attendees to be diligent in their almsgiving. He specifically referred to *Zakat*, the obligatory Muslim practice of contributing a portion of one's income to the poor. He reminded them *Zakat* was not voluntary but rather was considered a tax.

"Devout Muslims are required to pay two and a half percent of their income as *Zakat*, but they can also donate additional monies through *Sadaqah* donations," Ali whispered.

"These are voluntary, and people tend to give more during Ramadan because it's believed we'll find greater favor with Allah by doing so."

As the Imam was wrapping things up, Ali nudged Logan. "There," he pointed with his chin. "That's Akbar."

Logan looked in the direction Ali was pointing. He spotted a man roughly his age, slight in stature, with close-cropped brown hair and a short, wiry beard. Akbar caught Ali's eye and gave him a small wave of recognition.

When the Imam concluded the rites, Akbar came over to greet them.

"Are you a friend of Ali's?" he asked as he shook Logan's hand.

"Yes. Tim. Tim Hudson. And you are?"

"Akbar."

"Ali and I went to high school together in Virginia."

"Are you Muslim?"

"No," he laughed. "Actually, I was raised Catholic. I reminded Ali the only time I've ever been to a Muslim prayer service was when I went one time with his family in high school. I forgot what it was like and he offered to bring me."

"What did you think?"

"It's definitely different than a Catholic Mass. I spent some time in Afghanistan a few years ago and always wanted to learn more about Islam, but never had the time."

"What were you doing over there?"

"Military."

Akbar didn't register surprise, but Logan sensed the wheels beginning to spin.

"Are you still active duty?"

"No. There was this little problem with an AK-47 round taking out my knee. After that, the navy basically said sayonara."

"That's too bad."

"It worked out in the end. I started my own company outside of Boston doing security consulting. You know, things like VIP protection, training, tactical driving. That sort of thing."

Akbar gave Ali a knowing glance. "There's a pretty big

Muslim community in Boston. You ought to tune in to this one Imam I turned Ali onto a few weeks ago."

"Al Sadiq," Ali said.

"Yes, Hassan Al Sadiq," Akbar said.

"Is he in Boston?" Logan asked.

Akbar laughed. "No. Al Sadiq is in Kuwait. He does a weekly webcast from there. It's a little bit different than what you tend to get from the Imams here in the U.S."

"How so?"

"Most of them are running scared. These Imams don't really say what's on their minds, because Big Brother's probably listening, and it's not worth the risk of getting into trouble."

"So, you think the message in the U.S. is watered down?"

"Oh definitely. Right, Ali?"

Ali hesitated for a moment and then replied. "Akbar's right. Muslims in the U.S. make up such a small percentage of the population, they don't feel like they have a voice. They're afraid to rock the boat."

Akbar hesitated for a second, and then went to the place Logan was hoping for.

"So, you think you want to hear what a real Imam has to say?"

"I'm not sure. I—" He hesitated, to appear cautious.

"What do you have to lose? But I would urge you not to listen to this webcast from home. You would be better off tuning in from an internet café." He scribbled a web address onto a piece of paper. "I think he's scheduled to do one Tuesday afternoon."

"Maybe I'll check it out," Logan said.

He gave Akbar one of his Tim Hudson name cards.

"Nice talking to you, Akbar. If you're ever in the Boston area give me a call."

"Will do."

They shook hands and departed. As Logan and Ali walked away, Logan felt a stirring in his gut. It was the adrenaline rush that hits you before combat. Just before you engage the enemy.

Chapter 18

Azar brushed the hair out of her eyes as she scrutinized the last of the photos from the trip to Costa Rica. Her queries to a handful of travel magazines the week before resulted in *Condé Nast Travel* purchasing several for an upcoming article they were planning to run on the Caribbean vacation destination.

She checked her computer for messages and saw an email in her Dropbox account from Teheran. It was from her boss, the Unit 400 chief, Colonel Samadi.

> *"Greetings. Your colleagues and our commander, General Salehi, send their regards and congratulate you for the hard work you've been putting in. In particular, the New York lead who works for the NBA looks very promising. He just introduced a friend of his to our spotter, Akbar, at the masjid in New York City. It seems Ali and this fellow went to high school together.*
>
> *"We've developed some preliminary background information on the man, based upon a short conversation he and Akbar had after prayers at the masjid. His name is Tim Hudson, and he was a U.S. Navy SEAL with battlefield experience in Afghanistan but was released from the navy on a medical disability. Hudson has a business doing VIP protection and security training and has expressed some interest in Islam. He's not living in New York but outside of Boston in a town called New Bedford. I want you to go there and see what you can find out about him. If he's genuinely searching for something, we may have just what he's looking for."*

She could almost see the wheels spinning in Samadi's head. Recruiting a former U.S. special forces officer doesn't happen every day. Many of the ISIS recruiters go after the low hanging fruit, disaffected youth living in the Middle East. But this would be something entirely different.

She called her travel agent and asked him to book a flight to New York. First, though, she needed to wrap up the *Condé Nast* assignment. Then she would work on Samadi's tasking. There wasn't much to go on. Samadi provided a phone number and email address taken from Hudson's business card. And Akbar had managed to take a picture of Hudson with his cell phone. It wasn't a perfect likeness, but Azar immediately recognized the rugged features of the unidentified man who was with Ali Parandeh at the basketball game in New York a couple of weeks earlier.

Azar composed a brief message in response to Samadi's missive, providing her itinerary and flight information. Of necessity, she would fly through New York so she could retrieve her alias documentation. From there Azar planned to pick up a rental car and drive up to New Bedford, which, according to the map, was about an hour south of Boston. If traffic wasn't too bad, she could make the trip in three hours.

Azar felt the adrenaline rush in the pit of her stomach. Being on assignment was always exhilarating, but never more so than when the mission involved death and destruction, the currency she usually traded in. There was always an element of danger in those operations she didn't feel in her present role as a support asset to ISIS. But still, there were never any ironclad guarantees things would play out according to plan. In this work, you needed to be quick on your feet.

She spent the rest of the afternoon putting the finishing touches on the *Condé Nast* submission. When she was finished, she packed a bag and ate a light dinner before retiring for the night.

She arrived early the next morning at Pearson International for her 9:00 a.m. Air Canada flight. It was a light travel day, and she breezed through security without a problem. She was just settling into a seat in the departure lounge when she noticed a gate change flashing on the departure monitor.

"I knew this was too good to be true," she fumed. Once she made her way to the new gate, she was disappointed to see the departures display showing a two-hour delay. The gate attendant advised her there was a plumbing issue in one of the lavatories on their Embraer 175 aircraft, and they would get underway as soon as it was fixed.

Your World Awaits, Air Canada's slogan, was stylishly etched beneath a red maple leaf on the wall of the departure lounge. "You can say that again," she grumbled to herself.

The mechanics finished the job in just under two hours and in record time, the crew boarded the passengers. Moments later, they were backing out of the gate. The flight itself was uneventful, and by 12:30, they were descending from the clouds as they awaited clearance from the tower at LaGuardia Airport.

After retrieving her alias documents at the storage facility in the Bronx, she took a cab to the Hertz car rental on Stillwell Ave. There was a line at the counter, and it was nearly 30 minutes before she was on the road. She picked up I-95 north of the Throgs Neck Expressway and cruised at 70 mph all the way to New Bedford. Everyone else on the road was doing 80 mph or faster, but she literally needed to stay below the radar. She couldn't afford to raise her profile with a traffic stop.

Azar's reservation was at a B&B on Union Street not far from New Bedford's historic district. The Octagon House was built in the 1880s for a Captain Haskell of the whaler *Mercury*. She had a made-to-order cover for staying in the historic whaling port and would make sure she was observed taking photographs around town.

The illustrated pamphlet in her room depicted New Bedford as a flourishing historical whaling center and even today the home port of an active fishing fleet. The Whaling Museum and Herman Melville's historic house would be good subjects for a photo essay. She unpacked her bag and decided to take a shower before dinner.

Moments later, as she stepped out of the shower, she appraised her reflection in the bathroom's full-length mirror. Crow's feet wrinkles spread out from the corners of her eyes. But other than the barely discernable tell-tale sign of aging, she was pleased with her appearance. Her skin was warm and blemish free, and her hair, which hung below her shoulders, showed no signs of graying. She cupped a breast in one hand, appraising its round firmness. And her stomach was taut, her reward for all the stretching and crunches she endured in her morning fitness routine.

After she dressed, she decided to take a walk in search of dining options. Maybe with some food under her belt, she would be able to devise a plan for tracking down Tim Hudson and see what additional information she could develop about him. She would start first thing in the morning conducting reverse phone directory and internet searches. It occurred to her if Hudson was a freelance security consultant, he might work out of a home office.

Azar decided on a seafood restaurant at the pier. It was less than ten minutes walking distance from her B&B. As she sauntered towards the waterfront, she allowed herself a moment of rare self-pity. Around her strolled couples and families in the fading light. There were very few, if any, single people on the street.

Make no mistake about it. Azar loved her job as a freelance photographer, femme fatale in service to the Qods Force. Her former life as a dutiful military spouse was behind her, albeit not of her own choosing, after her husband was killed in the attack on his military base in Bandar Deylam.

But as fulfilling as her new job was, there was no accounting for the feeling of loneliness that overcame her at times like this. Unless she made an effort to get her emotions under control, she might slip into depression or even panic. She felt herself sliding in that direction and willed herself to snap out of it.

Azar felt relieved when she found a restaurant on the pier. She went inside and was escorted to an outdoor table with a view of the water. Nearby a ferry boat from Martha's Vineyard was disgorging passengers from the island. Fishing boats bobbed in their moorings. She ordered a seared tuna steak and grilled vegetable medley over couscous. She asked her waiter to bring her a fresh squeezed lemonade.

Azar relaxed for the first time that day. Most of the diners were inside the restaurant; aside from an occasional murmur from a nearby table, it was quiet. Her thoughts turned to the task at hand. According to a guidebook she was reading, New Bedford had a population of just under 100,000 people. Although that wasn't large by any means, it still presented a logistical challenge for her to comb through the city and get a fix on the whereabouts of the former navy SEAL.

Professionally, she was curious about the man. She was used to being in the company of military men, although for the most part, they were Qods Force personnel. She knew the operatives she worked with now, the assassins of Unit 400, were a particular breed. Trained in the dark art of assassination, they bore little resemblance to the special forces operatives from America's elite military units. *How would they stand up in a one-on-one contest?*

She suspected ISIS would be interested in Hudson on a wide range of levels, not least of which would be the propaganda bonanza they would reap if he were to come over to their side. And then there was the value of having a military operative conducting directed attacks on U.S. soil.

Azar thought back to the Las Vegas killings from the year before. Many thought the attack was ISIS-inspired. The gunman fired military-style semi-automatic weapons into a crowd of outdoor concert goers, killing 59 and injuring another 500 people. The shooter didn't appear to have any military training, but his personal arsenal was impressive. Imagine what a skilled special forces attacker could have accomplished. The death toll would have been staggering.

Ultimately ISIS would like nothing better than to have trained cells of fighters positioned all around the U.S.

Someone like Hudson could accomplish that. As she speculated about the possible role Hudson might play, the message light on her phone lit up, indicating she had a new message in Dropbox.

She keyed in her password and scrolled through a short follow-up email from Colonel Samadi. Apparently, General Salehi was anxious to bring the former navy SEAL on board. He wanted to dispense with the usual vetting process and cut directly to the chase. He instructed her to establish direct contact with Hudson as soon as feasible.

Chapter 19

Logan and Peter Breen were meeting to go over Logan's brief encounter with Akbar. They were sitting in a back pew at the Cathedral of Holy Cross in downtown Boston, an hour before the 9:00 a.m. daily Mass. There were a dozen early worshipers seated throughout the church, murmuring their rosaries sotto voce.

"How do you think it went?" Breen whispered, appraising him with a quick sideways glance.

"Pretty good. I think Akbar bought my story. At least he didn't seem suspicious. The way Ali and I engineered the encounter, it looked like Akbar was the one who approached us. I didn't push hard on anything he said. Just put a few things out there for him to see if he would bite. Former military. A little disaffected. Searching for meaning in my life."

Breen nodded. "After our last talk, I reached out to NYPD to see if they had anything on Akbar. I was purposefully vague about our interest in him, basically just saying he had come across our scope. Turns out they have a file on him as a person of interest, but so far, he's kept his nose clean. He hasn't done anything to justify bringing him in for questioning. Besides, we don't want to tip our hand.

"His full name's Akbar Maloof," Breen continued. "He's an engineer, late twenties, single. He lives in Brooklyn. Came to the U.S. from Iraq on an asylum request with his father in 2007. The old man was working for the American military as an interpreter. He and the dad got in on a special visa program for asylum seekers. His mother was killed in the spring uprisings in Karbala in 2004."

"Our friends from the Mahdi army," said Logan. His

sarcastic comment was not lost on Breen.

"Right. Muqtada Al-Sadr's militia." Breen hitched up one pant leg to scratch a dry patch of skin on his calf. His eczema was acting up again.

"Anyway, Akbar was pretty screwed up after his mom died, but he was able to get into an engineering program at City College once he got here, earned a degree in mechanical engineering, and has a pretty good job with the city—Department of Buildings. Working on cranes and derricks."

"Sounds like he's doing a lot better than most of the refugees who get into the States but can't find a decent job, even if they do have a degree. Why would Akbar risk everything he's worked for by getting involved with ISIS?"

"That's the sixty-four-thousand-dollar question," Breen said. "We may never get the answer. Hard to know what he went through in Iraq. Probably just a teenager when his mom was killed. Maybe he blames the U.S., and it's his way of getting back at us.

"Changing the subject." Breen glanced around. "I had a message from Langley yesterday." He stared pointedly at Logan.

Logan cocked an eyebrow. "Yeah?"

"Nice to know who we're dealing with."

"Sorry, Peter. You know how it is."

Breen remained silent. "I thought we had something special," he glared. Then he laughed and slapped Logan on the back. "Just kidding man. Good to know we're working with the 'A' team."

"Yeah," Logan said. He looked at his watch. "I better shove off. Al Sadiq's webcast begins at ten-thirty, and I don't want to be late."

"All right. Let me know if you need anything."

"Okay." The two men shook hands and departed the cathedral separately.

Logan drove back to New Bedford. He had checked out a list of internet cafés and was surprised to discover the majority were in donut shops. Dunkin' Donuts seemed to have a monopoly on them. One place on Union Street was a

135

regular internet café with actual workstations for rent.

Logan planned to follow Akbar's suggestion to use a public computer for the webcast just in case ISIS was monitoring him. It wouldn't hurt for them to think he was good at following instructions.

He decided to park his car at the apartment and walk to Union Street. It would take him about 15 minutes on foot to get to the place. By the time he got there and checked in, it was almost time for the webcast to begin. He logged on and typed in the web address Akbar gave him.

Logan was wearing earbuds for privacy. The last thing he needed was to draw attention to himself if anyone were to overhear him tuning in to an Arabic language program. It didn't look as if it would be a problem though, because he had the place pretty much to himself.

He checked the time. Ten-thirty on the dot. He hit the enter key and a sound, not unlike that of the muezzin, the crier who calls the faithful to prayer at a mosque, filled his ears. As the seductive sound gradually died out, the screen was filled with a stylistic depiction of the word *Allah* in green Arabic script. In the background, Logan could hear the faint sound of running water, and then the image faded to a picture of a mosque with the muezzin looking out over a wall towards a vast desert landscape. Logan leaned forward in anticipation.

* * *

Azar had spotted the internet café on Union Street while walking back from dinner. She made a mental note to stop by in the morning so she could do her background checks on Hudson without resorting to the use of her own computer.

She was out at first light, photographing the historic buildings in the old seaport. Satisfied she had a good start on a photo essay depicting the eighteenth-century whaling village, she decided to walk over to the internet café. *What is it called? Your Other Office,* she remembered.

She spotted the sign from a block away. Traffic was brisk

on Union Street at this time of day, and Azar wondered if the place would be packed. She paused in front of the front window display, with photos depicting New Bedford street scenes from the turn of the century and looked in. There were only a few customers working on computers. Just inside the entrance, there was a counter behind which a young woman was engrossed in a crossword puzzle. She greeted Azar with a warm smile.

"What can I get you?" she asked.

Azar ran her eyes over the coffee and tea offerings but decided on a bottle of water. They were also offering some baked goods—brownies and muffins—but she wasn't hungry.

"Just water," she replied. "And I'd like to use a computer for about an hour."

"Sure thing. That'll be $7.50."

Azar gave her a $10 bill. The woman gave her $2.50 in change, her water, and a piece of paper with an alphanumeric code.

"When you log on, the username is 'Other Office,' and the password is this code," she explained, pointing to the slip of paper. "You can sit wherever you like."

"Thanks." Azar looked around the café. As she made her way to an empty workstation, she passed a casually dressed man wearing earbuds, staring intently at his computer screen. He glanced up momentarily as she went by, and as their eyes met, Azar felt a sudden jolt.

Could that be Hudson? She forced herself to keep moving. *Did I detect a flicker of recognition as his eyes swept over me? How strange.* They had never met. *New Bedford must be smaller than I realized,* she thought. *What are the chances of randomly running into him like this?*

The sense of déjà vu she experienced the first time she saw his photo, taken at the basketball game in New York City, gnawed at her again. Maybe that's what she was reacting to, she reasoned. The photo of him next to Ali Parandeh. It hadn't been a great photo, but the likeness was striking.

If it were Hudson, he must be here for Al Sadiq's

webcast. Akbar would have cautioned him to stay off of his home computer when listening to the Imam's program, the better to avoid the possibility the FBI would find out about his browsing habits.

Azar surreptitiously glanced in the direction of her quarry and could tell by the way he was hunched over, staring at the screen, he was immersed in something. If it were Al Sadiq's sermon, she knew it by heart, and although the firebrand's exhortations did little for her personally, she knew, from witnessing him firsthand, how his preaching often resonated with these people.

These webcasts generally ran for about an hour. Azar's normal M.O. was to have a private investigator working with her to help with the background checks and, where warranted, surveillance. But in this case, she was on her own. As she mulled over her options, it occurred to her there was a ready-made pretext for establishing direct contact with him. If he ran his own security consulting business, she could approach him to advise her on personal security advice for a woman who spent a fair amount of time traveling to out-of-the-way destinations.

Azar turned to her computer and logged on. She might as well see what she could find on Mr. Hudson. There might be something useful, especially if he had a website, to suggest the best way to approach him.

She was engrossed in her search, and the hour slipped by before she knew it. Hudson's website outlined a range of security services his company provided. One of these was a tactical driving course, which could be completed in just four hours. If she could sign up for this class, it would allow her to observe him close up in an intense, short timeframe. She would have to call him later to see if she could schedule the course on short notice.

Azar glanced up to see what he was doing and was dismayed to discover he was no longer at his workstation. He must have left while she had been using the computer. She cleared the cache from her web browser. This would remove the cookies and related website data tracking her browsing history. She was diligent about cleaning up her online activity weekly from her home computer, but in situations like this, she did it every time she logged off.

Azar double checked her workspace to make sure she had everything. As she walked back up Union Street to the Octagon House, she was already rehearsing her call to Mr. Hudson. If when they met, he recalled their near encounter at the internet café, she would pass it off as a coincidence. The Qods Force operative didn't anticipate any problem handling Tim Hudson.

Chapter 20

Logan slipped out of the internet café right after the web-cast was over. Azar was so absorbed in her work, she didn't even look up when he walked by. Right now, Logan was eyeballing the entrance to Your Other Office. He had line-of-sight to the building from a coffee shop across Union Street. He decided for the time being to keep an eye on the place from afar, but he was going to need backup if he wanted to find out what she was up to without showing his hand.

He called his SEAL buddy, Le Brian Delray, who said he could be in New Bedford later in the afternoon. Logan was unable to get through to Ed Wozolski, one of the other SEALS from the operation in Iran, who had been on the *Fish Sniffer* with him a couple of weeks back. Wozolski, "Blackjack" to his friends, lived in Princeton, New Jersey and would have a hard time getting to New Bedford on short notice.

As he sipped his coffee, Logan tried to process this turn of events. Azar Ghabel was in New Bedford. His initial assessment was she was working alone. He hadn't detected anything unusual when he exited the internet café, and there weren't too many places in the area for a surveillance team to hide. He would conduct a long SDR before he returned to his apartment, just to be sure, but for now, his immediate goal was to find out what she was up to.

Logan couldn't make sense of her unexpected appearance. They locked eyes for only a second when she walked by him in the café, but there was no doubt in his mind it was her. Was he mistaken, or did she betray the slightest hint of recognition before she averted her eyes? His mind raced as he thought through the implications of her presence in New Bedford. He immediately ruled out the possibility of a chance encounter. There was no way she would randomly show up in the U.S. five years after their violent confrontation in Caracas. That wasn't even in the realm of possibilities.

Did it mean Unit 400 was still out there, seeking to avenge his team's attack on the Qods Force terrorist training camp? If so, why would Azar reveal herself to him in public in such an obvious way? Was it possible the assassin's reach extended to New Bedford, Massachusetts? What was she up to?

He was meticulous in his tradecraft when setting up the Tim Hudson cover. Could it be Ali double-crossed him? Maybe Ali was working for the Qods Force. Perhaps this whole scenario was a Unit 400 ruse to draw him out. He pondered that thought for a moment, but then shook his head.

Logan trusted his instincts. Despite his past differences with Ali and the latter's recent dalliance with extremism, he was confident his brother-in-law recognized ISIS for what it was and had pulled back from the abyss before it was too late. No, Ali wasn't the one.

The only logical conclusion was Azar was somehow connected to ISIS. After all, Akbar was the only person, aside from Detective Breen and Ali, who had his Tim Hudson contact information. Well, there were others –his realtor, the car dealer, Jason Summers at CIA. But none of them would have been in touch with the Iranians nor would they have any motivation to betray him.

It was probably a fluke, but could it be Unit 400 was in bed with ISIS?

It was such a ludicrous idea, given their inherent differences; he forced himself to repeat it. Was Unit 400 in cahoots with ISIS? Even more bizarre was Azar Ghabel's involvement.

He replayed the night in Caracas in his mind. He, Bruce Wellington and Norm Stoddard had been staking out the safehouse where Azar and Nouri Khorasani were holed up. His team broke into the building while the two Iranians were out, lying in wait for their return. The plan was to take

Khorasani down, but the wily killer gave them the slip. Azar was the only one to show up. It turned out her partner had been unexpectedly dispatched to Mexico City to assassinate a prominent Israeli author by the name of Simon ben Reznik.

Azar by herself proved to be a worthy foe. As she walked through the apartment door, she immediately sensed something was wrong, and when they sprung out of hiding, fought back with everything she had. She went after Wellington with an assassin's dagger when he showed himself, and that's when Logan drilled her in the neck with a taser.

He couldn't say for sure, but it was unlikely she ever registered his presence as the weapon's two metal probes struck her. The high-voltage electrodes lodged in her neck, and she collapsed with a thud. He doubted there was any way, five years later, she remembered his face. She was out cold when the team left her inert body in one of the bedrooms and escaped into the night.

They learned later, medics from the Centro Médico de Caracas responded to their anonymous phone call within minutes. A police informant advised them she was transported to the hospital, where she remained in critical condition for over a week before being airlifted to Teheran.

Logan mulled over these facts as he assessed the situation. There was another possibility, he conceded. The Qods Force had penetrated the Kuwaiti intelligence service almost a decade ago. Their agent, a Kuwaiti intelligence officer by the name of Simon, was the one who disclosed Hamid Subaie's covert intelligence affiliation to the Iranians. Simon was also in the room when Logan first met the Kuwaiti operative.

None of the Iranians at Bandar Deylam survived the attack, but Simon was able to alert Tehran after the fact that Kuwaiti intelligence was involved. He revealed to them that Logan and Hamid planned the attack together in Kuwait City.

Simon was aware of Logan's real name, and he passed it

on to the Qods Force. It was a simple matter for their agents in Kuwait City to identify the taxi driver who drove Logan from the airport to his hotel and then bribe the front desk manager to retrieve the particulars from his passport.

And while he never dismissed the possibility the Qods Force might come after him, it was a stretch to think they were able to link his Tim Hudson persona to Logan Alexander. Of that he was confident. Hell, CIA was as good as it got when it came to doing link analysis, and even they sometimes missed clues which, in retrospect, seemed obvious.

The only credible explanation for Azar's presence was the Qods Force was working with ISIS. Akbar was the front man, the one who drummed up the leads he fed to people like Azar. She might even be the conduit to an investigative team hired to conduct surveillance and do background checks. She'd be there to pitch the new recruit or shut it down if it smelled like an FBI sting operation.

As he mulled over these possibilities, his cell phone rang. He didn't recognize the caller ID, and he almost let the call go to voicemail, but he stabbed at the phone before it stopped ringing.

"Hello?"

"Yes. Is Mr. Hudson there?" Logan didn't recognize the caller—the soft, foreign-accented voice seemed vaguely familiar. He searched his memory and was startled to realize, although different, it reminded him of Zahir.

"Speaking."

"Are you the Tim Hudson with the security consulting business?"

"Yes. How can I help you?" His pulse quickened as it occurred to him he was talking to Azar Ghabel! What was she up to?

"My name's Alice Meens. I wanted to know if your company teaches tactical driving classes?"

"Yes, we do. What can I do for you?"

"I'm a freelance photographer, and I travel all over the world doing photoshoots, sometimes on short notice. I live in Canada, and I'm here for just a few days working on a piece about New Bedford's whaling history.

"My editor wants me to go down to Colombia next week on assignment," she explained, "but I'm a little nervous because of all the kidnappings they have down there. I was sharing my concerns with a friend in the business, who said she took a tactical driving course a couple of months ago. Even though she's never had to use it, it gives her a lot of confidence when she's working in some of these high-threat locations.

"How long does the course take?" she asked.

"The basic tactical driving course is four hours," he said. He gave the caller a brief rundown of the curriculum. "In that time, we mostly concentrate on the essentials. We'll teach you how to recognize an attack before it happens, how to use your vehicle as a weapon, and how to use a high-speed reverse, 180-degree maneuver to get away from the threat. We won't be teaching the forward 180-degree movement. That one's a little trickier and takes longer to master.

"Typically, we like to use the client's personal vehicle since it's usually the one they'll be driving. In your case, since you're traveling, we would just use your rental car. I'm assuming you have a rental, right?"

"Yes."

"So, we would simulate the part where we use the vehicle as a weapon. We don't want to ruin your relationship with the rental company." He chuckled at his own joke.

"Can you fit me in tomorrow?"

He paused and turned the pages in his notepad to make it appear he was consulting his calendar. "I think tomorrow should be fine. Ten o'clock?"

"Yes, that'll work. By the way, what's your fee?"

"Five-hundred dollars. Cash or credit card. A couple of other things. I'll have a release of liability form for you to sign, and I'll need to see your driver's license and proof of insurance."

"No problem. Where shall we meet?"

"In front of your hotel?"

"Yes, that's fine."

"Where are you staying?"

"I'm at the Octagon House. On Union."

"Great. One other thing. Do you know if your car's front- or rear-wheel drive?"

"I'm not sure."

"What are you driving?"

"It's a blue Toyota Corolla."

"Probably front-wheel drive. All right. I'll see you at ten."

"Thanks. See you tomorrow."

Logan sat there for a moment pondering this new development. Things were definitely getting interesting. A movement across the street caught his attention. It was Azar, departing the internet café. She turned right and headed up Union towards the Octagon House.

He waited until she was a block away and then discreetly fell in behind her to see if she met up with anyone and to confirm she was staying at the B&B. Bingo. There it was just up the street. She turned off the sidewalk and went inside.

Logan spent the next two hours slogging through New Bedford to see if anyone was tailing him. He wasn't as meticulous as he would have been in a hostile foreign country, given the remote likelihood anyone was actually surveilling him. He didn't want to be cavalier about it, given what was at stake, but it had to be a fluke Azar had run into him.

Later that afternoon, Logan drove 20 minutes south to Fall River, once the most prominent textile manufacturing hub in the country. He was meeting Delray at Battleship Cove, a maritime museum and war memorial situated near the confluence of Mount Hope Bay and the Taunton River.

As the two friends walked around the USS Massachusetts, a famous relic from World War II, he briefed Delray on Azar's unexpected appearance.

"Tomorrow, I'm meeting her at ten o'clock in front of her B&B." He pulled out a map of New Bedford and pointed out where she was staying. "The first thing we need to figure out is if she's here on her own or traveling with 'friends,'" he explained.

"If she's working for ISIS, this is probably some kind of vetting exercise, and I'm not too worried about that. I'll stick with my cover story and just run with it. Even if she's got backup, their goal is to recruit me, not take me out.

"But if she's coming after me because she's somehow linked Tim Hudson and Logan Alexander, that's a whole different ballgame. It could be about paybacks for killing her husband."

"You been talking to your man Breen, right?"

"Yeah."

"Can't he put some people on the street for backup?"

"I thought about it, but we need to be discreet. I don't know how good Breen's people are. If Azar spots anything squirrely, she could get spooked and ruin everything. I'll just have to take a chance. I can handle her."

"Yeah. You've got some experience with that," Delray joked.

"Will you look at this?" Delray abruptly changed the subject. He was stopped in front of another relic from World War II. It was a PT boat, one of a handful of surviving motor torpedo boats from those days, memorialized by President John F. Kennedy's PT-109. This one, PT-796, sported some fearsome artwork, a gaping shark's mouth in bright red and white with two menacing eyes causing the hair on the back of your neck to bristle.

As the men continued walking around the outdoor exhibits, they decided Delray would stage near the Octagon at nine o'clock the next morning to determine if Azar was bringing company with her. Since she wouldn't know their destination, it would be difficult, if not impossible, for her to set up an ambush once they got moving.

"I wish we could get inside her room. See if she's careless. Give us a clue as to what she's after. But the B&B's too small. They'd be all over us," Logan said.

"You carrying?" he asked.

Delray nodded. "Man's best friend. Glock-23."

"Good. Hopefully, you won't need it. I think we're good

to go. You want to grab a beer before we call it a day?"

"Sure."

They found a sports bar and grill on Davol Street. The bartender must have been a soccer fan because the TV was tuned to a World Cup match between Sweden and the U.K. Logan relaxed for the first time all day. It was hard to predict what tomorrow would bring, but he suspected it was going to get interesting from here on out.

Chapter 21

When she got back to her room, Azar fired up her computer to see if there were any messages from Teheran. There was a note from Colonel Samadi urging her to fast track her assessment of Tim Hudson.

> *"ISIS is fast approaching a situation where they'll be unable to hold their ground in Syria and Iraq. Baghdadi is fighting on other fronts as well. Against the Taliban and Afghan army. And in Libya. The only reason he has held on there is the civil war and the resulting power vacuum. ISIS is losing territory day after day.*
>
> *"At some point 'The Invisible Sheikh' will truly have to become a ghost if his Caliphate is to survive. More of his operations will, of necessity, take place outside of the area he now controls. This means cyber recruitments and attacks like the ones we've seen in Europe and the United States. It will be more 'lone wolf' attacks and small cell operations. They will be everywhere."*

She was surprised to hear Baghdadi was losing ground so fast. When the self- proclaimed Caliph staked out his claim to power in 2014, jihadists from all over the world flocked to him. It was a time when much of the international community had all but abandoned efforts to shore up their respective allies in the Middle East. In Syria—Russia, China, and Iran remained steadfast in their support of Assad, while the Americans, Saudis, and Turks provided reluctant aid to the rebels.

And if you could believe what you read in the papers, many Americans were suffering buyer's remorse for having cleaved to a policy that brought their combat troops home from Iraq and Afghanistan. The previous administration left but a small contingent on the ground to serve as advisors to indigenous forces in Iraq and Afghanistan and the poorly equipped militia in Syria. But, the new U.S. leaders seemed bent on reversing direction, and as a result, the Pentagon was gearing up to increase America's presence there again.

She smiled. America was tearing itself apart, with Republicans clamoring for the president to get back into the fight and Democrats insisting he keep U.S. troops home. It should be a perfect time for ISIS to wage war because America was at war with itself. And, the EU was fraying at the edges because some members treated it like a welfare program to prop up their lagging economies. The EU was beginning to deconstruct, with Britain leading the way.

Enter Iran's Ayatollahs, who, despite worldwide havoc, were playing a decidedly dangerous game. On the one hand, the Qods Force was secretly advising the Iraqi military, and covertly arming the Kurdish Peshmerga. But, behind the scenes, the operatives from Unit 400 were quietly helping ISIS achieve its objectives.

In public, Iran's leadership denounced ISIS, blaming its rise to power on the West for having created power vacuums in Iraq, Afghanistan, Libya, and Syria, as a result of their meddlesome foreign policy and warmongering.

She didn't fully understand geopolitics, and why Iran was playing both sides against the middle. In her heart, she believed much of it could be attributed to her country's complicated relationship with its neighbor, Iraq. The two nations shared a thousand-mile border. And both countries were comprised of predominantly Shia populations. On so many levels their interests were intertwined, in particular, their religious and economic ties. But the Iran-Iraq War, sparked by Iraq's invasion of Iran in 1980, destroyed any trust between the two countries. Now, decades later, many of the grievances left over from the eight-year conflict, still remained.

Azar was astute enough to understand this improbable

alliance between the Qods Force and ISIS had the potential to backfire. If it became public knowledge, the international community would have another excuse for tarring the republic as a supporter of terrorism. Or even worse, if ISIS should succeed in partitioning Iraq, this could weaken Iran's western border and the fraught, if not vital, economic relationship with its neighbor.

She pursed her lips. How would Tim Hudson fit into this scenario if ISIS succeeded in recruiting him? It was hard to know. The direct approach she was taking would be a first for her. With her previous targets, there was no one-on-one interaction. This was new territory.

"I'll have to test him, to see if he's as brave as they think he is," she concluded. She researched navy SEALS on the internet. Their BUD/S (Basic, Underwater, Demolition/SEAL) training was designed to weed out the weaklings. If he was indeed a graduate of this course, he must be one tough customer.

The first phase of SEAL training focused on intense conditioning and seamanship skills and then moved on to combat diving before finishing up with land warfare. Thinking about it made her slightly nostalgic for her own training days, learning the art of the assassin. Her coursework didn't cover tactical driving, so she was looking forward to tomorrow's program.

She glanced back at the screen and noticed there was another paragraph in Samadi's message.

"One other matter I would like you to look into when you finish up there has to do with Ali Parandeh. Akbar has been dead on with most of the leads he has given us, and this one seemed very promising, mainly if his recruitment were to result in a significant attack at an NBA game or on their headquarters.

But, Akbar has seen him a few times recently at prayer services, and, except for the time when he met Hudson, he's had the feeling Ali's avoiding him. Maybe he's on the fence or getting cold feet. If he's one of those intellectual types, he may have been turned off by Al Sadiq's message. We've seen this happen in other cases.

Another possibility is he may have monarchist connections. We have uncovered some evidence his mother may have been related to the Shah."

Azar wasn't surprised by Samadi's disparaging reference to the radical Imam's lecture. Of course, the colonel was Muslim, and he would follow whatever directives came down from the Supreme Leader. But he wasn't likely to be personally swayed by ISIS' conservative message.

She shut down her computer. She wasn't hungry enough for dinner but wandered down to the conservatory, where her hostess was offering refreshments. She poured herself a cup of tea and selected a piece of berry pie, which she took to a table overlooking the flower garden. She remained there for an hour, enjoying the quiet, before retiring to her room. Tomorrow would be a busy day.

Chapter 22

Logan's apartment was less than a mile from where Azar was staying. To avoid walking directly to the Octagon House, he decided to drive to Clasky Common Park and leave his car near the intersection of Pope and Purchase. The park was known for its Saturday farmers market in the summer; a decent place to kill some time. He reached into the back seat to retrieve a bag filled with a half-dozen orange traffic cones he planned to use in the class. They were from a sporting goods store in Taunton.

It was 7:30, and the market was in full swing. Small farmers from around the area were setting up stalls and unloading baskets. It was a little sparse on fruit and vegetables because it was early in the season. But there was honey, eggs and farm-raised meats from Falmouth and Sandwich. There must have been people from 40 different farms laying out their wares.

One enterprising vendor was selling coffee, and Logan wandered over to order a dark roast. While he was waiting, his phone vibrated; it was a text message from Delray.

Heading out now to have breakfast, Delray wrote.

That was code to let Logan know his man was on his way to conduct counter-surveillance against Azar. New Bedford's historic downtown district wasn't the most comfortable place to stage a surveillance operation. Delray knew where she was staying, Logan's planned route to the B&B, and the way he intended to drive to Falmouth.

It hadn't been easy to find a place on such short notice to conduct Azar's tactical driving class. The ideal spot required good asphalt, little to no traffic, and no distractions. He remembered a navy buddy of his, Randy Case, from the upper Cape, took over his dad's crop-dusting business after he got out of the service. He was situated on the Cape, close to Falmouth, and had his own private airstrip. Randy did crop dusting, seeding, and spraying and was pretty busy during the planting and growing season. It just so happened he wasn't working Saturday because he was the proud possessor of a Boston Whaler he loved to take out in search of tuna, striped bass, and bluefish. Logan found Randy's contact info in the white pages directory online. It was Friday evening, and Logan reached Randy at home.

"I'm not working Saturday," Randy said. "You'll have the place to yourself unless someone has to make an emergency landing. My cousin and I are heading out early to fish, so we'll probably miss you. Sorry, you can't join us."

Randy didn't ask any questions, which was just as well, because Logan didn't want to get into the whole Tim Hudson story and his work against ISIS.

"We'll have to get together one of these days. You remember Willy Blacklock?" Logan asked.

"Yeah. How's old Willy doing?"

"Great. Owns a charter business in Boston; fishes all around Boston Harbor. Took my dad, brother-in-law, and some SEAL buddies out a few weeks ago."

"Tell him I said hi if you see him again. Sounds like a fun gig. How long's he been doing that?"

"Since he got out. Seven, eight years, I guess."

"Nice. All right. I have to go. Give me a buzz if you need anything else."

"See you soon, Randy. I owe you one."

"Just make it a cold one, and we'll call it even." He chuckled.

Logan tossed his coffee cup into the trash. He walked south and then west out of the park and began working the streets in a zig-zag fashion to determine if anyone was tailing him. Walking in a straight line as the crow flies would put him at the B&B in a half-hour. But as he methodically worked the streets, sometimes backtracking and sometimes looping back on himself, he estimated he would get there right at ten.

An hour later, he turned onto Union and saw the Octagon House up ahead. He could see Delray's car parked a block up the street with line-of-sight to the B&B. As he moved forward, there was another text message from Delray giving him the all clear.

Here we go. Parked out front was a blue Toyota Corolla. Inside, behind the wheel was a woman. As he approached the car, he glanced around. There was some light traffic, but nothing to make his hair stand on end.

He tapped on the driver's window. "Ms. Meens?"

She rolled the window down. The woman looking back at him was definitely Azar Ghabel. She was very much the same as he remembered her from their encounter in Caracas. And if there was any doubt, the squiggly outline of a scar on her neck where the taser struck her, peeped out above the neckline of her blouse.

"Mr. Hudson?"

"Yes. You can call me Tim. If you don't mind, I'll drive. It's about forty-five minutes from here."

"All right." She stepped out of the car and walked around to the passenger side. She was wearing designer jeans and a round-neck blouse hanging loosely over the top of her pants. She had on sandals. Impossible to tell if she was armed.

Azar had the lithe body of an athlete. Dark hair below the shoulder, parted in the middle, swept back from an attractive face. Designer sunglasses completed her ensemble, making it difficult to read her eyes.

When they were in the car together, she removed the glasses and extended her hand.

"Please call me Alice," she said. She reached into her purse. "Here are the IDs you asked for." She handed him her license and insurance card.

He took the identification from her. *Wonder who forges documents for the Qods Force?* he thought. They looked authentic, although he was hard-pressed to tell the difference between fakes and the real deal. He gave them a cursory look and returned them to her.

"Thanks." He started the car and pulled away from the curb. "It's forty-five minutes to our training site. We'll be working in Falmouth, on the other side of Buzzards Bay." He reached into his pocket and withdrew a business card, which he handed to her.

"How'd you find us?"

"I was searching online for driving schools."

"You know there's a difference between defensive driving and tactical driving. In the business, we think of defensive driving as being more like driver's ed, a safety course, something parents put their kids through before they get their driver's license.

"Tactical driving requires more advanced driving skills. It's for experienced drivers who have safety concerns. Hostile environments with high crime, kidnappings, or terrorist threats."

"Everything in Toronto is defensive. I didn't find anything tactical, like what you're describing."

Logan sped up as they left New Bedford and approached the on-ramp for I-195. *It's too bad there's no car ferry service from New Bedford to the Cape,* he thought. There were passenger-only ferries from New Bedford to Nantucket, but that wasn't any help. He'd take Route 25 in a big loop around Head of the Bay and then cross the bridge over to the Cape at Bourne.

He glanced at her. *She seems pretty relaxed for someone on a mission,* he mused. He wondered what kind of training the Qods Force put her through and what she had been doing operationally since she started working for them.

"You said you were a photographer. Have you always lived in Canada?"

"Yes. Freelance. Actually, I'm from Iran. Shiraz. I immigrated to Canada three years ago."

"Family?"

"No. My parents are both dead, and my husband died unexpectedly several years ago. I was looking for a fresh start, a change of scenery. There's a relatively sizeable

Iranian expat community in Toronto.

"How about you? Are you from this area?"

"No. My family's from northern Virginia. Arlington. Just outside of Washington." It was a good thing he was used to operating in an alias. The fiction rolled off his tongue as smooth as butter.

"How'd you end up here?"

"I was in the navy. Thought about making a career out of it, but I was injured in Afghanistan and was medically discharged. Some of my navy buddies were from the Boston area. Decided to check it out. Met a girl from New Bedford, but it didn't work out."

They continued chatting as he looped north past Wareham, crossing the Bourne Bridge. It would have been more scenic to follow Shore Road but to save time he stayed straight after the bridge and merged onto Route 28. A few minutes later, he turned left onto Route 151 and soon was approaching the Crane Wildlife Management Area. It and the Mashpee National Wildlife Refuge to the east preserved several thousands of acres of marshlands and wetlands.

He turned onto an unmarked dirt road wending back to fields and what looked like a cranberry bog. There was a small Cape-style house with weathered gray shingles and white shutters. A Ford pickup truck was parked in the driveway, but there didn't appear to be anyone around. He drove to the back of the property where it opened up to a large meadow. A forest of pitch pine crept up to the south side of the pasture. To the north, there were several acres of cranberry bogs, narrow ditches running between rows of low evergreen runners.

"What are those?" she asked, pointing to the bog.

"Cranberries. We have a reputation for producing most of the cranberries in the U.S., but actually, Wisconsin beats us out hands down. Those low evergreen bushes will produce bright red berries by September. The farmers flood the bogs, and the berries float to the top."

There were several outbuildings behind the house to include a hangar, barn, and nondescript sheds. Running through the middle of the meadow was an asphalt runway he estimated was just under a thousand feet long.

He pulled up to one end of the landing strip and killed the engine. "Let's take a stretch, and I'll explain what we're going to do." They both exited the car and walked to the front. He had a pad of paper and a pencil to sketch out the maneuver he was about to teach her.

"The first thing we're going to work on is called a J turn. Being able to do this is critical when the attack is coming at you from the sides or head on. You can only execute this maneuver if the road behind you is open enough to make the turn.

"You can do this with either an automatic transmission or a stick. The manual takes a bit more practice and coordination because you have to clutch and shift. What do you drive at home?"

"An automatic."

"We'll work on that. In most cases where you'll be driving a rental, it will be an automatic, too."

"Just a couple of thoughts about attitude and preparedness when you're in a high-threat environment. You can't be complacent about your surroundings. All bets are off regarding what you think of as 'normal.' You have to learn to anticipate the unexpected. In driving, it means always being alert, leaving yourself escape routes should you be attacked and having the confidence you'll survive an attack because you know what to do."

He put the notepad on the hood of the car and sketched out a scenario similar to the one he was about to demonstrate. "You can see from this situation two cars have come up in blocking positions from side streets. Typically, gunmen will exit their vehicles. Depending on their motive, they'll either start shooting or confront you, hoping you'll freeze. That's when they'll either take you out or kidnap you."

"I don't see how you could get out of that situation alive," Azar said.

"I'll show you. They both got back into the car, with

Logan driving. He headed several hundred feet down the runway and stopped.

"All right. We just had two cars cut us off. The first thing we're going to do is look in our rearview mirror and see if we have room to maneuver.

"We do, so we put the car in reverse, and begin accelerating backward until we get it up to thirty to thirty-five miles per hour. We're not used to driving in reverse at high speeds, so most of us tend to be a little tentative. Remember time is essential. We need to get off the dime."

As Logan spoke, he slid the car into reverse and began accelerating. His hands were positioned on either side of the steering wheel at about the three and seven o'clock positions, and his eyes were fixed on the rearview mirror.

Azar pressed her feet against the floorboards and held her breath as they passed 35 mph. Suddenly, Logan took his foot off the gas and spun the wheel counterclockwise for three-quarters of a turn.

"The most important thing at this point is to keep your foot off the brake. The speed and weight of the car will swing it around," he shouted.

She slid sideways in her seat from the sudden motion, straining against the G-forces caused by the speed and violent shift in direction. If it weren't for the seatbelt, she would have landed in Logan's lap. As it was, her head banged into his shoulder, and she involuntarily clutched his leg.

The wheels were screeching, and the car seemed out of control, straining to hold the road in a dizzying flash. Midway through the turn, Logan swung the steering wheel back in the opposite direction, shifted into drive, and tromped on the accelerator.

The car stabilized and raced away from the scene of the notional attack. She let out a small gasp. He could tell from the look on her face she was startled by the surge of speed and the controlled spinning of the vehicle. But something in her manner told him she enjoyed the thrill. Her nostrils were flared and her breathing uneven. He looked down and noticed she was still grasping his leg.

"Oh. I'm sorry," Azar blushed. "It happened so fast."

"You ready to try it now? I can show you again if you want."

"No, it's okay. I think I've got it." They changed places, and she drove back to the starting point.

"Remember, the key thing is to be decisive when you're making the turn. It'll feel as though you're losing control, but the weight of the car and the momentum from the speed will whip it around. Also, coming out of the turn is just as important. You figure the car is going to basically do a 180-degree turn. You need to let the steering wheel come back the same amount, so you'll be headed straight down the road."

Azar nodded. She put the car into reverse and began accelerating—10, 20, 30 mph. Her mouth was set, and as she reached 35, she started her turn. She forgot to take her foot off the accelerator, and the car began to spin out of control, sliding sideways. Logan thought she was going to flip it.

"Slow down," he yelled. "Take your foot off the gas."

The car began to decelerate, and she hit the brakes. It came to rest; she slumped forward in defeat.

"I don't know what happened," she said, stammering. "It seemed pretty easy when you explained it."

"People don't usually get it on the first try," he said. "Why don't I demo it one more time and then we'll give you another shot at it." They traded seats, and he executed the maneuver, talking her through the steps as he transitioned from one movement to the next.

Azar had a determined look on her face as they again swapped seats and sped down the runway in reverse. She was initially tentative, but by the fourth attempt, Azar looked as though slinging cars around on asphalt was a cinch.

"All right. I think you have that down. Now let's try something else." He reached into the back seat and retrieved his bag, withdrawing a half-dozen lightweight orange cones.

"I'm going to line these up, and we'll combine steering

around an obstacle while you try to execute a J turn." He got out of the car and set up the cones so she would have to steer between them before executing the turn.

"This simulates a situation where there's something in the road behind you. A car, a person, an object blocking your way, and you need to get around it, so you can complete the J turn and get out of Dodge."

As she practiced weaving through the cones, he cautioned her to be sensitive to the aerodynamic forces coming into play and to learn how to maintain control of the car by understanding the limits of shifting weight and traction.

He spent an hour talking about techniques involving the use of the vehicle as a weapon. Using his sketch pad, he drew out several attack scenarios Azar could encounter in a congested area.

"Most people don't think of it, but your car is a powerful battering ram. A small vehicle can move a larger one blocking its way, by merely ramming it on the side, towards the front or the rear, but not in the middle. You basically turn the car on its axis, and it allows you to slip past.

"There's this natural hesitation too. You wouldn't dream of ramming your sixty-thousand-dollar Lexus into another car. But this is about saving your life. You can always buy a new car, so don't worry about it."

"What if someone pulls up beside you?" she asked.

"I'll say this again and again. You have to be aware of your surroundings. A student of mine went to live in Athens a couple of years ago. There used to be a domestic terrorist group there called '17 November.' One of their favorite techniques was to pull up next to their target on a motorcycle. Usually, it's two guys. A driver and a shooter. They would kill the target in congested traffic, and then escape in the havoc.

"Anyway, my student made a point of keeping his eye on the motorcycles as they wove their way through traffic, especially if they fit the profile of two riders. He would watch their hands. And he always left a buffer around him when he was at a stop light. An escape route.

"This one day, a motorcycle was coming up behind him, and he saw the gun before they got close enough to shoot. He ran them over. He had left several feet in front of his car when he was stopped at the light. He swerved to the left as they started to pull up, knocked the bike down, drove over the median strip and escaped."

By four o'clock she was able to demonstrate her mastery of the various tactical maneuvers he had taught her. They made small talk on the drive back to New Bedford. As they pulled up to the Octagon House, she pulled out an envelope with his $500 fee.

"Thank you for everything. I feel much better after that." She paused for a moment. "We didn't have time for lunch. Would you like to join me for dinner later?"

What is she up to? Logan wondered. This was too good to pass up.

"Yes. I'd like that. What time?"

"How about seven?"

"I'll pick you up here."

"See you then."

Logan had a few things to do before dinner. He wanted to shower and change, and he needed to debrief Delray and set up coverage for the evening.

Chapter 23

"Why not call him?" Rosana Parandeh pleaded with her daughter.

"I will, Mom. I'm just not ready." Rosana was driving Zahir to Reagan National Airport for her flight to Boston. Her extended stay in D.C. was over, although Cooper was going to stay on with his grandparents for another week.

Zahir's department head at Boston University reached out to her to see if she would be available to fill in for the rest of the semester. One of the other Arabic professors was rushed into emergency heart surgery earlier in the week and would be unable to return to his teaching duties until September.

Zahir was looking forward to getting back to work. She loved her parents. They were trying to be supportive, but in the last few days, her relationship with them felt strained because of their incessant harping on her separation from Logan. Her mother had taken to leaving clippings from advice columns on her bedside table and one evening even confided her own distress over a miscarriage she had suffered when she was younger, and the angst it had produced in her own marriage.

"It was our first child. A boy. Your father and I were still living in Teheran. Like you, I carried him almost to full term. It was the third trimester. January. Your father was in Paris for a conference, and I was at home, alone.

"I remember going to bed early that night because I felt so tired. I woke up at around three a.m. Something was wrong. The bed felt wet. When I turned the light on there was blood everywhere."

Tears began to trickle down Rosana's cheeks, and she

162

started to sob. She dabbed at her eyes with a tissue and fought to regain control. Zahir put her arms around her mother and lay her head on her shoulder as the older woman's body shook. They sat that way for several minutes. When she was able, Rosana continued her narrative.

"I was in so much pain. It felt like someone was stabbing me in my lower back. And I was so sick to my stomach I thought I would die. I called my mother, and she phoned for an ambulance.

"At the hospital, the OBGYN did some tests, but it was no use. The baby was already dead. Afterward, I was very depressed. The doctors will tell you one in four pregnancies ends in miscarriage. But most of these are in the first trimester. I think it's much harder if you've carried a baby for seven months."

"How come you never said anything to us?" Zahir asked.

"Some things are better left unsaid. I was having a hard time coping with it. And for a while, I blamed your father because he was not there to help me. Which is totally irrational because there was nothing he could have done.

"The thing is, you never get over it. If you let it, grief will destroy you. But you can overcome the way you look at it. If you consider the amount of grief you feel is proportionate to the love you felt for your child, you realize what a gift motherhood is."

Zahir reached over to touch her mother's arm. "Thanks, Mom. It helps to know you understand what I'm going through."

Her mother squeezed her hand. "I love you, my light."

"I love you too, Mom." With a start, Zahir realized she was daydreaming. They were on George Washington Parkway, fast approaching the airport exit.

"I spoke with Ali yesterday. He said he's going to be in Boston today," her mother said.

"That's what I heard. Meeting clients in from Brazil. They're interested in having an exhibition game between the Celtics and a team from Rio next winter. Their people wanted to meet with the Celtics' front office," Zahir said.

"Are you going to have a chance to see him?"

"We're supposed to get together, but it depends on his schedule. Maybe dinner. I could cook for him. But I'll probably have to do some shopping."

"Will Logan be there?"

"No. I don't think so. I asked him to move out of the apartment last week."

"What!" She took her eyes off the road. "Where's he staying?" she asked in an accusing tone.

"I'm not sure, Mom. I need to talk to him. Watch the road!"

"What about Cooper? He needs his father." Rosana wrenched the steering wheel to straighten the car and glanced sideways.

Zahir sighed. "I know." She started to tear up. She was already missing Cooper. He was at Frying Pan Farm Park in Herndon for the day with his grandfather.

They were pulling up to the Delta departures area. She leaned over to kiss her mom and got out of the car.

"I'll call you when I get in," Zahir said. She opened the tailgate and pulled out her bag. She was traveling light. All of their things from Hong Kong were in Boston.

She was already checked in, but once she got inside, security took forever. The three airports in the Washington Metro Area: BWI, Dulles, and National are always busy, and as gateways to the nation's capital, have comprehensive security procedures. *It's a good thing I'm early,* she thought. It took over an hour to navigate the line, and by the time she was through, they were already boarding the first-class passengers on her flight.

The trip up to Boston was without incident. Zahir had a window seat, and as she stared out at the clouds below her, she thought back to her mother's admonition to reach out to Logan. In the deepest recesses of her heart, she knew she was still in love with him; her behavior was selfish. Without a doubt, he felt as much grief over the loss of their baby as she did. They had been through so much in their short five years of marriage. Her eyes brimmed over with tears as she thought about their life together. She vowed to call him as soon as she got to Boston.

When she deplaned at Logan Airport Terminal A, Zahir took the shuttle to the airport subway station. It was only a half-mile from there to Porter Street. Her roller bag was light, and since it was such a beautiful day, she decided to walk. She crossed over to Breman Street Park and got on the East Boston Greenway, a twelve-acre park constructed along an abandoned railroad right-of-way.

Fifteen minutes later, Zahir was walking into their apartment. She bought the duplex penthouse before she and Logan were married, just before their operational trip to Iran. Not long after the successful conclusion of that operation, Logan proposed to her during a Christmas visit to his parents' home in Vermont. Over the last three years, they were in and out of Boston because of Logan's assignment to Hong Kong. She was looking forward to being back in Boston on a full-time basis.

Zahir walked around the apartment, touching a favorite photograph and taking in the panoramic view of the city. She paused in front of a desk with a photo of the two of them at Surin Beach in Phuket, Thailand. They were tanned and laughing at something the photographer was saying.

She wondered where he was now. Looking at the photo, her eyes began to well up, and suddenly she was consumed with an overwhelming urge to have him there, holding her. How could she have asked him to move out? And not even bother to ask where he would go? She resolved then and there to call him. To beg him, if that's what it took, to come home. She dug her cell phone out of her purse and called his number, but it immediately went to voicemail.

"Call me when you get a chance. I'm back in Boston. I need to talk to you." She hung up, wondering what he was up to. She knew he and her brother had been in touch. Maybe Ali knew something.

Later that afternoon, Ali called to say his clients from Rio missed their flight and wouldn't be in until the next day.

He was already in Boston and suggested they get together for dinner.

"Why don't you come over to our place? I can whip up something. It'll be more relaxing than going out."

"All right. What time?"

"How's six-thirty?"

"That works. See you then."

She tried Logan's cell again, but there was no response. "Where are you?" she muttered.

There was some food in the refrigerator, but there were still a few items she needed for dinner. She made a list and then walked to a neighborhood market just two blocks from the apartment.

Ali probably didn't have many opportunities to enjoy a home-cooked meal, she knew. She was planning to make something simple—a rice pilaf and a yogurt-based chicken dish. Shopping and preparing dinner was therapeutic. It took her mind off of her troubles.

Zahir was looking forward to seeing her brother. They were close growing up but had become estranged after he reacted poorly to her pregnancy out of wedlock. There was a gradual rapprochement between them after she and Logan were married, and recently it was almost like old times.

She was proud of Ali's accomplishments, an up-and-coming star in the NBA's New York City corporate head-quarters. She followed his progress, marketing American basketball in South America. There was no doubt about it. He was destined for success.

At six-thirty, the doorbell rang. "Whew. It's hot out there," Ali said. He gave her a hug and handed her a bottle of wine.

"That's a Shiraz. I think you'll like it."

"Let's open it up and find out."

Ali walked over to the large windows looking out over the city as Zahir searched for a corkscrew.

"Where's Cooper?" he asked.

"He's staying with Mom and Dad for another week. I have to fill in for one of the Arabic instructors at BU who's out on extended sick leave."

"Can Mom and Dad handle that? He's a handful, and they're not getting any younger."

"They love it. They missed him when we were in Hong Kong."

"Dad mentioned you and Logan are separated?"

"It's temporary. I need to work through some things. I was blaming Logan for—"

"The miscarriage?" Ali finished the sentence for her.

"Yes. I know it wasn't Logan's fault. I didn't take his feelings into consideration. Did you know Mom miscarried?" Zahir asked. The timer went off signaling the pilaf was done. She got up to check on it.

Ali looked surprised. "No. She never said anything."

"While they were still living in Teheran. Before you were born. It was a boy."

Both were silent for a moment. "Logan tells me you've been meeting some interesting people at your masjid in Tribeca." She scooped the pilaf and chicken onto two plates and set them on the table. "Come on let's eat."

Ali looked surprised as he took a seat at the table. "He did?" He unfolded his napkin and placed it in his lap as he digested her words.

Finally, he spoke. "There's this guy. Akbar. We got into it one day after prayers. I was just fed up with our Imam. He doesn't like to make waves. Sometimes I think he's sold out to the establishment."

"What did Akbar have to say?"

"He steered me to a website. It was this Imam in Kuwait. Al Sadiq. It turns out this guy probably works for ISIS and is out there trying to bring in new blood for them. I went into it thinking I would be interested in what he had to say, but nothing he was preaching has anything to do with the Quran as we know it."

"What do you mean?" She took a bite of the chicken and made a face. She needed to check the date on the yogurt. It didn't taste right.

"It was all twisted," Ali said. "Logan thinks it's a plot to recruit *jihadists* for ISIS. He even got me to introduce him to Akbar."

"What!" She felt an icy shiver run through her body.

"Yeah. Logan came up to New York and went to prayers with me. I introduced him to Akbar in some phony name. He pretended to be interested in Islam."

"Ali, these people are dangerous." She slammed her fork down for emphasis.

"I know." He held up his hands as if to ward off a blow. "Logan told me all about how ISIS uses these Imams to radicalize foreign recruits. I can see how if you weren't very educated and didn't have much going on in your life, it might have some appeal. But I'm not interested in their brand of Islam. They're way out there."

"Did Logan mention why he wanted to meet Akbar?" Zahir asked.

"I think he and his friend from Kuwait want to find out how ISIS is radicalizing all these people. He's hoping to get some leads from Akbar. Find out if they have cells here. I think Logan wants ISIS to try and recruit him."

Zahir put her hand up to her mouth. All she could do was stare at Ali in horror.

Chapter 24

It was a quarter to seven when Logan pulled up to the Octagon House. He went inside and asked the innkeeper for Alice Meens. A few minutes later, she strolled into the lobby. She was wearing a sleeveless mini shift dress with matching sandals and a clutch. *She looks very put together,* he thought.

"Did I keep you waiting?" she asked.

"No. I just got here."

He appraised her as they walked out to the car. She was also carrying a camera bag, which caused him a moment of concern. *Hope all she's packing is camera gear,* he thought. He was on high alert to find out if she was bringing company to their meeting, but so far everything on the street looked quiet. Maybe she was handling this assignment on her own.

"I thought we could take a ride over to Mattapoisett Village," he said. "Not too far from here. There's a great seafood place facing the harbor. We don't have a lot of light left, but you might get some good shots." He nodded towards her camera bag.

"That sounds perfect. I got some terrific pictures of New Bedford yesterday."

Before picking her up, Logan had logged onto the internet to see if he could find any information about her. Other than an obituary dated five years earlier for an Alice Meens, a chemical engineer from the University of Michigan whose entire career was spent perfecting the color orange for a favorite detergent bottle, there were no hits on that name. He found it odd for her to be using a cover legend with a name that didn't hold up under the slightest bit of scrutiny. Pretty sloppy of the Qods Force.

He extended his internet searches to Iranian expat photographers living in Toronto and discovered Alice Shirazi's online portfolio of photographs. There was a picture of the photographer, and not surprisingly it was the woman sitting next to him, Alice Meens AKA Azar Ghabel.

There were photo credits from well-known travel magazines ascribed to her. It looked as though the Qods Force had done a convincing job of backstopping Ghabel before her foreign deployment after all. *But why this extra level of buffering? Was Alice Meens a throwaway alias?* She did have a driver's license and insurance card in that name.

Wasn't she concerned he would find out she was involved in some kind of subterfuge? He was already thinking of the intel report he was going to write focusing on the Qods Force's use of business cover, and the extent to which they were capable of backstopping one of their officers with credible documentation and work portfolios. It would be of interest to the people on the Iran desk and would dispel any notions the Iranians lacked finesse in their conduct of field operations.

The CIA was good, but sometimes it suffered from what he liked to call "institutional arrogance" the assumption that, except for a handful of adversaries like the Russians, the Chinese and the Cubans, the opposing intel services were not quite up to par. Keystone Cops caricatures. But this revelation proved otherwise.

She was quiet as they approached Mattapoisett. "What kind of photography do you do?" he asked.

"Mostly travel. I do freelance, so I have a fair amount of flexibility in the assignments I choose."

"Any magazines I would recognize?"

"*National Geographic, Condé Nast, Travel and Leisure.*" She hesitated for a moment. "I write under my maiden name. Alice Shirazi."

He was taken aback. Why would the Qods Force operative give that up? Maybe she realized with his SEAL and security background, he was likely to check her out.

They were driving past Munro Park in Mattapoisett. He

turned onto Water Street, pulling into a lot next to Ned's Seafood.

"Who's Ned?" she asked.

"An old farmer who used to live in this area. Ned Dexter. See the lighthouse?" He pointed to the white structure at the end of the point. "Ned's Point Lighthouse. Built in the early 1800s. Named after him, too."

Azar shielded her eyes as she looked at the lighthouse in the distance. She got out of the car and took several photos. When she was done, they stood for a few minutes, taking in the tranquil scene of Mattapoisett Harbor, gulls circling overhead, the sound of their persistent cawing buffered by the waves splashing against a rock outcrop. They went into the restaurant and were seated at a table overlooking the water.

"Do you have any dietary restrictions? I mean, you're Muslim, aren't you?"

"Yes, I am. I eat just about everything though. Some people say all seafood is *halal*, (permitted) but there are those who say some kinds of fish are *haram* (not allowed).

"I don't believe the Quran is specific on this point, but some Imams from other sects have different interpretations." She shrugged.

This detour into Islamic dietary requirements offered the perfect opportunity for him to open the door to a discussion on Islam, and his flirtation with Al Sadiq's message. He needed to be cautious though lest she see through his ploy.

"One thing I've never understood is the hostility between Sunnis and Shias," he said. "I mean, I get the whole succession thing, but wouldn't it be better for Muslims, in general, to put it behind them and band together. Iran's mostly Shia, right?"

"Yes. Over ninety percent are Shia. I was raised Shia. Do you know much about Islam?"

Their waiter came up to take their order. The special of the day was swordfish with a choice of sides. Azar ordered the swordfish, and Logan chose a blackened sea bass. Their server collected the menus and left to place their order.

"Not a lot," Logan said. "The navy gave us the essentials in an area familiarization course we took before deploying to Afghanistan. My first introduction to Islam actually was from a high school friend back in Virginia. His family was from Iran, too. They were Shias. His parents were pretty religious. They made him go to special classes on the weekends, so he'd have a solid foundation.

"We used to talk about religion. It was before 9/11, and the hate talk about Muslims."

He and Ali concocted a story about his attending masjid with Ali's family when they were in high school, while they were planning for the meeting with Akbar. Now would be a good time to show Azar his flirtation with Islam had been years in the making.

"I remember once we took turns going to each other's worship services. We found there was something in common between Islam and Catholicism," he said with a straight face.

"What was that?" she asked.

"There's a lot of standing and kneeling between prayers," Logan said.

She shook her head and wagged her finger in mock disapproval, laughing at his lame joke.

"No. Seriously. There were more things in common than I would have believed," he said.

"Like what?" she asked. The waiter brought them two wine glasses and poured their Pinot Grigio.

"Well. Like the fact, both Muslims and Christians trace their beginnings to Abraham. And we both believe there were apostles who spread the word. And the word has been captured as scripture in the Quran and the Bible as the living word of God."

"How about you? Have you ever been to a Christian service?" he asked.

"I can't say I have. My parents were conservative, and so was my husband. Since moving to Toronto, I've been so busy with my photography work my personal life has been neglected." She sighed.

She swirled the wine around in the glass, her tapered fingers lightly tapping the crystal. "Did you stay in touch with your friend?" she asked.

"Who? Ali? We went our separate ways after high school, but I ran into him while I was doing security for a couple of NBA players in Boston. Turns out he ended up working for the NBA in New York. I just saw him last month."

"So many people left Iran after the revolution," she said. My family stayed. My father had a good position as a professor at the university in Shiraz. He tried to be apolitical. He was not pro-monarchist, but he wasn't a big supporter of the Ayatollahs either.

"It seems most Iranian expatriates assimilate in the countries they adopt. But a lot of Muslim refugees from other countries find it hard to settle in. Your friend seems to have done well."

"I think professionally he's on the fast track. But he has a chip on his shoulder. After 9/11 many Muslims in the U.S. felt they were treated differently because of the attacks on the World Trade Center. They felt as though the rest of America blamed them for it." He bent forward and lowered his voice.

"There seems to be less tolerance in American society these days. It's probably an exaggeration to say Muslims are being persecuted, but there is a perception among many of them they are being treated like second-class citizens. Ali keeps talking about wanting to do something."

"Like what? What could he do?" Azar asked.

"I'm not sure. Ali's met some people." Logan wanted to give her the impression he was flirting with the dark forces reaching out to Ali. But at the same time, he tried to come across as discreet, not a "tell-all" type.

"People with a more proactive agenda. People who want to make a difference," he said in a whisper.

"And how about you? How do you feel about these things?" she asked. Her tongue darted out, and she wet her lips.

"I was angry with the government after I was forced out

of the navy. I thought I would have a career as a SEAL, but once I got hurt in Afghanistan, it was all over. They couldn't wait to cut me loose." Despite his feigned anger, Logan's voice shook as those emotional scars were ripped open.

"After I got out, my attitude about these things began to change. I looked at what we were doing in Iraq and Afghanistan, and it didn't make any sense to me. We went into Iraq under false pretenses. Saddam Hussein didn't have weapons of mass destruction. Colin Powell got up in front of the whole world and accused Saddam of having WMDs, and it was a lie. The intelligence didn't support the analysis. And the inspectors never found a thing."

"Didn't the U.S. have a good relationship with Saddam at one time?"

"Back in the sixties, maybe earlier. We were pretty tight with Saddam in the eighties when he was at war with Iran." He couldn't help needling her.

"Maybe that's one of the reasons our government doesn't trust the U.S.," she shot back. "The military help the U.S. provided Saddam ended up killing a lot of Iranians."

"It cuts both ways," Logan said, trying to quiet his anger. "There was that little problem of occupying our embassy and holding our people hostage for over a year." He took a breath. She might be pushing his buttons to see if he'd bite. He couldn't afford to let her get under his skin.

"It's ancient history," he said. "We should've just stayed out of it. Billions of dollars down the tubes. And all for what? I wish—" He stopped.

She was still swirling the wine in her glass. She set it down and leaned forward, searching her quarry's eyes. "You wish what?"

Here we go, he thought. "That I could help make it right. Do something."

"Maybe you can."

"What do you mean?" He set his glass down and leaned back in his seat.

"I have friends. Friends there who are trying to do the right thing."

"Where?"

"In Iraq. Some of them are in Syria, Libya, Afghanistan."

Logan tried to look confused. "But—"

She pushed forward. They're trying to get rid of the dictators. They're fighting *jihad* against the real evil ones. They've even set up their own government."

"You're not talking about ISIS, are you?" Logan asked, straining to keep the incredulity out of his voice.

She nodded. "Yes. I know these people."

He looked uneasily around him and then leaned forward. "Why would they want to talk to me? I'm not even Muslim."

"You have skills they can use. And, you have an open mind. You should think about it. I can put you in touch with the right people."

They were quiet on the drive back to Octagon House. Logan turned off the ignition.

"Call me tomorrow if you want to follow up on what we were talking about," she said.

Without warning, she leaned in and kissed him on the lips. His initial impulse was to pull away, but the taste of her mouth on his excited something in him. The tip of her tongue explored his lips, and they remained locked that way for what seemed like an eternity before she pulled back. She was panting softly. Looking into his eyes for a moment, she seemed about to speak. Instead, she turned, and flung the door open, pausing to look back at him before she sped into the inn.

Chapter 25

Azar left New Bedford for New York the following day. The ride south on I-95 was frustrating, and she was afraid she would miss her afternoon flight to Toronto. Traffic crept along for an hour before she came upon the cause of the congestion. From the looks of it, a northbound tractor-trailer truck crossed the median strip south of Old Lyme and plowed into another semi traveling in the southbound lane. The ensuing inferno blocked traffic for two hours before rescuers were able to extricate the drivers, both of whom were dead, and clear the carnage from the road.

Parts of the highway were so torn up by the impact of the crash, a temporary detour onto U.S. Route 1 was set up while emergency road crews were brought in to repave the surface. Fortunately, she was on the road early enough, and although it was going to be tight because she had to stop in the Bronx to swap out her documents and return the rental car, she was confident there would be enough time.

Azar was mentally going over her encounter with Tim Hudson. As she reviewed their short time together, she felt it had gone well, although she was somewhat chastened and confused by her impulse to kiss the man. There was something about him though. He was handsome, and there was an element of lethality clinging to him like an expensive cologne, which she found attractive. If she had allowed their kiss to linger any longer, she was confident she would have given in entirely to her burning desire.

She thought back to the moment they kissed, the familiar longing rising in her as she tasted his lips. Nouri was her last lover. And their relationship had ended prematurely, given his untimely death. She missed the physical intimacy of their bond. She reflected on how strange it was. In many ways, the nature of her work stripped away her humanity, inuring her to the grotesque duties of the assassin. But she continued to cling to the possibility of intimacy in her life, of a lover's touch caressing her body. She trembled as she turned her thoughts to more pressing matters.

Mentally she began composing a note to Colonel Samadi; he would be very pleased they were about to bring on board a bona fide U.S. Navy SEAL. The propaganda value alone was worth the effort. And she felt confident Tim Hudson was as good as theirs.

There were no certainties in this business though, and plenty of room for second-guessing. From experience, Azar knew many volunteers experience moments of self-doubt or even buyer's remorse after their initial encounter with ISIS. Without being there face-to-face to reinforce the conversation leading to their eager acquiescence, uncertainty began to creep in, and with it, the likelihood they would walk away from what they had so eagerly embraced just hours or days before. The call to action must be decisive.

As much as she wanted to, she wouldn't initiate contact with Hudson, although more than anything, she longed to plumb the depths of his convictions. He would have to reach out to her first, even if it meant letting him go. Azar didn't want him to get the impression she was overly eager. It would be better if he felt he was the driver in the relationship.

As she sat there idly looking out the window at the unending line of stalled traffic, her phone rang. It was Hudson.

"Hello?"

"Alice?"

"Yes. Is this Tim?"

"Yes. How are you?"

"Fine. I'm sitting in traffic on I-95. It's a mess."

"Headed back to Toronto?"

"Yes. I'm flying out of La Guardia. It would've been quicker out of Boston, but I wanted to see New York. I'm starting to regret that decision now."

"You'll be fine. The road crews usually get the highways cleared up pretty fast." He paused for a moment and then continued. "I've been thinking about our talk yesterday."

"Yes?"

"Let's just say, if I were interested—I'm not saying I am but just suppose. What would the next step be?"

"I need to know if you really want to do this, Tim."

"I know. It's just so sudden."

"Do you have a passport?"

"Yes. Why?"

"I think you're the kind of person who would benefit from meeting these people in person. You'd get to see the sort of work they're doing over there. Someone with your skills could make a big difference.

"To meet them directly would mean traveling to Syria or possibly Iraq. There are a couple of routes Americans and Europeans have been using beginning in London. One way is to take a train to Turkey and meet up with a trusted contact to escort you across the border to Syria or Iraq. Another route that seems to be working is through Cypress. You take a ferry to Beirut and then meet someone to help you cross over the border into Syria."

"Let's just suppose I'm interested. How soon could we make this happen?"

She held her breath for a moment. It sounded as though Hudson was ready. She didn't have the benefit of all the background checks she would get under a best-case scenario, but given Samadi's order to fast track Hudson's recruitment, she was prepared to go out on a limb.

"As early as next week. If you can get your travel lined up and let me know whether you're going into Beirut or Istanbul, I can set up a contact who'll guide you to the right people in ISIS."

"Okay. Give me a few days to make some arrangements. How long do you think I should plan on being away?"

"It depends on how much you decide to take on. You could stay in Syria indefinitely, or ISIS may have some ideas for operations you could undertake here in the U.S. The leaders there will have a better idea of where you could be the most effective.

"If you can do it, I would plan for two weeks to a month. Can you take that much time off?"

"I have a pretty flexible work schedule. I have a couple of corporate training events in July, and I can move up a class I have in ten days to early next week. I'll give you a call in a couple of days. Is this a good number to reach you?"

"Yes, it's fine. And Tim…"

"Yes?"

"Nothing. Be careful."

The line went dead. Azar exhaled as she went over the call. Her bosses in Tehran were going to be thrilled with this development. And worst-case scenario, if their background checks dug up anything derogatory on Hudson, she could call off his trip when he rang her for contact instructions. She wouldn't have to tell him anything. Just that ISIS didn't have anyone available to meet him just yet.

She returned to mentally composing her note to Samadi.

"I made direct contact with our target two days ago. Initially, I phoned Hudson to set up a meeting for the following day. I told him I was interested in taking a tactical driving course he offers through his company. Later, he accompanied me to dinner, and I had the opportunity to assess him in a social setting. He followed up with me today. He thinks he could travel as early as next week. He's looking into reservations now, meaning we need to identify someone to escort him to ISIS.

Hudson exudes the image one has of a navy SEAL. He's rugged-looking and muscular in build. Also seems very athletic and capable. My impression is he's dissatisfied with his treatment when he was forced out of the navy. There was an injury during his last deployment to Afghanistan, and the doctors didn't think he would ever be capable of combat operations again. Military life is what he loved. What he trained for. So, I think he resented their letting him go so readily.

He was very professional in the tactical driving course. He's a good teacher. Maybe those are some skills he could put to use with ISIS — weapons training, tactics, bomb making. I did some research on the SEALS, and they are competent in all of these combat areas.

I don't get the impression he's a fanatic or is looking to be a martyr. He has a chip on his shoulder. On the personal side, I was somewhat surprised he's not married. Apparently, he was in a relationship, but it didn't work out. Too many deployments is my guess. All the better for ISIS. No one else competing for his attention.

Please let me know if any other information from your background checks surfaces."

She heard the sound of a truck downshifting and realized the logjam was clear. Traffic was being redirected to an off-ramp and onto U.S. Route 1. Her GPS told her she could get back onto I-95 about 15 miles ahead.

Azar picked up speed and 15 minutes later eased back onto I-95 southbound. It was about two and a half hours to New York City. She stepped on the gas and set the cruise control to 80. There were plenty of cars passing her, so she wasn't too worried about being pulled over, and besides, she had a lot to do before she checked in for her flight.

Chapter 26

Zahir's 10:30 a.m. class was at Boston University's Geddes Center on Commonwealth Avenue. It was only 8:30, but she needed to check in with her department chair and then meet with students from 9:00-10:00. It was just a short drive from her apartment to the Back Bay, where the language school was located. She usually took the summer semester off, and during the school year, taught advanced Arabic, but this was an opportunity to do something different, something to take her mind off of her personal problems.

She would be teaching one elementary modern Arabic class Monday through Thursday from 10:30 a.m. to 1:00 p.m. It was an intensive introduction to the language. With its focus on listening, speaking, reading, and writing skills, the students found it challenging. Walking into the building, she saw a number of them already hard at work in the language lab.

For those who did well in this introductory course, there was a level two class beginning the first week of July. By the time her students completed the two sessions, they would have over a hundred hours of Arabic to their credit. For those deciding to pursue the language as a major or minor during the regular school year, they would have the foundation to study more modern, formal Arabic with its sophisticated sentence structure and advanced vocabulary.

"Zahir!"

Bursting out of a classroom across the hall was Ava MacKenna, the unlikely chair of BU's Arabic department. In her forties, Ava was distinguished by flaming red hair, which cascaded around her freckled face like chokeberry in the fall. Her father had served as an Arabist in the foreign service. He was a career FSO, and she spent her formative years accompanying him on assignments all over the Levant, principally Egypt, Iraq, Syria, Jordan, and Lebanon.

By the time Ava graduated from Georgetown, with a PhD in Arabic language and Islamic Studies at the age of 27, she could pretty much write her own ticket.

"Thanks for stepping up, Zahir. I was desperate for help after Arthur's emergency heart surgery." She gave Zahir a warm hug and then held her at arm's length to study her face.

"How are you holding up?" she asked.

Ava knew about Zahir's miscarriage because they discussed it when she first reached out to see if she was able to fill in for Arthur.

"It hasn't been easy," Zahir replied. I'm looking forward to being back in the classroom. If I keep busy enough, maybe it'll take my mind off everything."

"You'll be fine," Ava said, with greater assurance than Zahir felt. "You're strong. Look how you managed after you got back from Iraq. With Cooper's death and your family turning against you, it was more than most people ever have to deal with."

Zahir sighed. The day she lost Cooper seemed so long ago. What she didn't admit, although it gnawed at her, was her more recent tenuous relationship with Logan and the rest of the Alexander clan following their separation. The Alexanders' love was there to pull her through those desperate weeks and months following Cooper's death. Now, because of her own selfishness, her relationship with all of them was at risk. Ava didn't know about her separation from Logan. Zahir hadn't confided in her because she didn't want to be a burden. There was no reason to weigh her boss down with personal issues.

Ava patted her on the shoulder. "Come to see me when you get a break this afternoon. We can catch up."

"Okay. I'll talk to you later."

During office hours, a number of students dropped in to introduce themselves. They were an eclectic bunch. Some were second-generation immigrants whose parents left the Middle East decades ago. They might speak a smattering of Arabic at home, but for the most part, they were a hundred percent American. Others heard the call when the Department of State declared Arabic a critical language after 9/11 and began offering scholarship money as an enticement to learn the language.

Zahir was initially drawn to teach at BU because they use the communicative method in their foreign language program. The idea is to get students started using the language from day one. For Arabic, teachers were required to use the *Al-Kitaab* textbooks to teach core language skills, but they were also encouraged to introduce cultural materials like newspapers and magazines, and music and movies to liven up their classes, giving the students a better feel for the cultures and daily life of the places where Arabic is spoken.

Zahir enjoyed being back in the classroom. The morning flew by, and before she knew it, it was 1:00.

"Want to grab a sandwich?"

She looked up from her desk. It was Ava.

"Sure. How's the pub sound?"

"You read my mind."

The two colleagues walked over to the BU Pub, a classic Boston alehouse, with an outdoor patio overlooking the Charles River. Located on the lower level of the Castle, a Tudor Revival mansion just a short walk from the Geddes Center, it was the foreign language faculty's favorite lunchtime spot. Last year, the restaurant was named one of the top 33 college sandwich shops in America, best known for its signature sandwiches.

Zahir ordered *The Lawyer*—tomato, fresh mozzarella, spinach, and pesto on a sourdough baguette while Ava opted for *The PhD*—chicken salad, bacon, cucumber, and sprouts garnished with cranberry sauce on whole wheat.

As they ate, they observed a fleet of sailboats from the Boston Sailing Center tacking back and forth across the Charles. "Must be sailing classes," Ava said.

"They are. The center's office is located in that old

riverboat docked at Lewis Wharf. I'm thinking about getting Cooper into a class when he's a little older. We belonged to a yacht club in Hong Kong. There was a sailing school in Repulse Bay at a place called Middle Island, not too far from where we lived."

"Did you sail much?"

"Some. Cooper loved to go out. And Logan has a skipper's rating. You know he was a navy SEAL. The club has dinghies at the Middle Island facility. Cooper was just starting to get the hang of it when we left.

"How about you? Did you do any sailing growing up?" Zahir asked.

"The closest thing to it was when we lived in Egypt. Two or three times a year my father would hire a felucca, one of those traditional wooden sailboats, with a crew and we would sail the Nile. Not great training for racing on the Charles. We didn't really have a chance to develop any boat handling skills. The crew always took care of everything."

The two fell quiet, content to watch the boats on the river below them.

"Zahir?"

She turned to look at Ava.

"Yes?"

"Is everything all right?"

"What do you mean?"

"You seem preoccupied." Ava pursed her lips and covered Zahir's hand with her own. "You know I wouldn't pry, but if there's anything I can do, all you have to do is ask."

Zahir looked back out over the Charles and swallowed hard before answering.

"It's Logan. I asked him to move out last week."

"Oh, Zahir," Ava exclaimed. "What happened?"

"It goes back to losing the baby. When I'm thinking straight, I know it wasn't his fault, but then I get emotional and blame him all over again." Her lips quivered as she continued.

"In my mind, I keep thinking if we were living in Boston instead of Hong Kong this never would have happened."

"Ava's perplexed expression begged for clarification."

"We had an intruder in our apartment one day," Zahir said. "Logan was at work, and I was home early because classes were canceled. He was Chinese. The police were never able to identify him.

"Anyway, he must not have been expecting anyone to be in the apartment at that time of day. When I went inside, I surprised him, and he barreled past me, knocking me down. I landed hard on my stomach. I started bleeding, and it hurt so much I couldn't get up. Fortunately, Logan got home shortly after that and called an ambulance.

"They rushed me into the ER at Adventist Hospital and did an exam, but it wasn't conclusive. I was spotting some, and my cervix was dilating. They also did an ultrasound but didn't hear anything. That just made me more anxious. I stayed in bed for a week or so and then went back to work."

"So, what happened? From what you're saying I thought everything was going to be all right."

"We did, too. Logan's parents came out to visit us in Hong Kong for Christmas, and we all went to Thailand. Phuket." She thought back to that idyllic week, basking in the sun, getting couple's massages on the beach, eating mangos, dragon fruit, and pineapples. It was the last time she remembered feeling happy. The last time she and Logan…

"A few days after we got back from Thailand, I began hemorrhaging. Logan took me to the hospital. The baby was stillborn an hour later." She replayed this scene in her head so often that when telling it she appeared unemotional. Only the quaver of her voice betrayed the depth of her anguish.

"So, what are you going to do?"

"I don't know. My brother was in town the other day on NBA business. Something to do with the Celtics. He saw Logan last week and said he looked fine. I tried reaching out to him yesterday, but he hasn't returned my calls. I think if we could just talk—"

"You'll work this out, Zahir." Ava hesitated as if to consider what she was about to say.

"How would you feel about taking on a new project?

You have the time, and I think this might be right up your alley. It might take your mind off—"

"What is it?" Zahir asked.

"I had a call the other day from the BPD. Their bureau of intelligence and analysis oversees this outfit called the BRIC. They're some kind of fusion center for sharing information between state and federal agencies and the military.

"Anyway, one of the units within the BRIC is responsible for field operations. The BPD wants to run some of their personnel through a survival Arabic course and also sensitize them to some aspects of Muslim culture. The idea is to make them more competent when they're dealing with Muslims in the bay area.

"I thought with your experience working for DoD you might have a feel for what the BRIC needs."

"What's the timeframe?"

"As soon as we can put a proposal together. Apparently, money's not an issue."

"Would we use our own classrooms?"

"They want to start small. Maybe ten students. We can accommodate up to fifteen. Plus, we have the language lab, which would be available to them."

"What about core competencies? What should they be able to do?"

"It's survival Arabic. Basic greetings. Enough to be able to break the ice when they go into the community to interview someone. Listening comprehension is important. Forget about reading and writing."

"I'm intrigued. It sounds like it could be fun."

Ava reached into her pocket and pulled out a name card, which she handed to her. "Why don't you reach out to them and see if they have identified who they want to take the course?"

Zahir glanced down at the card, and her jaw dropped in shock. The name printed in bold letters was none other than BPD officer Peter Breen. She ran her fingers over the letters. When they first met several years ago, it was *Detective* Breen, in charge of Hamid Al Subaie's murder investigation.

But now, according to Ava, he was in charge of the BRIC.

And perhaps even more interesting, he was recently in touch with Logan. Something to do with Nayef Al Subaie's visit to Boston. Money laundering in the mosques in Kuwait. And then she remembered Logan's revelation; her brother might be in touch with a radical Imam in Kuwait. Nayef was concerned ISIS might be attempting to radicalize him. All of this flashed through her brain in an instant.

She looked up. Ava was waiting for her response.

"Yes, of course. I'll reach out to Mr. Breen after lunch. From the sound of it, this shouldn't be too hard to put together. If they're ready to go, we could start as early as next week."

"Good. It's settled. Let me know how your conversation with Breen goes. Tell me what you need to get started, and we'll make this work."

Chapter 27

Logan scanned the room of familiar faces. Peter Breen from the BPD's BRIC, Jason Summers from headquarters, and Norm Stoddard and Bruce Wellington, both recently back from Hong Kong, returned his gaze.

The men were meeting at the Hyatt Regency Boston Harbor in a 14th-floor suite, reserved in Logan's Tim Hudson alias. It was only two days since his encounter with Azar Ghabel in New Bedford. When he recounted the outcome of his meetings with her to Jason the next day, the CTC chief suggested they all get together in Boston to game out how they were going to take the operation to the next level.

Logan was pleasantly surprised when Stoddard and Wellington joined them. From what his secretary, Alicia Gomez, told him, he didn't expect them back in the States until the end of the year. According to Jason, the DDO decided to detail the two to Logan's team for as long as they were needed. Logistically this made a lot more sense than bringing in Delray and Wozolski, his other two SEAL buddies.

Both men seemed eager to help out when Logan raised the issue on Willy Blacklock's boat. Delray was as good as his word, dropping everything to conduct counter-surveillance against Azar when Logan met her in New Bedford. But as a practical matter, both Delray and Wozolski were working full-time jobs and would be hard-pressed to travel on short notice. Besides, Stoddard and Wellington had current top-secret security clearances and were already on CIA's payroll.

Logan began the meeting by recounting his recent contact with Azar. Most of this was for Stoddard and Wellington's benefit.

"The Qods Force has gone to a lot of trouble to set her up in Toronto. She's living there undercover as Alice Shirazi and has established herself as a freelance photographer. She has a pretty impressive portfolio of photography work to back up her story.

"When I first ran into her in New Bedford, I was worried the Qods Force was on to me, but I gave it a low probability given the fact I've been spending a fair amount of time playing Tim Hudson over the last week and have been very careful to separate him from my real identity.

"Also, if the Qods Force somehow managed to link the two names, it would have taken some detective work on their part, given the short time Tim Hudson has been up and running. The more I thought about it, it was apparent to me Azar was somehow working with ISIS because it didn't take any time for her to come looking for me after I dangled myself to Akbar, the ISIS spotter in touch with my brother-in-law in New York.

"The most bizarre encounter was when I spotted her in the same internet café I picked to listen to the ISIS recruitment video. That had to be a coincidence because no one else knew I was going to be in there. The thing about that particular café is it has a lot more privacy than your average Dunkin' Donuts, which is where most of the internet cafés are in New Bedford."

"This is the first indication we've seen of Iran working with ISIS," Jason said. To date, the intelligence has consistently pointed to Iran going all out in support of Assad. They've been sourcing weapons and materiel for him and have ordered Islamic Revolutionary Guards Corps, Qods Force, and intelligence units into battle against ISIS and Syrian opposition forces."

"From what I've seen, it's a crowded playing field over there," Breen said. "I saw a report the other day claiming it's not just the Iranians. There are Lebanese militia and paramilitaries from Iraqi Shia militias joining the fight too."

"Don't you think it's strange for Iran to be in bed with Assad and at the same time be helping ISIS? Think about it.

Even though the Iranians claim not to have any troops on the ground in Syria, over 700 Iranian 'advisors' have been killed in combat operations there to date. It's conceivable ISIS fighters supported by Iran are responsible for some of those Iranian deaths," Logan said.

"Just goes to show you how far Iran is willing to go to play both ends against the middle," Stoddard said.

"I'd like to know if Iran's support for ISIS goes beyond recruitment operations," Jason asked.

"You mean, are they doing training or sending troops over there?" Wellington asked.

"Yeah. We don't have any reliable intel in that area," Jason said. "We'll be breaking new ground if Logan's able to penetrate ISIS," he added.

"Azar's a pretty cool customer," Logan said. "She had a good cover story for contacting me. She claimed she wanted to take the tactical driving course because of some of the high-threat areas she works in.

"We spent a whole day together and not once did she show her hand. Pretty confident. It was only later at dinner when I asked her something about Islam, that she opened up. She let me take the lead as far as asking questions. I was trying to plant a seed, give her the sense I was disaffected and looking for something else. I'm pretty sure she bought into it.

"So, let's talk specifics," Logan said, changing course. "I have a reservation to fly into London next week. From there I plan to take a train to Istanbul and then figure out how to get into Syria. I'm supposed to have a contact in Istanbul who will escort me across the Syrian border and hand me off to ISIS. I won't know who it is until she calls me with the information."

"Seems like a convoluted route," Breen said. "It'll take you five days at best just to get to Istanbul."

"Believe me, I know it," Logan said. "I'm trying to make it look as though I'm covering my tracks. If I just waltz into Syria from Boston, ISIS is going to question why I'm so comfortable flaunting my travel plans. I don't have a good excuse for being in the middle of a war zone, although I suppose I could dummy up a phony contract for some kind of security course," he said.

"What are you actually going to do when you get there?" Breen asked.

"Good question. It really is going to depend on how ISIS decides to handle me. Best-case scenario is they'll put me in touch with their leadership. Maybe we can find out if the rumors about Baghdadi being poisoned are true."

"He doesn't spend much time in the public eye," Jason said. "Remember in 2014, after he declared himself Caliph, there were rumors he was killed in fighting in Iraq? ISIS captured Mosul in June 2014, and there was chaos everywhere. Reports in November said Baghdadi was wounded or dead, but we were never able to confirm them. Same thing in 2015."

"One of the reasons his nom de guerre is *The Ghost*," Logan said.

Breen scratched his chin. "I remember those reports. It was in the fall, September, October timeframe. People were speculating ISIS itself was putting out those stories."

"Baghdadi has to be running scared," Jason said. "He knows the U.S. has set a twenty-five-million-dollar bounty on his head. And not only that, there's been a big push by coalition forces and the Iraqi military to take back Mosul. It started last October and has been going on now for months. We've all heard the rumors Baghdadi really is dead. Killed in one of these coalition attacks. But so far no one has seen the body."

"What are the Iraqis telling us?" Breen asked.

"They're reporting the army has now recaptured most of the territory on the west bank of the Tigris. Everything lost to ISIS in 2014. They figure it'll be easier for Iraqi reinforcements to consolidate their position as they plan their attack on the last stronghold ISIS controls in Mosul, the old city center. It's just a matter of time."

Jason shifted his attention back to Logan. "If ISIS does decide to put you into contact with Baghdadi, or whoever's running operations on the ground, you'll be in the thick of it."

"That's right, Logan," Stoddard said. "You could come under fire from the very same Iraqi troops our guys are advising."

"I don't see any other way around it," Logan said. "If the goal is to get close to Baghdadi, and he's at the front, that's where I need to be."

"One of the things we're doing to support Logan is to embed Bruce and Norm as advisors with a special forces unit. They'll be working out of Q-West in Mosul," Jason said.

"The old Saddam Airbase?" Logan asked.

"Yeah. Qayyarah West."

"What's their mission?" Logan asked.

"They're calling it Task Force Zeus. There are two platoons attached to the airbase. It's serving partially as a logistics hub, but also as a mobile rocket platform."

"HIMARS?" Wellington asked.

"Yep."

"What are HIMARS?" Breen asked.

"High mobility artillery rocket systems," Logan said.

"It's basically a multiple rocket system that fits onto the bed of a medium-sized tactical vehicle. I'll bet it's the 18th Field Artillery Brigade."

"Third Battalion," Norm said. "They switched from howitzers to HIMARS in 2014. It's a good choice for fluid situations like they're experiencing. HIMARS carries a six-pack of MLRS rockets, and they're very mobile, meaning you can get out of Dodge fast if things get too hot. They're also easier to transport than some of the bigger artillery. HIMARS fit into a C-130. Lets you deliver it to places where the big transports can't land."

"How soon will you be in place?" Logan asked Norm.

"Office of Military Affairs is cutting our orders even as we speak," Bruce said. We'll be in country before you get there. It's not like we'll be right next door though. Mosul's probably two hundred, two hundred-fifty miles from where you're likely to end up."

"What are we doing for commo?" Bruce asked.

"We're still working on it. We've had some compromises," Jason said.

"WikiLeaks just did a massive document dump on CIA's cyber program."

"Vault Seven?" Norm asked.

"Yeah. Headquarters hasn't commented, but if *The Times* story is true, this ranks right up there with the Chelsea Manning and Edward Snowden leaks. It's possible some of our covert communications systems have been compromised, although from what I've seen so far, it looks as though Vault Seven is mostly a catalog of tools and techniques we use for our tailored access programs."

"Tailored access?" Breen asked.

"Typically, it's been a function of NSA," Jason said. "But with the focus on cybersecurity, everyone has beefed up their cyberwarfare capabilities in the last few years. Tailored access was traditionally the tools and techniques used to monitor and collect intelligence from our targets' computer systems. Nowadays it could be any smart device connecting to the internet—smartphones, laptops, tablets, smart TVs, whatever.

"If any clandestine communications systems were compromised as a result of the Vault Seven release, we could assume our enemies, and that includes ISIS, will be able to figure it out. It could pose a major counterintelligence threat to our assets and officers working undercover."

"We're already starting to see ransomware attacks by cybercriminals using some of those tools," Breen said. "The *Wanna Cry* attack is an example of what happens when these capabilities fall into the wrong hands."

"We might just have to go with cell phones and open verbal paroles," Logan said.

"The Onion Browser (TOR) just came out with a new browser for IOS," Jason said.

"I was reading a tech journal about this software developer who came up with TOR for IOS in 2012. His goal was to make it available to people who needed anonymity in their communications, you know, dissidents or whistleblowers. So, he put it up on the Apple app store for $0.99, but he still felt it might be more than some people could afford. Now he's basically giving it away for free."

"Why don't we try it out before we all head out?" Logan asked. Let's download the software and try sending some messages."

"It may have limitations," Jason said. "I don't think there's voice privacy encryption at this point, although there has been some talk TOR will have a voice encryption capability early next year."

"Have you guys heard of Silent Phone?" Breen asked. "Some of my undercover operatives are using it. A company called Silent Circle puts it out."

"What is it?" Logan asked.

"It's an app. Gives you encrypted voice, data, and video on your mobile device. It doesn't matter if you're using IOS, Android, or Silent Circle's Blackphone. It's encrypted end-to-end as long as both people are using the Silent Phone application."

"Sounds perfect," Logan said. "What do you think?" He looked around the room.

"Let me run it by our tech people when I get back to headquarters," Jason said. "That is, assuming I can find someone not up to their eyeballs in this WikiLeaks disaster."

"I hope somebody strings Assange up by the balls," Norm said through clenched teeth. "Not to mention Snowden."

"You can say that again," Logan said.

He thought back to what little he knew about the notorious recluse. Julian Assange co-founded WikiLeaks in 2006. The internet publication established its reputation for publishing secret information, sensitive documents, and other forms of classified media from anonymous sources. Assange initially served as the organization's editor-in-chief but was forced to seek refuge in the Embassy of Ecuador in the U.K., out of concern he would be extradited to the U.S.

to face espionage charges following the group's publication of highly classified materials. He'd been holed up there for five years and counting, pending resolution of the case.

"Are we done?" Logan asked, looking around the room.

"That's all I had," Jason said.

"All right." Logan stood up. "Let me know what you find out about Silent Phone. I'm going to download the app and play with it. Maybe read some reviews."

Jason needed to catch a shuttle back to D.C., and Peter was hosting an interagency meeting at the BRIC at 2:00 p.m. After they said their goodbyes, Logan, Norm, and Bruce decided to call it a day.

"Let's get a brew," Logan said. "It may be the last one we have together for a long time."

Chapter 28

"Mommy, I want to talk to Daddy." The plaintive note in Cooper Alexander's voice clutched at Zahir's heartstrings. It was only a few days since she left him in the care of her parents. She made a point of talking to him every morning before she went to class, and every morning he asked for the same thing—to speak with his father.

"He's not here right now, sweetie," she said.

"But why?" he asked. "Where did he go?"

"He left early for work." Her voice quavered. Her stomach churned as the falsehood spilled out. Guilt washed over her like a rogue wave, nauseating and drowning all other senses.

She said goodbye. Sitting there gripping the phone in one hand, she massaged her brow with the other. Had it come to this? She was deliberately lying to her five-year-old. Not that he was capable of understanding her inner turmoil. But he deserved better. She was putting herself first to erase the pain caused by her miscarriage, and as a result, she was inflicting pain on others, those she loved the most.

Some mom you are. She sighed as she returned the phone to its cradle. There was no one else to blame but herself. In a few days, Cooper would be back in Boston, and it would be obvious his Daddy wasn't here. What could she tell him? How could she make him understand why he was gone?

As she dwelled on her self-imposed predicament, she remembered she was scheduled to meet with Peter Breen at his office at 1:30. She was going to go over her proposal for BPD's survival Arabic course, and just needed his formal concurrence to move forward.

There was a second, hidden agenda for her conference

with Peter. Logan met with him over a week ago, when he shared the concerns raised by Nayef regarding ISIS recruiting in the U.S. After the meeting, Logan, promised her he would not reveal Ali's flirtation with extremist websites to Peter or anyone else. Knowing Logan though, he wasn't one to just sit on information if he felt he could use it to get to the bottom of a potential threat.

"Oh, Logan!" She suddenly began to cry. Deep sobs wracked her body as she gave way to her inner turmoil. She collapsed in a heap and, unlike the other times she felt consumed with grief, she didn't resist the pull of her emotions. She gave in to them, welcomed the cathartic release, and allowed it to wash over her.

She lay there for several minutes until the sobs subsided. She was spent, but at the same time, felt a certain lightness, as though a heavy burden was lifted from her shoulders. She understood there was no textbook solution for dealing with grief, and based upon her mother's shared experience, knew this would be something she might have to live with for the rest of her life.

But how she chose to live the rest of her life was something she could control. Shaking off her torpor with newfound resolve, Zahir rose from the floor and went into the bathroom. Looking in the mirror, she barely recognized the stricken figure gawking back at her. Deep hollows framed her eyes, and pallid features elicited a sharp breath. She turned on the cold water and splashed it across her face, sending shivers down her spine. Drying off, she detected a faint hint of color returning to her otherwise weary features. Although she seldom used makeup, she pulled a tube of liquid blush from her makeup drawer and with two deft sweeps across her cheekbones transformed her appearance from despondent to sanguine. She daubed some lipstick on her lips. *There,* she thought, satisfied with the transformation. She dressed and left for BU.

At 1:30, after her classes were over, she drove to the BPD. Peter was in the lobby to greet her. As he escorted her to the BRIC's workspaces, he gave her an appreciative smile.

"It's been what? Five years since we first met?"

She thought back to the tumultuous events leading up to that fateful day. She and Logan were living in Boston a year after the operation in Iran. He was just getting set up in his maritime consulting business, and she was working on her PhD in Arabic at BU.

He came home from work one afternoon, drenched in blood, to tell her their friend, Hamid Al Subaie was murdered on the steps of a Boston eatery, moments before Logan was to meet him for lunch. She and Logan got to know Peter during the ensuing murder investigation.

"It seems so long ago," she said.

"Let me give you a quick tour," he said.

"We were set up in 2005 as an urban fusion center under the direction of the BPD's bureau of intelligence and analysis. Since then, we've become nationally recognized as a model liaison-driven fusion center.

"You did some liaison work with the military, didn't you?" he asked, as they stepped into a room humming with activity.

"I was a civilian translator for DoD and the multinational forces in Iraq. I would go out on patrol with different units and help them deal with civilians and local police. It was grassroots community liaison for the most part."

He led her deeper into a large bullpen with a couple dozen workstations.

"I think I'm most proud of what we've accomplished here," he said, as they entered the nerve center of the BRIC. "Early on we decided to co-locate our analysts with our investigators, so when they're out on the street, they have the best information available to do their jobs."

"What's your main focus?" she asked.

"Basically, our mission is to reduce criminal activity and get a handle on terrorism threats. DHS funds these fusion centers all across the country. Boston's a little different than most of them. We're considered a major urban area fusion center. If it helps, visualize us as a hub, with nine other communities in the Metropolitan Boston homeland security region attached like spokes.

"We're able to leverage our partnerships with local law enforcement, federal agencies, and the private sector so we can better manage the threat environment."

He steered her through the bullpen and into his office. Do you want some coffee or tea?" he asked.

"Tea would be nice," she said. "Did you get a chance to look at the proposal we sent over?" she asked as he rummaged around for cups and a tea bag.

"Yes, thanks. I think you have a good understanding of what we're trying to accomplish. We're not looking to create the next generation of classical Arabists at the BPD, but rather to give our investigators on the street some basic Arabic language so when they do interact with the non-English-speaking Muslim community, there's better communication."

"We can do that with two weeks of intensive instruction. We also have self-study materials, including a whole series of listening comprehension exercises the students can access through BU's foreign language portal.

"I'd also like to work up some special vocabulary lists based on the kinds of interactions you anticipate your investigators will be having," she added. "If you could get those to me this week, I'd be able to do the translations and then work them into the materials we'll be using in class."

"Great minds..." he said, as he handed her two pages of typed vocabulary words. "I asked the guys for their input last week, and this is what they came up with."

"Excellent." Zahir glanced at the sheet.

"Camel jockey?" She fought to soften her tone, but she could feel her face flushing in indignation.

"What?" he asked, with a confused look.

"That's what it says. Camel jockey," she shot back stony-faced.

"Let me see that."

Zahir handed him the pages and sat back in her seat, fuming.

As he looked down the list, she could sense the anger

rising up in him. "I have to admit I only glanced at this just before I gave it to you. I think I know the culprit," he said with a scowl on his face.

"Would you like me to include a module on cultural sensitivity training?" she asked, as calmly as she could.

"We actually do our own in-house sensitivity training, although you wouldn't know it from this." He creased the offending list in his hands. "Twice a year we bring in an Imam and some local Arab business owners to talk to the group about Islam and life in the Middle East. There's always some lug head who thinks *True Lives* is an accurate portrayal of Arab culture."

"Funny you should mention that film. A couple of years ago we hosted a guest lecturer at BU who wrote a book entitled *The TV Arab*. In it he cited a report, *100 Years of Anti-Arab and Anti-Muslim Stereotyping* that argued the way Arabs are portrayed in popular culture can be summed up as 'the three B's'—bombers, belly dancers, and billionaires.

"If anything, post 9/11 anti-Arab sentiment and today's toxic political environment have only made things worse."

"How do you conduct your sensitivity training?" he asked.

"Typically, we'll ask the students to participate in some situational role-playing. We'll give them a scenario and have them act it out. It's designed to bring out those stereotypes. And then we talk about why we hold our particular views and how negative stereotypes are perpetuated in popular culture to the point we accept them as the norm."

"Why not? It can't hurt my people to get some additional exposure."

"All right, consider it done. Will you be ready to start next week?"

"Yes. We've identified fifteen investigators we want to run through this training. If it goes well, I can see us doing one or two of these a year."

"Okay. If you could get a complete roster to me by the end of the week, that would be great. Ava talked to you about location, right?"

"Yes. The Geddes Center."

She nodded. "One last thing. This is personal." As she was about to speak her mind, the expression on Peter's face turned from welcoming to wary.

"It has to do with Logan. He told me he stopped by to see you a week or so ago. Something to do with Nayef Al Subaie and a radical Imam in Kuwait."

Breen's face remained impassive, but she sensed he was calculating how to respond to her. Eventually, he spoke.

"Uh huh. Logan came by about ten days ago. Mr. Al Subaie was in Boston to see your sister-in-law, Millie, on some business matter and then got together with Logan to see what he knew about ISIS recruiting in the U.S. It seems there was an ISIS-provoked attack on a mosque in Kuwait City, and a radical Imam there is stirring up trouble by proselytizing for ISIS.

"Was there a U.S. angle with the Imam?"

Peter squirmed, just perceptibly.

She could read body language as well as the best of them. Much of her work in Iraq involved translating for Iraqi civilians the U.S. military detained under suspicions they were aiding and abetting the enemy. This part of her work was so time-consuming, the army put her through a special seminar on non-verbal communications as a means of identifying deceptive physical behaviors suspects might exhibit while being interrogated. Later, when she applied these observations, she and the interrogator would double down on a person displaying deceitful body language and more often than not elicit a confession from the suspect. Often, they turned out to be in touch with or working for, Al Qaeda. Meanwhile, what was Peter up to? He started speaking again, although more guardedly.

"Mr. Al Subaie told Logan an Imam by the name of Hassan Al Sadiq is trying to recruit in the U.S. It turns out we didn't have any dirt on him, and the fact ISIS was trying to recruit in the U.S. wasn't actually news to us. We've seen evidence ISIS has inspired some of the attacks here over the last few years. Hell, right now the bureau has over a thousand active cases against people living in this country who support ISIS in one form or another."

"But nothing specific?"

Peter hesitated. "I can't—"

"Come on, Peter. I know Logan told you about Ali."

This was a shot in the dark because she didn't know for sure if Logan talked about her brother's flirtation with the very same radical Imam Peter was talking about. If not, she had just exposed Ali to possible scrutiny by the BPD and most likely, the NYPD. Maybe even the bureau.

Peter snorted, massaging both temples with his fingers. He was avoiding eye contact with her. At last, he looked up and spoke.

"Logan told me about Ali, but not right after he spoke with your Kuwaiti friend. It was later."

She shook her head, looking perplexed.

"We got to talking about his relationship with Al Subaie, and he let me in on your little operation in Iran. He told me the Kuwaitis have your family information in a security database because of some alias documents they provided you."

"Yes, I remember filling out some forms for them."

"Well they archived it, and it's supposed to be purged from their system after five years, but for some reason never was. When they ran name traces on this Al Sadiq fellow, your brother's name came up."

Her expression was determined. "I need to talk to Logan," she said.

"I'm afraid that won't be possible," Peter replied.

"What do you mean?" she asked.

"He's on his way to Syria, even as we speak."

Chapter 29

The flight into Heathrow was bumpy from clear air turbulence slamming into the Boeing 787 aircraft 30,000 feet over the Atlantic. The pilot began to climb above the subtropical jet stream after a strong downdraft left the passengers feeling queasy, as though the bottom was being jerked out from under them. The turbofan Dreamliner pitched and shuddered from the buffeting winds, and Logan wondered briefly if the aircraft was going to come apart.

They hit another stretch of turbulent air and passengers around him were wide-eyed as they maintained white-knuckled death grips on their armrests. The effect was not unlike the rollicking, swaying movement common to some amusement park rides. But nothing was amusing about this.

"Ladies and gentlemen, we'll be climbing to 40,000 feet to get above this weather. Please remain in your seats and check to make sure that your seat belts are fastened. We'll see if we can get around this bumpy patch for a smooth ride into Heathrow." The captain's voice was reassuring but failed to have a calming effect on those passengers seated in the main cabin.

Thirty minutes later, they were lining up for the final approach into London. Logan silently went over his Tim Hudson cover story—he was exploring opportunities to expand his security consulting business with American firms having offices and personnel in England. The only thing that had him mildly concerned was whether or not the U.K.'s use of biometrics at security checkpoints would trip him up as he transited passport control.

The last time he transited London was five years ago when he stopped over on his way to Kuwait, where he and his special operations team rehearsed their ops plan just before going into Iran to annihilate a terrorist training camp. That time he flew in from Boston using a valid passport and then switched to an alias Canadian passport in the name of Logan Campbell, which he then used for the remainder of his travels.

He wasn't as concerned the Brits would connect the dots between Tim Hudson and Logan Campbell, the name on his Canadian documentation. That passport was slipped to him in a document exchange with a member of the Kuwaiti intelligence service, after clearing border control in his real name. If anything, the authorities might be able to connect Hudson with Alexander. The only saving grace was his Tim Hudson papers were legitimate and should not elicit a second look from the border force officer.

There were two queues at Heathrow. One was for EU, European Economic Area, British and Swiss nationals, and the other was for everyone else. He got into the non-EU line, idly wondering how the EU residents would feel when Brexit (the British exit from the European Union) finally took full effect.

The U.K.'s decision to abandon the EU took the world by surprise, and some Brits. The move appeared to enjoy broad support among British nationalists, although pundits speculated racial intolerance and xenophobia borne out of years of African and Middle Eastern immigration were the real drivers behind the move to reclaim their sovereignty.

As he approached the head of the line, he was mindful of the border force officer, a Sikh gentleman, in his mid-forties. He wore a black turban and a neatly trimmed full beard. Logan recalled seeing a story a few years back about a Sikh member of the Scots guardsmen, those soldiers charged with guarding the Queen at Buckingham Palace, who made history by wearing a turban instead of the traditional bearskin cover while on duty at the royal residence. *These days that would hardly raise any eyebrows,* he thought.

As it turned out, his concern about entering the U.K. in alias proved unfounded. The border force officer gave his passport a cursory look and waved him through. Although Logan was prepared to say he would be in the U.K. for several days, staying with a friend in an apartment off of Kings Road in Chelsea, he actually planned to leave immediately for Paris.

He would be following the route of the old Orient Express—Paris to Istanbul. Along the way, he would transit Munich, Budapest, and Bucharest. When planning his trip, Logan discovered the original service, established in 1883, during the heyday of luxury passenger train travel in Europe, no longer appeared on regular European rail schedules. Nowadays there was a privately run company, using the Orient Express name and restored carriages from the 1920s and 30s, catering to the luxury travel market. But he wouldn't be using their service.

After clearing customs, he took the Piccadilly Line on London's famed "tube" from Heathrow to Kings Cross/St. Pancras. An hour later, he was at the Eurostar Station, where he purchased a one-way ticket to Paris Gare du Nord. Trains were scheduled to make the 300-mile trip every hour. His was scheduled to depart at 10:25 a.m. so he had about an hour and a half to kill. Looking around, he was perplexed by the heavy security presence in the station. Putting aside his concerns, he decided to check out Albertini Restaurant, just down the street from the train station, for some breakfast.

He found seating outside and ordered. It was only 9:00 a.m., late for the breakfast crowd, but there were several tables with people lingering over their coffee. While he was waiting for his meal, he checked the headlines on his cell phone's *New York Times* app. An article describing a terrorist incident in London the day before leaped out at him. *Must have happened while I was in the air.* He clicked on a video and watched with mounting concern.

"We are reporting from just outside MI 6 headquarters, where we have new details about yesterday's attack. The person who plunged into a crowd of pedestrians near the secret intelligence service headquarters, injuring scores and killing three, has been identified.

"Witnesses report after crossing Vauxhall Bridge, the assailant turned onto Albert Embankment and crashed his car into employees on their way to work. After exiting the vehicle, the attacker stabbed one guard several times before being shot dead."

The camera then panned the scene from the day before, showing chaos in the area near the headquarters building, where victims lay on the ground as emergency personnel and bystanders rushed to their aid. A bright red air ambulance hovered near Vauxhall Pleasure Gardens, looking for a place to set down close to several of the injured.

Logan was stunned, as he stared at the grisly images. While it was too early to know for sure, there was a good chance this was an ISIS-inspired or ISIS-directed assault. This type of terrorist attack was becoming the new normal, as ISIS was determined to extend its reach beyond the modest territory in the Middle East to which it laid claim. London's last terrorist incident was a little over a year ago when a knife-wielding man slashed passengers at Leytonstone tube station in an ill-conceived act of reprisal for victims of the fighting in Syria.

When will it ever stop? he wondered. He ascribed to the view that cutting the head off the snake, in this case, self-proclaimed Caliph, Abu Bakr Al Baghdadi, was the best way to sow disruption and chaos among the rank and file of ISIS. It was an immutable truth, like the nine-headed Hydra of Greek mythology, the terrorist group continued to demonstrate remarkable perseverance. This, even as its leadership was dispatched on the battlefields of Syria, Iraq, and Afghanistan. Omar the Chechen, Abu Sayyaf, Hajji Imam, and many more—a veritable roll call of sadistic zealots who got what was coming to them, mostly in drone strikes in recent months.

He was in a somber mood as he paid his bill and left the restaurant for the Eurostar Station. Now he understood why there were so many security personnel in Kings Cross. Armed Metropolitan Police officers, army personnel, and special counterterrorism forces from Scotland Yard were patrolling the entrances and exits to the station as well as the platforms.

Logan nonchalantly checked out their hardware. Most were equipped with SIG 516 semi-automatic rifles and Glock 9mm pistols. He could tell by the way they carried themselves, they were on high alert. Passengers, for the most part, seemed to be going about their business, although there was palpable tension in the air. A dozen people were clustered around a TV monitor in the departure lounge watching the BBC, where the British prime minister was responding to the bloodbath, assuring the world that Britain would not be cowed by this senseless act of terror.

Just before 10:00, his train began to board. He scanned his ticket at the gate and walked out onto the platform to his car. A marine architect by training, he had an intense appreciation for structures of every stripe, even those on land. St. Pancras Station was a marvel, with its Gothic facade joined seamlessly to a sprawling glass and steel train barn arching 100 feet above the platform. Contoured rail cars, capable of speeds of up to 180 miles per hour, idled in their bays.

The sleek Eurostar Express departed at precisely 10:25 a.m., cruising through London, and then accelerating past rural Kent's picturesque villages with names like Ashford, Broadstairs, and Canterbury, before plummeting 250 feet into the Channel Tunnel at Dover. The high-speed train emerged 20 minutes later at the French border town of Calais. Logan dozed briefly, waking as the train turned south and raced by Lille, the central city in France's Nord-Pas-de-Calais region. As the town came into view, Logan could see what appeared to be large manmade hills off in the distance.

"Do you know what those are?" he asked his seatmate.

"Slag heaps," the man replied. "Actually, a UNESCO World Heritage site. Some of them are over three hundred feet high. It's from all the coal mined here for centuries."

"Amazing."

"There are over a hundred of them just in this area alone."

"Do you live near here?" Logan asked.

"No, but I have a sister who does. There's maybe three thousand or so Brits living just this side of the channel. If you have the time, it's worth visiting."

"I'm on my way to Paris. Maybe on the way back. What's there to see?"

"The Palais des Beaux-Arts museum is second only to the Louvre. The old city is colorful, with picturesque squares and pedestrian walking streets. You must go to the Wazemmes Market in the old town. They have anything you could possibly want there."

"Sounds nice." Logan turned back to the window, musing how ordinary everything seemed. It caused him to think back to the scene near MI 6 headquarters from the day before. It was an average day, too, but in a flash, civilized society plunged into chaos when a cold-blooded sociopath unexpectedly struck down innocent passersby.

And yet, as has been the case in other terrorist events, the citizenry remains resilient. Initially registering shock, most people experience a range of emotions, which quickly morphs into fear with the adrenaline rush typical of such occasions. At the end of the day, the majority resolve not to be victims. No, they choose to be survivors.

Arrival at Paris Gare du Nord station was at 1:30 p.m. Logan was not planning to tarry here. His mind wandered back to the day he and Zahir transited Paris on their return from Iran. It seemed so long ago, and in some ways, was a much less complicated time.

They had laid over in Kuwait to take inventory of their spoils before heading back to the U.S. via Europe. It was an emotional period in their relationship, especially after Zahir discovered a video of the attack on Cooper's unit by one of the Qods Force-trained IED teams. It was hard for both of them to watch, especially for her since she was actually there, with Cooper's unit, when the attack took place.

As he was consoling her, they found comfort in each other's arms. Restrained emotions, percolating beneath the surface over the several weeks spent together were ignited.

Paris, the city of love, would have been a fit place to explore their new-found passion. But, there were pressing matters to attend to, and they transited separately from Paris to London where they conducted reverse document exchanges, allowing them to slip back into the U.S. unchallenged. Paris wasn't in the cards for them then, and, as matters now stood, was unlikely to be anytime soon.

Logan consulted a local map in the station. His seatmate suggested he walk to Gare de l'Est to catch the train to Munich, rather than take the metro one stop.

"If you go by Rue d'Alsace you'll be there in ten minutes," he said.

It felt good to stretch his legs after sitting for three hours. As he approached Gare de l'Est, he was struck by its grand forecourt and facade. Inside he found the main concourse and located a TV screen with arrival and departure information. The next train to Munich was at 3:55, putting him into the Bavarian capital at 9:30 p.m.

He picked up his pace. There was a little over two hours to kill before his train was scheduled to depart. Enough time to grab a bite and pick up a few personal items for the journey. For the first time all day he felt a sense of anticipation. Each leg of the journey was taking him closer to his objective—ISIS.

Chapter 30

"When's Cooper getting in?" Ali asked.

He was in Boston for meetings with the Celtics front office. He had the commissioner's blessing to pitch a proposition to dispatch several marquee NBA players to Brazil during the off-season to participate in exhibition games and serve as goodwill ambassadors for the NBA. This was a key component of Ali's marketing strategy to cement the lash-up between the NBA and Brazil's Liga Nacional de Basquete. He was finished with his meetings by 3:30, so he and Zahir were enjoying an early dinner at her place.

"Dad's bringing him up tomorrow," she replied.

"They flying or driving?"

"Eight hours in the car is too stressful for Cooper. He gets restless after just an hour or two. No, they're flying in. I considered getting him an unaccompanied minor ticket, but I keep hearing horror stories about airlines dropping kids off at the wrong airport, or strangers molesting them in the air. So, Dad offered to accompany him."

"Is Dad staying over?"

"Just for the day. They get in early afternoon tomorrow, and he has a Sunday afternoon flight back to D.C."

"Maybe I can change my flight and spend the weekend here. I haven't seen Cooper since you guys got back from Hong Kong."

He winced inwardly at his indirect inference to Logan. He hadn't spoken with her about their situation recently and wasn't sure he should bring it up if she didn't. The thought evoked memories of their days together in high school. Growing up in Arlington, they were close. After he left for college, they saw each other less often, although when he moved back to D.C. following graduation, they picked up like it was only yesterday.

In retrospect, things began to change when he started spending time with a conservative group from the masjid. Also, it didn't help their relationship after she left for Iraq and got pregnant, that he reacted so poorly. There was something in him still not entirely accepting of her situation, but six years was a long time to hold a grudge. She was the person he was closest to in his family, and he knew that she was in pain.

"That would be fun," she said. She got up to refill Ali's glass. "Maybe we can go to brunch Sunday. There's a popular little kid-friendly place on Hanover Street not too far from here."

"I didn't bring a change of clothes," he said. "I was just planning to be here for the day."

"No problem. You can wash your stuff here. And there's plenty of room if you want to stay with us."

While she cleared the table, Ali called Delta to see about changing his flight. With his platinum rewards account, the airline treated him well. They tended to waive change fees because of the amount of business travel he did.

"No problem," he said, getting off the line. "Sunday must be a light travel day." He and Zahir moved into the living room.

"Do you want to watch a movie?" he asked.

"No. Actually, I want to talk to you about something," Zahir replied.

She began slowly, chronicling her bout with depression and how it, in turn, led to her separation from Logan. "I understand now that I was laying all of this blame on him, but that's not fair. I'm sure he was just as hurt by the miscarriage as I was, and for me to accuse him of being responsible, just because we were in Hong Kong for his job, was wrong."

"I don't get it. Why would you accuse Logan in the first place?"

"Did you hear what happened to me?"

"Something about getting mugged? I mean, I heard you

were just back from vacation in Thailand with Logan's parents and had to go into the ER."

"It started earlier. I wasn't just mugged. Worse. We had an intruder in our apartment during my first trimester. I surprised him by coming home from work earlier than usual. I was by myself. We don't know to this day what he was looking for. He didn't steal anything. But when he heard me come in, he ran out, knocking me down.

"I guess my thinking was, we live in a nice area in Boston. Nothing like that has ever happened to us here."

"That's not true. Remember the crazy Iranian guy who killed your friend, Hamid? What was his name? Khorasani? He went to Logan's office and tried to kill him."

"Good point," she said. "I guess at the time we tried to downplay it. It did make the front page of *The Globe*, especially after Khorasani ended up diving out of a window on the 16th floor."

"It sounds like what happened in Hong Kong was a random event. It could have happened anywhere."

Zahir wanted to make the point it wasn't random. They were targeted, precisely because the Chinese suspected Logan was working for the CIA. But she couldn't go there. Although Logan was no longer with the Agency, Zahir wasn't at liberty to discuss his work, especially if Norm and Bruce were still in Hong Kong managing Alexander Maritime. If the Chinese learned of Logan's relationship with the CIA, it could expose the others and their entire clandestine operation.

"I guess so," she sighed. They remained silent for a moment, lost in their own thoughts.

"Ali?"

"Yes?"

"Have you had any more contact with the Imam from Kuwait?"

"Al Sadiq? No! I told you last time we talked I didn't want anything to do with him or ISIS. They've hijacked Islam for their own perverted agenda."

"Do you remember telling me Logan met the guy from

your masjid in Tribeca? Akbar?"

"Yeah, I introduced them a couple of weeks ago."

"Just like that? I'm surprised he would meet these people and put our family at risk."

"No, it's not like that. We didn't tell Akbar we were related. And he gave Akbar a phony name. He was adamant he didn't want Akbar to know anything about our family."

"What name?"

Ali squirmed. "Tim. Tim Hudson."

"How were you supposed to know him?"

"He cooked up this fake story about us being in high school together in Arlington, and after graduation, going our separate ways. We reconnected a few years later after he started this private security consulting company and did some VIP protection for a couple of NBA players in Boston."

Zahir jumped out of her chair and went in search of her laptop. She found it in the study. She returned to her seat and began typing.

"What's up?" Ali asked with a quizzical look.

"Just a second."

She hit the enter key. There it was. Hudson Security Consulting. It was a professional-looking website listing a range of services and training. The address was listed as Dartmouth Street in New Bedford. She didn't recognize any of the phone numbers. The photo of Logan showed him behind the wheel of a sedan, conducting a tactical driving class. A ball cap and sunglasses changed his appearance perceptibly. The casual observer would not immediately link the photo she was scrutinizing to Logan Alexander.

The site didn't offer any customer testimonials. There was some stock language: *Due to customer privacy, references are only available upon request.*

Dunn and Bradstreet listed the firm's year of incorporation as 2010. This has all the earmarks of a CIA operation, she fumed. There's no way Logan could have put this together without their help, particularly with the official backdating of the company. Or, had Logan set this up in 2010 and just not mentioned it to her?

"Did you know Logan's on his way to Syria?" she asked her brother.

"What! The last time I talked to Logan was when I introduced him to Akbar. We talked, and they exchanged contact information. Logan came up with this story saying he wasn't happy about the way the navy cut him loose after he was injured in Afghanistan. I think Akbar bought it and told him how he could reach out to Al Sadiq."

Ali paused for a moment before continuing. "You know, Logan told me sometimes ISIS puts people into these internet cafés to monitor their targets' reactions to the broadcasts. They might even have guys outside the café to follow the person and see what they can find out about them."

"You mean like detectives?"

"Yeah. Private investigators. They want to see if the person contacts the FBI, or local police after they've seen the webcast. Find out if they're truthful about where they live and work. Logan said ISIS has been burned by police informants who put themselves out there as recruitment targets so they can find out how these guys are operating in the U.S.

"I got the impression Logan's trying to do something along those lines. Figure out if ISIS has any organized cells here in the U.S. I never thought he would try to go to Syria."

"All in, all the time," she said.

"What?"

"It's something he and his SEAL buddies used to say. An attitude they have about the mission. Nothing halfhearted. And I didn't even know him when he was in the SEALS.

"Did Logan ever mention a Detective Breen here in Boston?"

"He's with the BPD?" Ali asked.

"Yeah. He heads up a fusion center for them. Called the BRIC. They have investigators and analysts working on terrorism issues.

"I don't remember him mentioning that name, but he did say he has some friends in the BPD. Why?"

"Logan and I first got to know Breen when he was

assigned to Hamid's murder investigation. I think Logan probably reached out to him after Hamid's father came to him with information about Al Sadiq trying to radicalize Americans and get them to set up cells in the U.S. to commit terrorist attacks.

"Anyway, as fate would have it, Breen recently approached my boss at BU with a request to set up a survival Arabic language course for some of their investigators. She asked me to take the lead on it, and I met with him earlier this week.

"That's how I found out Logan's on his way to Syria. I guess I was so shocked I didn't know what else to say."

"You don't think Breen is involved in sending Logan to Syria, do you?" Ali asked.

"I mean, he's concerned about what's happening here in the Boston metro area. He doesn't have the resources or the mandate to be mucking around overseas."

"I've heard about these fusion centers," Ali said. "Our security people in New York talk to them from time to time if they have threat information to share. The thing is, they're not just local police. They have the FBI and intelligence people working in those centers.

"Maybe Logan's working for the CIA," he said.

She caught her breath. If Ali only knew. "I don't think so," she lied. In the recesses of her mind the refrain, "All in, all the time," reverberated. A mantra to take action. "All in, all the time."

"I need to talk to Breen again," she said. "Maybe he knows something."

In reality, she was already moving beyond Breen. Maybe there was a clue in Logan's office. She would stop there Monday to see what she could find out. It might also be worth reaching out to the Agency. She had an emergency contact number for the OMS. No, that was likely to be a dead end. CIA already thought she was a nut case because of her demand that Logan terminate his assignment early.

She looked up from her reverie. Ali was staring at her. "Where were you just now?" he asked.

"I'm sorry. I'm just rattled by all of this. I feel responsible. I asked Logan to move out, and now he's on his way to Syria. I'll call Peter on Monday. Maybe he can tell me something."

She snapped her notebook shut. "So, what else do you want to do in Boston this weekend?"

Chapter 31

Several days after returning to Toronto from her meeting with Tim Hudson, Azar received a text message from him, advising her of his travel itinerary. He was flying into London and would be hopscotching by train through Europe to Turkey. It looked as though he would be getting into Istanbul on April 30th.

She composed a short message to her boss, Colonel Samadi, requesting contact instructions to provide the former navy SEAL in Istanbul. His response came back within 24 hours.

"Azar,

I want you to personally meet Hudson in Istanbul. From there you'll both travel by plane to Sanliurfa where you'll pick up a car for the drive to Raqqa. You can make the travel arrangements to Sanliurfa and Raqqa once you get to Turkey. We want to keep your Canadian travel documents clean. We'll have someone meet you in Istanbul with papers for you to use getting in and out of Syria. Once you hand off Hudson to ISIS, your job will be done. Things are very fluid in Raqqa right now so you must be careful. The Americans want to take it back. They want to drive ISIS out of their so-called capital.

From your correspondence, it sounds as though Hudson is eager to join the fight, but I don't want to risk him getting cold feet at the last minute. This's where you come into play. You're a known quantity to him, and you have some level of rapport. You should know General Salehi has closely followed your progress. This is precisely what he was thinking about when we started down this path with ISIS."

She was astonished Samadi was directing her to accompany Hudson into Syria. His reasons were sound though, and she agreed it made sense to handle the new recruit with special care, particularly given General Salehi's personal interest in the operation. That would only leave a couple of days for her to work out her travel arrangements. She wrote Samadi back to advise him she was clearing her calendar to concentrate on this alone. She also included a specific request—that her contact in Istanbul bring a Glock 9mm pistol with spare ammo and a tactical fighting knife.

This would be her first trip to Turkey. She decided to cover her travel there under the guise of a freelance photo assignment. The Canadian security intelligence service had shown no interest in her since taking up residence in Toronto, and she didn't want to give them grounds to start now. If she was on their radar, and there was no reason to suspect she was, they should be accustomed to her comings and goings to far-flung locales, followed by the inevitable travel piece in a travel magazine or newspaper.

What was going on in Istanbul this month? She pulled up the home page for a Turkish travel agency, the Stamboul Travel Group, to see if there were any unique festivals or holidays in April for her to photograph.

As she read, she grabbed a pen and paper and began jotting down a few ideas taken from the website. The city had a tulip festival in April. With over 30 million tulips in bloom, Istanbul would be awash in flowers. That might be of interest. As she read on, Azar discovered tulips were thought to have originated in Turkey, among other places. Even the scientific name *Tulipa* came from the Turkish word for "turban."

There was an international Turkish film festival. She would have to check the dates to see who was attending. No, it took place earlier in the month. Here was something. *Gülhane Parkı* was initially the grounds of the Topkapi Palace, built nearly six hundred years ago by Sultan Mehmed II after he conquered what was then Constantinople. Now the grounds were a public park where, every April, storks return from wintering in sub-Saharan Africa to lay their eggs. That could be interesting. She remembered reading about Turkish superstitions having to do with storks. She would have to check back copies of *Condé Nast* to see if they had done any features on Turkey recently.

When she was finished perusing the tourist information, she booked a direct flight out of Toronto on LOT-Polish Airlines. Even though there was only one stop in Warsaw, it was still going to be a weary 13 hours of travel. It would put her into Istanbul on the 29th, giving her time to get the lay of the land and check out locations to photograph. She booked a single room in the Neorion Hotel for two nights and added an adjoining room to accommodate Hudson. The hotel was situated in the *Sultanahmet* area, within walking distance to the *Hagia Sophia* mosque and the *Capali Carsi* (Grand Bazaar).

When she was done making her travel arrangements, Azar sent a text message to Hudson, who by now was already en route to Istanbul. She told him to be at Gate 1 to the Grand Bazaar on April 30th at 5:00 p.m. where he would be contacted. She did not let on she would be his contact, preferring to keep him slightly off balance and giving her more control over the initial meeting.

Thus far, there was no reason to suspect Hudson's motivation for volunteering. Everything about him checked out, and her Qods Force bosses seemed convinced he was a perfect candidate to advance their goal of striking at the heart of the Americans. She grimaced as she reflected on her own particular animus towards the U.S. They were responsible for the murder of her beloved Barzan in his prime, a mere 37 years old, butchered in Bandar Deylam in a commando-style raid.

She felt the bile rising in her throat as she dwelled on the moment she learned of his death. His body riddled with AK-47 rounds and his intestines spilling out from where he lay, gutted like some animal. He was her husband, her lover, her friend.

She pushed these grisly thoughts aside, concentrating

on the meeting arrangements with Hudson. He would be surprised to see her. And unlike their first encounter in New Bedford, where he was on his home turf, she would be the one with the language, connections, and know-how to navigate him securely into the waiting arms of ISIS.

Two days later, she stepped off the plane in Istanbul. It was drizzling, with temperatures in the mid-forties. Despite the gloomy weather, it was a respite from Toronto, which, despite a recent warming trend, could easily have snow showers and freezing temperatures at this time of year.

After she checked into the Neorion, she asked the concierge for a map of the city. She had a rendezvous in *Ümraniye*, a sprawling working-class district about 30 minutes by cab from her hotel.

Azar directed the driver to a tea garden on Hatip Street. Tea houses were the strict provenance of men, but for some reason, tea gardens were more hospitable towards women and families.

"What's the name of this bridge?" she asked as the driver pulled onto an arching suspension bridge.

"The E 80."

"Doesn't it have another name?" she asked.

"Yes. It's the Faith Sultan Mehmet Bridge. It was completed in 1988 and is over three thousand feet long. It's part of the Trans-European Motorway."

As they crossed the Bosphorus, she felt it would be nice to have more time in the former capital. She thumbed through her Fodor's Guidebook to Turkey, looking forward to spending what little free time she had exploring the city. Here and there, lining the waterfront on both the European and Asian shores, were magnificent *Yalı*, traditional palaces, some dating back to the early days of the Ottoman Empire.

As they sped over the strait connecting the Black Sea and the Sea of Marmara, Azar was overcome by a feeling of nostalgia. Iran was not far away. Indeed, closer here than it was to Canada. There was nothing to take her back there though. With Barzan and her parents gone, there was no compelling reason to return. Besides, the Qods Force was inclined to keep her where she was. She was valuable to them in Canada. Just consider the current operation.

The driver pulled up to a full garden backing onto an ancient mosque. She paid him and walked in, not sure whom she would be meeting. A young woman standing by a Palladian window distinguished by a colorful mosaic design at its peak, gestured for her to follow. Her name was Yazmin, and she worked undercover for the Qods Force at Iran Air's Istanbul office.

"How'd you recognize me?" Azar asked.

Yazmin pulled out her cell phone and showed her a text message with Azar's photo attached. "You look just like your picture," she said as she led her over to a table for two in a far corner. Given the gloomy weather, they decided to remain inside.

They each ordered a Turkish black tea. After the waiter served them, Yazmin fished Azar's alias documents out of a bag and handed them to her. "No need for us to meet on your way out," she shrugged. "Just destroy them." She reached into her handbag and pulled out a small package, which she slid across the table. "These are the other things you asked for.

"I'm not briefed on what you'll be doing here," Yazmin said. "You shouldn't have any problems with the Turks. Traditionally we have a lot in common with them, but it doesn't help they are members of NATO and sometimes take actions harmful to Iran's interests. When that happens, things can heat up pretty fast, so pay attention." They chatted for a few more minutes and then departed the tea garden separately.

Azar made a stop in the toilet, and while in the stall secreted the documents within a concealed space inside her camera bag. Usually, she wouldn't have two incompatible sets of papers on her person, but this trip was anything but ordinary. She opened the package and found a Glock 9mm pistol and two magazines of ammunition. Azar checked and noted with approval there was a round chambered. The safety was on.

The tactical knife was a lightweight, foldable design. Azar flicked it open, testing its weight and balance in her hand. The steel blade was inscribed Apache TAC 1, and the handle had a hard rubber feel to it. It was a far cry from her own knife, the one custom-made for her in Caracas. The handle on her weapon was constructed from a solid block of titanium, and the blade was made of stainless raindrop Damascus steel. That's the difference between a 40-dollar mass-produced knock-off and the 400 dollars she spent on her custom blade.

She stowed the hardware in her bag, checked the time, and with surprise saw it was only 2:00 p.m. Looking outside, she noticed it was no longer raining and the sun was out.

Azar hailed one of the official bright yellow taxis cruising outside and asked if the driver could take her to *Gülhane Parkı*. She observed he already had two male passengers in the back seat. She slipped into the front, remembering it was common in Turkey for cabs to pick up multiple fares at the same time; she wasn't really worried about the two septuagenarians shouting to be heard over the pop music blasting out of the driver's CD player.

Her interest in going to *Gülhane Parkı* was to see if any of the famed storks were arriving on schedule. A story about nesting storks without any actual photos would be of little interest. She was mindful of the fact her ability to continue operating unimpeded out of Canada depended upon her cunning role playing the international freelance photographer she purported to be.

Minutes later the driver let her out near the south entrance to the park, but not before a quarrel erupted over the correct fare. Turkish taxi drivers are known for their guile when it comes to extorting excessive charges from their customers. She took note of the meter, barely visible beneath the gear shift on the dash, when she entered the vehicle and told him, in no uncertain terms, he was a scoundrel and would not get one lira more than what was owed to him. She muttered something about *polis* under her breath, and he took the proffered bills without further argument and sped off.

Azar strolled into the park. The light might not be particularly suitable for photography this afternoon, but she could get the lay of the land, and sell her cover story, not to the Canadians, here and now, but to the Turks. They were the ones she needed to worry about over the next few days.

Chapter 32

Logan stretched, barely suppressing a tired yawn as he gazed out the window of the train. Except for a one-night layover in Budapest, he'd been traveling non-stop ever since departing Boston.

It was a good idea he decided to rest up overnight in Budapest. He went out for some Hungarian goulash and then killed a bottle of local wine in the catacombs, an ancient burial place repurposed as the Faust Wine Cellar, beneath the Hilton Hotel, on the west (Buda) side of the Danube River. It would have been pleasant to explore the narrow, winding streets snaking upward to the Buda Hills the next day, despite a lingering hangover, but there was work to do.

He was scheduled to arrive in Istanbul at 11:30 a.m., plenty of time to make his 1:00 p.m. meeting with Bruce Wellington and then his 5:00 p.m. meeting at the Grand Bazaar. Azar had texted him with instructions to be at Gate 1 precisely at 5:00 p.m., but he didn't plan to make initial contact until he met with his backup. He didn't have a clue who ISIS was sending to meet him but assumed his point of contact would have been given his physical particulars.

Jason Summers was running this operation out of CIA headquarters, and his recommendation was to keep a low profile in Turkey. No one at the embassy, not even the ambassador or the COS, knew he was in country. Wellington was going to pick him up in a rental car several blocks west of Halkali, on the western side of Istanbul. Normally he would have taken the train to the end of the line at Sirkeci Terminal, but it was closed for renovations.

He and Bruce would drive around until they worked out a counter-surveillance plan for his initial meeting with the ISIS contact. Bruce was also supposed to be bringing him some protection—a Glock 9mm with ammo, tactical fighting knife, and a collapsible baton.

Thirty minutes later the train began to slow, and the conductor announced their imminent arrival at Halkali Station. A patchwork of nondescript one and two-story houses bordered the tracks. The station itself was in need of a makeover. Tanker cars idled on a siding adjacent to the tracks where the train was beginning to disgorge passengers. A white wrought iron fence with blue stanchions separated the passengers from the freight area.

The station was drab; a one-story concrete affair whose dull beige facade gave the impression it was last painted during the waning years of Atatürk's reign. Logan retrieved his bag and headed out into the street. He had about an hour to kill before he was due to meet with Wellington. Their rendezvous site was only six blocks from the station. He began walking north. From what he could see, Halkali had little going for it. Vehicular and pedestrian traffic was heavy. There was a loud, clanging vibration in the air around him.

After an hour spent window shopping, he spotted Wellington in a Toyota Land Cruiser, pulled over to the side of the road.

"I never thought I would be so happy to see your ugly mug," Logan said as he stowed his bag in the back seat and climbed up front.

"Nice to see you too, buddy," Bruce said.

"Where's Norm?" Logan asked.

"Got to Mosul a couple of days ago. He's already embedded with Task Force Zeus. Soon as we get you squared away here, I'm headed over there to check in too."

"How you getting there?"

"Commercial into Baghdad, Emirates probably. I'll catch a MILAIR ride from there to Mosul." He reached onto the back seat and handed Logan a small bag. "Brought you some presents."

Bruce slipped the car into gear and pulled away from the curb. "You still set to meet this guy at the Grand Bazaar?"

"Far as I know. I forwarded the text message I got from Azar to you guys the other day. Haven't heard anything else from her since." He rummaged through the bag, satisfied everything he needed was there.

"Thanks for this," Logan said as he hefted the bag. "I'm glad headquarters gave us the go-ahead to use Silent Phone. Don't get me wrong. The proprietary stuff the Agency makes is good, but with everything going on with Wiki Leaks, it's hard to know what's secure and what's not."

"We'd be in a world of hurt if we couldn't talk to each other," Bruce said. "And the other nice thing about Silent Phone is we can also securely send videos and photos. TOR wouldn't let us do that."

"Right," Logan said. "It's only set up for text. I don't expect to be sending many images, but you never know."

Bruce navigated onto the E 5. "Should be a little less than an hour to Istanbul. I can't believe this traffic." He swerved suddenly to avoid an overladen donkey cart.

"How do you want to manage the counter-surveil-lance?" he asked.

"I'll be honest. This is my first trip to Istanbul, so I'm not really sure what to expect. The Grand Bazaar's in *Sultanahmet*, which is the main tourist district. So, there'll be a lot of tourists, restaurants, and shopping. That should work to our advantage. We won't stand out as foreigners. But once I make contact, we'll be flying blind."

"Aren't you supposed to go in through Beirut?" Bruce asked.

"That was the original plan, but it's over six hundred miles to Beirut from here. That's probably thirteen hours driving. We may go into Syria on Turkey's eastern border."

"Maybe he'll want to fly," Bruce said.

"We'll see what happens. Do you want to grab something to eat before we get into town?" Logan asked. "There's less chance of us being spotted together out here."

Bruce turned off the E5 onto a side street and found a small family rooftop restaurant open for lunch. Fifteen minutes later, they were tucking into doner kebabs, a kind of roasted meat wrapped in flatbread, with a side tomato and onion salad. They were quiet as they gulped down their food. Logan leaned back in his seat when he was done eating and burped.

"You heard about the attack in London the other day?" he asked.

"It was all over the news before I left," Bruce said. "The initial take is it was ISIS-inspired. Why would they go after MI6 headquarters?" he asked.

"ISIS has been putting threats out on social media through their propaganda arm, *Al-Wafa*. There was a message last month entitled "England, You Are Next," where they basically said they were going after them.

"Think about it. England's been part of the global coalition to fight ISIS since 2014. And they're second only to us in the number of airstrikes against ISIS in Iraq and Syria.

"I don't think ISIS cares how many people died in the London attack," Logan continued. "Symbolism is what matters most to them. They were able to take the fight to the Brits in their own backyard. And what better target than MI6, who, by their own admission, has penetrated ISIS headquarters in the past? They've probably been responsible for derailing a dozen ISIS plots over the years."

The men paid their bill and headed back out to the car. Bruce eased into traffic. The

E5 was like a parking lot. Nothing was moving. Thirty minutes later, they came upon the accident. A taxi rammed into a horse cart carrying a load of melons, causing it to overturn and spill its contents into the road. It was going to be tight making the meeting on time.

A mile from the Grand Bazaar, Bruce pulled over to let Logan out. They agreed he would park the car first and find a spot with a good visual on Gate 1. He knew Logan's approach route to the meeting site and would be able to see who made contact with him.

If it looked like a setup, Bruce would back him up. Absent any kind of distress signal, he would maintain visual contact on the meeting for as long as possible without exposing himself.

Logan started to get out of the car, but Bruce held him back. "I wanted to mention something before you go. You know last week when we all met in Boston?"

"Yeah?"

"Well, after we finished our beers, Norm and I decided to stop by the office to see how Alicia was doing."

"How was she?"

"Everything was cool. We got caught up on Hong Kong. Told her the old dragon boat buddies were going to pull out of this year's race because they couldn't find another cox-swain to take her place. Anyway, while we were there..." He paused as if to consider what he was about to say.

"What is it, Bruce?"

"While we were there, Zahir stopped by."

Logan's heart skipped a beat. His brow furrowed as he considered what Bruce had just said. Bruce knew about their separation. "What did she have to say?"

"She was all emotional. Blaming herself for making you move out."

"Did she say anything about Cooper?"

"Yeah. I guess he was at her parent's house for an extra week. Your father-in-law brought him up to Boston, and she was enrolling him in a summer program at a Montessori school near your apartment."

"What was she doing at the office?"

"I think she was hoping to catch you there. She went over to BPD to see Detective Breen because her boss asked her to put together a survival Arabic course at BU for some of his investigators. Anyway, seems like she pried your trip out of him. She was steamed when she heard you were on your way to Syria."

"Shit! What the hell was Breen thinking?"

"I don't know. Norm and I kept pretty quiet. She wanted to know if we had your contact info, but we played dumb. I think she sensed we were holding back. She left in a huff."

Logan massaged his brow as he pondered this unexpect-ed turn of events. It sounded from what Bruce was saying, that Zahir was ready to reconcile, or at least talk. He'd reach out to her when he got home. Maybe they'd be able to work it out after all.

He fumed as he thought about the timing of this revelation. He didn't need any distractions. When he left Boston, he turned off the "family" switch so he could focus a hundred percent on the mission. If he let his mind wander now, he might make a mistake. And that was something he couldn't afford to do.

"Thanks for telling me, Bruce." He took a moment to load the Glock and conceal it in the small of his back. He bent down and strapped the tactical knife to his left ankle and stowed the collapsible baton in his pocket.

"All right. Let's do this." He stepped out of the car, retrieved his bag from the rear seat and began walking towards the tourist district.

Bruce watched him until he was swallowed up by the crowd. "Stay safe out there," he whispered to himself.

* * *

Bruce eased back into traffic and headed towards the Grand Bazaar's Gate 1. When he'd reconnoitered the meeting site earlier in the day, he was struck by how crowded the place was. It was going to be really tough to figure out if there was anybody out there working with Logan's contact.

There were 21 gates into the bazaar, five of them major ones. There was no parking on the street in front of this gate, so he'd have to park the car a block away and walk to a place where he could observe the meeting. When he scouted the location earlier, he noticed there was a carpet shop across the street with stacks of carpets outside. He would set up there just before 5:00.

It took him longer than he expected to park the car, but he still had five minutes to get to his observation post. As he approached the carpet shop, he could see Logan standing just outside the gate. He looked relaxed. Bruce thought the area looked less crowded than it did in the morning, making him comfortable he would be able to spot anything untoward.

He scanned the pedestrians, and his eyes were suddenly drawn to an attractive woman walking towards Logan. She looked vaguely familiar. And then it hit him. The last time he had seen her was five years ago. She was coming after him with a knife in a Qods Force safehouse in Caracas. He, Logan, and Norm had surprised her when they were searching for Unit 400 assassin Nouri Khorasani, who'd killed their Kuwaiti friend, Hamid Al Subaie. It was Azar Ghabel.

She walked up to Logan, and Bruce could tell by the shocked look on his friend's face he wasn't expecting this. They spoke briefly and moments later began walking in his direction. He didn't know if she would recognize him, but he couldn't take a chance she might.

That night in Caracas as she came into the apartment he was the one who took her down with a sweep kick. She was a fighter though and sprang right back at him. That's when Logan hit her in the neck with a taser shot. She went down hard and was out cold when he reached for her. Now she was only a few feet away. Bruce ducked his head and entered the carpet shop as they walked by.

Chapter 33

It had been two days since her visit with Norm, Bruce, and Alicia at Alexander Maritime, an emotional reunion to say the least. The three of them were in Hong Kong with her when she miscarried. They even went back further than that, all the way back to the operation in Iran. They were like family to her.

But something felt different this time. Maybe it was because Zahir had violated an unspoken trust, breaking with Logan. After all, the four of them were a tight-knit group with their work for the CIA in Hong Kong and China. They were conducting black ops, but she was on the periphery of their operational activity. She knew, as an Agency wife, her job was to support Logan, and at times maybe even be involved operationally.

Zahir learned early on her role was to remain in the background. And it was ok. From her days as an interpreter in Iraq, she understood the "need to know" principle. The fact was, she really didn't need to know what they were working on. But the closeness the four of them enjoyed now was her adversary. She recognized the look in Bruce and Norm's eyes when she asked them for Logan's contact info. They shut down, shut her out. She understood, but it didn't make her life any easier.

That's why at 9:00 p.m. on a Wednesday night she was walking into One Marina Place at Fan Pier explaining to security she needed to pick up something for her husband. She suspected it was a long shot that there would be information just lying around, particularly with Alicia's CIA training, but maybe, just maybe, there would be contact information for him in Alicia's desk.

Zahir rode up to the 16th floor and held her breath as she unlocked the door and scurried in to disable the security alarm. She got the all clear signal and heaved a sigh of relief. It was an eerie feeling being in the office at this hour. She felt a stab of guilt given the underhanded nature of her mission. She paused before Logan's office and looked in. There were some mementos and SEAL paraphernalia as decorations, but what drew her into the room was a family photo on the desk. It was taken at The Peak in Hong Kong, overlooking Victoria Harbor. She and Logan both had their arms around Cooper. *A happier time,* she reminisced.

Zahir went back out to Alicia's desk and began poking around. She spotted her Rolodex and found a cell phone number under the letters "T.H." *H for Hudson,* Zahir surmised. Tim Hudson. She copied the number down, shut off the lights, and left the building.

A part of her wanted to dial the number right away so she could hear Logan's voice. But she knew enough from being in the company of Logan and the others to understand when he was working undercover in a foreign country she couldn't just reach out to him.

How many times in the past was she on tenterhooks when he was operational with no way of contacting him? She wasn't sure how she was going to use the number, but it gave her some comfort, rustling there in her pocket.

The phone was ringing when she got back to her apartment. She waved to the babysitter and grabbed the receiver before it went silent. It was her father.

"Hi, Sweetheart. How are you?"

"Fine." It was unusual for her dad to call, especially this late in the day. "Is everything all right?" she asked.

"It's your brother."

"What? Did something happen?"

"He was at a Knicks game tonight, and there was a disturbance in the stands. They say it was racial taunting. Anyway, he came to the defense of this Iraqi man and his son, who were being hassled by several white fans. It seems they were drunk, the Knicks were losing, and these Iraqis were cheering for the other team.

"It started to get physical, and that's when Ali intervened. According to witnesses, one of the hecklers called Ali a 'rag head' and cold-cocked him. Ali fell into the bleachers and hit his head. He's in a coma at Lenox Hill Hospital."

"Oh my God," she said. "What's wrong with these people? Is he going to be all right?"

"It's too soon to tell. Your mother and I are flying up to New York tonight. There was a call from the commissioner's office. He's making a statement on the 11:00 p.m. news."

She looked at her watch. It was 10:45. She and her father talked for a couple of minutes. "Call me if his condition changes. It doesn't matter what time it is."

"Is everything all right, Mrs. Alexander?"

She was so absorbed in her phone call she forgot all about the babysitter.

"It's my brother. He's had an accident." She rummaged in her purse and pulled out a twenty. Thanks, Lauren. It's too early to tell."

Lauren gave her a hug. "I hope everything turns out ok."

"Thanks." After she closed the door, Zahir poured herself a glass of wine and sat down in front of the TV. There was another incident of racial taunting at Fenway Park just last week. A bi-racial family was insulted in the stands, and in that case, the offender was banned from Fenway Park for life.

The basketball commissioner was being interviewed on ESPN. It was the lead story. She was surprised to see a photo of Ali displayed as a backdrop on a screen behind him. She turned up the volume.

"Commissioner, thank you for being with us on this late breaking story out of Madison Square Garden. For our viewers, Ali Parandeh, an NBA marketing executive here in New York City, was ruthlessly attacked this evening at a Knicks game while coming to the assistance of an Iraqi immigrant and his son, who were being taunted with racial epithets. We have just learned Mr. Parandeh is in a coma at Lenox Hill Hospital. Commissioner? Any updates on his condition?"

"We have no updates at this time. First, though, I would just like to say my heart goes out to Mr. Parandeh and his family. He is a valuable member of the NBA franchise. He's been working very hard this year to expand the NBA's brand and image in Latin America."

"Brian, let me say unequivocally, the NBA doesn't tolerate racism. From our players. From our personnel. Or from our fans. The NYPD has taken into custody the persons responsible for the racist remarks and the unprovoked attack on Mr. Parandeh. We are working closely with the police commissioner's office, and we will prosecute these people to the full extent of the law.

"I would add, anyone involved in this incident proven to have used racist remarks will be banned for life from Madison Square Garden. There's no place for racism in America, and as one of the great sports venues in the world, there's no place for racism at the Garden.

"This is a sad day for American sport. Indeed, this is a sad day for America."

She turned off the TV, checked on Cooper, and then went to her own room. As she lay down, her heart was heavy, thinking about Ali. For the first time in months, she didn't go to sleep thinking about her own problems. She was praying silently for Ali's recovery.

Early the next morning, after dropping Cooper off at his Montessori school, she stopped in to see Ava before class.

"Hi, Ava. Got a minute?"

"Sure, come on in."

I wanted to give you an update on the BPD class. We're three days into it. It's a little slow, but I'm starting to see some progress. The one thing that has me pulling out my hair is an undercurrent of anti-Muslim prejudice I sense coming out of a couple of the male students.

"I hate to say it, but this just got very personal for me." She went on to explain Ali's violent encounter the night before.

"Oh my God. That's terrible. Can I do anything for you?"

"If his condition worsens, I may need to go to New York. My parents both flew up from Washington yesterday. They'll stay until his situation is resolved.

"It's made me really want to put more emphasis on our cross-cultural segment. And I think we should be brutally honest in our evaluations for Mr. Breen if we're not comfortable with the way the students handle it. The last thing we need in Boston is law enforcement alienating the Muslim community. There is tension enough as it is without throwing fuel on the fire."

"I support you one hundred percent. Just let me know what you need, and we'll make sure it happens."

"I'd like to move up our cross-cultural exercise to tomorrow. Do you think it'll be a problem getting our usual role players a couple of days early?"

"Shouldn't be. They're pretty flexible. Talk to Sarah and ask her to reach out to them."

Sarah Appleby was their resource manager. She began working in the language school over a decade ago and could be counted on to get the job done, no matter how complicated.

"Changing the subject, how's Cooper settling into his new school?"

"He's so excited. Loves his teacher. I think it's the perfect place for him."

"Great. Let me know if you need anything."

"Thanks."

Zahir walked down the hall to her office. She felt a renewed sense of purpose. On one level, she believed combating prejudice, even on a small scale like this, could make a difference. Maybe Ali wouldn't be lying comatose in a hospital bed if there were more emphasis on breaking down cultural barriers in programs like theirs. In a way she wasn't just doing this class for the BPD, she was doing it for her brother and all minorities who were victims of racial prejudice.

Chapter 34

Logan sensed from the smug look on Azar's face, she was pleased with herself over his surprised reaction to her appearance. It never occurred to him she would show up in Istanbul.

"What are you doing here?" he asked. "Why didn't you tell me you'd be the one meeting me? I was expecting someone else."

He didn't like surprises, and he had to admit he was rattled moments earlier when she walked up to him in the bazaar. It was unusual for him to be caught unaware, so thorough was his attention to detail. *What is she up to?* His brain was on fast forward as he considered the implications of her arrival on the scene.

Logan scanned the street in the direction of Bruce's observation post as they began walking through the dense crowd, away from the Grand Bazaar. But there was no sign of his friend outside the carpet shop, meaning he was probably watching them from inside. By now, Bruce surely would have recognized Azar, given their past history, and was, without a doubt, just as confused as he was by her perplexing arrival on the scene.

"A photo shoot opportunity came up in Istanbul, and I contacted my friends in Syria to tell them I was available to meet you here."

"What are you shooting?"

She explained the background of the stork migration from Africa to Europe.

"It's one of the great migration stories. These white storks spend the winter in sub-Saharan Africa, and in the spring, they return to their breeding grounds in Europe.

Most Turks believe storks mate for life, so for them, the stork is a symbol of marital fidelity. In reality, scientists believe the birds return to the same nest every year, not necessarily the same mate, although they do seem to prefer monogamy from what I've read.

"Turkey itself only has about twelve thousand storks. But because Istanbul is right in the middle of the migration route to other nesting grounds in Europe, hundreds of thousands of storks cross the Bosphorus every year around this time."

They were moving away from the Grand Bazaar, but the crush of people continued to press in from every direction. Logan was on high alert as he scanned the throng for anything out of the ordinary. So far, he sensed nothing unusual.

"Where we headed?" he asked.

"We're staying at the Neorion Hotel; not too far from here. I booked you into a room next to mine. I thought you might want to rest up tomorrow. I need another day of work here, and then we can leave for Sanliurfa, which is near the border with Syria.

"How far is it from Istanbul?"

"Thirteen hours driving, but it's only an hour and a half by air."

He nodded his head as he considered the prospect of spending 13 hours ensconced in a car with the mysterious woman at his side. He still didn't grasp how the Qods Force could be in cahoots with ISIS, given the regime's support for Assad. And how this woman, who five years ago was a housewife living in a backwater on the Persian Gulf, was now working as an undercover conduit to the Islamic State.

"What are you thinking?" he asked.

"Initially I thought it best for us to drive to the border, so you wouldn't have to use your passport. Then I remembered I have a friend working for one of the airlines here, and she offered to get us onto a flight to Sanliurfa without having to go through security."

"Isn't that risky for her?" he asked.

"She knows what she's doing," Azar replied with an

offhand wave of her hand. "She's been here for a few years. More importantly, she's made some friends."

"Whatever you say," Logan said. In his mind, however, he was trying to think of a title for the intelligence report he planned to write describing ISIS/Qods Force abilities to breach security protocols at Istanbul Atatürk Airport.

He could see the sign for the Neorion just up ahead. The facade of the hotel had a series of window arches in the Ottoman style, highlighted by blue mosaic tiles. *It must be named after Neorion Bay, on the Golden Horn,* he thought. As they approached the main entrance, Logan scanned the street for signs of any unusual activity. He didn't see anything out of the ordinary. Azar paused to fish a key from her purse before they went inside.

"Here's the key to your room. You're next to me. Room three forty-seven. Let's get together after you've had a chance to rest. Seven o'clock? Maybe we can get something to eat. By the way, I meant to ask you if you had any trouble taking time off?"

He accepted the key and stuck it in his pants pocket. "No. I moved up two courses scheduled for May and June and left word I would be out of town for a couple of weeks. I said I was meeting some heads of security for U.S. companies with offices in London. I figured they'd be on edge because of the uptick in terrorist attacks in Europe.

"Did you hear about the attack on MI 6 headquarters in London the other day? The train stations were full of police."

She stepped away from the entrance and motioned for him to move out of earshot of the doorman. "Yes, I saw it on the news. I think you'll see more of this type of attack in the months ahead. ISIS has been on the defensive in recent months, ever since the U.S. renewed its offensive ground campaign. In Syria alone they've lost half the territory they captured in 2014. Over a million Syrians who were under ISIS command are now under the control of Assad or the Syrian militias.

"They have to take the fight to wherever they can be

most effective," she said emphatically. "The plan is to do more of these attacks abroad, inspiring supporters through social media and publications like *Rumiyah*."

"*Rumiyah*?" He left the word hanging.

"Yes. It's an abbreviated version of ISIS'S first publication, *Dabiq*. This one's flashier. It's translated into English, Russian, and French and is distributed online through Twitter and different blogs." She brushed her hair back.

"ISIS has been making a big impact just by using social media. In one of their earliest issues, they encouraged lone wolf attacks using knives, guns, and cars in outdoor places where people tend to congregate: markets, festivals, restaurants and bars with outdoor seating, concerts, and rallies. Right after it was posted, we began to see a spike in these kinds of attacks in Europe and the U.S. The London attack against MI6 headquarters was probably inspired by this kind of social media campaign. They're going to try many different things in the coming months. You'll be impressed."

"What kinds of things?" Logan asked.

"Maybe you'll become an ISIS insider and will be telling *me* these stories," she laughed, deflecting the question. Turning serious for a moment, she cautioned him about watching what he said indoors. "Turkish security is excellent, and they keep an eye on foreigners."

"Point taken." They entered the hotel and took the elevator up to the third floor. Azar paused outside his room.

"I'll rent a car when we get to Sanliurfa. We'll make the border crossing into Syria and drive up towards Raqqa in the afternoon. My friends tell me the situation is very fluid there, so I'm not sure how close we'll be able to get, or exactly where we're going to meet up with my contacts."

"Any idea who we'll be seeing?"

"They didn't say, although I know it'll be someone with connections to the leadership. They move around a lot for their own safety. We'll find out when we get there." She glanced at her watch. "I'll leave you for now. See you at seven."

He nodded and went inside. He was careful to maintain

a neutral expression on his face as he nonchalantly cleared the room. Thus far, in his interactions with the Qods Force, they had shown a preternatural level of operational finesse and capabilities. He wouldn't be surprised if there were bugs in his room—audio and video—so they could observe him with his guard down.

What they didn't know, or at least he hoped they didn't know, was who he really was—a highly trained CIA operations officer who was about to infiltrate ISIS. And with any luck, his new contacts would steer him right to the mother-lode—Al Baghdadi himself.

Logan busied himself sending an Eyes Only encrypted text message to Wellington and Aaron Cousins, advising he was in Istanbul, was in contact with Azar Ghabel, and provided a brief synopsis of their conversation.

After hitting the send button, Logan typed a quick cover text to a notional business contact, saying he was in London for the next couple of weeks. The purpose of this message was to give him cover if anyone challenged his story about why he was on the phone.

Before he left the U.S., the technical people at the CIA manipulated the software in the commercial phones they were using, so encrypted messages were invisible to anyone who didn't possess a specific passcode—a sequence of random numbers. Without the passcode, all anyone could see were his overt cover messages.

After a shower and shave, he felt almost human again. He got dressed and saw it was nearly seven. There was a light knock on the door, and there stood Azar.

"Ready?" she asked.

"Yes." He pulled the door closed and joined her in the hallway. "Any idea where you want to eat?"

"My friend suggested a place called *Güler Ocakbasi*. It's a grill restaurant not too far from here. The family who runs it has been there for almost forty years. They have their own farm and bring in their own meat."

"That sounds good," Logan said. "In the States, we call it farm-to-table."

In the lobby, Azar asked the bellman to order a taxi. The restaurant was located in a section of Istanbul known as Sisli. Ten minutes later as they neared Sisli District, their driver pointed out a sprawling shopping mall.

"Cevahir Istanbul," he announced with proprietary immodesty.

"It's the largest shopping mall in Europe," Azar explained. "This entire area, all the way up to Taksim Square, was undeveloped until around 1800. Before then it was rural, and people would come out here to hunt."

"That's hard to believe," Logan said as they passed by upscale neighborhoods and well-appointed hotels. Moments later, the driver pulled over in front of *Güler Ocakbasi*. The wooden facade of the restaurant and adjoining hardware store gave the place a decidedly down-to-earth feel.

They went inside and were seated at a table for two. The restaurant was packed with tables of multi-generational families and friends. Among them, young Turkish males were the dominant demographic.

Logan filed away a question to ask Azar later about women's rights in Turkey. He knew for the most part, in conservative Islamic countries, women were discouraged from being alone outside the home unless accompanied by a male relative. That practice seemed to be borne out from what little he had observed in his short time in Istanbul.

Logan sniffed the air. An enormous copper hood suspended above a charcoal fire pit dominated one wall. Several spits strung with chicken, lamb, beef, and fish sizzled above the hot coals as their juices dripped on the white-hot embers. A large copper pipe connected to the hood was venting the smoke from the fire pit outside.

Logan and Azar ordered a mixed shared platter. While they were waiting for their food to arrive, Azar sipped from a tulip-shaped glass of *Cay*, a strong, black tea and Turkey's national drink, while Logan nursed a glass of *Rakı*, an anise-flavored alcoholic beverage.

Logan swirled the milky liquid around and whet his lips. "Have you spent much time in Turkey?" he asked.

"No, this is my first trip," she replied. Quite a few Turks are living in Canada, and I think the two countries get along all right. I'm sure the Turkish police talk to the Mounties from time to time, so I'm going to try to keep a low profile here." She paused as if to consider what she was about to say.

"I'll be using a different name for getting around Turkey and for when we make the border crossing at Sanliurfa into Syria."

Logan raised an eyebrow. "You think that's necessary?"

Azar shifted uncomfortably in her seat. "I've worked very hard to establish myself in Canada since I immigrated from Iran. I wouldn't want to do anything to jeopardize my situation there."

Logan leaned forward in his seat. "Do you think the Mounties keep tabs on you in Toronto?" he asked.

She gave her head a furtive shake. "No, not me in particular. But even though they have allowed a large number of Iranians to immigrate to Canada in general, the two countries don't have a stable relationship. The Mounties and Canadian security service have been known to be aggressive towards Iranian immigrants in the past.

"Anyway, the point is, if you hear me using a different name, that's why."

Their waiter brought their food, and Logan raised his glass in a toast. "To our success." He downed the drink and ordered another.

Logan decided to push her a little harder to see how she handled herself. "Are you working for the Iranian government, Alice?" he asked.

"What do you mean?" She challenged him.

"It just seems unusual for a journalist living in Canada to be introducing foreigners to ISIS. Is Iran supporting ISIS?" he asked.

"Don't be ridiculous," she said. "Iran is a predominantly Shia country, and ISIS is Sunni. What could the two sides possibly have in common?" she asked. "Besides, the Ayatollahs have ruined Iran. Why would I want to support them? Maybe what I'm trying to do," she said in a conspiratorial whisper, "is to ruin *them*."

Logan dropped the subject. Azar was a convincing storyteller. He felt confident she was an ardent supporter of the regime, but to hear her tell it, she loathed the clerics.

They were quiet on the ride back to the Neorion. She paused outside of his room. "I'm going out at first light to take some pictures," she said. If you're awake and up for it, you can meet me in the lobby at six thirty. Otherwise, I should be back at about ten."

"All right. I'll see you in the morning."

Logan found the BBC on TV and watched the news for 20 minutes before brushing his teeth and crawling back into bed. Things were beginning to get interesting. He turned out the light and waited for sleep to overcome him. Just as he was dozing off, he heard the door between the adjoining rooms creak open. He reached for his Glock. *What the hell is going on?*

Azar stepped into view, and in two strides she was standing beside his bed. Her hands were empty. As his eyes adjusted, he could tell from the sensuous shadow, she was naked. Reason cried for him to get out of bed, demand she leave. As he opened his mouth to speak, she slid in next to him and pressed her fingertips against his lips.

Chapter 35

The next morning, Logan was reflective as he waited for the elevator to take him down to the lobby to meet Azar. It was 6:15. He was going over the previous night's events in his mind. Sleeping with your agent is a big no-no in the CIA. But then, Azar wasn't really his agent. It was more like sleeping with the enemy. He shook his head. A self-deprecating admonishment that he'd crossed a line.

And then there was the question of what this would do to his relationship with Zahir. He knew she would be hurt, angry with him if she found out what he'd done. Hell, she was already mad at him. Maybe this wouldn't have happened if it weren't for her insisting on the separation. He probably wouldn't have been so quick to volunteer for this assignment if they were still together in Boston.

As soon as the thought crossed his mind, he realized it was gutless of him to try to lay the blame on Zahir. No, this was all his doing. His alone. He heard the elevator door closing on the floor above him and realized he'd forgotten to push the call button. He stabbed at it but was too late as the car bypassed the third floor. He decided to walk, head down, and trudged towards the stairwell at the end of the corridor.

He and Zahir had been through a lot in their short five years together. Despite their travails, he was always faithful to her. It was because he loved her too much to behave otherwise.

Logan thought back to his first encounter with Azar in New Bedford, the night after dinner when she unexpectedly kissed him with so much passion. It hadn't seemed contrived or calculated at the time. It was spontaneous, and she seemed surprised by the fire it ignited between them.

He doubted Azar was using their encounter last night as a way to blackmail him in the future or as a means of establishing control over their relationship. It seemed unlikely she would have an ongoing role handling him in the future if the introduction to ISIS went well. There would be a handoff in Syria tomorrow, and that would be the end of it.

His instincts told him Azar was lonely. She would have to be one cold customer to be an assassin for the Qods Force. He conceded it was possible there wasn't a shred of human compassion within her, after what she'd been through, but the passion and warmth she displayed last night made him wonder.

As he came out of the stairwell into the lobby, he spotted her sitting on a sofa, cradling a cup in her hands. He decided to let her take the lead on whether or not to mention their encounter from the night before.

She looked up as she heard him approach. "Tim, I wasn't sure if you'd be up so early." She stood up and seemed about to say something else but instead took a sip from her cup.

"I'm an early riser," he said. "Besides, after you talked about the storks, I thought it would be interesting to see. Who knows if I'll ever be back here again."

She nodded. "Do you want something to eat?"

"Just coffee. How about you?"

She raised her cup. This is my second one. I'm not hungry."

Logan ordered a cup of coffee to go. Azar gathered her photography gear, and they strolled outside in search of a cab to take them to the ferry terminal.

"Everything I've read says the Bosphorus cruises are a must see. I thought we would check out the southern Bosphorus from the Golden Horn and take the ferry up to the Black Sea," Azar said. "We can do it in a couple of hours, or, if we decide to get off anywhere, take longer."

Traffic was heavy with the morning rush hour. Their taxi driver gunned the engine to get around a lumbering truck and sped in the direction of the Galata Bridge. Looking out the window, Logan could see clear skies up ahead.

"Looks like you'll have good light for photography," he said.

"I checked the weather report before we left," she said. "It's supposed to get cloudy later in the afternoon, but they said clear and sunny this morning."

"Did you want to take a hop-on hop-off cruise, or stay put?" Logan asked.

"Maybe we can decide if we see something we want to get off and explore," she said.

"I think you have to commit one way or the other. Some ferries don't make any stops, and some are hop-on hop-off."

"All right. Why don't we try the hop-on hop-off? We don't have to get off, but it gives us the option if we see something interesting," Azar said.

The ferry terminal was bustling with activity. The blast of horns as boats announced their arrivals and departures, and a cacophony of languages as Turks and foreigners jostled their way on the docks. Many Istanbul residents commute daily by ferry, but for the tourists, it's a once-in-a-lifetime opportunity to gaze upon Ottoman palaces along the shores of the Bosphorus, looming fortresses, and the famed *yalis*, those wooden seaside mansions dating back to the time when Istanbul was known as Constantinople.

They boarded their boat and within minutes, were cruising by the *Topkapı* Palace and the Scutari Barracks, a Turkish army garrison where, in 1854, during the Crimean War, Florence Nightingale is said to have cared for the wounded.

Almost as if on cue, as they passed beneath the Bosphorus Bridge, thousands of white storks appeared above them, wheeling and circling in an avian dance, their long necks outstretched and streamlined bodies built for flight, coursing through the air.

Azar pulled a camera from her bag and began photographing. She worked fast, concentrating on the spectacle.

The storks seem to be in communication with one another making shrill cries, not unlike the raucous sound of gulls at the beach. Logan wondered at their ability to avoid mid-air collisions as they flapped their enormous wings and glided close to each other. He estimated they were flying at least several hundred feet above them.

"Did you know they can fly up to two hundred miles a day?" Azar asked. They were both silent as they watched the storks flying, their white color contrasting with the cerulean sky. There wasn't much traffic on the water at that hour, and by ten o'clock, Azar had taken over three hundred photos.

"I think between these and the ones I took the other day at the *Topkapı* Palace, I have enough. How would you feel about moving up our departure a day if we can change our flight?"

"That's fine with me," Logan said. "Are you sure there's a flight this afternoon?"

"Hold on. I'll give my friend a call." A moment later she was on her cell phone, speaking Farsi. Listening to their conversation, Logan wondered if the Qods Force had a cover position in the local Iran Air office. Or, it could be they had co-opted a friendly employee at Iran Air to help them out when needed.

"It won't be a problem," Azar said, as she put her phone away. "There's a four o'clock direct flight to Sanliurfa that gets in at five-thirty. We might even be able to make the border crossing tonight. They're not expecting us until tomorrow, so we'll have to see. What do you think?"

"It's fine with me," Logan said. "The sooner, the better." He was itching to get on the road, but he didn't want to appear too eager.

It was noon when they sighted the Galata Bridge looming into view. Since they hadn't eaten breakfast, they decided to have lunch nearby. Despite the area's designation in several guidebooks as a tourist trap, there were some promising-looking fish houses in the area. The Yaka Balik was right on the water and offered the freshest fish around, or so they claimed. They passed by a nargile café, en route to the eatery, where patrons sat smoking traditional Turkish water pipes. The pungent odor of Latakia tobacco laced with apple wafted out the open doors.

Logan and Azar didn't linger over lunch, a shared plate of fresh calamari and the catch of the day, a blackened red mullet. Gulls screeched overhead, and fishing lines dangled in the water not far from where they sat. When they finished their meal, they returned to the hotel to pack their bags.

It was two o'clock when they arrived at Istanbul Atatürk International Airport. Named after the founder and first president of Turkey, Mustafa Kamal Atatürk, it was a sprawling transportation hub located 15 miles west of the center city.

"Which terminal?" asked the driver, as he punched the meter.

"Domestic, please," said Azar.

Once inside, Azar placed a call to her friend at Iran Air, and ten minutes later, she appeared to show them the way. Her name was Yasmin, and she and Azar spoke in hushed Farsi as they navigated the stairs to the upper floor. Yasmin stepped behind the Pegasus Air counter and whispered with an employee. The latter affixed baggage claim tags to their suitcases and placed them on a conveyer belt. Yasmin thanked her. She took two boarding passes from the woman and looked at her watch. Motioning to Logan and Azar, Yasmin guided them towards the security gate, handing them both security badges and their boarding passes as they walked. "Put the badges here," she said, touching her breast pocket.

"If there's any problem, let Yasmin do the talking," Azar said. Logan noticed a shift change taking place as they neared security control. Yasmin held them back until the new officer was in place. He gave her a barely perceptible nod as she ushered them through. None of the other passengers seemed to notice their special treatment. Although neither he nor Azar were wearing distinctive clothing, the others probably assumed they were airport employees.

Once through security Yasmin took back the security badges. You're on Pegasus 2420," she said. "It's boarding at 3:55 from gate 112. Good luck."

The flight to Sanliurfa Gap Airport was bumpy but otherwise uneventful. Logan marveled at the vast expanse of the desert below them. Most of the other passengers were men—Turks, Arabs, and Kurds. Many were dressed in traditional attire, baggy pants held up with a wide sash, a plain shirt and a vest for the Kurds, and thwabs (a type of tunic) worn with a pajama bottom, for the Arabs. Nearly all of the Turks were wearing Western dress.

After they disembarked, Azar went in search of the Europcar desk to check on rentals while Logan decided to send a text message to Bruce and the Washington team to let them know about their changed itinerary. He wasn't sure when he would be able to communicate with them next. GPS tracking was enabled on his phone so they would know where he was, as long as the phone remained in his possession. Nothing was guaranteed though.

Arrived Sanliurfa today at 5:30 p.m. Plans are to make border crossing into Syria this p.m. Will attempt to make contact with ISIS tonight or tomorrow. Will advise.

Logan walked over to the baggage claim area and retrieved their two suitcases. He was curious to know where his ISIS contacts would want to meet up. When he'd hatched this plan weeks ago, Raqqa seemed to be, symbolically at least, the most likely place to have an encounter with them. It had, after all, been the de facto capital of ISIS since Al Baghdadi declared his Caliphate in 2014.

But for several months now, Raqqa had been under siege, in a ground war led by Syrian Democratic Forces supported by airstrikes and ground support from a coalition led by the United States. Raqqa had fallen to the SDF, and ISIS no longer controlled vast swaths of territory in Syria or Iraq.

He spotted Azar walking towards him. "Any luck?" he asked.

"Yes. We have a mid-sized sedan. We'll have to take a shuttle bus to pick it up."

Azar took her bag from him, and they began to walk in the direction of signs pointing towards ground transportation.

"I called my ISIS contact while I was waiting at the car place," she said. "I'm sure you know Raqqa's no longer an option."

"I seriously doubt if ISIS has anyone there," he said. "Where did they suggest we meet?"

"They mentioned an area west of Ash Shaddadi."

"ISIS used to control that part of Syria," Logan said as they left the terminal and walked towards the shuttle. "But if I remember correctly, last year they began evacuating women and children from Ash Shaddadi because the Kurdish YPG captured the Hasakah Dam and was beginning their push towards the city."

"We have a limited window to make contact with them," Azar said. "We'll take the highway east and enter Syria at Al Qamishly. From there we'll make our way south to Ash Shaddadi. We'll get the final location for the meeting when we get there."

Their car was a four-door Kia sedan. "You drive," Azar said. "It'll be less alerting than if a woman is driving."

"How about the border crossing?" Logan asked as he backed out of the parking space.

"The border is pretty loose in that area. I think our best bet will be for you to go in on foot a couple of miles from the border and make the crossing on foot. I'll pick you up on the Syrian side." She pulled a map out and showed him the spot on the ground. "If we're questioned later inside Syria we'll tell them we're journalists. I'm coming in to take some photographs, and you're gathering material for an article you're writing."

Logan nodded his understanding. He headed south from the airport towards Sanliurfa's city center with its ancient walls and Urfa Castle dominating the skyline. Too bad they didn't have time to visit the ancient sites. But they had more pressing matters to tend to. Urfa, as it was called by Turks, dated back to 400 BC and possibly even 500 years earlier.

Fifteen minutes later, he turned east onto the E90 towards Kızıltepe, a two-hour drive. Then he stopped the car and got out. Azar slid over into the driver's seat as Logan struck out off-road in the direction of the border. He walked 45 minutes before coming to the spot Azar had identified on the map. She was already there waiting for him, apparently having made the border crossing into Syria without incident.

Logan was on high alert as he got back into the car and resumed driving. He turned onto the D950 and began to drive south. There was destruction everywhere. With more than 11 million displaced persons, six million of whom had relocated within Syria, he expected to see death and destruction everywhere, but this was disturbing.

In the fading sunlight, they could see once barren desert crushed with rows upon rows of white tents. Ragged children stood off the road, watching the occasional car or truck roar by. Some of this seemed vaguely familiar. Maybe it was from his time spent in Afghanistan. There he had been in the middle of a war zone. But this felt different. *This must be what hell feels like.*

Just south of Al Hasakah, he noticed the motorcycle keeping pace with their vehicle, several car lengths behind them. In his rearview mirror, he could see two people on the bike, from their shape and clothing, both males. Logan increased his speed, and the motorcycle sped up too.

"We may have company," he said to Azar.

She looked over her shoulder. "They're picking up speed," she said.

Logan reached behind his back and pulled his Glock out of its holster. He flipped off the safety and held the gun in his right hand as he steered with his left.

'It may be nothing," he said. "I just don't like the way they're hanging back there." As he said it, it occurred to him this might be an ambush, and Azar could be working with the men behind them. As soon as he thought it, he discounted the idea. *Why would she go to all the trouble of traveling to Syria, when she could have taken him out in Istanbul without even trying?*

He glanced over at Azar and was surprised to see a pistol in her hand resting in her lap. It looked not unlike his own Glock. He cocked an eye and said. "Nice weapon."

She smiled. "I'm not taking any chances. It would be crazy to come here without some protection."

"Here they come." Logan gritted his teeth as the motorcycle pulled out and picked up speed. He lowered the driver's side window and gripped his Glock. The rushing wind and whine of the bike as it drew near made his heart race. He took a quick glance to his left, prepared to swerve into the bike, but to his relief, it sped by, both riders scrunched down, focused on the curve in the road ahead.

"Whew," Logan said, as the acrid smell of exhaust emissions blew in through the open window.

"Thank God," Azar said.

Logan looked in her direction and could tell she was pumped up by the incident. Her chest was heaving, and her face was flushed. He was relieved it was nothing more than an innocent encounter on the road.

A moment later, he realized they had declared victory too soon. As he passed by a rock outcrop, the motorcycle reappeared in his rearview mirror. They must have pulled off when they realized there were foreigners in the car. Logan increased his speed.

"I don't like the look of this," he said, his mouth a grim line.

He looked at the speedometer and realized he was doing nearly 80 mph. The road took a dip and a sharp curve to the left. Fighting for control as he came out of the curve, he saw a roadblock up ahead, a lone pickup truck diagonally straddling the median strip. There were several figures crouched behind it, brandishing weapons.

Logan braked hard, skidding to a stop a couple of hundred feet from them.

"Get down," he shouted to Azar, as the men behind the truck began to open fire. Looking in his rearview mirror, Logan could see the motorcycle closing the distance. He was in the kill zone, and his well-honed survival instinct kicked in.

"Hold on," he shouted. Logan slipped the car into reverse and began speeding backward, away from the truck. His breathing was relaxed as he kept an eye on the mirror, his hands light on the steering wheel. At 35 mph, Logan reversed direction, and the vehicle lurched around, centrifugal forces ripping across his seatbelt. He allowed the steering wheel to spin, grabbing it midway through the turn, and tromped on the gas.

He let out a sigh as the car righted and sped in the opposite direction. They were now heading straight for the motorcycle. The driver was braking, attempting to make an arcing turn in the road when Logan hit him broadside. Logan was close enough to read the terrified look on the passenger's face, right arm outstretched, firing a semi-automatic pistol at them as, with a sickening crunch, bike and riders were suddenly airborne.

The impact of the motorcycle slightly altered the direction of the car, and Logan momentarily lost control. As he fought to keep it on the road, it plunged off the berm into a trough, bounced twice, and flipped over. He lost consciousness for a moment. When he came to, he called out for Azar. There was no answer.

Extricating himself from the wreckage, he found her lying 30 feet from him, immobile. He could hear the slamming of doors and hushed whispering coming from the road. When he reached her, he whispered her name but got no response. He felt for a pulse and detected a very weak beat. She was alive. He pulled her to cover and then crouched down behind an outcrop. There was the sound of rocks sliding on the limestone bedrock as their pursuers slipped on the desert pavement. They were coming for him.

Chapter 36

Zahir was just wrapping up her class with the BRIC investigators. They were taking part in an activity designed to test their empathy for people from other cultures. It was a simple enough exercise. The students were given a list of ten common behaviors such as smiling, gift giving, hygiene, and punctuality, and asked to make assumptions about how a typical Muslim would behave in those situations.

"How would you expect a Muslim man to react to a female investigator knocking on his door?" Zahir asked the class.

"Given the way they normally treat women, not very favorably," one of the female students said.

"That's probably true," Zahir said. "Muslim men typically don't want to interact with women, particularly in a professional environment. And that's because in most cases, women in predominantly Muslim cultures don't have any authority. Why would those men want to deal with a woman who isn't in a position to make a decision?

"It's not always cut and dried though," she said. "You need to take into consideration other factors. What's the person's age? Did they grow up in a rural area or a city? What's their level of education? Did they study or travel abroad during their formative years? All of these factors can impact behavior towards women."

One of the male students raised his hand. "So, what you're saying is we shouldn't be too quick to judge what's going on. There's probably a cultural context we need to consider when we sense a conflict."

"Exactly," Zahir said. "Often people have this sense of cultural elitism. If you're an insider, i.e., from that culture, you tend to feel your ways are 'best' or that you are some-how superior to anyone who's outside your group. This doesn't just happen in the U.S. It's common everywhere. But since we live in such a multi-cultural world here, there are more opportunities for misunderstandings to arise."

Zahir took a few more questions before dismissing the class. As she was gathering her materials together, her cell phone rang. She looked at the caller ID and recognized her father's number. She experienced a moment of fear. Maybe it was about Ali.

"Hi, Dad," she said. "Is everything all right?"

"Hi, sweetheart. I called to let you know how Ali's do-ing. He's going to be fine, but he'll need to take a couple of weeks off before he's able to go back to work. The doctors performed a CT scan last night and found swelling in his brain."

Zahir clutched her hand to her chest. "Are you sure he's going to be OK? That sounds serious."

"The trauma from the fall caused the tissue in his brain to swell and push against the bone in his skull. In his case, the swelling wasn't too severe, so they were able to treat it by putting a drain in to remove fluids. They're going to monitor him here for a few days, and if everything's all right, they'll send him home."

"How's Mom doing?"

"She's fine, considering. We're going to stay with Ali af-ter he's released to make sure he gets to rest. A week or two at least."

"Give him my love."

"We love you."

Zahir looked up from her phone and realized her boss was standing in the doorway.

"Is everything all right?" Ava asked. She came into the room and sat down next to Zahir.

"That was my dad. Ali had to have surgery this morn-ing to relieve pressure on his brain. He just came out of it a little while ago, and so far, so good. They need to keep monitoring him to make sure there's no more swelling."

"If you need to go—" Ava's voice trailed off.

"I think we're fine," Zahir said. "Ali has to rest. I'll let you know if I have to take some time off."

"All right. Keep me posted. Tell me how the cross-cultural segment went this morning."

Zahir spent the next 15 minutes going over the class with the BRIC students.

"I polled them before we did the exercise. A few of the students had traveled internationally, but none to the Middle East. Most of them live in the suburbs, which, as you know, is not particularly diverse. None of them claimed to have any Muslim friends."

"Not surprising," Ava said.

"No. But what surprised me was how the students seemed to get it once we got into the exercise. They understood the concept of cultural elitism, and at least they were making the right noises once they understood why some of these cross-cultural differences exist."

"Maybe there's hope after all," Ava said. "Make sure to keep Mr. Breen up-to-date on their progress. He asked us to let him know how it is going."

"Sure thing."

* * *

Bruce looked up from the computer he was monitoring as Norm walked into the modified shipping container they were using as their base of operations within Task Force Zeus.

"Look at this," he said, as Norm secured the door behind him. They weren't in a CIA-approved sensitive compartmented information facility, but it was about as good as you could expect in a war zone. The thick metal walls would make it difficult for anyone to conduct electronic surveillance against their computers.

"What you got?" Norm asked, walking over to the makeshift desk where Bruce sat in front of a computer screen.

On the screen was a map of the Middle East highlighting

Turkey, Syria, and Iraq. Norm was running a GPS software program allowing him to track Logan's movements in real-time. The software updated Logan's progress with a degree of precision measured in feet. Unlike programs that obtain data from cell towers, GPS signals are collected off of multiple satellites. The algorithms then employ a process called trilateration to pinpoint the exact location of the target GPS signal. To get this level of accuracy, data from four satellites in real-time has to be available.

Bruce turned the computer screen around so Norm could see it. He then reached for a pad of paper where he had been making notes. "We know Logan arrived in Sanliurfa at five-thirty this afternoon. We got his text message saying they were going to try to make the border crossing into Syria tonight, right?" He turned back to the computer and pointed to Sanliurfa on the map.

"Yeah."

"I've been tracking his cell phone since they left the airport, and it's mostly made sense to me. They took the E90 towards Kızıltepe and made the border crossing into Syria without incident. They did something a little strange before the border, but I think I figured it out."

"Strange? How so?" Norm asked.

"I suspect she drove across the border and Logan went in on foot here." He pointed to a spot on the screen. "I timed it, and she wasn't at the border for more than five minutes." He pointed to a highlighted red line on the map. "The red line shows her route." He used his finger on the computer screen to trace Azar's direction.

"Look over here, and you can see where the one on foot, and I'm assuming that's Logan, goes in. Forty-five minutes later they lash up again.

"From the border, they get onto the D950 heading south. So far so good. But take a look at this," he said, jabbing his finger at the map. "This was about twenty minutes ago."

The program Bruce was using provided a record feature for the session. He clicked on another tab and pulled up the live recording. "What do you see?" he asked, pointing to the area just south of Al Hasakah.

Norm grabbed a chair and pulled it up to the desk next to Bruce. He looked at the screen for a couple of minutes before speaking.

"It looks like they were going along real steady, pretty much from the time they left Sanliurfa. There was the one stop at the border and then this."

"That's what I mean," Bruce said. "They turned around and headed back north." He had a perplexed look on his face.

"Yep. And stranger still, they haven't moved in twenty minutes."

"Could be anything. Maybe they got lost or decided to find something to eat."

"That was my first thought too, but then I ran another feature this program has, a kind of time-lapse recording. Using that I was able to figure out Logan's been traveling on average about 55 mph give or take. But in this segment south of Al Hasakah, he reached speeds of 80 mph. And now he's just sitting there."

"That's weird. Are you recording Azar's phone too?"

"Yep."

"Why don't you pull that up?"

Bruce switched to another view, and in a moment, the details of the collection against Azar's cell phone were there for them to see. Bruce created a side-by-side look of the two GPS signals and hunched over the screen.

"This is strange," he said, pointing to a portion of the display. "Their phones have been in lockstep ever since they left the airport in Sanliurfa, except for the border crossing. But look here," he said, pointing to the end of the display. "There's some separation. I'd say thirty, forty feet for several minutes, and then they come back together."

"I don't like this," Bruce said. "I have this feeling in my gut something's gone wrong."

"I've got an idea," Norm said. "Let's find out if any drone missions are flying in that area tonight and see if we can add on a tasking."

"What kind of package are we looking for?" Bruce asked. "I'd say at a minimum we need an infrared surveillance package and some firepower if Logan's in trouble."

Bruce got on a secure line to Creech Air Force Base, the command and control facility about 50 miles northwest of Las Vegas, home to the 432nd Wing and 432nd Air Expeditionary Wing "Hunters." He spoke for circa five minutes with a captain in the operations center, who confirmed the air force had aircraft in the area Bruce had described. He estimated they could deliver a Reaper drone equipped with infrared video and four Hellfire missiles within minutes.

Both Bruce and Norm had the authority, delegated in advance by the DDO and chief/CTC, to schedule these missions, but if they were going to task the pilot to pull the trigger on those Hellfires, they'd have to get somebody further up the food chain to approve it. There was a lot of debate in Washington about the ethics of targeted killing from drones.

It was starting to look like it was going to be a long night. Norm got up to put on a pot of coffee, while they waited for the video feed from the Reaper to begin. Five minutes later, they grabbed their mugs of java and linked the computer with the video feed from the Reaper crew, now known as Reaper 1.

The Reaper was coming in at about 300 mph at an altitude of 25,000 feet. These aircraft were capable of flying as high as 60,000 feet but based upon known conditions in the area this evening, it didn't need to fly so high. The ops center at Creech checked back in to verify the mission coordinates.

"36.5079° north by 40.7463° east," Bruce said. He also gave the ops center Logan and Azar's cell phone numbers so they'd also be able to track them real-time in the event there was any movement. As Bruce was about to hang up, his cell phone rang. He looked at the number in surprise. It was Logan.

"What the f—" Bruce said. "Are you all right?"

"Yeah. About as good as a shit sandwich," Logan said. "Can you see me? No? Hold on a second." A moment later, a blurry picture filled Bruce's screen.

"We got ambushed. Motorcycle with two guys on it working in tandem with a pickup truck with three guys. Managed to take out the motorcycle. Two bad guys are dead. The guys in the truck have me pinned down. Not sure how long I'll be able to hold them off. Azar's out cold. She's breathing, but she's going to need medical attention."

"We've got help on the way. Got a bird coming in about five minutes. Reaper 1. They're listening in on our feed so you can talk directly to them."

"Reaper 1. Comms check. Do you read me?" Logan asked.

"Roger that. Read you loud and clear. I think we've got eyes on you too. Looks like a four-door sedan off the road. About fifteen miles south of Al Hasakah. Flipped over or something. Two people crouched down about twenty feet from the car. That you?"

"Yeah, that's us."

"I see the bike about fifty feet from your location. No sign of any bodies," the drone pilot said. "Let me take a look over here," he said. "Oh. There they are. They're not moving."

"No, I think those guys are dead. We were probably doing eighty when we hit them."

"There's a pickup truck on the road about two hundred feet south of your position. You said there were three bad guys in the truck?"

"Affirmative." Logan looked over at Azar, but she was still unconscious. He could see her chest moving up and down, so he knew she was alive. She didn't have any other visible signs of injury.

"If it's possible, I'd like to salvage the truck. It's the only transportation we have out of here."

"Roger that. We need to confirm there are no targets in the vicinity of the truck. If we start shooting, they may try to make a run for it, and you'll be out of luck. Let's see."

Logan could hear the pilot consulting with the sensor operator in the ground control station.

"All right, we're going to see if we can find the hostiles

using our onboard thermal camera."

It took the crew less than a minute scouring the area, to identify the location of the three hostiles.

"Got 'em," the pilot said.

While Logan and Reaper 1 were talking, Bruce was on a separate line to Langley. It was early afternoon in Washington, and he got patched through to the DDO's office immediately.

"Logan's in a jam, boss," he said. He went on to give him a rundown of recent events. "Request permission to use lethal force if necessary, sir."

It went quiet for 30 seconds. Bruce could hear the DDO's voice urgently calling out to his secretary. When he came back on the line, he was calm. "Permission granted. I'm going to have you link up with chief/CTC. Try to patch him in so he can follow you in real-time. And, Bruce?"

"Yes, sir?"

"Good luck."

"Thank you, sir." Bruce got off the phone and immediately placed a secure call to Jason Summers.

"Jason?"

"Hey, Bruce."

"Did you get a chance to talk with Aaron?"

"Yep. I was actually in his office when you called in."

Bruce could see Norm waving to him. "Jason, do you mind holding for a second?"

"No. Go ahead."

Bruce cupped his hand around the mouthpiece and looked inquiringly at Norm.

"Things are moving fast. The three bad guys have left the truck and are heading in Logan's direction. The good news is they're bunched together, so Reaper One thinks one shot will take out all three without damaging the truck.

"All right. Let me throw out something that's been bugging me before we move forward," Bruce said. "What if these guys are ISIS? What if they're the people Logan's supposed to be meeting?" He shifted uncomfortably in his seat.

"If they are, that was a pretty shitty welcoming

261

committee," Norm said. "I don't think so. The guy on the back of the bike was firing away when Logan hit him."

"We have no way of really knowing," Jason interjected. "It could have been ISIS. We don't know for sure where Azar was planning to do the handoff. If the guys on the bike were ISIS, it's unlikely they were part of the handoff team. The other possibility is Kurdish militia. The Syrian Democratic Forces control a lot of this area."

"Aren't we providing them military support?" Bruce asked.

"Look," Norm said. "We don't have time to screw around. These guys are closing in on Logan, and they don't look like friendlies. "

"Go," Jason said. "Get it done."

"Reaper One, that's a go," Bruce said. "Take them out."

"Reaper One. Roger that. We've had continuous eyes on. Three males. All armed with rifles. Moving in stealth mode towards the crashed vehicle." The pilot requested final verification from the sensor, and a safety observer from ground control confirmed what they were seeing.

When the pilot initiated the firing sequence, the Hellfire Romeo's single stage solid propellant Thiokol TX-657 solid-fuel rocket motor ignited, delivering ten Gs of initial thrust. As it sped away from Reaper 1, reaching a velocity approaching 900 mph, all eyes were on the three figures on the ground, less than 200 feet from Logan's position. Suddenly there was a burst of light in the night sky, and a second later the three men were vaporized.

Logan's phone line was open throughout the bombing sequence, and the others could hear the impact when the Hellfire struck, followed by the noise of debris raining down for what seemed like an eternity. And then it was silent.

"Nice shot," Logan said. "I've got to get moving. I don't know if these guys have any backup in the area. And driving this pickup truck may be about as good as putting a bullseye on our backs. I need to get Azar some medical attention."

While Logan was talking, Norm was scouring the

internet. "There's a hospital in Al Hasakah—the National Hospital. If you have to leave her there, the closest Canadian consular office is in Beirut."

"All right. Thanks," Logan said. As soon as I know more, I'll be in touch."

As Logan was about to sign off, Reaper One came back on the line. "This is Reaper One. Just to let you know, we've done some reconnaissance around your location, and it looks pretty quiet. We're going to break off for now. Good luck and Godspeed."

"Thanks, guys. That was an awesome job." Logan rang off and pocketed his cell phone. Out of the corner of his eye, he detected a slight movement ten feet to his left. He looked up. Azar Ghabel had risen to a sitting position. In her hands was a Glock pistol, and it was pointed squarely at him.

Chapter 37

Logan wasn't used to being on the wrong end of a fire-arm. He couldn't be sure, but he was confident Azar didn't overhear his conversation with the base and Reaper1. If she did, it was game over.

"Who were you just talking to?" Azar asked, steadying the gun with both hands.

"I was trying to find out if there's a hospital in Al Hasakah. I was going to take you there. You need to see a doctor." He stood up and moved towards her.

"Stop." Azar kept the pistol trained on him as she put one hand to her head, gingerly touching the side of her face. "I can't remember what happened. I remember seeing the motorcycle and then..." She gestured vaguely with the gun.

"We were trying to get away from the roadblock. We got turned around and were heading back towards Al Hasakah when the motorcycle came back after us. There was a shooter, so I rammed him with the car. We lost control and crashed. We both blacked out when the vehicle rolled, and you were thrown about thirty feet from here. When I came to, I could hear the men in the truck coming this way. I was getting ready for them.

"I got us over here off the road and was getting set up when I heard a loud explosion. Must have been an IED. I was just going to go over to see what happened. I haven't heard anything, so I doubt if anyone survived it." He held his arms out in a plaintive gesture.

It was a long shot. Hopefully, Azar was woozy enough to believe his version of events. If any missile fragments were lying around, he'd have some explaining to do. And besides that, there was the minor problem of making any sense out of why in the hell there would be an IED planted out here in the middle of the desert. Azar must have been reading his mind.

"What makes you think it was an IED?" she asked.

"What else could it be? There was a lot of fighting in this area in the last few years," he said. "Kurdish Militia, Syrian army, ISIS, Syrian Democratic Forces. I can't say for sure, but I'd bet money this area was contested and someone, probably SDF, buried the IEDs. They just never got around to cleaning up when they pulled up stakes."

Azar continued to search his face, processing what he'd said. Finally, she let the gun drop. "I'm sorry, Tim."

Inwardly, he heaved a sigh of relief. That was touch and go. Maybe they'd be able to salvage something out of this fiasco after all.

"Can you walk?" he asked.

She tried to stand and gasped in pain, sinking back down to the ground. "I'm not sure what's going on," she said. "Something's wrong with my knee."

"We need to get you out of here," Logan said. "Before someone comes looking for us. We don't know if these guys were operating on their own or were part of a larger group. Let's go back to Al Hasakah and see if we can find a doctor to examine you."

Azar didn't protest. She shifted painfully. Logan bent down to prop her against the rock outcrop. After she was comfortable, he walked towards the crash site. "I'll just be a minute," he called over his shoulder. "I want to see what's left of our 'friends' and bring the truck up if it's still there. We need to get back on the pavement. If there was one IED out here, there could be others."

As he walked towards the truck, he suddenly realized there was a full moon. The sky was cloudless, lighting the desert up for miles around. He could see the vehicle parked on the road about two hundred feet from his position.

Logan gingerly picked his way around a rock outcrop, searching for any signs of disturbance in the desert sand, where an IED might be concealed. He already knew the men from the attack were all dead, thanks to Reaper 1's after-action report, but he made a pretense of searching around the impact zone for Azar's sake.

When he got to the truck, he was relieved to see the keys in the ignition. He could hotwire it if necessary, but having the keys there made life simpler. He started the engine and drove up to a point opposite where Azar sat. He opened the passenger-side door and walked back to where she was waiting.

"Tell me if this hurts," he said. He scooped her up off the ground. She wound her arms around his neck, leaning her head against his chest, gasping as he hoisted her in his arms. He could sense she was gritting her teeth in pain, but she was too much of a pro to complain. Once she was settled on the front passenger seat, he closed the door. He searched her face, feeling sympathetic despite her earlier outburst. She leaned her head against the window, beads of sweat glistening off her forehead, and closed her eyes.

Logan stepped over to the wrecked Kia and rummaged around until he found their bags. They were stowed in the trunk and had somehow survived the crash. The motorcycle and two dead bodies lay 50 feet away. Logan was concerned about them. They posed a risk to their safety because they could be linked to the rental car, which was too battered to be moved. He'd have to carry them out of there.

He struggled to hoist the motorcycle onto the truck bed. When it was entirely inside, he closed the tailgate. Then he dragged the two bodies, one-by-one, over to the rear passenger-side door of the truck and jammed them inside onto the floor. Then he covered them with a frayed drop cloth lying on the back seat.

Azar roused herself to ask what he was doing. He explained his thinking about the bike and the bodies, and she nodded in agreement. "We'll have to be careful in Al Hasakah," she said. If anyone makes the connection between us and the truck, we'll have a hard time explaining these two dead bodies."

"Right. We should try to find someplace to dump them

first. Let's keep an eye out on the way into town."

Logan picked up their bags and tossed them into the back. It took them 20 minutes to get back to Al Hasakah. The National Hospital was located at Number 7 Qamishli. Azar called the emergency room while they were en route and was told there was a resident on duty who could see her.

Logan found the drab three-story hospital, split system AC units protruding from the exterior walls, with little trouble. The front of the building was too well-lit for him to park the truck. Although there were hardly any pedestrians on the street at this hour, he couldn't take the chance someone would spot them getting out of the vehicle, or, God forbid, discover the bodies on the floor.

Driving to the rear of the property, he came upon a narrow alley. It was dark, and in the shadows, he spotted a construction dumpster parked next to a corrugated gate leading into the back of the hospital. Getting out of the truck, Logan walked over to the trash container and lifted the lid. Although the alley was dimly lit, he could tell there was adequate space to conceal the two corpses. Moving quickly, Logan dragged them out of the back seat and heaved them into the dumpster, arranging the tarp over them to provide some concealment. He closed the lid and breathed a sigh of relief. One less thing to worry about.

Logan then drove down the alley and turned on the next side street, paralleling the hospital. He pulled over to the curb and parked. He carried Azar into the emergency room and set her down in a chair.

A nurse came over and spoke to them in Arabic. Azar grimaced as she sat up and answered her questions. The RN made a note on the clipboard she was carrying and told them to wait. There were two other people ahead of them, a whimpering child whose bloody foot was bandaged with rags and an old woman grousing at a young man accompanying her. She stamped a scarred cane on the cement floor repeatedly to emphasize a point she was making.

"I'm going to find someplace to get rid of the truck,"

267

Logan whispered. "The sooner we distance ourselves from it, the better off we'll be. We'll talk when I get back; see if we can figure out what we're going to do."

Assuming he could ditch the truck without being seen, the only thing left to explain was the wrecked rental car in the desert. Logan had been thinking about what they could say if questioned. Maybe something close to the truth.

They were on assignment to do a story about the war. While driving south of Al Hasakah, a truck forced them off the road, and they crashed. The driver continued on, leaving them abandoned in the desert. Hours later, a good Samaritan picked them up and dropped them off at the hospital.

Logan rehearsed the story in his mind until he was comfortable with it. It was believable. The rental car might be salvageable, although the insurance company would probably write it off. As long as the authorities didn't investigate the crash site too thoroughly, it might just work.

Logan left the bags with Azar and drove the pickup in a circuitous route. At one point he passed through a darkened neighborhood where he dumped the motorcycle after removing its license plate. With that out of the way he proceeded to the Al Meridian neighborhood. There he left the truck parked in front of an old bathhouse oozing bathwater onto the street. It was after 10:00 p.m., and there was no one on the road.

He walked for 30 minutes without seeing anyone, passing a mosque, a bank and then a supermarket before he spotted a taxi cruising. The driver didn't speak English, and Logan's limited Arabic from his navy SEAL days was rusty. He thrust the address of the National Hospital Azar had written out in Arabic at the driver. He nodded his understanding, and they drove in silence for several minutes.

* * *

It was an hour before the doctor examined Azar. While she was waiting, despite her throbbing head, she sent a text message to her bosses in Tehran. She explained the events of the last several hours, intimating the handoff to ISIS would likely have to be to be postponed for a day or more. She didn't elaborate on her medical situation, explaining she was being examined at the National Hospital in Al Hasakah.

Despite downplaying her situation, the duty officer in Tehran must have felt her condition was dire enough to warrant awakening Unit 400 chief, Colonel Samadi. His text to her 30 minutes later expressed alarm and concern. He requested she let him know immediately if her condition worsened.

Azar then placed a call to her ISIS contact, known to her only as Rifat.

"We were ambushed outside of Al Hasakah. Right now, I'm being evaluated at the National Hospital there. I doubt we'll be able to meet you tonight. Can you come here?"

"That's not possible. Security in Al Hasakah is too dangerous for us right now. It's better to meet in Ash Shaddadi when you can.

"Ever since the Americans began providing air support to the Syrian defense forces, we've suffered grave losses," Rifat said. "I was in Al Hasakah in 2015 when the people's and women's protection units announced their alliance. Kurdish bastards," he spat out.

"How far are you from here?" Azar asked.

"Maybe an hour, give or take," Rifat said.

"I'll call you tomorrow," Azar promised. "By then I should have a better idea of my condition and if it'll be possible to travel."

"*Insha'Allah,*" Rifat said.

Moments later, a harried doctor, accompanied by the nurse she had spoken with earlier, came into the reception area. They transferred Azar to a wheelchair and rolled her down a dimly lit corridor into an austere examination room.

"You may call me Doctor Evana," she said. "And this is Roshan." She gestured towards the RN.

"*Evana.* God is gracious," Azar said.

With the nurse taking notes, Doctor Evana questioned

Azar about the accident and asked her to describe her symptoms.

Azar described her condition as best she could. "I have a pounding headache, and my whole body hurts, especially my right leg. I'm finding it difficult to walk."

The nurse gave her a hospital gown and asked if she needed any help changing out of her clothes.

"No, I think I can manage."

After Doctor Evana was through with her examination, she told Azar to get dressed.

"You were fortunate from what you told me," she said, coming back into the room. "You said you were using your seatbelt, but we often see cases where the seatbelt fails. Your face is bruising because of the airbag, and other ejection injuries you sustained when you were thrown from the car."

"Often, these accidents result in severe injuries or death. You appear to have landed in a relatively soft area, and you avoided being crushed by the vehicle as it rolled over. I believe you have torn ligaments in your right knee—ACL, and you have a concussion."

"I'm traveling. What do you recommend I do?"

"We need to stabilize the knee. Unfortunately, with our situation here, even the most basic medical supplies are scarce. I don't have any knee braces. I would recommend you get medical attention in Turkey. Sanliurfa is the nearest airport from here. Where's home?"

"Canada," Azar said.

"Are you traveling by yourself?" the doctor asked.

"No. I'm with a colleague. We're on assignment. I'm a photographer."

"My greatest concern right now is the concussion. I strongly recommend you get a CT scan as soon as possible. We don't have the equipment here."

"Why are you recommending that?"

"Your headache may be an indication of internal bleeding or swelling of the brain. The cognitive and neurological exam I just did leads me to believe your injury isn't severe. Still, I want to keep you under observation for twenty-hours

hours to make sure there's no swelling.

"We'll give you some acetaminophen for your head-ache, but right now the most important thing is rest. Both physical and mental. Your brain has received a shock, and the best thing you can do for it is to rest."

"Is it safe for me to travel?" Azar was concerned about making the meeting with ISIS. At the end of the day, Tim had proven himself to be resourceful, and he could prob-ably make the trip to Ash Shaddadi without her.

"Let's see how you're feeling tomorrow," Doctor Evana said. "Rest is the best thing for now."

Chapter 38

Rifat placed his cell phone in airplane mode, turned it off, and pulled out the battery. He learned long ago, while fighting with Al Qaeda in Iraq, to share his contact information with only a select number of trusted associates, and when possible, to shut his phone down as he just had. This was to prevent the Americans from tracking him and blowing him to smithereens when he was least expecting it. Over the years, many of his comrades suffered this fate because they were careless or were betrayed by someone from within their inner circle.

Rifat was standing in the shadows of a building reduced to rubble on the outskirts of Ash Shaddadi. He hitched up his pants, and following the road, walked a half-mile to where his battered two-door sedan was parked. It was getting late, and he needed to report back to his boss.

He had lived in Iraq in the late nineties and early 2000s combating the Americans and Shiite militias backed by Teheran. In 2004, he was swept up in a raid and imprisoned at Camp Bucca, near Umm Qasr, along with 26,000 other detainees.

Rifat spent 11 months there, living in Compound 6 of the vast complex, shrouded in concertina wire, with around a thousand other detainees. Concertina wire could shred a man to pieces, so his fellow inmates rarely attempted to escape. Instead, they spent their time radicalizing new prisoners, inculcating them in the virtues of Sharia law, and instructing them in the tools of the modern-day terrorist—bomb making, weapons training, and military tactics. He also learned to speak English from a Pakistani rug merchant detained during a business trip to Iraq on money laundering charges.

But by far, the most relevant contact he made during his incarceration was a fellow captive by the name of Abu Bakr Al Baghdadi, the current leader of ISIS. He and Baghdadi were incarcerted at roughly the same time and shared a tent in Compound 6. He became a trusted lieutenant to the Caliph, nowadays functioning as the commander of Al Baghdadi's security detail.

It was in this capacity Rifat was planning to meet the new recruit his Qods Force contacts were bringing to him. Not that he trusted the Iranians. They were Shias after all and had fought a decade-long war with Iraq. But Al Baghdadi was intrigued by the recruit's pedigree. It wasn't every day ISIS had the opportunity to welcome a navy SEAL into its ranks.

Rifat knew something about the SEALS from his reading. They were an elite military force. He had already thought of several ways he might put Tim Hudson to work. Assigning him to Al Baghdadi's security detail, sending him back to the U.S. to set up an ISIS cell, and training new recruits in Syria. He would have to get additional details about his military and civilian work experience and evaluate him firsthand before proposing anything specific.

He reached his dusty, two-door sedan, and after peering under the hood and giving a cursory look underneath the vehicle, he started the car and pulled onto the road.

The recent emphasis on recruiting foreign fighters is a mixed blessing, he thought, as he skirted a large crater in the road. Many of them were coming in through Europe, and since Turkey shared a 500-mile border with Syria, it provided many inconspicuous entry points of entry. In the last month alone, eight new recruits had made the trek from Turkey. Typically, they were picked up in Istanbul or some other Turkish city and driven to the Syrian border, where they were told to find their way across on their own.

One of his associates picked them up on the Syrian side and drove them to a safe site where they were required to fill out paperwork and undergo a personal interview. Soon after that, they were transferred to a training base where they could spend up to three months. The first part of their training was ideological in nature, with in-depth lessons in Sharia law. When they were ready, the volunteers received military training, not unlike what ISIS provided new recruits when he and Al Baghdadi were interred at Camp Bucca.

There were probably fewer than a hundred American jihadists who had made the dangerous journey to Syria to join the ISIS cause. Most of them were American Muslims; it was rare to find a non-Muslim committed to taking up the sword for ISIS.

"If only they were all like Abshir Suleman," Rifat grunted. A Somali-American, Suléman earned his stripes fighting with the jihadist fundamentalist group, al-Shaabab in Mogadishu before fleeing in 2011 because he was targeted for assassination by government forces. Suléman's exploits on the battlefield were legend, and Al Baghdadi promoted him to command *Jaysh al-Khalifa*, the Caliph army, an elite special forces unit made up entirely of foreign fighters respected for their military prowess.

Rifat leaned on one cheek and let loose a thunderous fart. He sighed in relief and wound down the window as the foul odor filled the car. He was troubled by indigestion, and passing gas was a rare relief.

His destination tonight was a compound 15 miles south of central Ash Shaddadi. It was not unusual for Al Baghdadi and his inner circle to change locales frequently. There were informants, even traitors among themselves, eager to collect the reward offered by the Americans for the Caliph's head. Sometimes they were just hours ahead of the fire that rained down from the sky, the dreaded Hellfire missiles that struck without warning.

His mind turned back to the American recruit. *What is his name? Hudson. Tim Hudson.* Al Baghdadi would be displeased about the delay in his arrival. *What were the Iranians thinking? Entrusting such a critical mission to a woman.* He would convey his displeasure to the Qods Force the next time he met his contact.

Moments later, he was approaching the walled compound. He flashed his headlights twice, and after a brief pause, the gate opened, allowing him to pass through. Two guards scrutinized him as he entered, peering into the dim interior of his car and nodding as they recognized him.

This complex was one of many recently liberated by ISIS, after having lost control of the area to the Kurds during the previous year's offensive by the SDF and the American-led coalition. There were over a hundred airstrikes in one month alone, allowing the SDF to reclaim over three hundred villages formerly under ISIS control. This see-sawing back and forth was concerning. With the Americans and Russians in the fight, Rifat sensed ISIS was back on its heels. It would take a miracle to turn their circumstances around.

There were several other vehicles parked in the courtyard. A cluster of a dozen beehive mud huts, some for dwelling and others for storage, made up their quarters. These huts, made of mud bricks stacked in a huge circle, tapered off in a conical shape, leaving an air vent at the very top. They had no windows, but there was a door for privacy. Mud and straw, plastered over the inside and out, had hardened from the scorching desert sun.

Their living space wasn't lavish by any stretch of the imagination, but these abodes had been keeping desert dwellers cool in a part of the world where it was not uncommon to see summer temperatures rise to 140 degrees Fahrenheit.

Rifat grunted as he clambered out of the car. One of Al Baghdadi's personal bodyguards emerged from the shadows, looking quizzically around. It was Simon, a Syrian fighter formerly from Aleppo.

"Where's the American?" he asked.

"His escort was injured in a car crash, and they're at the hospital in Al Hasakah," Rifat replied. "*Insha'Allah*, he will be able to join us tomorrow."

"How is he?" Rifat asked, inclining his head towards the door.

"He's resting," Simon said.

Al Baghdadi was wounded in one of the foreign

airstrikes near Raqqa the year before and was forced to relinquish day-to-day command and control to one of his trusted lieutenants for several months. Even now he tired quickly, leading Rifat to question his ability to keep up the fight.

"Maybe we should wait until tomorrow to brief him on the American," Rifat said. "There's nothing we can do right now."

Simon nodded and returned to his post. Rifat walked to the adjoining hut and ducking his head, entered the darkened room. He waited a moment until his eyes adjusted to the dim light. Several motionless figures were reclining on mattresses on the floor. He found his space and silently stripped down to his underwear. Lying down on the stuffed mattress, he stared at the moonlight coming in through the opening in the roof. The only sound was the shallow breathing of the others. His last thought before surrendering to sleep was what kept him going day in and day out. It was the image of his wife and three-year-old son, blown up in a car bomb attack meant for him two years before. He shuddered involuntarily, falling into a fitful sleep, his drawn-out gasps joining the slumbering chorus around him.

Rifat awakened before dawn to the sound of his comrades rising for *Salat al-fajr*, the pre-dawn prayer ritual recited by circa two billion Muslims around the world. He washed up and headed out to the courtyard where the others were already gathered facing Mecca. Al Baghdadi led them in the five-minute ritual. Afterward, the group broke up to begin their morning tasks.

Today was important. A car bombing was planned at Saint George Cathedral in Al Hasakah. It was Sunday, and the patriarch of the Syriac Orthodox Church was expected to celebrate Mass there later in the morning.

The car bomber, as always, was an aspiring martyr, eager to die for the greater good. He had responded to the call for volunteers during his indoctrination class six months before. Born in Tennessee, and recently accepted into an undergraduate program in engineering at the University of

South Carolina, he was nevertheless, disenchanted with his life in the U.S.

The car he would use was a nondescript four-door sedan of a particular vintage. The trunk had been packed with two thousand pounds of explosive material at a bomb-making facility on the western outskirts of Al Hasakah the night before. It was primed and would be detonated by a triggering device wired into the console. There was a lookout stationed near the cathedral whose job was to confirm the arrival of the patriarch.

Rifat approached Al Baghdadi after prayers and told him about the events of the night before. The Caliph shared Rifat's sentiment that the Iranians were not doing them any favors by assigning women to these critical tasks.

"Is there any reason Hudson can't get here on his own?" Al Baghdadi asked.

"It seems the Qods Force operative was injured in a car crash, and he wants to make sure she is taken care of before he leaves. I spoke with her last night, and the doctors at the National Hospital are conducting some tests. The extent of her injuries is unknown at this time."

"Keep me advised, Rifat. We need this man now."

"Your wish is my command, sir."

Rifat had a small but crucial role to play in today's operation. He would be transporting and providing security for one of their technical people outside of Al Hasakah who would be flying a drone to photograph the attack on Saint George Cathedral.

It was impractical to get physically close enough to film the event on the streets of Al Hasakah. Instead, they would be shooting from a position five miles west of the target area. It was almost too close for comfort, but the technical limitations of the remote controller precluded them being farther away.

There were reports from sympathizers in the city indicating security for the patriarch's visit was tight. Only a year ago a suicide bomber attacked the Syriac Orthodox Church in Qamishli, where the patriarch was commemorating the genocide of 250,000 Assyrians, victims of the Ottoman Turks during World War I. The patriarch survived that attack, but three of his bodyguards died in the blast, and five others were severely wounded.

After a breakfast of Fava bean salad, hummus, olives and pita bread, Rifat went to find Wahid, the Iraqi technician who would pilot the drone. He saw him outside one of the huts, where he was examining his equipment.

"Is that a new drone?" Rifat asked. "It looks tiny."

"Yes. When we fold it up it's no larger than a water bottle," Wahid said.

"I wish we didn't have to be so close to the action," Rifat said. "The security net may extend some distance from the target. We must be vigilant."

"Commercial drones are worse," Wahid said, straightening up. "They're only good up to a couple of miles. At least this one gives us five."

"Well, we better get going," Rifat grunted. "The celebration is supposed to begin at ten a.m. The plan is to initiate the attack after the service has begun. We should be able to kill more of the bastards."

ISIS was a frequent user of technology. It allowed them to extend their reach way beyond the limitations imposed by their reduced numbers and geographic constraints. Today's video would be released all over the internet in time for the evening news cycle.

It was 8:30 when Rifat and Wahid left the compound. Twenty minutes outside of Al Hasakah, he noticed a wrecked vehicle with Turkish plates lying on its side just off the road. That must be the car Hudson was driving, Rifat speculated, craning his neck to look at the mangled wreckage. He would have liked to stop to have a look, but it was getting late, and they needed to get set up for the photoshoot.

Their destination was a farmhouse five miles west of Al Hasakah city center. The owner was an ISIS sympathizer, a Syrian who fervently hated the Assad regime, and yet hated the Kurds almost as much.

It was 9:30, and Rifat left Wahid to set up the drone

while he placed a call to the spotter outside the cathedral. "How's it going there?" he asked.

"Our friend has just arrived," the spotter said. "He's going inside now and has brought many friends with him."

Rifat took that to mean the patriarch was accompanied by a large security contingent. "When you talk to our comrade, please wish him our best." That was the agreed upon code to let the driver of the car know they were set up and ready to film.

Timing was crucial in this operation. The time when the patriarch arrived at the cathedral. The time it would take the driver to reach the target. The time when Wahid should begin flying the drone. The time for the drone to fly to the target area. The time for the drone to fly back to the farm. The time for them to get away from Al Hasakah. Time was everything.

At 9:45, Rifat received confirmation the suicide driver was on his way to the cathedral. They had a description of the car and knew the route he was taking into town.

Wahid launched the drone, climbing to two thousand feet before directing it towards the rendezvous point on the road leading into the city. He spotted the car two miles away from the target area and began descending until the device was flying at an altitude of four hundred feet.

The video camera on this drone had 4K ultra HD technology, meaning they would be getting resolution along the order of 4,000 pixels. Rifat checked his watch. The driver had less than a mile to go before he reached the target. From 400 feet, the image was clear, but he couldn't see inside the vehicle, and he had no idea how the man from Tennessee was feeling about his impending encounter with Allah.

These things had gone wrong in the past. The bomb was only as good as the bomb maker, and ISIS had some very talented ones working for them. The human being driving the vehicle was the real wild card, despite having volunteered and undergone intensive indoctrination. Sometimes they could not will themselves to pull the trigger. The human instinct for survival was too powerful.

The vehicle was picking up speed as it navigated towards the city center. Rifat could make out the shape of the cathedral in the distance, its white dome prominent above the brown facade of the main church. There was an iron fence around the place of worship, but the main gate was still open as worshipers made their way inside.

Rifat felt his pulse quicken as he watched the suicide bomber speeding towards his mission. He was less than a hundred feet away when a delivery vehicle pulled out in front of him. The driver swerved to avoid crashing into the truck then steadied the car, accelerating towards his target.

At the appointed time, he plowed into the gate, sending several bystanders flying. Part of the iron gate became wedged under the chassis, and there was a moment of churning before the car suddenly exploded, sending debris and plumes of black smoke up into the air. There was a secondary explosion as the gas tank in the vehicle caught fire and ripped apart.

The drone continued to film the destruction. Maimed bodies were scattered like chaff around the entrance of the cathedral, spilling into the street. Pedestrians could be seen fleeing the scene, and a melee ensued as drivers fought to navigate their vehicles away from the smoldering ruins of the car.

"How much time do you have left?" Rifat asked.

"Maybe fifteen minutes. I'm bringing it in," Wahid said.

Rifat nodded his agreement. "The sooner, the better."

Chapter 39

Logan slipped back into the National Hospital through the emergency room entrance. The same nurse on duty when they first came in was manning the admissions desk. She gave him a quizzical look but then recognized him from earlier in the evening.

Speaking in halting English, she directed him to Azar's room. "Your friend…room two twenty-five," she said.

Logan took the stairs to the second floor and checked in at the nurse's station. The person on duty shrugged her shoulders when he asked for Azar by name. He offered her the piece of paper with the room number written on it, and she pointed down the hall with her chin.

As he walked towards room 225, he was struck by the severe conditions surrounding him. There were several blown out windows along the corridor, jagged remnants of glass clinging to the frames. What was left was covered in micro-thin layers of adhesive vinyl to protect the windows from shattering on impact.

Wash buckets and mops lay abandoned in a corner, the sour smell moldering on the filthy tile floor. A neglected gurney, listing to one side, awaited its next hapless occupant. He gagged as he strode past a plastic bench where an old woman with an oozing head wound stared vacantly ahead.

Outside of room 225, he paused and then knocked. There was no answer. He opened the door and stepped inside. The conditions inside the room were no better than the corridor outside. Sandbags were stacked irregularly in a window frame, and crumpled blinds hung listlessly from a valance. A chair was overturned near the bed and debris littered the floor. Several electrical outlets and plugs sprouted from one wall but appeared to serve no useful purpose. A call button dangled from the wall, touching the floor.

Azar was lying in bed, a dirty gray sheet pulled up to her chest. Her clothes were folded in a pile by her feet, and she was wearing a frayed hospital gown. Her hair was disheveled, and she had not been bathed. Logan walked over to the side of the bed and stared down at her. Her breathing was slow and labored. Her eyes fluttered, as though she was instinctively aware of his presence, but she rolled onto her left side and continued to sleep.

Logan set the chair upright and placed it close to the bed. The luminous dial on his watch said 12:30. It was after midnight; he was doubtful he could do anything before morning. He was eager to find out what the doctors told Azar. Fatigue suddenly enveloped him; he was having trouble keeping his eyes open. He decided to sit with her for a while before deciding where to spend the night. He fell asleep to the cadence of Azar's soft moaning.

It was the sound of morning asserting itself that woke him. Voices wafting up from the street, the clatter of traffic beginning to move, and the drone of an aircraft flying overhead.

He looked at Azar and saw she was awake. She was watching him with a curious expression on her face. He broke the silence first.

"How do you feel?" he asked.

"I've been better," she grimaced, putting her hand up to her head.

"How'd it go last night?" she asked.

"I think we'll be all right," he said. "I ditched the motorcycle in a neighborhood and left the truck near a bathhouse on the other side of town. It'll be hard for anyone to tie them to us."

"I hope so," she said.

"What did the doctor tell you?" he asked.

"She wanted to keep me overnight, to make sure there's no swelling in the brain. I have a concussion, and it seems the ACL in my right knee is torn. I need a brace, but they don't have much in the way of medical supplies here."

"Did they give you something for your head?" he asked.

"Tylenol. It feels a little better, but I'm supposed to rest."

"What do you want to do?" he asked.

She considered his question before answering. "I don't think I'm going to be much use to you as I am," she said with a self-deprecating wince. "I spoke with my contact, Rifat, while you were out, and told him we wouldn't be able to make our meeting last night. He was disappointed but seemed to understand.

"He told me it wasn't advisable for him to come to Al Hasakah to meet you. It's too dangerous for his people to be seen here now. It's better for you to meet him closer to Ash Shaddadi. He said to call him after twelve."

"What about you? Are you going to stay here?"

"I'll find out from Doctor Evana today if it's safe to travel."

"You can't drive," he said.

"That's true." She tried to prop herself up in bed, wincing from the exertion.

"Do you want some help?" Logan asked.

She nodded. He lifted her into a sitting position and adjusted the pillows.

"There, is that better?"

"A little."

"Your best bet is to find a car service to drive you to Sanliurfa. At least once you're back in Turkey, you'll be able to get better medical care. If you can get back to Istanbul, there's probably a Canadian consulate. They'll be able to help you.

"Are you hungry? They must be serving something."

As if on cue, an attendant came into the room with a wash basin and towel. She was going to give Azar a sponge bath first and then bring her breakfast.

"I'm going to find a bathhouse and then get something to eat," Logan said. I should be back before ten."

Logan found a public bathhouse, *a hammam*, two blocks

from the hospital. A bath attendant gave him a striped towel and showed him where he could undress. After he stowed his clothes in a locker, the man then led him to the hot room, where he sat sweltering for 15 minutes.

When he felt he was about to pass out, a masseuse led him to a central platform where he soaked Logan with warm soapy water and followed with a massage. Afterward, they moved to one of several large water basins, where the attendant vigorously scrubbed him down with an exfoliating glove.

The procedure concluded with a final soapy bath, followed by a dousing with cold water. When he was finished, Logan dried off and donned a fresh striped towel, lounging with the locals in any airy room furnished with benches draped in carpets. Piped in music provided a restful ambiance, and everyone seemed to be enjoying the respite from the chaos outside.

Logan dressed and asked one of the attendants if there was any place nearby to grab a bite to eat. His stomach growled, and he realized he was famished. His last meal was lunch with Azar on the Bosphorus. It was only yesterday, but so much had happened since then that it seemed a lot longer.

He walked for a couple of blocks and found the restaurant specializing in local cuisine the attendant had recommended. Surprisingly there was an English language menu, and he decided to order a traditional Syrian breakfast. Ten minutes later, he was tucking into fresh pita bread, hummus, stuffed eggplant, olives, and pastries. Logan was feeling decadent after his bath and meal, but he knew there was unlikely to be much in the way of creature comforts in the weeks ahead.

A Syrian family was eating a late breakfast at the table next to his, and the young boy squirming to get away from his mother reminded him of Cooper. He was howling because she wouldn't allow him to run around the other tables. The father admonished him gently, and the youngster sat sulking, pushing a small plastic truck back and forth on the table in front of him.

Maybe he is one of the lucky ones, Logan mused, as he paid his bill and left the restaurant. So many children were suffering because of this war, which began in 2011 when anti-regime activists opposed to Syrian President Bashar Al-Assad started their peaceful uprising. And there was no end in sight. Logan stepped off the sidewalk to make way for a blind man and his wife, edging their way down the street.

More than 500,000 people had died in the civil war's horrific fighting, and of course, ISIS was there because power abhors a vacuum. Other proxies—the Russians, the U.S., the Iranians—were there as well, sometimes uncertain who they should be supporting, or what outcome they should be seeking. At a minimum, the slaughter of innocent civilians should end. What possible future was there for the child in the restaurant?

As he turned into the entrance to the hospital, he heard a loud explosion, followed momentarily by a secondary explosion. Racing back out to the street, he saw a black plume of smoke billowing skyward several blocks from where he stood. He knew from his navy SEAL training, the blast radius for a 2,000-pound bomb was on the order of 400 yards. His gut told him it was a car bomb, but he didn't know for sure.

Moments later, the wailing screech of alarms rent the air as emergency vehicles, lights glaring, raced in the direction of the blast. Logan was not inclined to investigate. He knew a favorite terrorist tactic was to stage a second bomber near the scene and when curious bystanders and emergency responders showed up, the terrorist was there to welcome them with more death and destruction.

He went back into the hospital and up to Azar's room. This time she answered his knock.

"Come in." Azar was resting in bed. Her color was better, and she seemed alert.

"What was that?" she asked.

"Car bomb, I think," he said. "Can't say for sure, but it sounded like a big one. The nurse may know something later on, especially if they bring any of the victims in here. In all likelihood, they'll be doing triage.

"You feeling any better?" he asked.

"Some. I didn't eat much, but it felt good to get cleaned up. Doctor Elena came by earlier. She said it would be all right for me to travel this afternoon. They found someone to drive me to Sanliurfa. There's a flight to Istanbul at 4:30. I called my friend Yasmin, and she's taking care of the travel arrangements." She grimaced as she shifted positions in bed.

"Are you sure you'll be all right?" Logan asked. If you want, I can go with you to make sure you don't have any issues. I can always come back here on my own."

Azar contemplated him from heavy-lidded eyes. She suddenly seemed tired. *Maybe all the talking is wearing her out,* Logan thought.

"No, I should be all right," she said. "They made sure the car service had a comfortable vehicle. And Yasmin is going to pick up a brace for me, so I can move around a little bit. I may take a few days to rest in Istanbul. Maybe go to the hospital there and see if they think it's safe to make the trip back to Toronto."

They had been sitting in silence when Azar's cell phone rang. She cupped her hand over the mouthpiece. "It's Rifat," she said.

Logan listened as she spoke to her ISIS contact with practiced ease. He wondered where she had picked up her Arabic language. From Zahir's studies, he knew Persian and Arabic have almost nothing in common. Arabic was a Semitic language while Persian was Indo-European. Persian was closer to English than it was to Arabic.

Moments later she hung up. "It's set," she said. "Rifat will meet you a mile or two south of where we left our car." She proceeded to give him a description of Rifat's vehicle. "He'll be expecting to see you around four p.m."

"Good. That reminds me. What are we going to do about the car?"

"I took care of it already. I gave Europcar a call and

explained what happened. My friend Yasmin will drop the keys off at the rental office. They'll have a local contact here take a look to see if it's worth shipping back to Turkey. I think they'll probably just write it off and bill the insurance."

She fell silent. The rhythmic cadence of her breathing told him she was asleep. He was tempted to steal her cell phone to see if there was any actionable intelligence on it. But he didn't want to take the chance she would become suspicious of him when she found it missing. His meeting with ISIS was the most important thing right now.

Logan sat with her until 11:00 and then tiptoed out of the room. Before closing the door, he took one last look at her. Who knew if their paths would cross again? Despite the fact he detested the Qods Force and everything they stood for, he and she had been through a lot together. He was under no illusion though. She was the enemy. But at this moment, he bore her no ill will.

Chapter 40

Logan was riding south on the road to Ash Shaddadi. His ostensible purpose for being there was to survey the damage to the rental car. His driver was a twenty-something engineering graduate from Georgia Tech named Mahmood, who planned to put his degree to work in Damascus a year before the outbreak of the civil war. But his family was from Al Hasakah, and he moved in with his parents a year after hostilities broke out in Syria because they refused to move and leave the family business behind. There weren't any engineering jobs in his hometown, so he was driving a taxi to earn his keep.

"What was that explosion this morning?" Logan asked as he paid the fare.

"A car bomb. Probably ISIS. They were targeting the patriarch from the Orthodox church who was celebrating services at St. George's. The driver didn't get close enough to kill the patriarch, but there was damage, lots of damage. Initial reports said twenty-two people died and maybe seventy-five were injured. The numbers are bound to go higher."

"I'm sorry," Logan said. "I'm meeting a guy from the car company out here, and I don't want to hold you up. I'll get a ride back to Al Hasakah with him."

"Good luck with that," he said, jutting his chin in the direction of the car. He shrugged his shoulders and headed back into town.

Logan looked in the direction Mahmood indicated. There wasn't much left of the car except for the frame. It was picked clean. As he got closer, he could see the interior was stripped of seats and gauges. The tires were gone. Side mirrors and the rear bumper were missing. The front bumper was so severely damaged in the collision it wasn't worth stealing. Looking under the hood, he wasn't surprised to see the thieves had made off with the engine and transmission too. "Azar's going to have a tough time explaining this to the rental company," he said out loud.

When he was finished examining the car, he walked a couple of hundred feet over to the impact zone from the Hellfire missile. To the practiced eye, the impact crater was reasonably easy to read. The earth was discolored and disturbed. Out here in the desert, the blast radius would have been around 400 yards since there was nothing to absorb the impact. There was a discernable stench of burned flesh in the area. And looking closely, he spotted bone fragments here and there.

A shadow passed over him. Peering up, he shaded his eyes and could just make out a kettle of vultures circling high in the sky above. He must have disturbed their feeding. Better to keep moving south towards Ash Shaddadi and let them finish their grisly banquet.

It was a little before four when he continued his journey south on the desert road. He was ten minutes into his walk when his cell phone vibrated. Pulling it out of his front pocket, he squinted to read the caller ID in the bright sunlight. It wasn't a number he recognized, and he was tempted let it go, but with everything going on, he figured it would be wise to pick up.

His heart stopped when he heard the voice on the other line. It was Zahir.

"Is this Tim?" she asked.

His pulse quickened, and he was tempted to disconnect. *How the hell did she get this number?* He swallowed hard before taking her call.

"Yes."

What followed could be suicide. Zahir knew when he was operating in alias, he couldn't link back to his real-life persona. Anyone listening in would be able to connect the two personalities and figure him for a spy. The fact he didn't recognize the phone number was a good sign. Maybe she was calling from a public phone that couldn't be traced back to her personally. She knew the drill.

"It's been a long time since we talked," she said. "I just wanted to let you know, everyone here misses you."

"Me too. I've been on the road. Maybe when I get back, we can get together."

"Yes. I'd like that. Why don't you stay with us? When do you think you'll be in town?"

"I'm not sure," he said. "I just got here, and there's a lot of work to do." He wanted to say more—how much he missed her and Cooper, how much he loved them both, but there was too much at risk.

"I hope to see you soon," she said. And then, so softly Logan barely heard it she whispered, "I love you."

The phone went dead. Standing there in the Syrian desert, trying to comprehend what just happened, Logan felt an intense burst of yearning. It was as though someone just ripped a hole in his heart. Maybe there was hope for them after all. He heaved an exasperated sigh and put the phone back into his pocket.

He began walking south again towards Ash Shaddadi. The temperature was hot, but not unbearable. This area, traditionally known as Al-Jazira, and in the history books as Mesopotamia, referred to the island formed between the Tigris and Euphrates rivers. The region had a complicated history with Assyrian Christians and Kurds vying for decades for a place to call home.

Logan paused to take a sip of water. Wiping his brow, he saw sunlight reflecting off of a vehicle coming from the direction of Ash Shaddadi. Straining his eyes, he made out the shape of a car racing north towards him. *Could this be Rifat, my ISIS contact?* He continued walking south in anticipation.

* * *

Norm Stoddard and Bruce Wellington were packing their bags. Logan's brush with death was a sharp reminder of just how far out on the pointy end of the spear their buddy was. Of course, they both knew this going in, but the attack in the desert made them reconsider their stand-off support to him.

It was pure serendipity the air force was flying in the skies over northeastern Syria when Logan and Azar ran afoul of the hit team in the desert. If the response time for Reaper 1 to engage the targets had been even minutes longer, there was a good chance Logan and Azar would either be dead or captured.

In their current situation, Bruce and Norm had everything you could want for a behind-the-lines support element. But Logan needed somebody closer to the front line if things went south again. The problem was, the way wars are fought today, there was no front line. That was why they were on the move.

When they broached the idea with the DDO's office and chief/CTC, both immediately lent their support for the change of plans. The Office of Military Affairs worked out the approvals with DoD, and in 24 hours, Bruce and Norm had their orders.

They caught a ride over to the Flight Ops Center at the old Saddam Air Base, where they were about to catch a hop to Ash Shaddadi in the southern part of Al Hasakah Governorate. Q-West in Mosul was light duty compared to where they were headed, a small forward operating base (FOB) manned by special ops personnel training Kurdish opposition infantry.

They walked out to the flight line where the crew chief was just beginning his pre-flight safety briefing. Norm and Bruce were wearing combat fatigues but had no rank insignia, indicating they were not active duty military.

The crew chief looked them up and down with an unflinching stare. "You men ever been in one of these birds before?" he asked, jerking his thumb at the UH-60A Blackhawk helicopter.

"A couple of times," Norm answered.

The crew chief shook his head and muttered something

about civilians under his breath. Norm and Bruce looked at each other and shrugged. If this army puke had a hard-on for civilians, that was his problem. They were supposed to be flying under the radar, so they let his comment pass. Besides, navy SEALS weren't in the business of blowing their own horns.

They boarded the helicopter and found their seats. Almost immediately the twin GE turboshaft engines began to whine, and they were cleared for liftoff. This baby was carrying an extra fuel tank, giving it a range of 1,200 nautical miles, so they'd be flying directly to their destination.

Norm and Bruce donned full muff comm sets to suppress the noise. Aside from the three-man crew, there were six combat-ready assault troops on board. Two, one on each side of the bird, were flying as door gunners. The open doors elevated the ambient noise in the main cabin.

They didn't try to talk in flight. It was impossible to be heard over the incessant *thump, thump, thump* sound of the rotors and the whooshing wind. Both men sat back, looking out over the expanse of desert.

Ten miles out from Ash Shaddadi, their rear rotor blade failed. The pilot put out a Mayday alert and began to initiate procedures for an emergency landing. He cut power to the two engines because without the rear rotor working to counter the torque from the main rotor blades, the Blackhawk would almost certainly spin out of control.

Landing without power was nobody's idea of a picnic, but these pilots practice auto-rotations often enough they can do them in their sleep. Once the rotors disengaged from the engines, the pilot lowered the pitch, selected the right glide path given their rate of descent, and searched for the best place to put down.

The tension in the air was palpable as the wind shrieked through the open doors and the ground rose up to meet them. Just when it seemed they were doomed to crash into the desert floor, the pilot flared the rotor blades while pitching the nose up. They hit the ground with a light bump and rolled forward before coming to rest.

Everyone on board let out a collective sigh of relief. The assault troops clambered out of the helicopter to set up a defensive perimeter around the bird. The pilot established comms with the FOB and explained their situation. Meanwhile, the co-pilot climbed out of the cockpit to take a look at the tail rotor.

The crew chief was walking through the cabin. He stopped in front of Norm and Bruce. "You two don't seem too shook up," he said.

"I told you it wasn't our first rodeo," Norm said.

"Oh yeah? Where else you been?"

"Oh, Yemen, Somalia, Ramadi, Abbottabad. Places like that," Norm said.

The crew chief assumed a different attitude, sizing the two men up. There was a tone of respect in his next question that wasn't present before. "What branch were you in?"

"Navy."

"Navy?"

"Yeah."

The crew chief had a quizzical look on his face. "What unit?"

"Special Operations Command," Bruce said.

The crew chief's face reddened as he realized who he was talking to. "You guys are SEALS?"

Sensing the man's discomfort, Bruce laughed and landed a light punch on his arm. "It's ok, brother. We're all on the same team."

"Between CNN, Congress, spooks, and all the other damn civilians running around here, you never know who you're talking to," the airman said. "I didn't mean nothing," he apologized.

"No offense taken," Norm said. "So, what's the drill, now?" he asked.

"I'll get an update from the chief," he said, heading back to the cockpit.

While they were talking, Bruce and Norm kept an eye outside the bird. They knew the longer they sat on the ground, the less tenable their situation would be. If any locals sympathetic to ISIS saw them go down, it wouldn't take long for the bad guys to show up.

The crew chief was back in five minutes. "There are a couple of maintainers at Ash Shaddadi, but they aren't equipped to do much of anything in the field except inspections and minor repairs.

"The co-pilot thinks it's more than they'll be able to handle. Worse case, the mechanics will put a band-aid on it and fly it back to Q-West for repair."

Fifteen minutes later, the men heard the familiar sound of an incoming helicopter. They shielded their eyes from sand kicked up as it came in for a landing.

The two maintainers piled out with their rapid-deployment toolkits. It took them 30 minutes to figure out that a pitch link in the tail rotor swashplate had malfunctioned, making it impossible for the pilot to change the pitch angle on the tail rotor blades.

They were able to come up with a temporary fix, allowing the flight crew to safely ferry the downed bird back to Q-West. The other men unloaded their gear and transferred it to the bird from FOB Ash Shaddadi. Moments later, the other Blackhawk's engines began to whine, and it started to climb. The pilot held it in a hover at 100 feet and then began to gain altitude before peeling off in the direction of Mosul.

Chapter 41

Logan eyed the approaching car with practiced noncha-lance. Inside though, his stomach was churning, and all pistons were firing. The extensive planning over the last few weeks came down to this moment. This meeting could very well determine the success or failure of his mission—to penetrate ISIS.

He was walking into oncoming traffic on the left-hand side of the road. The nondescript two-door sedan slowed as it approached, and Logan peered through the dusty wind-shield. It appeared ISIS had dispatched a welcoming committee of one. The driver stopped the car, leaned over to the passenger side and wound down the window.

"Are you Hudson?" he asked.

"Yes," Logan said.

"Welcome," he said. "I'm Rifat. Get in."

Logan got into the car. Rifat was carefully scrutinizing him, seeming to take in every detail.

"Do you have any weapons or cell phones?" he asked.

Logan anticipated there would be a shakedown, espe-cially if he were going to meet anyone high up in ISIS. He didn't like it, but he knew he was going to have to give up his hardware to gain their trust. If Logan could ingratiate himself with them, maybe they'd return his weapons in due time. He wasn't too worried about their ability to exploit the cell phone. With its encryption algorithms, even NSA would be stumped trying to extract any data from it.

"Here you go," he said, pulling the items from their re-spective hiding places. "I want these back. I'm not thrilled about being in this environment without protection."

"Don't worry," Rifat said. "We have an intake process.

You'll get a security briefing and go to some classes. Once you know the drill, we'll return your items. With your background, you should understand we have to take precautions."

He stowed Logan's possessions in a soiled canvas bag and leaned back to set them on the rear seat. Looking in the rearview mirror, he swung the car around and began the drive back towards Ash Shaddadi.

There was a lag in the conversation, and Logan took the opportunity to size him up. Rifat looked to be in his forties. He was going soft in the middle, but Logan sensed it would be a miscalculation to underestimate him. Beneath the middle-age spread was a toughened warrior. Rifat's face was hard, bronzed from living life outdoors. He had a curly black beard and kinky hair glistening with oil. His shuttered brown eyes were inscrutable. He was stocky, broad in the shoulders. It was hard to tell with him sitting down, but Logan judged him to be around five foot eight to five foot ten.

"How's the woman?"

"What?" Logan was startled by the sudden question. "Oh, you mean my friend? She got pretty shaken up. Concussion and messed up knee."

Logan wasn't sure precisely what Azar told Rifat about their "accident," so he refrained from providing too many other details. "She's on her way back to Turkey this afternoon. Got somebody to drive her to Sanliurfa. She may rest up in Istanbul for a few days before she heads back home."

Rifat's eyebrows arched upwards. "Syria's a dangerous place," he said. "It's fortunate you were there to handle the situation."

"Where are we headed?" Logan asked.

"We have a base, not too far from Ash Shaddadi. I'm sure you know from news reports, the situation in Syria is very fluid right now."

"Was that your guys with the car bomb in Al Hasakah this morning?" Logan asked.

Rifat was noncommittal. "Maybe," was all he said.

Logan decided to try a different tack. "Where do you call home?"

Rifat grunted. "I come from an area outside of Damascus. Ghouta. My parents were shopkeepers. They had a hardware store in East Ghouta. My two brothers and I worked there, even when we were in elementary school.

"We're Sunnis. We went to our local masjid, and we got along with our neighbors, some of whom were Shia. It was a good life." Rifat reached into his pocket and extracted a pack of cigarettes. He offered one to Logan, who declined, and then lit one for himself. He inhaled deeply and then blew the smoke out of the side of his mouth.

"The whole time I was growing up, my family lived under the Assads. First, it was Hafez al-Assad, and when he died, his son, Bashar. They're Ba'athist bastards, and they were corrupt from the very beginning. They ruined this country. Many people think the civil war in Syria is sectarian, but the people just got fed up with the Assads. They wanted a change.

"When I was eighteen, I decided to leave Syria and make *jihad* in Iraq against the Americans and Iranians. I was young, and it began as a kind of adventure. But war changes you," he said, grounding his cigarette out in the ashtray. "You should know that."

"Yes, it does," Logan said. "Who knows? Could be you and I were in Iraq at the same time."

Rifat reacted with a mirthless snort. "You were navy, right? Navy SEAL?"

"Yep."

"What happened to you? It seems like a big switch to go on *jihad* for someone with your background."

Logan paused a moment before responding. Traffic was light on the road, and he cracked his window to let a little air in because it was getting stuffy.

"I guess it started when I was injured in Afghanistan. Navy pretty much told me not to let the door hit me in the ass when they gave me my walking papers.

"I was in rehab for a year, and I had a lot of time to think about what's going on over here and why the hell the U.S. is even involved. We need to get the fuck out of this fight. Now we've got a president who's anti-Muslim. He's a xenophobic son-of-a-bitch."

The fiction rolled off his tongue like oil, but in reality, it was anathema to his true beliefs. Logan hoped he sounded convincing. He didn't agree with many of this administration's policies, but he couldn't remember the last time he was this critical of a sitting commander-in-chief.

"Anyway, I've got a handful of Muslim friends. We go back to our high school days. I think they're getting a raw deal. I just want to do my part." He held his breath to see how Rifat would respond to his tirade.

Rifat turned to give him an appraising stare. "We'll see." He wound down his window and spat a speck of tobacco off his tongue. It was warming up outside, and the hot desert air permeated the interior of the car. The wheezing air conditioner struggled to keep up. Dog days were cooler than this.

A few minutes later, Rifat slowed and took a left turn onto an unpaved road. He navigated around what appeared to be a bomb crater, and then picked up speed, careening down the rutted path for 30 minutes.

Up ahead on the right-hand side was a mud hut, outside of which stood two men armed with automatic weapons. They signaled for the car to stop and approaching the driver's side, peered in. Recognizing Rifat, the sentry shouted a greeting. "*As-Salaam alay kum.*"

"*Wa alaykum as-salaam,*" Rifat replied. The men spoke for a few minutes, joking in rapid-fire Arabic. Logan was always mesmerized by the sound of spoken Arabic—guttural, but at the same time, poetic. He knew a few phrases, however, despite the fact Zahir earned a PhD in Arabic and made a living teaching it, he was not conversant in the language.

Rifat rolled the window back up and turned right past the guards. Up ahead a row of towering pine trees grew along the banks of a creek. Beyond the tree line, Logan could make out a mud-walled compound. The metal gate to the compound magically swung open as they approached. *Must have eyes on the entrance from an observation post,* Logan noted. Or maybe the sentries called in their approach.

There were several structures constructed of mud on the compound. It had the feel of a farm, with the main house, a barn, and other outbuildings. In the center was an ample open space where a dozen men were drilling in hand-to-hand combat. He spotted what appeared to be several foreigners among them. He and Rifat got out of the car and stood to watch for a couple of minutes.

"You want to give it a try?" From the way Rifat looked at him, Logan sensed this was both a challenge and a test. Saying no was not an option.

"Why not?" He took off his shoes and socks and removed his shirt.

There was a murmur from the men standing around the drill ground. Logan was a physical specimen in any culture. Even SEAL culture. He was six foot two, and 185 pounds of sinew. Muscles rippled across his taut frame. He wore his hair short, and his chiseled features gave most people second thoughts about getting on his bad side.

Rifat signaled to one of the men, a lithe, dark-skinned Arab with a ragged knife scar on his cheek.

"This is Faisal. He's one of our best instructors in hand-to-hand combat. The first one to disarm his opponent will win. We'll be using these wooden practice daggers. One of the students brought the knives over and handed them to the two men.

"Good luck," Rifat said, as the other men began to shout their support for Faisel.

This is bizarre, Logan thought as he and Faisel sized each other up. His last hand-to-hand combat encounter was in Afghanistan, where his life depended on it. It might just be that his success or failure in this mission against ISIS hinged upon how he handled this unexpected test of his fighting skills.

Logan gripped the wooden dagger in his right hand and

began to circle clockwise around his opponent. His favorite school of hand-to-hand combat was *Krav-Maga*, a style of street fighting developed in the 1950s for the Israeli army. SEALS are exposed to other hand-to-hand fighting techniques, like boxing, Muay Thai, and combat Jujitsu during their training, but *Krav-Maga* remained his go-to fighting system because it incorporated the best parts from a variety of martial arts.

Faisel was stepping lightly on the balls of his feet, in time with Logan, circling clockwise. He moved confidently, his dagger thrust out in front of him, his left fist raised to provide a counterbalance to his raised right arm.

Logan shifted direction, and Faisel adjusted accordingly. He parried and thrust a couple of times to test Logan's reflexes, but the former navy SEAL brushed these aside with little fanfare.

Footwork and balance are vital skills in hand-to-hand combat situations. And speed. You could have great footwork and balance, but if you're outmatched in speed by your opponent, your back will be up against the wall.

Faisel suddenly lurched at him, slashing in a vertical line left to right through Logan's upraised left arm. Logan parried and reversed direction again, this time pivoting towards his opponent. As Faisel raised his knife again to slash at him, Logan came in close and delivered a jarring thrust with his left elbow to Faisel's jaw. The Arab's head snapped back, and his eyes opened wide at the surprising ease of Logan's attack. He pulled back and continued moving in a counterclockwise direction, shaking his head to clear his brain.

Logan darted in, feinting to the left and then delivering a sweep kick, knocking Faisel to the floor. His knife fell to the ground, and Faisel lay there for a second. Logan turned his back on him and walked over to retrieve the wooden dagger when he heard a gasp from the men in the crown. Whipping around, he saw Faisel, now armed with an actual combat knife moving towards him.

"What the hell? Where did that come from?" Someone

in the crowd must have tossed it to him.

Now, the other men were shouting for blood, and Logan cast a quick look in Rifat's direction. The ISIS fighter was standing on the fringe of the group, an impassive look on his face.

Logan turned back to his assailant. The Arab was gripping the knife so he would be able to plunge it into Logan's torso. As Faisel launched his attack, Logan closed with him. A false move on his part could result in death, given he was fighting with a piece of wood, while Faisel was armed with a blade of steel.

As the ISIS fighter plunged the knife towards him, Logan blocked it with his left arm, and using his right knee, delivered a forceful blow to Faisel's groin. His attacker dropped the knife and rolled to the ground, moaning and clutching his privates in agony.

Logan was breathing heavily as he circled away from Faisel to retrieve the knife. What he did next could determine his survival in this world. ISIS's world. His inclination usually would be to walk away from this piece of dog shit. But this wasn't normal. Far from it.

Grasping the knife in his right hand, he walked over to the writhing man and straddled him. Faisel began to whimper, struggling to escape from Logan's iron grip on his arms and legs, but he was no match for the former SEAL. Looking into the man's eyes, Logan raised the knife over his head and in one quick motion, plunged it into Faisel's chest, piercing his heart.

Chapter 42

Logan stood up and surveyed the throng gawking at Faisel's body, splayed out on the ground in a pool of blood. They'd gone quiet and turned their sullen eyes on him. He wiped his face with the back of his hand and looked in the direction of Rifat, who wore a somewhat surprised, but strangely satisfied, expression on his face.

Finally, the Syrian spoke, motioning to two of the trainees. "Take care of this."

Two men stepped out of the group and, each taking an arm, dragged Faisel's body away from the drill ground towards an open field behind one of the buildings. It was still quiet, the only sound being the scuffling of the dead man's heels as they dragged him through the dirt.

"Come with me," Rifat said. "The rest of you, back to work." The men returned to their drills, their sudden nervous chatter breaking the silence.

After putting on his shoes and socks, Logan struggled into his shirt, trotting to catch up with the Syrian, who was striding towards a one-story, rectangular building near the rear of the property.

Logan knew this was going to be a mission fraught with danger going in; he just hadn't anticipated it would escalate that fast. The people who make up ISIS are a cutthroat bunch. It was apparent from their warped ideology and the gruesome videos they circulated on social media that the group reveled in vicious, even, inhumane actions against their opponents.

While he might lose some sleep over the needless taking of a life, most of these aspiring *jihadis* probably just take it in stride. Logan knew he was going to have to watch his back. If Faisel had any friends among the others, they might already be plotting their revenge.

Logan caught up with Rifat just as he reached the entrance to the building. "This is the barracks where you'll be staying." Shoving the door open, the security chief ducked his head, pushing his way past a heavy drape hanging from the doorframe. He stopped just inside the entrance to light a lamp hanging from a nail.

Logan followed him into the squalid structure. The flickering lantern cast shadows on unfinished mud brick walls. Sleeping pallets stuffed with straw covered in dirty cloth were scattered about the room. Meager possessions were strewn around many of the pallets, marking those already claimed.

"Pick one that isn't already taken," Rifat said. "You can leave your things here. Follow me." They exited via another door at the other end of the room, which led to an open-air latrine and bathing area.

Gesturing to another building a hundred feet from where they stood, Rifat said, "That's where we take our meals."

Leading Logan away from the latrines, Rifat approached a squat hut Logan took for an outbuilding, but which turned out to be a makeshift office.

"I need to get some paperwork from you. Take a seat," Rifat said, as he rummaged through a cardboard box on the floor. "Ah, here it is." He thrust a sheet of paper towards Logan and slid a pen across the table.

"You'll see I've already filled in some of the answers, but I need some additional personal information."

Logan poured over the form. In his preparation for this moment, he'd learned ISIS had a standardized intake process for new recruits. In fact, a year before, thousands of ISIS documents were inexplicably leaked to the British media by a disaffected member of the terrorist organization. Many of them were the personnel records of the *jihadis*. The form before him seemed to conform with what he remembered reading about. Much of it consisted of standard bio information: name, date and place of birth, parent's names, citizenship, military service, date of discharge, marital status, education, and so on.

It was apparent to him either the Qods Force or Akbar, the spotter Ali introduced him to at the New York mosque, provided ISIS with the information already inked in. He had only met Akbar that one time when he gave him his alias business card. He'd had much more contact with Azar, but of course, Rifat would be loath to disclose her true identity as a hired gun from the Qods Force.

After filling in the blank spaces, Logan checked the form one more time and pushed it back across the table to Rifat, who didn't bother to read it, but tossed it back into the cardboard box and closed it up. He sat contemplating Logan for a moment before speaking.

"Faisel was one of our better drill instructors," he said with a frown on his creased face.

"I'm sorry about your man," Logan replied. "I couldn't take a chance. I don't think he was just trying to intimidate me with that knife. He meant business."

"It was foolish of him to do what he did. He should have accepted defeat gracefully. But, we Arabs are a proud bunch." He shook his head in consternation, drawing a cigarette out of his pack and tamping it on the desk.

"What do you know about Islam? What we're trying to do here?"

"Well, I had a couple of Muslim friends in high school growing up outside of Washington. I took a world religions course at Annapolis, and then when I was active duty, I got some area fam training before I shipped out to Afghanistan. It wasn't much, but it gave me a sense of how wide-spread Islam is, who some of the major players were throughout history, background on the Sunni-Shia divide. Pretty basic stuff.

"I think I began to question the U.S.'s role in the Middle East during my assignment to Afghanistan. Originally, I was pretty gung-ho, particularly after 9-11, but now, sixteen, seventeen years in, I think it's time for us to get out."

Rifat nodded his head. "If only your leaders thought the same way," he said with a wry face. "You'll have a chance over the next couple of days to learn more. And you'll be learning from true believers, not some PhD who only read a few books."

There was a knock on the door, and one of the men Logan recalled seeing earlier came into the room. He walked over to Rifat and spoke to him in hushed Arabic. The security chief's brow furrowed, although he nodded his head in seeming agreement. The visitor left them, and for a moment, Rifat stared at the table, absorbed in thought. Abruptly he stood and motioned for Logan to follow him.

"Where to now?" Logan asked.

"Al Baghdadi wants to meet you," he replied. "He takes an interest in all of his fighters, but he's especially mindful of the foreigners."

"Why's that?" Logan asked.

"You play an important role, spreading the word about the Caliph's vision, to places where, for obvious reasons, we don't have a presence."

They left the hut and walked by the open field, where many of the fighters lay stretched out on the ground, resting. Some glanced up, and Logan sensed their hostile stares piercing him like darts as he passed by. He didn't dwell on their anger, although he knew it was something he needed keep an eye on. Right now, he was focused on his upcoming encounter with Al Baghdadi.

Rifat skirted a couple of the beehive-shaped huts, pausing before one before rapping his knuckles sharply on the wooden door.

"Come in," was the muffled reply.

When they entered, it took a moment for Logan's eyes to adjust to the dim light. He had done his homework on the ISIS leader but wasn't prepared for the underwhelming reaction he had to their first encounter.

The man standing before him did not look like the world's most wanted man with a $25 million bounty on his head. And that figure was just the state department's incentive to bring in the specially designated global terrorist. There were probably other countries offering their own rewards to bring him in dead or alive.

Abu Bakr Al Baghdadi wasn't his real name. It was his *nom de guerre,* intended to add to his mystique. Many believed Al Baghdadi took the name Abu Bakr, to create a sense of affinity with the first Caliph, Abu Bakr, who was the father-in-law and advisor to the Prophet Muhammad.

Al Baghdadi didn't resemble photos of the star soccer player from his college days. His penetrating brown eyes scrutinized Logan from beneath bushy black eyebrows. The unruly black beard, laced with white strands of hair on the sides, stood in sharp contrast to his olive complexion. It was difficult to get a sense of his proportions because of the flowing robes he wore. Despite reports, he was gravely injured in fighting the year before, he gave no indication of that as he moved forward to greet his visitors.

"Tim Hudson?" he asked, as he took Logan's hand in his own.

"Yes. Pleased to meet you." Logan wasn't sure what the protocol was for addressing Al Baghdadi. So many Muslims considered him a false Caliph. He decided to refrain from calling him by name.

"I understand you experienced a little excitement coming into the camp," the ISIS leader said as he led them over to a carpet on the floor. Everyone sat down, and Al Baghdadi asked one of the attendants hovering by his side to bring tea.

Logan made an effort to appear contrite, although Faisel's death was a win for the good guys as far as he was concerned. "Yes. It got out of hand. I thought we were having a friendly contest and all of a sudden Faisel was coming at me with a real weapon. I couldn't take a chance that he was just trying to scare me."

"It's of no importance," the Caliph replied, waving his hand dismissively. "He should have shown better judgment. Where did you learn to handle yourself like that? Faisel was one of our better instructors."

"SEALS. We spend months learning hand-to-hand combat techniques, and we drill a lot."

"If I remember correctly when I first read about you, you left the navy over five years ago. That's a long time to be out of shape."

"I can't explain it. It just becomes who you are. You're always ready for the unexpected."

Al Baghdadi was silent for a moment, stroking his beard. Finally, he spoke. "Rifat will take care of you over the next couple of days. There are some classes you must attend. These will be with the other foreign fighters, most of whom speak English.

"Afterwards I want you to spend some time with my personal bodyguards. You're planning to stay for some time. Is that correct?" The question came across more as a statement than a query.

"I want to help any way I can. I can justify being away for a month at the most. I have a business back home, and the story I put out there was I was going to England to drum up some new security-related business with U.S. companies in the U.K. Anything longer than a month will likely attract attention. I was hoping maybe there's something you want done in the U.S."

Al Baghdadi searched his face. "We'll see," he said, rising. "First thing's first."

Rifat and Logan took their leave and completed the tour of the compound. Rifat showed him the classroom where he would receive his indoctrination into ISIS ideology. Then, returning to his car, Rifat retrieved the canvas bag from the back seat and withdrew Logan's Glock, fighting knife, baton, and cell phone.

"You may be needing these," he said, handing them over. "Get some rest. Dinner is at six."

Chapter 43

The trip from Al Hasakah to Sanliurfa Gap Airport was monotonous yet agonizing. Azar's driver displayed a knack for finding every bump in the road, and by the time they reached the Turkish airport, her head was throbbing. Unable to walk unassisted, she gratefully sank into the wheelchair awaiting her curbside outside the departure hall. A porter pushed her inside and facilitated check-in. An employee from Pegasus Air helped her navigate security and board the plane.

The flight wasn't crowded; Azar had an entire row to herself. She tried to nap, but the lacerating pain from her knee made it impossible. She'd have to wait until her arrival in Istanbul for relief. With any luck, Yasmin would be there to help her. She had called her before leaving Al Hasakah to confirm her itinerary and ask the Qods Force operative to schedule a doctor's appointment for her in Istanbul.

As Azar stared at the desert landscape from 25,000 feet, her thoughts turned to the bungled effort to deliver Tim Hudson to ISIS. *What must Colonel Samadi be thinking?* He couldn't really blame her for the botched attempt on their lives. They were lucky to have come out of it in one piece, shaken though she was.

Her bosses were acutely aware of the security risks in Syria. Thousands of Iranian Revolutionary Guard Corps advisors had perished fighting there since 2013. Qods Force threat-reporting in the war zone was plentiful, but it wasn't omniscient. Her present circumstances were a testament to that.

Did Hudson succeed in making contact with ISIS? He was resourceful; the way he handled the ambush was the work of a seasoned pro, although she remained dubious over his explanation for the detonation. *An IED?* She knew something about IEDs, having been married to the commander of a Qods Force bomb-making school. Granted, she was knocked out in the attack and not thinking straight. Something about the episode was off kilter, though.

Although Samadi would not fault her for the unforeseeable encounter on the road from Al Hasakah, he would be less forgiving if he found out she had bedded Hudson. She couldn't help herself. Loneliness was an occupational hazard for a covert operator in the field. Besides, it was worth it. Hudson was an energetic lover, more than satisfying. But he was also very tender. Dare she say it? She felt needed.

The plane was beginning its descent into Istanbul's airspace. Thirty minutes later, after all the passengers deplaned, she spotted Yasmin rolling a wheelchair down the aisle.

"What happened to you?" she asked, helping Azar out of her seat.

"It's a long story," Azar replied. "We got to Syria without any problems but were ambushed south of Al Hasakah. We don't know who did it. A couple of guys on a motorcycle and several men in a pickup truck. There wasn't much left of them when it was all over."

"And your friend?"

"He decided to stay for a while."

Yasmin nodded, understanding. She navigated the chair down the aisle and into the arrivals hall. "I have a car waiting for you downstairs. You have two appointments tomorrow morning at Florence Nightingale Hospital—the first is at eight with an orthopedic specialist, and the other is at nine-thirty with a neurosurgeon. I'll have a car pick you up.

"Oh, one more thing. I put you in the same hotel you were in before—the Neorion."

"Thanks, Yasmin. I don't know what I'd do without you."

"No problem. You have one checked bag, right?"

"Yes." Azar handed her the baggage claim ticket. After

Yasmin retrieved her suitcase and helped Azar into the waiting car, she squeezed her hand. "Call me if you need anything," she said. "You still have my number, right?"

"Yes," Azar said, holding up her cell phone.

The following morning, Azar ate a light breakfast in the Neorion's dining room before leaving for her appointment. She was able to navigate around the hotel on crutches Yasmin had rented from a local pharmacy.

At the hospital, both the orthopedist and the neurosurgeon confirmed Dr. Evana's diagnosis. After ordering x-rays and a cat-scan, they prescribed bed rest, anti-inflammatories, and pain medication.

Back at the hotel, Azar decided to call Samadi, using the encrypted feature on her phone. She knew he would be worried about her and would be looking for an update.

His secretary picked up on the first ring. Even though she was using the encrypted feature on the phone, Azar gave her code name rather than her actual name to identify herself.

"This is Hafez calling for Colonel Samadi."

He picked up almost immediately. "Hello?"

"It's me."

"Where are you?"

"I'm in Istanbul. Got in yesterday and had doctor's appointments early this morning. I'm back in my room."

"What did they say?" He sounded concerned.

"They confirmed what the doctor in Syria told me—concussion and the ACL in my right knee is torn." She winced as she shifted positions and realized she needed to take her pain medication.

"How do you feel?"

"There's some pain. I'm still a little woozy, and I can't walk without crutches."

"How soon can you travel?"

"The doctors suggested I wait a week before going anywhere. The problem is, I'm not going to be able to do much except rest."

"Don't worry about it. Just get well. Have you heard

anything from your friend?"

"No. I set up contact with ISIS for him outside of Al Hasakah yesterday around four. I think they are going to be very pleased. He's definitely a pro. I don't know if I would have survived the ambush without him."

Samadi paused a moment before replying.

"I have something to tell you. It's very preliminary, but one of the analysts in the counterintelligence division has been reviewing some old files and believes he has found something concerning about our Mr. Hudson."

Azar felt her stomach tighten. "What is it?"

"This may be hard for you to listen to."

"Go on. I can take it." She waited expectantly.

"You recall several years ago after the attack on Bandar Deylam, we did an all-out investigation into who was involved?"

"Yes." She felt a knot tighten in her stomach.

"We already knew about the Kuwaiti Nouri killed in Boston—Hamid Al Subaie. We found him because of a penetration we had in the Kuwaiti intelligence and security service. Simon. Simon was Hamid's handler when Hamid was conducting covert operations in Iran. We ran Simon for several years before he suddenly passed away. Pancreatic cancer.

"We knew the Kuwaitis didn't pull off the Bandar Deylam operation on their own. They don't have that kind of capability. Our analysts felt it was CIA or U.S. military. At one point before he died, Simon met an American who traveled to Kuwait for meetings with Thamir Alghanim, the director of operations for the Kuwaiti intelligence and security service.

"This person also met Hamid Al Subaie at a safehouse in Kuwait City. He was traveling under an alias as it turns out—Logan Campbell. We were able to bribe the driver who met him at the airport and drove him to his hotel, where we discovered he was traveling under another name, Logan Alexander."

"But what does this have to do with Tim Hudson?"

Azar asked.

"Maybe it's a false alarm," Samadi replied. "We don't have anything definitive, but the analyst thinks it's possible Logan Alexander and Tim Hudson are one and the same."

Azar clutched her stomach as a spasm of pain jolted her. "What makes you so sure?" she asked, as she tried to control the trembling in her voice.

"Partially it's geography. Alexander's based in Boston, as you know. He's the guy Nouri was going after when he was killed. Tim Hudson is close by. New Bedford isn't that far from Boston.

"Both men have navy SEAL backgrounds. We haven't been able to definitively confirm either one's affiliation though. We know Alexander went to Annapolis because he was a football star there. It's a safe bet he went on to serve in the navy, but we can't crack into their personnel records. There were some online posts by Logan Alexander on a navy SEAL forum, but there hasn't been anything like that from Hudson.

"What about Hudson's business in New Bedford?" Azar asked.

"That all checks out. But, we know from intelligence reporting, the CIA and even the FBI can do that sort of backstopping to make a business look valid. Just the fact he has a legitimate looking business isn't definitive."

"Do you have a picture of Alexander? Azar asked.

"Simon was able to get a copy of Alexander's passport from the hotel. Unfortunately, it was never entered digitally into our system and was destroyed in a record purge a couple of years ago. The analyst is doing public records searches to see if there is anything out there, but so far he's come up empty-handed."

"What about the picture of Hudson taken by the surveillance team in New York?" Azar was castigating herself for not taking pictures of him during their time together.

"That was taken from a distance, and Hudson was wearing sunglasses and a ball cap. Not a good likeness and as I said, we don't have anything else to draw a comparison."

Azar silently fumed, wanting nothing more than to return to Syria to confront Hudson. But traveling now was out of the question. On a deeper level, she was experiencing a sense of self-loathing. Was it possible she had given herself to her dead husband's killer?

"What next?" she asked through gritted teeth.

Samadi was quiet. Azar was about to repeat her question, thinking he hadn't heard her.

"How long do you think it will be before you're well enough to travel?" he finally asked.

Her leg was cramping, and she shifted in her seat, trying to find a comfortable position. "I don't know. Weeks probably. I can't even walk by myself right now. Hudson's not planning to be in Syria for more than a few weeks. A month at the most."

"I'm hesitant to say anything to ISIS at this point," Samadi said. "Mostly, what we have is unsubstantiated conjecture from one of our analysts. If we develop any additional information, I'll let you know."

Azar said goodbye and sat for a moment digesting Samadi's revelations. She struggled to her feet and found the bottle of pills her doctor had prescribed. She poured out two and searched for a bottle of water in the mini bar. Returning to the sofa, she carefully lowered herself onto the cushion and leaned back with her eyes closed.

She searched her memory for any clues Hudson was anyone other than who he purported to be. There was nothing. If this was a charade, he had played the role masterfully. Her eyes opened wide, and she sat up as she contemplated the implications of that possibility. If that was the case, Hudson probably knew full well her real identity.

Azar gritted her teeth in determination. For his own sake, Hudson better not turn out to be Logan Alexander. She would hunt him down, no matter what it took. And kill him.

Chapter 44

Logan could hardly believe a week had flown by since Rifat first picked him up on the dusty road outside of Al Hasakha. Despite initial misgivings about his own security in the camp following his fatal encounter with Faisel, the other men, for the most part, steered clear of him. It seemed he had attained a certain level of notoriety because of the incident and the way he handled himself.

He was grouped with a half-dozen other English-speaking volunteers from all over the world. There was Matthew, a lanky college-dropout from Alberta; Ernesto, a fisherman from a small town outside of Barcelona; Gregory, a brick mason from Londonderry; Oleg, a petty thief from Warsaw, who was in and out of jails for years; Anthony, a moody barista from London; and Ethan, a foul-mouthed mechanic from Sydney.

In Logan's earlier discussion with Rifat, regarding his mastery, or lack thereof, of Islam and what ISIS was all about, he admitted to little depth in understanding of the religion or ISIS's broader agenda. But if he felt lacking in these areas, his fellow volunteers, with the exception perhaps of Matthew, were woefully ignorant about the most fundamental aspects of the religion and what ISIS was attempting to accomplish.

Anthony admitted to having purchased a copy of *The Koran for Dummies* to fill in gaps in his knowledge, while most of the others relied upon programs on TV and reports in local newspapers. Matthew, who was the only one besides Logan to attend college, had actually memorized the Quran.

Their routine varied little from day to day. Everyone

followed the Islamic practice of *Salah*, the recitation of prayers five times throughout the day and evening. While non-Muslims were not required to pray, everyone was roused from their beds before dawn. After prayers, there was an hour of physical exercise followed by a light breakfast of tea, bread, and fruit.

While the rest of the camp went about their chores, training, or conducting military operations, the seven foreigners were subjected to orientation classes consisting of fighting skills and political and Sharia ideology.

The military training took place outdoors. It consisted mainly of conditioning drills—navigating obstacle courses, simulating hand-to-hand combat, running and doing calisthenics. Following noon prayers and lunch, the would-be militants were herded into a classroom where a visiting Imam or young cleric would lecture them on Sharia law or make them watch ISIS propaganda videos.

It was evident to Logan, as he participated in these activities, how shallow the religious convictions of his fellow *jihadis* were. They seemed to be there more for the excitement and sense of camaraderie than any deeply held religious beliefs.

Today the young cleric running their class was showing a video about the origins of the Islamic State. In his introduction, he announced ISIS was an outgrowth of Al Qaeda, although he hastened to distance the organization from Osama bin Laden's successor, Ayman al Zawahiri, who did not acknowledge Al Baghdadi as the legitimate Caliph.

After the video was over, the cleric explained that although there was some tension between the leaders of Al Qaeda and ISIS, on a doctrinal level the two organizations were in synch with each other.

"True jihadists are Sunni Salafists, or 'pious forefathers,'" he explained. "We should make every effort, in all aspects of our lives, to model the Prophet Mohammed. By this, I mean the way we comport ourselves in our everyday lives, how we dress, and how we make *jihad*."

Matthew raised his hand. "Why does ISIS issue so many

excommunications? What do you call them? *Takfir?*"

The cleric peered at the young Canadian for a moment before responding. Folding his arms across his chest, he took a defensive posture before the group. "There are many forms of apostasy," he began. "The most obvious, blasphemy against the sacred writings or the Prophet himself is an egregious form. Shiites are an entire class of apostates because they do not strictly follow the Quran. Instead, they have put themselves above it because they change the real meaning to suit their whims. They have put humans before God.

"But, there are other transgressions as well," he continued. "Those who sell forbidden substances, such as drugs and alcohol for example, or shave their beards, or marry a non-Muslim. These and many other crimes can, and do, lead to *takfir*."

Logan raised his hand. "What can you say about those Muslims who haven't pledged allegiance to the Caliph?" he asked. "I don't mean the Shiites, because I understand they are a class by themselves. I'm talking about Sunnis who, in every other way are living their faith."

The young cleric considered the question before responding. "As Al Baghdadi declared in his June 2014 proclamation in Mosul, there is a communal obligation among all Muslims to revive the Caliphate. By that, he didn't mean the Ottoman Empire, which was a false Caliphate. You would have to go back in history 1,000 years to find the last true Caliph, one descended from the Prophet himself.

"Al Baghdadi comes from that tribe. He is Qurayshi. And he meets all of the other conditions under Sharia law. He has moral and physical integrity. And he is mentally fit. Under these conditions, if he were to fail to declare the Caliphate, he would be in violation of his moral obligation to do so.

"Just as he would fail to meet his moral obligation, so, too, those Muslims who have not pledged their allegiance to his Caliphate have failed to meet their moral obligations." He scrutinized the group with the barest hint of a frown on his face.

"If there are no more questions, that will be all for this afternoon." The men filed out of the classroom. Some of them had chores to do. There was a rotating schedule of cleaning, food preparation, and caring for the sick and wounded. Logan had a free hour and decided to reach out to his support team for an update.

While in training, the recruits were forbidden from leaving the camp unaccompanied. There was no real privacy on the compound, but Logan noticed most of the men retained their cell phones and used them when they had an opportunity to do so. He found a quiet spot and eased himself onto the ground, leaning against the mud wall of a building.

After entering the code and switching his phone to its encrypted status, he punched in Wellington's number.

"Bruce?"

"Logan. How you doing, buddy?"

"The food sucks and the beer tastes like camel piss," he joked.

Bruce laughed. "Glad to hear you haven't lost your sense of humor."

"How's it going at Q-West?" Logan asked, keeping an eye out for anyone who might wander in his direction.

"Q-West is history. After the close call you had, we decided to relocate. We're at an FOB about twenty miles from your current location."

"What!"

"Yep. I've had you on a GPS tracker since you got there. So, really, how's it going?"

Logan gave him a rundown of his activities from day one, including the training schedule, the layout of the camp—although Bruce ought to be able to pull up specifics on imagery—and the number of combatants and trainees.

"I think those who aren't training are going out on missions, but they're pretty closed-mouthed about what they're doing around the trainees. I suspect the car bomb attack in Al Hasakah last week was the work of this group, but I'm not sure."

"So, what's the game plan?" Bruce asked.

"I've got a week, maybe less, of training and then I'm supposed to hook up with Al Baghdadi's security detail."

Bruce let out a low whistle. "How'd you land that gig?"

Logan explained the run-in with Faisel, and the Caliph's respect for the level of training SEALs get.

"You can tell people back home that reports of Al Baghdadi's demise are flat out wrong. Unless this guy's his twin. He seems to be in pretty good shape, but we don't see a lot of him. He keeps to himself. This Syrian, Rifat, who's in charge of Al Baghdadi's security detail, meets him regularly. I think they go back a few years from when they were both detained in Iraq.

"Anyway, I should get a better sense of his movements in another week or so, if they do decide to put me on his security detail. Why don't you get with Jason and find out if they'd rather take him dead or alive? Either way, we're going to need an extraction, because I have no intention of spending any more time here than I have to."

Logan could hear some noise in the background. He heard Bruce say, "Why don't you tell him." There was some shuffling as the two men on the other end changed places. Then Norm Sherman's voice came on.

"Logan?"

"Yeah."

"Norm here."

"I thought I recognized your voice. What's up?"

"I just got out of a meeting with the base commander. He had an Eyes-Only Top-Secret Night Action (NIACT) cable from headquarters he wanted to show me."

Logan felt his breathing still, as he waited for Norm to deliver the message. This had to be significant. Night Action messages are the second highest precedence the Agency uses. The only one higher is Flash, which bumps every other lower precedence message to make sure it goes to the top of the communications' queue. He could hear the crinkle of paper as Norm unfolded the message.

"It's from Jason's office in CTC. Apparently, they're

running an Iranian asset who works in the counterintelligence area for the Iranian Revolutionary Guard Corps. Anyway, this guy told his case officer his office received tasking from the Unit 400 people, asking him to conduct some name traces. He said the specific request was to find out if there were any links between two names."

Logan could feel his stomach muscles tighten. "Go on."

"The names were Logan Alexander and Tim Hudson."

Logan's breathing had gone so quiet he wondered if he'd involuntarily stopped altogether.

"Logan? You there?"

"Yeah." *Whew.* He let out a breath as the enormity of what Norm said hit him full force. The Iranians were looking for connections between Logan Alexander and Tim Hudson. His mind raced as the implications of their search hit home. Did that mean Azar had her doubts about him and somehow managed to put two and two together? Was there a leak at the Agency? Did he screw up?

"There's more," Norm said. "Our Iran desk has had this standing requirement for a couple of years to question their assets about any operations they are aware of against U.S. citizens. Anyway, there's this new, un-vetted source working out of Istanbul. She works undercover for Iran Air. She's the one who helped you and Azar get through security. She saw your passport, but the really bizarre thing is, she was working CI in Tehran when you did the dirty deed in Bandar Deylam. She was assigned to the case and is the one who figured out you were Logan Alexander and not Logan Campbell."

"Whoa. What are the chances?"

"Exactly. Yasmin's her name. She made the connection when she met you at the airport. Anyway, one of her analyst buddies in Tehran is working on this now. He told her the Qods Force isn't convinced there's a link between the two names. She was pretty sure it was you when she met you in Istanbul but claims she didn't confirm it for him.

"The Qods Force doesn't plan to report this to ISIS unless they can definitively ID you as Alexander. But the DDO isn't too happy about you being out there with the possibility the Iranians will connect the dots.

"He's not the only one," Logan laughed. "Holy shit."

"We're going to be all over this. If there's even a whiff of trouble, we're pulling you out."

Logan let that sink in. He wasn't afraid to take risks. He'd been doing that pretty much his whole life. But this was for keeps.

"Oh. One more thing," Norm said. "Your girlfriend made it back to Istanbul in one piece."

What the hell is Norm talking about? His stomach sank. There's no way he could know about his midnight liaison with Azar in Istanbul.

"Who?" he asked weakly.

"Just kidding," Norm laughed. "Azar. Ms. Iran Air passed that info on when she met her case officer."

Logan forced a laugh. "It's a small world. All right. I'll get back to you in a few days. I'll try to work up an extraction plan based on what I find out. Why don't you guys get some imagery of this place and do a little recon? I'll talk to you early in the week."

Chapter 45

A zar remained in Istanbul for a week, recuperating from the ambush. Her colleague from Iran Air, Yasmin, was particularly helpful—arranging transportation, setting up medical visits, shopping, and just spending time with her.

The life of a field operative living abroad under cover can be stressful. Azar had been in Toronto for several years and even lived in an Iranian enclave, but she rarely had the opportunity to associate with colleagues or speak in her native tongue. She forgot how much she loved the sound of Farsi.

This afternoon she and Yasmin were basking in the sun on a balcony off of Azar's room. Yasmin had brought some Persian snacks—pistachios, *lavashak* (a kind of fruit leather), and *ajeel* (Persian trail mix) for them to share. Azar ordered hot tea from room service.

It was a perfect summer day without a cloud in the sky. Azar's room faced east, and because it was early in the afternoon, they were shielded from the sun. From their perch three floors up from the street it was quiet. Many people were walking in and out of the entrance to the bizarre, visible from where they reclined on overstuffed pillows. Azar's leg was propped up on a low stool, and she was idly wondering how long it would be before she could return to a full range of activity.

"So, you're off to Toronto tomorrow?" Yasmin asked.

"Yes. I'm not actually looking forward to the trip, but it'll be good to be home."

"Do you have anyone there to help out?"

Adjusting the position of her leg on the pillow, Azar sighed. "Not really. I live by myself. I can get groceries delivered, and it shouldn't be a problem going to medical appointments. There's just so much to do though."

"Does photography take up a lot of your day?"

"I have to spend a fair amount of time on it, just so the Canadians don't come sniffing around. Last year there was a big story about an Al Qaeda recruiter who was wrapped up by the Mounties in Montreal. Apparently, he wasn't doing any cover work to justify his presence there. He didn't have a real job, so eventually, his neighbors became suspicious and reported him to the police. How about you? You have a full-time job at Iran Air?"

"Timewise it's not much different than working out of an embassy. There's usually more cover work than you would want. But, in this job, I have an excuse to get out and about and take care of requirements like yours last week."

Azar nodded knowingly. "That was very helpful. Just getting through security without any hassles took a load off my mind."

She scooped up a few pistachios and cracked one between her teeth. The purple skin parted to reveal a meaty, light green nut. She savored the taste and felt the sensation of being transported back to her youth in Shiraz where she and her father would sit on the floor in their apartment, sharing a bowl of nuts and sipping tea as he quizzed her on her studies.

"Do you think he made contact with ISIS?"

Azar was startled by Yasmin's question. She hadn't discussed why she was escorting Tim Hudson into Syria. Then she realized she was overreacting. There couldn't be too many reasons for an American, accompanied by an undercover Qods Force operative, to be traveling to the war zone.

"I don't know. I imagine we would have heard something if Hudson went missing. ISIS has my contact information."

"He's not volunteering to be a suicide bomber, is he?"

"I don't think so. We didn't talk specifically about how he might be useful to ISIS. He has a military background, so he might go back to the U.S. and carry out an attack there. He's not planning to stay in Syria. He has a business in the

U.S., and it would be unusual for him to be away for an extended period."

"There have been others." Yasmin lowered her voice to a whisper. "I can't go into detail, but travelers have favored this route over others this year." She glanced at her watch and jumped up.

"It's getting late. I have to go. I'll have a car come by tomorrow morning. I'll get you through security so don't worry about getting there too early." She gave Azar a hug and let herself out.

The next morning Azar arrived at the airport at 10:00 a.m. She didn't notice the young CIA officer in the departure lounge using a concealed camera to take her picture.

By early afternoon, the photo and a description of Azar's conversation with Yasmin were on their way to Langley. Sometimes, compartmentation leads to unnecessary duplication of effort. In this case, the CIA office in Istanbul was unaware CIA officer, Logan Alexander, was in direct contact with Azar, nor the nature of their relationship. They would receive a NIACT message in reply, telling them to stand down on any tasking regarding the covert Qods Force operative or Alexander.

Yasmin got her colleague settled onto the plane for the fifteen-hour flight. Azar was flying KLM and would have a four-hour layover in Amsterdam. Under different circumstances she would enjoy spending some time in the "Venice of the North," but her lack of mobility made traipsing around impractical.

By the time she reached Pearson International a day later, she was exhausted. She took a cab from the airport directly home and immediately went to bed. She slept for 12 hours.

The evening was not entirely restful. She went to bed tormenting herself with thoughts about Tim Hudson, and the possibility he might actually be Logan Alexander, her husband's murderer. Azar was conflicted by the realization she actually was attracted to the man. The fact she made love to him might have colored her feelings, but it wasn't everything. No, it was his intelligence, his operational skills, his masculinity.

She didn't know what she would do if, at the end of the day, Hudson proved to be Alexander. Was everything he told her a lie? Maybe Hudson actually had a family. He apparently had a military background, so that part at least must be genuine.

She spent a couple of days working on her photo spread of the stork migration. The images were striking; she was confident her editor at *Condé Nast* would be able to use them. One, taken of a stork coming in for a landing was breathtaking in detail. Its wings were splayed out fully, legs dangling low, and eyes fixed intently on the landing spot.

Another bright spot in an otherwise monotonous day was the diagnosis her doctors at Humber River Hospital provided following her physical. They concluded her concussion was not as severe as described by the physicians in Syria and Turkey. And as for her ACL, it would take time to heal, but her age and excellent physical condition made her a promising candidate to begin physical therapy right away. The doctor gave her the name of an outpatient rehab clinic in her neighborhood; they had an opening available that afternoon.

Azar was feeling tired by the time she got to her appointment, but she was in good spirits about the prospect of speeding up the healing process.

"From what you told us, your initial treatment right after the accident was spot on," Dr. McClellan told her. "Cold compresses over the first forty-eight hours makes an enormous difference in reducing swelling in these soft tissue areas." He pointed to a life-like mock-up of the knee.

"And you said the hospital in Turkey was using a DTR wrap?"

"Yes. Deep tissue rehabilitation. The doctor told me it was a way of getting more blood circulating in the knee without the risk of causing more damage through exercise."

"That's right. We use a patented product. Targets conditions like meniscus tears, sprained ligaments, osteoarthritis, bursitis. We've had a lot of success with it. The particular model we use is manufactured in the U.S. Within days our patients see very positive results. They have less stiffness in their joints, and greater flexibility deep in muscle tissue. And because there's increased blood circulation, inflammation is decreased, causing a reduction in pain."

"Do you know where I can find one?"

"We stock them here. Typically, your insurance will cover the cost. Would you like to purchase one?"

"I think so."

"Good. Karen, one of our therapists, will show you how to use it."

When she got back home, Azar took the device out of its box and programmed it. She wrapped it around her knee and sat at the kitchen table as it went to work. Azar might be on the sidelines for now, but this much she knew. The sooner she healed, the sooner she would be able to get back to work. And get to the bottom of the Tim Hudson mystery.

* * *

Zahir was on her way to pick up Cooper from his Montessori school. Two weeks had passed since she first learned Logan was on his way to Syria to establish contact with ISIS. She would be fooling herself if she didn't acknowledge the concern she felt for his safety. Such was life with Logan Alexander. Not one to be found sitting in the bleachers. No, her husband had to be on the playing field, in the thick of it. He hadn't been able to say much to her in their short conversation, but she prayed he understood she wanted him back.

Meanwhile, the Arabic language mini-course for Peter Breen's employees was finished. Today, in their final role-playing exercise, she was pleased to see the students' progress. They weren't going to be Arabic scholars or candidates for the Nobel Peace Prize, but they were going to be more effective police officers in their communities.

She and Cooper were flying to New York to spend a

week with Ali. He had been home for two weeks, and her parents were there to help him, but they needed to get back to Washington for a prior commitment. The timing was perfect for her. She had some time off before her next class was scheduled to begin and besides, she was worried about her big brother.

At Cooper's school, the teacher, Ms. Lucille, pulled her aside, asking her aid to help Cooper put his things away in his cubby.

"Ms. Alexander, I just wanted a word with you before you leave."

"Yes?"

Ms. Lucille seemed uncomfortable with what she was about to say. "I just wanted to ask if everything is all right at home?"

"What do you mean?"

"It's Cooper. He's normally such a happy little boy. But lately he's been withdrawn and prone to little crying spells. He seems sad. He told me he misses his father." Ms. Lucille creased the hem of her skirt and looked at Zahir expectantly.

Zahir felt a stab of pain. She knew Cooper missed Logan but didn't realize it was spilling over into his interaction with others outside of their home.

"My husband's been traveling a lot for work," she said. "As you know, we just got back from Hong Kong, and he's had to do a lot of contact work with clients outside of town. He's in Europe this week," she added.

"I'm glad that's all it is," Ms. Lucille said.

"What do you mean?"

The teacher squirmed in her chair. "Cooper seems to think it's something else. He's under the impression you and Mr. Alexander are separating."

Zahir was shocked and embarrassed by Ms. Lucille's statement.

"I, I don't know what to say—"

The older woman looked at Zahir with sympathy and understanding. "Children are much more perceptive than we give them credit for. They hear and see things we think have gone over their heads. I don't want to embarrass you or in any way intrude on your personal situation. My only concern is for Cooper's well-being. I'm not sure if he internalizes his feeling at home. Sometimes they'll do that, thinking they're protecting Mommy."

Zahir nodded her head, wiping away a tear sliding down her cheek. "We lost a baby a couple of months ago. It's caused a lot of tension at home."

Ms. Lucille reached over to take her hand. "I'm so sorry. I didn't know."

Their ride to Logan International was uneventful, and the shuttle to LaGuardia was on time. A couple of hours later, she and Cooper were walking into Ali's Chelsea condo. Azar was shocked by Ali's appearance. His ordinarily ruddy complexion was sallow, and his lustrous hair and mustache were dull and limp.

"I'm sorry I couldn't come earlier. I had to wrap up a special class we put on for the BPD." She gave him a hug, and Cooper wrapped his arms around Ali's knees."

"What's wrong, Uncle Ali?"

"It's no big deal. I fell down and banged my head. I'll be okay." He reached down and tousled Cooper's hair. He smiled faintly at Zahir.

"Mom and Dad just left a little while ago. Thanks for coming."

"What do the doctors say?"

"I should be able to go back to work in another week. I'm supposed to take it easy. No exercise or foreign travel until the end of the month."

"What's happening to those men?"

"Who? The ones responsible for this? The commissioner's going after them. Lifetime ban at the Garden and assault and battery charges. They're looking at doing time."

"Serves them right." She rubbed her brother's shoulder.

"Did Mom do any shopping while they were here?"

"Some."

"Let me check the fridge. Tell me what you feel like eating, and I'll run out and pick up some things." This was something she was good at. Her nurturing side took over. This week would be good for her and Cooper. It would take her mind off Logan, and she'd be helping her brother out.

Chapter 46

ISIS didn't hand out graduation certificates when the foreign volunteers completed their last day of training. They received assault rifles instead. Two of the men, Anthony and Ethan, were singled out for additional indoctrination at another camp. They packed their bags and left without a word right after breakfast.

"You know what those two blokes signed on for, don't you?" Gregory whispered, nodding in the direction of the departing *jihadis*.

"No, what?" Logan asked.

"Suicide training," said the Irishman.

"No way," Logan said. "How do you know that?"

"I was washing up outside a couple of days ago, and I heard the two of 'em talking. Ethan was telling Anthony he was having second thoughts about it, and Anthony was trying to convince him a martyr's death was the way to go."

"I didn't think either one of them was that committed," Logan said. "Or big believers for that matter." He was puzzled by Gregory's revelation.

"No, don't you get it, man?" Gregory asked. "It's the timid ones who go for martyrdom. They're nobodies at home. Invisible to most people. But here in the Middle East, there's this cult of the suicide bombers. They're the rock stars."

Logan watched as the two men got into a truck and drove off the compound. He felt an urge to shout after them, "Stop! Don't do it!" But that would be folly.

During breakfast, Rifat told Logan he would be moving into a hut next to Al Baghdadi's, used by his personal bodyguards. When he finished eating, Logan walked back to his sleeping quarters to pack his things. As he walked, he thought more about Gregory's comments.

Suicide must be a tough sell to non-Muslims, he reflected. Most Americans tend to think of suicide bombers as psychopaths, but in reality, the majority of them come across as average people. He remembered seeing a *60 Minutes* special called "Mind of the Suicide Bomber" several years ago. In it, a Muslim psychiatrist from Gaza evaluated dozens of suicide bombers over the years.

He developed a theory about how the cult of the suicide bomber, and its accompanying pre-suicide rituals, ultimately gave the attacker the courage to go through with the act. Those directly responsible for his preparation have a well-honed routine for lulling the bombers into the right frame of mind. This includes writing final letters to family members, photographing the martyrs in full suicide regalia for posterity's sake, and videotaping them explaining why they had chosen this path.

It only took him a couple of minutes to pack his things. When he got to his new quarters, Rifat was there waiting for him.

"You can take that spot over there." He nodded to an empty mattress on the floor. After Logan dropped his bag on the floor, Rifat handed him some clothing—a black sweatshirt and black, baggy trousers. When he was dressed, Rifat led him outside to a small armory and issued him a couple of extra magazines and ammunition for his AK47.

"You're going to spend the next couple of days shadowing me, learning your duties. The first thing is, despite the fact Al Baghdadi seemed pretty friendly when you first met, he doesn't want his guards to talk to him unless he initiates the conversation. He may be interested in your navy SEAL background. But unless he says something to you, it's best to keep quiet."

"How many guards are on duty at the same time?" Logan asked.

"If we're here in camp, it's generally two, one at each of the entrances to his quarters. If we're traveling outside, it'll be different. We'll have a lead car and a trailing car with bodyguards, and there will be two in the vehicle with him besides the driver, who's also trained as a bodyguard."

"Do you do any advanced recon if he's going outside?"

"It depends on the situation. You know there's a big price on his head, so we never make public announcements about his schedule. If he's going to a masjid to say prayers, we count on the local Imam to secure the area for us. We'll send an advance team to scout out the arrangements, and we also get intel from our people regarding security on the ground."

"Are there plans for dealing with an assault on the camp by air or ground forces?"

"Come with me," Rifat said. He pushed through the heavy curtain covering the doorway and walked outside to an area behind the hut. This place was used for collecting trash. He pulled two large plastic tubs off to one side to reveal a hole in the ground, broad enough to accommodate someone of Logan's stature. The Syrian handed him a flashlight, which Logan shined into the hole.

"This leads to a tunnel system. Inside there's a ladder that goes down twelve feet to the entrance. It runs west from here 200 feet. We've also hollowed out three rooms down there, big enough to serve as living quarters during an air attack. We have a second tunnel branching off from this one that opens up just on the other side of that hill." He pointed to a spot north of their position. "That one is over 400 feet long."

"Do you have guards monitoring the entrances?" Logan asked.

"That one yes, since it opens to the outside."

"How'd you dig these out?"

"We rounded up everyone in this village and put them to work."

"Isn't that risky? What if someone were to talk?"

"That's not a problem."

"Why? You can't be sure."

"Yes, I can. They're all dead." He pointed to a spot

outside the camp.

"After they finished digging, we had them dig their own mass grave, and then we shot them all."

"Go on. Take a look around."

Logan started down the ladder with some trepidation. If Rifat was tricking him, he was as good as dead. He touched bottom and shone the light on the rough-hewn walls. A cramped tunnel stretched out before him. He had to crouch so as not to bump his head. This produced a shuffling, sliding gait. The air was cool but musty; after about ten minutes of this, the tunnel opened up, to a kind of anteroom as it were. Off of it, there were three roughly hewn out rooms capable of accommodating a dozen fighters in each.

Logan began walking down the other branch of the tunnel to see how long it would take him to reach the exit, making mental notes of everything he saw. His flashlight cast a broad beam; with any luck, the batteries were fresh. Even if they died out before he got back, he wasn't too worried. It was pretty much a straight shot all the way.

Twenty minutes later, he detected a gradual upward incline to the tunnel. In the distance, he could see the light from the entrance. He emerged into sunlight, startling a sentry sprawled on the ground. Logan recognized him from the camp. They nodded to each other, and Logan surveyed his surroundings.

The entrance to the tunnel was well concealed with the desert brush. Turning south, Logan saw the camp in the distance, partially obscured by undulating terrain. A plan was beginning to form in his mind. *This might just work*, he thought.

Thinking it would be nice to get some fresh air after being in tight quarters, Logan took the overland route back to camp. It was mid-morning, and the temperature was still tolerable. He judged it would be no more than ten minutes. He was chary of walking in the desert, given uncertainty over what might be lying just below the surface—an IED or some unexploded ordinance. There was no one on the road. It was a good idea to check this area out anyway if his plan was going to come to fruition. No reason to leave anything to chance.

The sentry at the camp recognized him from training and gave him a quizzical look as he opened the gate. Logan found Rifat waiting near the rabbit hole he'd gone down. He wore a surprised look on his face as Logan appeared.

"I was beginning to think you got lost down there," he said.

"No. Just decided to see where it came out. That's a pretty decent tunnel. How long did it take to dig?"

"Two months. We worked round-the-clock shifts, from opposite ends. One of the men here was a civil engineer in civilian life. He worked out the calculations and figured out a system to keep everything going in the right direction."

Logan nodded his head in appreciation. Inwardly, he was marveling at the engineering work given the primitive conditions. As a marine architect, he appreciated the skills of the engineer who conceived and executed the tunnel project.

"It's pretty well concealed too. I wouldn't even know it's down there if you hadn't pointed it out to me."

"We have a special mission tonight," Rifat announced.

"Al Baghdadi's wife and children are going to be visiting. About twenty miles from here. He'll be spending the night."

"We have another camp so close?" Logan asked.

"No. It's a private compound. One of our supporters owns it and is making it available to us for a couple of days."

"Isn't that dangerous?"

"There's always some risk when we move him," Rifat explained. "He feels it would be riskier to bring his family to the camp because it has a higher profile."

"Where are they coming from?"

"His wife lives in Mosul. The family never appears in public with him. It's too dangerous given the number of enemies he has. Most people don't even realize he's married."

Logan nodded his understanding. Bits and pieces of the puzzle about Al Baghdadi's private life were beginning to fall into place.

"We'll set up out here," Rifat said, pointing to a shaded area just outside the entrance to the hut.

"Challenge anyone trying to gain access. Al Baghdadi's personal secretary keeps his schedule and will let us know of anything out of the ordinary. Sometimes he receives visitors during the day—Imams, district commanders, local leaders. Occasionally he'll talk to the press. We bring them in blindfolded so they can't figure out his location.

"Is there anyone who has unrestricted access?" Logan asked, taking up his position.

"Only his secretary, Sayid, and myself. Anyone claiming otherwise is lying and should be detained. Some of them are harmless, perhaps looking for a favor. But others may wish to harm him."

"We do eight-hour shifts. You may be assigned other duties if needed and of course, there will be opportunities for training and exercise every day. You will be going with us this evening. Right now, I have a meeting with several of the district commanders. You're in charge here. Let me know if you have any problems."

Rifat went inside, and Logan remained at the entrance. The irony of his situation didn't escape him. Here he was, guarding the most wanted man on the face of the earth, while in his mind, he was plotting his annihilation.

Chapter 47

Sunlight was fading as the three-vehicle convoy set out from camp. Logan was riding in the trailing car, with one other bodyguard and the driver. Up ahead, he could see the lights of the lead vehicle, a dented pickup truck, probing the rutted road. In the car immediately in front of his, Logan could make out four shadowy figures, although, in the dim light, there were no discernible features. Aside from the driver and bodyguard in the front, he knew Rifat and Al Baghdadi occupied the rear passenger seats.

The convoy turned right outside the camp and right away picked up speed. Logan's window was wound down to relieve the stuffiness; he sat in the back seat by himself. His driver, an Iraqi named Mustafa, and the other bodyguard, a former mujahideen fighter from Afghanistan by the name of Ali, conversed in raucous Arabic. Ali's native tongue was Dari, but he had been living in Iraq and Syria since 2005, and his Arabic sounded natural. They were listening to a local radio station, playing ISIS propaganda tunes. Logan recognized one called *Saleel-al-Sawari* — a *nasheed*, or jihadist chant; the seductive a cappella timbre was meant to captivate listeners and propel them to greater fervor.

At this hour, the moon was low in the sky. There was no other traffic on the road as they raced away from Ash Shaddadi. Logan was left to his own thoughts, as neither Mustafa nor Ali spoke English, and he possessed limited knowledge of Arabic or Dari. Just as well, he was busy taking mental notes of everything he saw. They would come in handy later.

It only took them 30 minutes to reach their destination. Like most of the desert compounds in this part of Syria, baked mud brick walls form the outer perimeter of the complex. As they came to a halt in front of the gate, an armed guard materialized from the shadows. There was a momentary delay as verbal paroles were exchanged, and then the metal barrier swung open to allow them passage.

The convoy pulled up before what appeared to be the main house. In the dim shadows cast by lighted kerosene lamps by the front door, Logan could make out the still silhouette of a slender woman dressed in conservative attire. A *niqab* covered her face while the rest of her body was enveloped in a black *abaya*. She gazed expectantly towards the vehicles, clutching three small children to her as they came to a halt.

Al Baghdadi's door opened, and he stepped out of the car. There was a moment's hesitation, and then the children broke free from their mother and raced to the robed cleric. He clutched them in an embrace, but his penetrating gaze was for the lithesome figure dressed in black who was already turning away to enter the house.

Al Baghdadi said a few words to Rifat and then, smoothing his robes, he shooed the children in the direction of a grandmotherly looking woman who shuffled over to lead them towards another building. The Caliph turned to survey the courtyard before entering the house. His eyes met Logan's momentarily and then looked away. He went inside and closed the door.

Rifat began issuing orders to the others in Arabic. The vehicles were moved to the rear of the complex, and the men delegated to guard duty took up their positions around the perimeter. Logan was assigned to a spot near the back door opening into the house. He took up his post as the camp began to quiet down. There was an outdoor kitchen not far from where he stood, and there was some chatter there as the cooks prepared the evening meal.

An hour later, a kitchen worker brought him a plate of food. There was a mound of pilaf, a chunk of what tasted like goat meat, and a cloth napkin containing several pieces of warm flatbread. Despite the austere conditions, the food was savory, and he devoured it in minutes. He wiped his face on the sleeve of his uniform and offered a burp in appreciation. It was good to have a full stomach because it looked like it was going to be a long night.

The Hare Moon made for unwelcome conditions to mount an attack. That was the first mistake the two would-be assassins made. It was just after 1:00 a.m. and the full spring moon was at its apex, traversing east to west above the Syrian desert. Aside from the occasional rustle of a foraging creature outside the desert wall, there was a profound stillness to the night air.

The silence was abruptly broken by the scuffling sound of a dislodged rock crashing into a brush. The noise came from just outside the rear perimeter wall about 200 feet from Logan's location. It suddenly went quiet; his ears strained to pick up any manmade sounds outside the compound.

Five to ten minutes passed before he detected any movement. There was definitely somebody or something lurking around just outside the enclosure. Logan was loath to raise the alarm because he didn't want to reveal his position. Whoever was out there had persuaded themselves they had the element of surprise working in their favor, but little did they know he was waiting for them to make their move.

Logan lay down on the ground and silently crawled over to a well 20 feet away. It would give him cover once they made their move. He took up a defensive position and waited.

Moments later, there was a dull thud, and he could just make out a grappling hook dangling on his side of the mud wall. The hook didn't set into the surface, and as the person on the other end hauled on the attached line, it scraped across the top of the wall and landed with a plop on the other side.

Logan could hear hushed whispers coming from the other side, which was the first indication he was dealing with more than one intruder. He heard a grunt as the hook came sailing back over. This time, when the person on the other end tugged on the rope, the hook dug into the surface and held. Seconds later, a black-clad figure hauled himself to the top, pausing momentarily to survey the lay of the land before dropping ten feet to the ground.

A second person grappled with the rope as he dragged himself up. Logan could hear him breathing heavily as he struggled to heave one leg over the wall. He dropped to the ground like a bag of wet cement before clambering to his feet.

There didn't appear to be anyone else. Both had on backpacks and were armed with automatic rifles. He considered his options as they began moving in his direction.

He felt confident these were not friendlies. Bruce or Norm would have called if there was a planned operation against Al Baghdadi. As far as he knew, they didn't have a fix on his exact location. And besides, the U.S. military wouldn't be party to something as amateurish as the inept operation unfolding before him.

He eased the safety off of his weapon. By now the two men were in a low crouch trotting towards the back of the house. At this distance and under these conditions, accuracy was not a problem. He had no intention of letting them get any closer, not knowing what they were carrying in their backpacks. For all he knew these guys could be suicide bombers.

The first intruder was 150 feet away when the burst of automatic fire from Logan's AK-47 tore into his chest. The impact spun him around, and he toppled to the ground. His companion was caught in the open with nowhere to hide. He dropped to the ground, taking refuge behind his buddy and attempted to return fire. He managed to get off a single burst generally in Logan's direction before the former SEAL's spray of bullets caught the prowler in the head.

As Logan stood up, some other security personnel charged around the corner of the building. They came to a stop just short of his position. Rifat was running towards him, half-dressed, and barking orders to the other guards. They began to fan out, searching the rear perimeter of the compound. He directed several others to extend their search outside the compound. Finally, he turned his attention to Logan.

"What happened here?" he asked.

Logan filled him in. "I heard a noise a few minutes ago, and then these two came over the back wall. They were running for the main house, so I figured they might know Al Baghdadi's staying here."

Rifat looked grim. "That or maybe they were after the owner of this place." He and Logan walked over to examine the two bodies. Rifat began to go into one of the packs when Logan stopped him. He'd been around enough improvised demolitions during his SEAL career to know you didn't just tear into an unknown backpack without taking precautions. They didn't have access to high-tech bomb detection gear or a water cannon, so the next best option was to pour some rounds into the bags to be sure.

"Why don't we clear the main house? Get everybody to the other end of the compound. We can use that rope and grappling hook to drag the bodies over towards the back wall. Get them as far away from the house as possible. Once we get them over there, we can pour some rounds into the backpacks and see if we can blow them up."

Rifat nodded his agreement. He instructed two of the others to move the bodies to the back. When he received confirmation Al Baghdadi and his family had moved to safety, he ordered the men to start firing at the backpacks. For a moment the rounds tore into the men, shredding them, their clothing, and possessions. Without warning, one of the packs exploded, spattering blood and body parts against the wall.

Logan guessed it was probably military grade C4. There was a good chance one of their rounds ignited a detonator, which in turn would have set fire to the primer and main charge.

It was a half hour before the men clearing the outside perimeter returned. They had discovered a two-door sedan parked on the side of the road a half-mile away from the compound. There were no tags on the vehicle and no registration inside. Whoever was behind the attack had gone out of their way to conceal their identities.

Maybe they were suicide bombers, Logan speculated. There wasn't much left from the two corpses, making it unlikely ISIS would be able to assess who was behind the foiled plot. Just as well for their families. If they were able to figure out who was behind the attack, those family members were as good as dead.

"Why don't you get some rest?" Rifat suggested. "You've had enough excitement for one day."

Chapter 48

L ogan was exhausted. Despite the successful resolution of the assault on the compound, Rifat convinced Al Baghdadi it would be unwise to stay where they were. It was clear their position was compromised, and uncertainty remained over who was behind the foiled attack.

Given the late hour, Al Baghdadi decided to bring his wife and children back to the camp. Their grandmother bundled them into the rear seat of one of the cars, and Al Baghdadi and his wife scrambled in behind them. The smallest one was sniffling over her interrupted sleep, but moments after setting out, she was snoozing on her mother's lap.

Rifat was driving; he told Logan to ride shotgun, having proven himself by the way he dispatched the two intruders. Logan could feel Al Baghdadi's eyes boring into his back as they raced through the night. It made him uncomfortable, but he didn't turn around.

"Thank you for what you did back there."

Logan thought he imagined it, but Al Baghdadi was speaking to him in a soft whisper so as not to awaken the children. He half-turned in his seat and acknowledged the praise with a slight nod of the head. "I'm glad I was there to help out," he said.

"Without your quick action, our work here would possibly remain unfinished. And these little ones. Who knows?" He nodded his head thoughtfully. "Many people want to see us fail." He leaned back in his seat and closed his eyes.

Logan shifted his gaze to the diminutive figure seated next to the Imam. Her *niqab*, loosened around her face, revealed a delicate jawline and slender neck. Olive skin and dark eyebrows gave Al Baghdadi's wife a decidedly Mediterranean appearance. Charcoal colored-eyes flickered open, appraising him with a frankness he was unaccustomed to from women in the Middle East. The look was fleeting, but it felt as intimate as a caress. She adjusted the *niqab* without speaking and then closed her eyes.

What a strange place this part of the world is. Although he and Zahir were married over five years ago, there were times he just didn't understand where she was coming from. She was born and raised in the U.S., but her roots were in this part of the world.

What must it be like for this woman sitting behind him? Could she be as much of a fundamentalist as her husband? Did she know what she was getting into when she married him? Their eldest child appeared to be seven or eight, meaning Al Baghdadi was probably making *jihad* years before they were even married.

Rifat called ahead to let the guards at the camp know they were ten minutes out. When they arrived, the gates swung open and the cars rolled through without pausing. Logan helped unload the car, carrying one of the sleeping children into the hut, and then going back out for their bags.

He returned to his quarters. It was three hours before daybreak, and he needed to get some rest. He sank to the mattress on the floor and was out as soon as his head hit the pillow.

In the morning, the sound of the others beginning their day with morning prayers awoke him. He kept his eyes closed, wishing he could roll back over and sleep for about eight more hours. But then he decided to get up.

He felt better after washing up and eating a light breakfast. As he walked around the camp, he felt all eyes were on him, appraising him, judging him it seemed. One of his fellow trainees, Gregory, the Irishman from Londonderry, enlightened him.

"Word got back to us mate. You're a hero."

"What?" he asked.

"Yeah. You saved Al Baghdadi from certain death.

Everybody's talking about it."

"It was a turkey shoot," Logan replied. "These two guys came in over the back wall, and apparently never even considered the possibility there would be extra security."

"So, what happened?"

"I was on guard duty behind the house, and I saw them sneak in. They used a grappling hook to get over the wall. I shot both of them. They were wearing backpacks, and I couldn't take a chance they were suicide bombers.

"Afterwards, Rifat went over to check them out, and if I hadn't stopped him, he would have blown us all up. Both of them were carrying undetonated IEDs."

"Whoa. You're a real chancer, Tim. Sounds like a close call."

"Close enough. Not a very good night for the Al Baghdadi family."

Al Baghdadi's wife and children left the camp under armed escort later that afternoon. According to Rifat, they were heading back to Mosul, where her extended family lived.

Right after they departed, Logan found a quiet spot and placed a call to Bruce. He gave him a quick rundown of the last couple of days.

"I've got something for you. I don't know if we want to pursue this, but Al Baghdadi's wife and kids just left here by car for Mosul. I'm sending you a description and picture of the vehicle. Three children are traveling with her. She also has a driver and a bodyguard. The bodyguard is sitting up front. They've got side arms and AKs.

"I doubt she's on any kind of kill or capture list, but if we want to mess with Al Baghdadi's head, picking her up might get his attention."

"Let me run it by Langley and the commander here at the FOB. We could authorize putting up a surveillance drone to track her car right away and then work the approvals from Washington. It's about four, maybe five hours drive from where you are to Mosul. You sure she's not going to pick up some additional security along the way?"

"I was talking to Rifat, the security chief here, and he said Al Baghdadi thinks it safer for her to travel without a convoy. Lower profile."

"The tricky part would be intercepting her car without getting into a shootout," Bruce said.

"I was thinking about that. I don't know where they're planning to cross the border into Iraq," Logan said.

"Probably at Rabia. That's on the Al-Shaddadah—Mosul Road. We could put up a Predator surveillance mission to track the car and have a team at the border to pick them up coming through. The tricky part will be separating the driver and bodyguard from the family, so nobody gets hurt. Let me make some calls.

"Before I forget, there's one thing from Jason. He'd like to take Al Baghdadi alive if possible."

"Got it. I'm going to send you a note on a tunnel system ISIS has under the camp. Might come in handy in an exfiltration scenario. Let me know what you think."

"Roger that."

* * *

After getting off the phone with Logan, Bruce huddled with Norm for five minutes to discuss their options. When they were done, Norm went in to talk to the FOB chief to get authorization for the Predator mission, and Bruce put in a call to Washington. They were seven hours ahead of D.C., and he was hoping to catch Jason at his desk. Eventually, he'd have to put this proposal down on paper, but given the short time fuse, there were a lot of wheels to set in motion.

"Summers."

"Jason? It's Bruce." He gave the counterterrorism chief a quick rundown of Logan's intelligence and proposal to pick up Al Baghdadi's wife at the border. As he waited, he could envision the bear of a man drumming his pencil on the desk as he weighed the pros and cons of the proposition.

Finally, he said, "Let's do it. I'll clear it with the DDO and talk to CENTCOM. I'll also touch base with Baghdad to make sure they're on board with it. Why don't you go ahead and get the wheels turning on your end? It's easier to ask forgiveness than permission, and we don't have a lot of time."

"Right. We know the guys at Q-West pretty well. They're about 100 klicks from Rabia."

And with that, the CIA and the Pentagon's efficient machinery kicked into high gear. The Predator surveillance operation was already underway. This particular mission was being flown out of Creech Air Force Base. Given Logan's timely information, within an hour, the drone picked up the target north of Al Hasakha and began relaying intelligence feeds to operators at Q-West, FOB As-Shaddadi, CENTCOM, and CIA headquarters.

The 27-foot long unmanned aerial vehicle had a wingspan of 49 feet and could fly at an altitude of 25,000 feet. With its payload of electro-optical and infrared cameras and synthetic aperture radar, the Predator was able to operate in all kinds of weather, providing resolution to one foot, which was more than enough capability for this particular mission.

The commander of Operation Inherent Resolve, Central Command's combined joint task force set up in 2014 to defeat ISIS in Iraq and Syria, gave the go-ahead for a combined force to pre-position in Rabia no later than 6:15 p.m. By 6:00 pm. a navy SEAL unit was on site and in direct communication with the pilot of the Predator UAV, who estimated the vehicle Al Baghdadi's family was traveling in, would reach the border at roughly 7:00 p.m.

Shortly before 7:00, the dusty Mercedes 300 SL sedan pulled up to the border crossing. The head of the Iraqi border crossings department was briefed on the operation, and his men were instructed to cooperate with the U.S. military.

An Iraqi interpreter working with the special forces unit asked the driver of the vehicle to step outside so the immigration officials could examine the trunk. At the same time, two navy SEALS dressed as local women walking across the border breached the passenger side of the vehicle and immobilized the bodyguard. The driver went for his sidearm but was taken out with a blow to the head by one of the other SEALS.

Al Baghdadi's wife began screaming at the intruders, who by now, had discarded their costumes, revealing themselves to be foreign soldiers. She clapped her hand over her mouth as the three children cowered around her.

Within three minutes, two of the SEALS commandeered the car, and it was escorted away from the border area to a military airfield five miles away. There, an awaiting helicopter picked up the three passengers and made the short flight to Mosul. The family would be detained at Q-West, pending a decision by the White House. The CIA was arguing to have the family rendered to an undisclosed location in the U.S. where a team of operations officers and intelligence analysts would seek to gain Mrs. Al Baghdadi's cooperation in exchange for possible asylum. The only problem was no one knew anything about her, not even her name. Was she an ardent ISIS disciple, or a victim? Only time would tell.

Chapter 49

The loneliest time of day is from 1:00 to 5:00 a.m. Most of the camp was sleeping, and there was a stillness to the surrounding area. Normal breathing seemed loud enough to wake the dead. But tonight, Logan was primed for action. Operation Ghost Rider was a go. Some hotshot at Langley came up with that name. Al Baghdadi was known as "The Ghost" because it was so rare for anyone to see him. And if things went well, he'd be riding out of town this very evening.

Emboldened by the successful operation against Al Baghdadi's wife two days earlier, Jason Summers was looking to score another big win for the good guys. It would make things a lot easier when he traveled up to The Hill, hat in hand, if he had some success stories he could share with the congressmen. Taking Al Baghdadi off the playing field would rank right up there with killing Osama bin Laden.

The operation was scheduled to kick off at 2:15 a.m. Logan was working the 12:00 to 8:00 a.m. shift and was stationed just outside the entrance to Al Baghdadi's quarters. The second bodyguard was positioned at the far end of the hut. They swapped positions every two hours to vary the routine and help them stay awake.

The camp was silent as Logan casually moved to take up his new position. The other guard was a young Syrian by the name of Jamal. He nodded as they passed each other, but he was unprepared for what happened next.

Logan pivoted and landed a crippling blow to Jamal's head. He clamped his hand over the Syrian youth's mouth to muffle the surprised grunt that escaped from his lips, and expertly snapped his neck, easing the limp body to the ground. The plan called for Jamal's body to serve as a decoy, once Logan had his hands on Al Baghdadi. There was just too much at risk to allow Jamal to live. He maneuvered the slack corpse onto his shoulder and returned to the front entrance of the hut.

From here on out, time was of the essence. If anyone were to get up and notice Jamal was not at his post, it could be problematic. He had to get himself and Jamal into Al Baghdadi's hut without waking his prey. If the Caliph were to sound the alarm, Logan knew he was as good as dead.

He decided to leave the body in the shadows outside the hut as he eased himself inside. Al Baghdadi was alone, and Logan could tell from his even breathing, he was fast asleep. He crept over to the side of the bed and stared down at his prey. Perhaps it was a sixth sense or Logan's faint breathing that awakened the Iraqi cleric. His eyes fluttered open and widened as he grasped the fact he was not alone. He started to sit up but was thrust back as Logan flung himself at him, clamping a hand over his mouth.

Al Baghdadi was a star soccer player in high school and college, and still retained a certain level of athleticism. He fought back with surprising strength. He tried to bite Logan's hand, and in the process the two men rolled off the bed, crashing with a thud to the floor. Logan came up on top and, straddling the cleric, began pummeling him in the face with bone-crushing blows. After a combination of three vicious shots to the head, the ISIS leader lay there, as limp as the corpse just outside his door.

Breathing heavily, Logan secured his captive's hands and feet and skillfully knotted a cloth across his mouth. So far so good. He went back out to retrieve Jamal's corpse, lugging it across the threshold and dumping it onto the bed. He returned to his post, shutting the door when he heard footsteps nearby. A moment later Rifat came into view.

"Having trouble sleeping?" Logan asked as he braced himself for questions.

The security chief stopped in front of him and squinted in the poor light. "I got up to use the toilet and thought I heard something." He looked around. "Is everything all right?"

"I haven't heard anything. Jamal and I just swapped positions. We were talking. Maybe that's what woke you up. Sorry."

"No problem." He paused for a second, but then continued walking. Logan held his breath. If Rifat went looking for Jamal, things could get nasty fast. Instead of going left towards Jamal's post, the security chief took a right and walked back to his own quarters.

Logan checked the time. He was startled to see only 15 minutes had passed. He pulled out his cell phone and sent a text message to Bruce and Norm, to let them know the first phase of the operation was a go.

Back inside the hut, he covered Jamal's body with blankets. The idea was to buy time if anyone decided to look in on the cleric while Logan was making his escape. The corpse wouldn't fool anyone for long, but it might give him precious minutes to get away.

He looked down at the figure on the floor; Al Baghdadi was still out. Logan checked the ropes securing his hands and feet again and tugged on the cloth covering his mouth. There had been no opportunity to rehearse what he was about to do, but this was the best shot he had of secreting the Imam out of the camp.

He bent down, and straining under the weight, shouldered the unconscious cleric like a 100-pound sack of potatoes. Only he probably weighed closer to 220.

Grunting, he stooped down to retrieve his AK-47 and stepped out into the night air. He closed the door and, keeping in the shadows of the building, edged his way around to the recycling area and the entrance to the tunnel. He had hidden the rope from the grappling hook behind some trash. Retrieving it, he fashioned a lasso which he looped under his captive's arms and pulled taut around his chest.

Al Baghdadi was groggy and was beginning to move around. He didn't have the strength to resist what Logan was doing, but he might be able to make it difficult to navigate the tunnel.

Bracing himself on one side of the hole, Logan lowered the limp figure into the tunnel. The dead weight made it difficult for him to control the descent. He wasn't wearing gloves, and the friction from the rope slicing through his hands produced a searing pain. After what seemed like an eternity, he heard a thud and felt the line go slack. Peering over the side, he saw Al Baghdadi sprawled face down on the ground.

Logan pulled the camouflage back over the top of the hole as he made his own descent into the tunnel. This part was going to be tricky. Because of the narrowness of the passageway, there was no way he could lug his human cargo on his back. He would have to physically drag the cleric along the tunnel floor, using the rope. Unlike the rough-hewn walls, though, the ground was sandy, given the amount of foot traffic passing through. It was doable, but Al Baghdadi was going to have a raging headache when he woke up.

Logan rechecked the ropes and positioned Al Baghdadi, so he was faced head first on his back entering the tunnel. As Logan prepared to set out, he felt the Caliph's eyes upon him. He was struggling with the restraints, shooting daggers at his captor.

Logan stared at him for a moment before setting out. "You'll get a chance to have your say," he said. "Only not now."

He turned and began to trudge through the tunnel. It was hard work, and despite his physical conditioning, he found himself gasping for air as he marched forward.

* * *

Bruce and Norm made up two of the 14 commandos about to board the stealth-modified Blackhawk helicopter preparing to take off from FOB Ash Shaddadi. One other Blackhawk was warming up nearby. It also had one less than the full fifteen-person compliment; that seat was reserved for their quarry.

The men had received confirmation from Logan 15 minutes earlier that phase one of the extraction plan was successful, and he was making his way into the tunnel with Al Baghdadi in tow.

Based upon Logan's intelligence, the team had located the entrance to the tunnel. Imagery from a drone tasked to photograph the camp and its environs enabled them to geo-locate the tunnel entrance and identify the ISIS fighter charged with securing it.

The target was ten minutes by helicopter from their base. They would be approaching the camp fast and low, enabling them to evade enemy operational radar. Moreover, because of special modifications to their helicopters' tail booms and the use of newly developed high-tech materials used in the stealth aircraft, it would be virtually impossible for anyone on the ground to hear their approach.

Two snipers on the lead aircraft would be carrying suppressed semi-automatic rifles. Their job was to take out the tunnel guard before he had a chance to raise the alarm. Once on the ground, they would secure the entrance. Norm and Bruce were tasked with going inside to assist Logan.

Since capturing Al Baghdadi was their primary mission, the extraction team did not plan to engage with the enemy unless absolutely necessary. As soon as they were safely out of range, two MQ9 Reaper Hunter/Killer UAVs, each armed with a payload of four 500-pound bombs equipped with laser and GPS guidance systems, would reduce the ISIS camp to rubble.

"All right. Let's saddle up men," said the flight commander. Moments later, they were strapped in, and the two birds took off into the night sky. Five minutes into their ride, lights from the town of Ash Shaddadi were visible several miles to the east.

"I wonder what that is?" Norm nudged Bruce and pointed out the window. It appeared to be a flame, spurting up into the night sky.

"Burn off from a gas plant," Bruce replied. "Back home that's a pretty common sight." Bruce was from Custer City,

Oklahoma and had seen a few oil wells in his day.

"Five minutes to target," the captain said. He swooped down until they were less than ten feet off the deck, flying nap-of-the-earth. This type of rollicking, swerving flight at 100 miles per hour, is not for the faint-hearted. These men had all been on countless missions where nap-of-the-earth was the standard operating procedure, but it never failed to produce a sense of awe watching the pilots maneuver their birds.

The two snipers got into position to take out the sentry as they came in.

"There he is," the captain said. "Eleven o'clock." He gained altitude, leveling off at 100 feet and went into a hover.

Bruce could see the ISIS fighter down below on his side of the aircraft. The man was on his feet looking around. He probably sensed rather than heard the two stealth helicopters. He looked up, and when he saw the two aircraft, raised his weapon, only to be propelled violently backward as the sniper's bullet found its mark.

As soon as the two helicopters touched down, the men piled out and set up a defensive perimeter. Bruce and Norm ducked down low and scurried over to the tunnel entrance, barely visible in the low light conditions. They went inside and, moving at a half-jog, ran for five minutes before encountering Logan. He was sitting on the ground, wincing in pain, and Al Baghdadi was propped up against the tunnel wall with his eyes closed. When he heard them approach, he gave them a hate-filled stare.

"Oh man, am I glad to see you guys," Logan said. "My knee just gave out. Can't put any pressure on it." Logan's knee had been blown out by machine gun fire in an ambush when he and his navy SEAL unit were on patrol in Afghanistan years ago. That injury ended his navy career and earned him a brand-new knee. It was good, but it wasn't meant for this kind of wear and tear.

"You should have called, man," Norm said.

"I tried, but this thing's no-good underground," he said,

holding up his cell phone.

It took them fifteen minutes, hobbling, dragging and clawing their way back to the entrance, but they made it. Figures emerged from the dark and rushed to help them aboard. Al Baghdadi was bundled into one Blackhawk, never taking his eyes off of Logan the entire time. His smoldering stare evoked a sense of hatred Logan had never before experienced. He joined Bruce and Norm in the other helicopter and sank back into his seat. They were airborne in minutes.

Bruce turned to him. "You did it, brother," he said. "You got him."

But Logan didn't hear him. He was already fast asleep.

Chapter 50

Logan winced as he eased himself into a chair in the DDO's office. It was two weeks since his return to the U.S. from Syria. The day after Al Baghdadi's capture, an Agency aircraft transported Logan to Frankfurt, Germany, where he was transferred to a commercial flight to Dulles International. Following successful surgery to repair his knee at George Washington Hospital, Logan was spending a few days getting reacquainted with his wife and son at her parents' home in Arlington.

Today, Norm, Bruce, and Jason were with him, to do a wrap up for the DDO. Plans called for him, Zahir, and Cooper to fly up to Boston in the morning.

Jason took the lead. "First I'd like to give you an update on Al Baghdadi's wife. It turns out she's less disciple and more captive than we thought. She's being debriefed at one of our safe sites in Maryland. It's a very controlled environment. We've brought in some Arabic speakers to help with the children, and our counterterrorism people have been talking to her.

"She's obviously wary and hasn't completely opened up, but the feeling is we're making progress."

"Al Baghdadi's at Guantanamo Bay. He's been subjected to steady interrogations, but so far, he isn't cooperating. We haven't disclosed the fact we have him to our allies. Conventional wisdom on the Arab street is Al Baghdadi was killed in our assault on the camp at Ash Shaddadi." Jason pulled up imagery of the camp taken immediately after it was bombed; it was flattened.

"It's doubtful anyone survived the bombing," he said. "But to be certain, forces went into the camp at daybreak.

They cleared the tunnel system and determined no one was hiding in there. As you can see from the imagery, no one above ground could have survived."

"Intelligence from around the region indicates Al Baghdadi's disappearance has created havoc in ISIS. There's a power struggle going on, but no clear successor. This, in effect, marks the end of ISIS as we know it," he said with satisfaction. "He may very well be the last Caliph."

"Regarding the intelligence operative, Azar Ghabel: we advised the Canadian government she was actually a clandestine operative for the IRGC, posing as a freelance photographer.

"Without going into Logan's contact with her, we gave the Canadians a very compelling case. As a result of our intelligence, the security service picked her up in Toronto last week. She is currently under arrest and is facing terrorism charges. Ottawa has reached out to Teheran to see if they will claim her as one of their own, but so far, the Iranians haven't responded.

"Because she has Canadian citizenship, Ghabel is considered a Canadian person, and thus enjoys certain rights that may make it more difficult for them to prosecute her."

"Even if she got her citizenship under false pretenses?" Logan asked.

"That's the kicker," Jason replied. "She has built up an impressive cover portfolio as a freelance photographer. The Canadians will have to do some digging to prove Alice Shirazi is actually Azar Ghabel.

"We have a new asset inside the Qods Force, who might be able to help, but it's risky because any information she gives us could point right back to her."

"How about Akbar? The spotter in New York City?" Logan asked.

"Peter Breen is talking to his counterparts at the NYPD. Based on Akbar's approach to you and your brother-in-law, they are going to the FISA court to request approval to conduct electronic and physical surveillance against him."

The DDO thanked them for the update and then

requested they accompany him down the hall. Logan gave the others an inquiring look, but they shrugged their shoulders. No one seemed to know where they were going.

Logan recognized the well-worn path to the director's office. They entered his conference room, and he was surprised to see Zahir and Cooper sitting around the conference table along with his parents and sister.

"What...?"

At that moment, the director came out of her adjoining office and asked everyone to be seated.

"It gives me great pleasure to have all of you here today to recognize one of your loved ones, a hero whose selfless courage has dramatically enhanced the security of our nation. I can't go into the details of what Logan and his colleagues did, but I can tell you this: it has severely degraded the capabilities of one of our most potent enemies and was carried off at significant personal risk. Logan please come up here."

Logan made his way to the director's side. He was embarrassed to be recognized this way. From his perspective, he had just been doing his duty.

"It is with great pleasure I present to you the CIA's Intelligence Star for actions of extraordinary heroism." The director pinned the medal, the civilian equivalent of the U.S. military's silver star, to Logan's lapel. After the applause subsided, she shook Logan's hand and, taking him aside, expressed her personal gratitude for the risks Logan had made on behalf of a grateful nation.

After the ceremony, there followed a brief reception and lunch in the director's dining room.

As he and Zahir were leaving, the DDO pulled Logan aside and said, "You know our offer is still open, if you decide to come back."

Logan was about to respond when Zahir chimed in.

"I want him to say yes. We haven't had a chance to talk about it, but I've changed my mind. I don't want to stand between Logan and the CIA. He has so much to offer, and I want to be supportive."

"Are you sure?" Logan asked. "We don't have to make a decision right now."

"Yes, I'm sure. I've already told Ava I won't be back in the fall. We can put our place in Boston on the market, and start house hunting in D.C."

"I guess it's settled then," he said to the DDO with a grin on his face.

Cousins clasped his hand. "That's great news. Why don't you take some time to get your personal affairs in order? We'll see you sometime next month."

After bidding goodbye to everyone else, Logan, Zahir, and Cooper exited the building.

As they walked to Logan's rental car, they stopped by the memorial garden, where Cooper ran off to chase a butterfly. Zahir rested her head on Logan's shoulder.

"You know how much I love you, don't you?" she whispered.

"Yes, sweetie, I know." He stroked her hair, lost in thought.

* * *

Two weeks after Logan's meeting with the DDO, the Canadian government used a back channel to Teheran via Pakistan's ambassador in Washington, D.C., to advise the Iranian government Alice Sherazi was to be arraigned in court on terrorism charges and suspicions of being a foreign intelligence operative. The Iranians replied via the same channel, for the first time acknowledging Alice Sherazi was actually Azar Ghabel, an official Qods Force officer. After some bartering, an offer of exchange was accepted. Ghabel was to be repatriated to Iran in exchange for three Canadian journalists who were being held at Evin Prison on charges of espionage. Ghabel's Canadian citizenship was revoked, and she was declared persona non grata; she was given one week to settle her affairs.

During the same period, FISA coverage against Akbar, the alleged ISIS spotter, began. Within days, evidence suggested he was engaged in illegal activities in support of terrorism against the U.S. He was arraigned on 15 counts at the Manhattan Federal Court and was being held without bond pending trial.

Al Baghdadi's wife was now cooperating with the U.S. government. She was responding, albeit reluctantly, to questions posed in intelligence debriefings. She denied any interest in conjugal visits with her spouse and was bargaining with the government for a resettlement package to an undisclosed non-U.S. location of her choice.

Al Baghdadi remained secluded at Guantanamo Bay. His refusal to cooperate with the government led some to raise the specter of employing enhanced interrogation techniques to gain his cooperation. Others proposed turning him over to the International Criminal Court (ICC) for crimes against humanity. The U.S. has had a troubled relationship with the ICC over the years, particularly as it relates to the court's jurisdiction in matters affecting the U.S., and thus this was not viewed as a viable alternative.

Al Baghdadi presented a dilemma for the U.S. Despite existing authorities, conflicting views regarding the detention of high-value targets, held by Congress, the Supreme Court, NGOs, and international organizations, make long-term incarceration without trial, a public relations nightmare. It is likely his imprisonment will go on for years, although no one can predict the outcome with any certainty. But, despite the quandary, the U.S. remains resolute on one issue. Al Baghdadi will indeed be the last Caliph.

The End